THE PROTECTORS

JOLYNN ANGELINI

iUniverse®

THE PROTECTORS

iUniverse books may be ordered through booksellers or by contacting:

iUniverse
1663 Liberty Drive
Bloomington, IN 47403
www.iuniverse.com
1-800-Authors (1-800-288-4677)

ISBN: 978-1-5320-6391-6 (sc)
ISBN: 978-1-5320-6393-0 (hc)
ISBN: 978-1-5320-6392-3 (e)

Library of Congress Control Number: 2019900950

Print information available on the last page.

iUniverse rev. date: 03/12/2019

For my mom and dad, who are my biggest fans;
To my husband, for all your support; and
To my sweetheart Isabella, never stop persisting!

Prologue

I can feel my eyes trying to open as I lie there awake but barely able to move. I am telling my body to move, but nothing seems to be happening. I am so tired, but I feel like I need to get up. My eyes finally flicker open, and I realize that my surroundings are very familiar. Even though I don't quite know where I am, the panic that I felt earlier has now washed away.

When I finally become fully awake, I realize that I am in my own bedroom. I look out the window and see the sun just starting to peek up behind the house across the street. I look at the clock, and it reads 6:40 a.m. I try to sit up and notice that my head is pounding. I have the worst headache, and my mouth feels like I licked a cotton ball. Flashes of the night before start racing through my head, and I sit bolt upright in the bed and wonder what the hell happened.

I race down the steps and nearly break my ankle when I get to the bottom. I run right into the garage and find my SUV gleaming clean and in the bay where I usually park it. I open the driver's side door and climb in to see if there is anything out of place or anything in there that doesn't belong. There is nothing out of the ordinary that I can see at first glance, and my seat is in the programmed position of #1. I drift off for a little while. I think about the #2 position and can't help but feel the sadness but yet some anger. I'm still very confused but now for a completely different reason.

I decide to calm down and collect my thoughts—try to anyway. I head back inside to make myself a cup of coffee. I try to pull up any memory from last night. It doesn't help that I'm in my silk pajamas and anything that I would have worn out last night is either in the hamper or put away. Not that I can remember what I wore out, but it's not lying all over the floor, so it must be somewhere … and how in the world did I get into my pj's? I don't even remember getting into bed, not to mention how I got changed.

I'm so lost in thought it doesn't even occur to me to check my cell phone. My whole life, like everyone else's in the world, is in my phone, and it took me this long to dig it out and check it. I am definitely not thinking straight.

I scroll through my phone. I don't see anything out of the ordinary—same old text messages, a very nice one from my mom just checking up on me, but the last one was at midnight, and I replied like usual, saying, "Good night," and that I would text in the morning. I look over at the clock, and it is now 7:15 a.m. She's probably wondering where I am. I'll wait until later when I know she's up.

I go back upstairs to look around the bedroom for my clothes and maybe a clue, and out of the corner of my eye, I see something shining in the sunlight on the floor at the edge of the bed. I shoot over there to see what it is, and my stomach flips but oddly in a good way. It's Derrick's cigarette lighter. Wait ... Derrick's lighter? In my bedroom? And it hits me like a brick to the face! Derrick put me to bed last night and, oh no, changed me into my pj's? What in God's name did I do last night, and why can't I remember it?

I go back to my text messages just to see if I missed something. There aren't any from Derrick. This makes me certain that I was with him last night. But where is he now? I was only looking for odd numbers or someone I hadn't spoken to in a while, so I begin reading through the most recent ones from last night. There is one from my daughter, Isabella. I miss her and Gavin so much while they are away. Their father's idea after ...

My mind drifts again to the #2 position. Normally, the thought of him makes me so happy. This time, I'm just angry. Clips of the last few weeks start racing through my head. A specific scene creeps into my thoughts.

I close my eyes thinking that will help me remember. I walk out of my bedroom and look down the hallway. Last night floods back to me, jammed into one memory. I slowly walk down the hallway. I turn the handle on the spare bedroom door. I open it, and my body breaks out into a cold sweat.

Chapter 1

"Jeff, do you really think it's a good idea to come and work with you in our family business?"

"Yes, Angie, I do. I think it's a great idea. You hate your job, and you continue to get disgusted with the lack of respect your boss has for you and your coworkers. Why not come and work with me? Your education in management and your experience in sales will bring a lot to the table in the business. Since the kids are still young, you will have more freedom to be home if they need you, and you won't have to travel so much anymore either."

"I don't know, Jeff. I think it's taking a major risk. What if we fight constantly and don't see eye to eye on things?"

"We are going to fight sometimes, and we are not always going to see eye to eye all the time, but we work really well as a couple, and there is nothing that we can't accomplish together. Look how we finally ended up getting together. Better late than never, but it took us a while to get where we are today.

"Also, since I own a residential exteriors company and you have always wanted to get into the design business, you can help clients design their new project, and maybe we can eventually add an interiors side of the business."

"Really? You would do that for me?"

"Of course, but you'll have to work for it, you know."

"I know. You see how hard I work now, so I will work even harder for something I enjoy doing, especially if it allows me to control our future together."

"I want a partner in crime, and who better for it to be than you? I would like for you to travel with me though, so you will still have to travel but nowhere near as much as you do now, and you won't have to come with me all the time."

"You do travel quite a bit, Jeff, and I'm not real crazy about that at all."

I wondered why he had been traveling so much just in the last two years. I didn't push the issue.

"I know, but now that you won't be traveling, you'll be home when I am, and we won't have to pass each other on the front porch coming and going to the airport on separate trips."

"That's a really good point, Jeff."

"I know, Angie, and don't forget the three months you helped me when my office manager left."

"How could I forget that? It was a mess back then, and those employees you had … *yikes*! You're right, Jeff; that was a lot of fun, and we really worked well together when the stress level was through the roof. No pun intended," I said with a sly smirk.

Jeff laughed at me and engulfed me in his big bear hug.

"Well, I guess I'll write up my resignation letter and give my two weeks' notice on Monday."

"Angie, if you think that will make you happy, then it will make me happy."

"I guess it's a done deal then, partner."

We shook hands and laughed. He took me in his arms again and kissed me.

I was so thankful that Jeff had become more loving in the last few years. I was puzzled as to why, but I wasn't complaining.

Chapter 2

When Jeff and I agreed on me working with him, we both thought it would be a good idea to take a week off before I jumped right into the new job. I thought this would get me in the right frame of mind for taking on a new job and allow me to quickly get adjusted to my new life.

I dropped the kids off at school and went and bought myself a coffee. I would be able to do this every morning from then on, and I was completely ecstatic. This was what I had been missing all along at that high-stress corporate job.

My best friend and cousin, Elle, lived right across the street from us in the development. She had a newborn, and because her husband owned a massive grocery store and a hardware store in town, she was able to stay home with the baby. I was not sure whether she'd go back to work, but for the next few years, she'd be home with the new princess. She'd been talking about writing a cookbook. It would consist of the old Italian family recipes with an updated twist. She wanted to entice our generation and the younger ones to come to keep up with the traditions. She was a great cook, so this would be a great project for her while she was home.

She was thrilled that I was going to be home all week because she would have an adult to talk to during the day. I called her that first day I was off and asked her and Bianca to come over and visit. They wandered over after Bianca woke up and was fed.

"Angie, what are you going to do all week?"

"Well, I really want to get the house in order. You know, get rid of all the clothes that don't fit all of us and go buy some things that I've been wanting to get for a while. I want to decorate the front porch for the spring and summer, get the rocking chairs and the other furniture out there, and maybe get some flowers for the planters I bought and never filled."

"I was wondering when you were going to finally do all that," Elle said and rolled her eyes. We burst out laughing together. Her house was always decorated for each specific season. It looked like Martha Stewart had come to decorate it herself.

"Are you really sure this is what you want to do, work with Jeff? What if you don't see eye to eye and start fighting all the time?"

"I'm not worried about it. It's funny you should say that, Elle. Jeff and I said the same thing. We work really well together as a team, and he has set up very defined processes, as well as a flowchart, so there won't be any confusion on who reports to who and what needs to get done during the day-to-day functions."

"You will be in a whole different industry though. How do you feel about that?"

"I think it will be a great experience, and I'm not worried that I won't catch on very easily. I've already worked with him, so I know a large portion of the business. I also know that he will take my side when necessary and tell me when I'm being irrational if needed."

Elle said, "Well, at least you know most of the workers."

I said, "Yes, I suppose so. I don't know them well, but I'll certainly get to know them."

She laughed at the silly face I made, and I laughed at the one she made back at me because I knew what she was going to say.

"What about McHottie?" she said.

And there it was. The comment I was expecting.

"What are we, in an episode of *Grey's Anatomy*?"

She laughed again and made sure to remind me of the incident at the company Christmas party I told her about involving a very good-looking employee who worked for my husband. We started laughing like schoolgirls, and I replayed the whole thing in my head. I didn't think Jeff knew about it, which was just as well because I wouldn't want to upset him or make him do something unfair to his employee—not that I believed he would, but I wouldn't want to test the waters.

"He only said some very kind, innocent words to me and didn't lay a hand on me."

"Remember what it was like back in the day when we thought a boy was cute and hoped he would like us or at least flirt with us?"

"Yes, but I am so happy now that different things excite me. Like nights to ourselves without the kids."

"I agree with you on that one. I've had B now for only a few months, and I feel like I don't even know my husband anymore."

"Oh, I know. I've been there, but once she starts sleeping through the night, you will get right back on track."

I slowly drifted deep into thought about how Jeff and I met so many years ago. We were so young and stupid back then but so much in love with each other. We met in college and both thought we were going to save the world. I was a finance major, and he was studying business. We had so many of the same ideas but then butted heads on other issues. Of course, being young and in love, we thought that was the perfect balance for a great marriage. Our biggest challenge had become what we should eat for dinner. I was thankful it was not how we were going to afford the groceries for dinner. We had hit a few speed bumps along the way but made our way back to each other.

Elle said, "Hello? Are you in there?" She was talking to me, and I was so lost in thought about my husband that I totally tuned her out.

"I'm so sorry. I was just lost in thought, I guess."

She laughed at me and said, "You must be thinking about McHottie."

I wasn't exactly thinking about him. I was happy, but something was definitely off. It was not like it used to be. I was not worried, but I was missing something. I couldn't put my finger on it, but it was there, sometimes sort of eating at me. This change of pace might help me figure it out. For the sake of my marriage, I hoped it just went away.

I laughed, trying to hide my concern, and threw a tennis ball at her. "Help me bring these bags to the car so I can drop them off at the Salvation Army for the clothing drive next week." She jumped right up to help me, and we got moving.

Chapter 3

I spent my week off between jobs doing exactly what I was hoping to do. I needed to get the house together and figure out what we didn't use anymore, what we needed to give away, and what we could contribute to the neighborhood yard sale. I made my way through the whole house, and once I was done, I felt a huge weight lifted off my shoulders. I really felt like I was ready to start the new job and not have anything holding me back.

I even had enough time to read a book that I had been wanting to read. I also had enough time for a spa day. I really felt rejuvenated and ready to go.

I pulled up to the house and parked in the driveway instead of pulling into the garage, as I was going to be heading back out after getting changed and having a quick bite to eat for lunch, and that was when I saw him. I stopped dead in my tracks. The hair on the back of my neck stood straight up. My skin started to crawl so badly it felt like it did when I was afraid I was going to get stung by a bee. I was fairly certain he didn't see me—at least I thought he didn't.

There was a beautiful house three doors down from us on Elle's side of the street. It was painted a soft Georgian-home-style yellow. In the ten years we'd lived there, we had yet to actually meet our neighbors. We didn't know who they were, what they did, or how long they had actually lived in that home. A few neighbors had been there longer than we had but only by a few years. We had all built our homes and lived there since, except this one house. The couple who built it had a terrible family tragedy and ended up selling the house before they had the chance to call it home. That was the story anyway.

No one was certain of what actually happened, but they'd heard a few stories over the years. It was even said that the gentleman who built the home had a wayward half brother who bought it from him after the family tragedy. Everyone questioned, of course, how wayward could he have been if he bought a $500,000 home? I would get such an eerie feeling just looking at it.

One story made the most sense, and that was that the husband was involved in many illegal operations. It was not believable from our perspective, as we had never seen any strange activity or police at the home. We had never had any issues at all with them. We'd even heard that they were both working professionals and traveled most of the month. The neighbor who lived right next door to them had spoken to them many times, but they were very secretive about their personal affairs. He mowed the lawn, and she gardened, but they didn't interact much with anyone. They had children, but they were both grown and out of the house, so they said.

As all of this was flowing through my brain, I realized I was still frozen in the driveway. Thankfully, I noticed my SUV was between my five-foot-three-inch body and the house, so if he was looking at me out the window, he wouldn't be able to see me. I raced into my house and dialed Jeff at the office. I hung up after the first two rings because maybe I was just overreacting. I also didn't want to get him upset or thinking I was crazy. I left it alone and moved on with my day. If it was who I thought it was and I saw him again, I would have to tell Jeff.

Why was he at the yellow house? What did he have to do with them? Seeing him there was starting to confirm some of the rumors about our shady neighbors in the pretty house. What was he doing there? Why was he so close to my family? I definitely couldn't tell Jeff. The first thing he'd say was "Thank God you're not a housewife. You would stay home all day and make shit up about the neighbors."

We don't exactly see eye to eye on what happened either.

Chapter 4

The alarm went off at 5:25 a.m. Monday morning. Jeff kissed me good morning and got out of bed to head to the shower. I turned off the alarm, and I was thrilled because I could sleep an extra hour with my new job. Even with getting the kids off to school, I could sleep in later. Jeff was off to work about two hours before I even needed to leave the house with the kids. Now they could sleep in two hours longer without having to take that dreaded bus to day care for an hour before the actual school bus came to pick them up for school. This was a win-win for the whole family, and I was really feeling good about life in general.

I got up at 6:25 a.m., worked out for thirty minutes, got in the shower, and then got dressed for work. I woke the kids up, and they got dressed and ready on their own. I made a cup of coffee and sat and read a book until the kids came downstairs. I thought buying a cup every day would be a little much. We all ate breakfast together and talked and laughed. It was a wonderful morning.

Isabella said, "Mommy, I love that you are home with us in the morning like this. It's so great."

I kissed her on the forehead and said, "Me too! Good thing I quit that crazy job."

I texted Jeff after I dropped the kids off at school and told him I was on my way to the office.

He replied, "Great! I have a story for you when you get here."

I sent the emoji blowing a heart kiss back to him. As much as he loved me, he refused to use emojis. I didn't know why, but he just wouldn't.

While I was driving to work, I thought life couldn't get any better than this. Normally, I would be a neurotic mess, wondering what bad was going to happen to screw it up for me, but not this time. I drove along my merry way with not a care in the world … Maybe I should have worried.

Chapter 5

I got to the office for my first day of work and walked into Jeff's office.

He gave me a big bear hug and said, "Are you ready for your big first day in the family business?"

With a big smile, I said, "Yep, put me to work, boss."

We laughed together and gave each other a kiss. He said he had a surprise for me. He led me to the other side of the building, to the area the customer service department called their home away from home. As we came around the corner, I noticed immediately that there was a brand-new office constructed. He had an office built for me. He said, "Surprise!"

"How did you pull this off so quickly?"

"I have a guy," he said and smiled his cute little smile, the one that I fell in love with from the beginning.

My mom teased him because he always "had a guy." You need a plumber? Jeff "has a guy." You need an exterminator? Jeff "has a guy." You need a landscaper? Jeff "has a guy."

Jeff had just acquired a new electric/plumbing/HVAC company. Financially, they were in ruins, but they had been a household name in the area for over sixty years. They had a very large client list, and that alone was worth the money. The old man had run the company effortlessly and made a very good living. The oldest son, Carl, took over the business ten years earlier. Since the father died three years before, the son hadn't been able to keep a handle on things trying to run it his way. He approached Jeff, knowing that he was a second-generation business owner and clearly very successful from the financial investment in radio and television for marketing and advertising. He pitched his business plan to Jeff. The plan consisted of Jeff buying the company for a very modest amount, given the debt we would incur. The plan also included Carl staying on to run the company under Jeff's constant advisement. Carl had a really great team of employees who worked for him, and keeping them on was part of the plan as well. This would make our job much easier. In our current company, we offered a number of benefits to our employees, and Carl did not, so they were more than willing to stay on board after the acquisition.

Jeff thought the business plan was very intriguing and knew he would be able to turn the company around in no time so it would be turning a profit again in less than one year. I sat in the initial meetings, and while I knew Jeff would be able to completely transform the company and make it profitable again, something just seemed off with Carl. I couldn't put my finger on it, but something just wasn't right. This was a reoccurring feeling for me these days. Jeff and I discussed it, and he agreed, but he wanted to keep it professional. We both thought he was a little squirrely, but that really didn't have anything to do with us making money. Jeff was confident that with me with my finance background, him with his business background, our accountant, and our attorney all combing through Carl's books, we would find a red flag if there was one to find.

Jeff stressed that we wouldn't buy the company if all parties did not give their blessing. It took six months for us to all come to an agreement and get all parties on board. We, of course, made some changes, and being that Carl was almost bankrupt, he didn't have much of a choice.

Since Jeff and I owned all the companies together, I came on board as an owner rather than an employee, and it stirred some hesitation from our staff. We set everyone straight from the beginning by presenting them with a flowchart, much like the one we already had for our existing company. This was to show them that I was not going to disrupt anything in their day-to-day activities. My role was to be there as support to Jeff and to begin implementing our company policies in the newly acquired company. With regard to the staff, I would only be in charge of the office staff, whom I would be hiring myself.

Years before, we had decided to change our business model in order to make more money and provide more benefits to our employees. Even though I was working full-time with my old company, I spent nights that I wasn't traveling and weekends either in the office with Jeff or in our home office helping him with the transition of everything. We planned out all the changes from how we were going to answer the phone to how we were going to change our name and the lettering on the work vehicles.

Yet again, it was another perfect fit for me to join the company and work in the business every day. I never thought I would be a part of the day to day. Was I happy to actually be a part of it, or was I just happy not to be at my old job? I grappled with that question every day.

Chapter 6

My mom offered to pick up the kids from school since my working hours had changed. She always wanted to spend more time with them, and she always hated the idea of them going to day care before and after school. This was a big help for me, because she would just take them right to my house after school so I would come home and there they were.

Jeff was now going to travel less often, but his trips would be at least ten days long. When he traveled in the summer, we usually went with him and made it into a family vacation. This time, however, the kids were still in school. I didn't like when he traveled, but we were safe in our neighborhood—or I assumed we were before my possibly delusional sighting.

I pulled into the driveway, and as I glanced down the street, I saw him again. My blood went cold, and I couldn't believe what I was seeing. I was sure it was him this time, and I didn't know what to do. So many thoughts went racing through my head again. I had a huge argument with myself. *Why do I care, and do I actually need to be worried? I know what he is capable of and what a monster he is from the things that he's done.*

I pulled into the garage and closed the door almost before the SUV was all the way inside. I pulled myself together before I walked into the house. The last thing I wanted was to worry the kids and my mom. I was thinking of a fail-safe, just in case. My mom and dad didn't live too far away from us, so I could always bring the kids there to sleep for the time Jeff was away if I really felt unsafe.

I walked into the house to greet everyone, and I think my mom noticed that something was wrong right away but knew better than to ask in front of the kids. She didn't want to upset them. She had a big smile on her face until she saw mine, and then it faded a bit.

Since it was Friday, she asked me for a quick recap of my first week at the new job, and I told her how great it was and how happy I was to have better hours to be home more with the kids. I was overjoyed that I wasn't going to have to travel anymore unless I was with my family. I could actually have some time to myself in the morning to drink some coffee and read a book. She was really glad for me. She asked if I wanted to bring the kids over and have dinner with them. Friday was order-out night. It had been at my parents' since before I was born.

"Yes!" came out of my mouth before she even completed the rest of the question.

The kids were very excited.

I thought this would be a great way to make sure no one would be following us over to my parents' house. I wasn't sure what might happen. I was very thankful Jeff convinced me to put the alarm system in the house when he started traveling. I armed it when we left to go to my parents' to make sure no one could get in while we were out. When we got back, I armed it and also called the local police to let them know that Jeff was traveling. I spoke to Chief DeNardo, and he informed me that Jeff had already let them know he would be away. I was silent.

I managed to say, "Excuse me?"

The chief said, "I'm sorry, ma'am. I probably shouldn't have said anything, but Jeff always lets us know when he will be out of town just for extra security."

I heaved a sigh of relief, as my radar was up after the two sightings from down the street.

"Ma'am, are you still there?"

"Yes, I'm sorry," I said. "Thank you so much. We really appreciate it."

He said, "Anytime. You know where to find us."

I went back and forth in my head to decide whether I wanted to tell Jeff or not. I thought, *Why worry him while he's away?* Since I knew for sure it was Justin that I had seen, there was no doubt that Jeff had to believe me. I'd tell him when he got home. God knew he didn't answer his phone all that often when he was traveling anymore. Why not?

Chapter 7

One month had gone by, and we were in the thick of setting up our new company. Jeff and I worked all day, and after we got the kids to bed, we picked up with it again in the evening. We worked so well together it was more like fun than work. It was even better knowing that we were going to make a good amount of additional money from the new company once it was all set up with our current business plan.

Carl came into the office, and he was a disheveled mess. His shirt was misbuttoned. His hair was definitely not even combed, so he most likely wasn't showered. I would even go as far as to say that he had slept in the clothes he was wearing the day before. He was very on edge and really short with everyone. We kept asking him what was going on, and he wouldn't admit that something was up.

He just kept saying, "I didn't sleep well, and I feel overwhelmed."

Jeff and I exchanged a shared eye roll, as Carl wasn't really contributing at all after the acquisition, even though the plan he approached us with showed him heavily participating in his company integrating into our business plan.

Jeff finally had to sit him down and set him straight.

"Carl, you have not been holding up your end of the bargain here."

Carl said, "What do you mean?"

Jeff said, "Do you feel as though you are focused and working hard to get this company up and running the way we agreed?"

"No, Jeff, I guess I haven't been working as hard as we agreed. I've had some personal issues, and I'm not quite sure how I am going to overcome them. My brother is involved in a life that isn't exactly on the straight and narrow. I've been trying to get him to walk away from that life, but he's not budging."

"Carl, you have to just let it go. Is his life starting to overlap into yours?"

Carl looked Jeff right in the eye and said, "No, not at all. I'm just really worried about him, and my nephew, Junior, is beginning to get involved. Well, at least I think he is. I'm assuming he is because he's been hanging around him again."

Jeff said, "So you're worried that he's involved because he's been spending time with his father?"

"Yes, I know how crazy it sounds, but I can't help but think that I need to try to get him out of there."

Jeff and I needed for Carl to focus. If we were going to keep paying him the large salary for the work that he agreed to do, he would need to step it up pretty quickly. Jeff told him that he understood that he was worried for his family, but something had to give and he needed to choose. Carl wasn't happy but eventually agreed to work harder and try to stop worrying and meddling in his brother's life.

Things turned around in the next few weeks, and Carl seemed to be much more focused. He took some work off my plate as well as Jeff's. We, of course, double- and triple-checked his work just to make sure he was doing it correctly and actually completing the tasks he agreed to do. We needed to make sure he was focused and on track. We eventually stopped checking his work because everything seemed to be moving forward smoothly.

I thought, *If he keeps this up, we'll be in good shape.*

Chapter 8

I headed over to Elle's one Saturday morning to have some coffee and chat. The kids and Jeff were eating breakfast and watching cartoons. I stepped out the front door and saw that there was a work vehicle parked out in front of Elle's house. She didn't mention that she was having any work done that day or at all for that matter. Then again, she and I hadn't spoken a whole lot since Jeff and I had been working for what felt like twenty-four hours a day.

I walked through the front door and into the kitchen and saw Elle feeding Bianca. She was such a little cutie-pie and a great new addition to the family. I hugged and kissed them both and thought how lucky I was to have them right across the street from me.

We chitchatted for a while and talked about work.

"How are things going at the stores?"

"Very well. It's so interesting to see how people react to the new trends. I'm so glad we are on top of things like that, because it really keeps the business going."

Elle was so stir-crazy she began getting involved in more of the marketing and sourcing of new products to offer at the stores. Going back and forth from food to hardware, she was always learning something new, and there was never a dull moment. I was so glad for her. I was afraid she was going to start getting depressed. Being home with not much to do all day but talk to a very small child can get pretty boring.

"How are things with the new company and those employees taking on the new business model? Are you still happy working with hubby?"

"Yes, I definitely think it was the right decision, and the employees from Carl's old business are ecstatic to have processes in place, benefits, and training programs. They don't have to fly by the seat of their asses all day and hope they did the right thing on the job."

"That's wonderful. I'm so glad to hear that things are moving along so smoothly. I see your lights on all hours of the night, so I know you guys are working so hard."

"We really are, so it's so nice to come over here and catch up with you and laugh. I'm sorry I haven't made more time to do so."

I didn't hear anyone moving around in the house, so I asked her what the deal was with the work vehicle outside.

She said, "You know how the property extends into the trees in the backyard?"

"Yes," I said.

"Well, there are a number of dead trees back there, and Dean wanted to have them cut down so we could use them for firewood in the winter."

"Oh, so you have a tree trimmer back there?"

She said, "Yes," and proceeded to tell me that a few months ago he was working at the "yellow house" down the street, and she just walked over there and asked him if he would be able to do some tree work for her a few houses down.

My body completely froze, and I'm pretty sure my face was a ghostly shade of white because Elle said, "Oh my, Angie, are you okay?"

I didn't want to frighten her or the baby so I said, "Yes. Why?"

She said, "You look like you've seen a ghost."

"Oh, I didn't have any breakfast so maybe it's just too much coffee."

I immediately knew who it was in her backyard, trimming her trees. It was Justin. He had a tree-trimming business before he crossed our path. I wasn't about to leave her alone with that monster, but I also didn't want him to see me or know that I was associated with Elle. I certainly couldn't tell her what I knew about him or how I knew what I knew.

She said, "Let me get you something to eat so you don't pass out. What do you want?"

I didn't want her to go to any trouble, so I said, "Do you have a granola bar?"

She said, "Of course," and went to the pantry to get me one.

Elle and I both looked out the window and saw Justin coming up through the backyard. She said, "Oh, he must be finishing up."

I waited until he was almost at the back door to come inside, and I headed to the bathroom so he wouldn't see me.

While I was in the bathroom, he told her he had just finished up and was expecting payment upon completion. I heard her get up to get her checkbook, and then I heard him say something about cash, so I assumed she paid him in cash. That was Justin for you. He insisted on cash so he didn't have to claim it as income and pay the taxes on it. What a shady cat.

I could hear him talking again, but this time, I couldn't quite make out his words. I felt the hair on the back of my neck stand up. If it were possible, my skin would have crawled right off my body. I heard Elle say thank you and goodbye. His footsteps through the front foyer passing the bathroom were not loud, and they weren't quick either. He wasn't rushing to get out of there. The front door closed, and he was gone. I was hoping he was out of the neighborhood for good, but I had a feeling I wasn't that lucky. At least this would explain why he was in the neighborhood to begin with.

I came out of the bathroom, and Elle looked at me a little funny.

She said, "Are you okay?"

I said, "Yes, why?"

She was still looking at me funny, and then she finally said, "Justin, the tree guy, said to tell Ang Toph said later." Elle could tell by the look on my face that I wasn't very happy with the comment left behind by that jackass. I felt like I was going to pass out. I didn't know what to do because, again, I didn't want to tell her the history behind it all and what that monster was capable of doing.

Finally, she said, "What was that about?"

I just looked at her and said, "Who's Toph?" I hated playing dumb and essentially lying to her, but I needed to keep her out of it and—not to sound dramatic—but out of danger as well.

She said, "The tree trimming guy." She asked me if I knew him, and I said, "I don't know. I didn't see his face."

Elle was a very smart woman, and I could tell that she wasn't buying any of my antics, but she obviously decided not to push the issue. Thank God for the mutual respect.

I needed to make it look as inconspicuous as possible and get out of there and back to my own house. I was just going to walk right across the street and tell Jeff what had happened. He needed to know. Although I was going to tell him when he got back from his last trip, I didn't, and I guess that was a mistake. Even if he got mad at me for not telling him, he needed to know. I needed him to know. I was thankful when my phone rang and it was Jeff.

I answered, and he said, "When are you coming home?"

I said, "I can come home now."

He said, "Yes, that would be a good idea."

I hugged the girls and got out of there as fast as I could.

When I got home, Jeff looked at me like he was ready to rip my head off. I said, "What's the matter? What is it?"

He said, "Do you mind telling me why I just saw Justin coming out of Elle's house?" He made it sound like he was pissed at me and like I knew he was going to be there.

I said, "Are you kidding me?"

My expression must have made him realize my level of anger because right away, he said, "What's happening?" in a much calmer, less accusatory tone.

"I wasn't going to say anything because I thought I was just paranoid, but a few months ago, I thought I saw him walking into the yellow house. I assumed I was just being paranoid, so I never mentioned it to you, but about two months after that, I saw him going into the house again. You were traveling, and I didn't want to worry you while you were away.

This time, I was sure it was him, and I was standing on the other side of the SUV so I was positive that he didn't see me."

He said, "Why didn't you tell me?"

I said, "I told you I didn't want to say anything because I didn't want you to worry. I also didn't want to argue about it because I wasn't sure if you would feel the same way as I do or not."

"Angie, all of this still doesn't explain why he was over at Elle's house this morning."

"I know, Jeff. Nothing explains why he was at Elle's this morning except that he was cutting down some trees in her backyard. Better yet, she said she saw him working at the yellow house, and she just walked right over there and approached him. She asked him to trim back the trees on her property. She wanted it to be done the same way he was doing it at the yellow house."

"*What*?" yelled Jeff.

Chapter 9

Jeff was beside himself, and I could see the anger building in his eyes. He was usually a very calm man and not much got him angry. He had had a pretty rough childhood, so since he was successful and we had a good amount of financial freedom, he was very happy with life. This was clearly a situation that had him furious, and as angry as he was, I could tell he was planning on what his next move would be.

I wasn't going to tell him what the chief of police told me either, but I wanted Jeff to know that I knew and also tell him how much I loved him because he cared about us so much.

"So when you were on your last business trip, I called the chief of police." I saw his eyes soften because he knew what I was about to say. "He told me that you always let them know when you are out of town."

He smiled at me and said, "Come here." He engulfed me in his big bear hug and kissed me on the forehead.

"I need to know you are all safe when I'm out of town. I have him watch over your parents as well. I know, I know, your dad's the mayor, and they watch over him anyway, but I just want to make sure you are all safe."

"I love you so much, Jeff. I can't help but feel uneasy about all this."

Jeff said, "I would usually feel just as uneasy, *but* it's just Justin."

"How can you say that, Jeff? Especially after your head was ready to blow off a few minutes ago when I told you what was going on?"

"Let's really take a minute to think about it, Angie. Let's take a step back for a moment and really think this through. We didn't have any issues with Justin, and as I recall, the employees always thought he had some odd sister-like connection to you."

"All the more reason to worry about it, don't you think? Not only that, but don't you remember what he went to prison for after his employment with us ended?"

"I do," Jeff said, "but I just don't see how that would affect you, being his sister and all."

"That is not funny, Jeff!"

"I know, Angie, but I don't believe he raped that woman while he was robbing that house. He robbed how many other homes in those few months and didn't rape anyone else? Why would he do that?"

"How can you say that? He went to jail."

"I know, but it doesn't make a lot of sense. I just don't see it. He's not a rapist. Drug addict and thief but not a rapist. Don't you think it's a little odd that they didn't even have that much evidence and he took a deal? He pleaded guilty when the evidence was crap. I just don't buy it. What do you want me to do about this?"

"I don't know, Jeff, but I don't like that he's hanging around the neighborhood. How did he get mixed up with the yellow house, and what is the connection?"

"Elle said he was cutting down trees for them. Isn't that why he was there?"

"I suppose," I said. "I'm pretty certain that he didn't have that work truck when I saw him there the first time."

"Maybe he was just giving them a proposal to do the work and didn't use the work truck?"

"Maybe, Jeff, but the whole thing sounds strange to me."

"Angie, it could really be just a coincidence that he's in the neighborhood."

"I guess you're right, but I just feel like there has to be more to it than that."

—⚊⚊⚊—

Jeff looked away from Angie because he didn't want her to see the concern on his face. He was just as worried as she was, but he wanted to keep her calm. The best way to do that was to show that everything would be okay and not reveal his concern. There were things that Jeff knew about Justin that he was not about to share with Angie, especially not now. Justin making an appearance was one sign of what was to come. Jeff wasn't sure if he was ready for this. No matter what, he knew he didn't have a choice. He needed to be ready.

Chapter 10

It was very calm in the office for a Monday morning, and the work crews were just about ready to leave the shop when Carl came into the office completely frantic. He was a disheveled mess, physically and emotionally. His clothes looked like he had slept in them, and it didn't look like he'd shaved in days. He was bouncing off the walls almost like he was on something. There was no history of drug use that we knew of with Carl, but he seemed high as a kite. Maybe he was really afraid of something or someone. Maybe he was being followed. We had seen him like this before but nowhere near as bad.

He ran into his office, slammed the door shut, and locked it. We gave him some time to settle down, and then Jeff and I knocked on the door. We figured we should talk to him together. He opened the door and almost slammed it in our faces, but Jeff, being such a large man, put his body between the door and the door frame before it had the chance to close.

Carl was all flustered and said, "What do you want? Can't a guy get some peace and quiet around here?"

Jeff said, "Carl, you are the one disrupting everyone. This is a place of business, and you are acting like a madman today. What's going on?"

Carl tried to avoid eye contact and continued to pace around the office. He was shuffling through papers as if he was looking for something.

I asked, "Carl, can we help you find something?"

He barked at us, "What the fuck? I asked you to leave me alone."

Jeff said, "Listen, if you can't pull yourself together, I am going to send you home for the day or I'm going to call the cops. Your choice."

This seemed to set something off in Carl, and he looked at Jeff with pleading eyes, saying, "Okay, okay, jeez, maybe I should just get out of here."

Jeff said, "If you need help, we will help you. We are in this together, and you should probably tell us what's happening being that you are completely frantic. Since you are here in the office, can I assume this is office related?"

Carl looked at Jeff and said, "I wish it was that easy."

Jeff said, "I would hope that I wouldn't have to say this to you, but if you are in some kind of trouble, you can talk to us, and maybe we can help. Also, if you are in trouble, I would hope you are not bringing it into the business. You cannot put our employees at risk either. Is it your family again?"

——m——

Carl looked at Jeff helplessly, not sure what to say. Jeff knew that something was seriously wrong. He had spent enough time with Carl to know when something was really out of whack, and this was one of those moments when Jeff could see that Carl was seriously rattled.

Jeff looked right in Carl's eyes and knew this was the beginning of a very tough road ahead, a road that could take many different turns—some good and some really bad—in the end. Jeff knew this was it, and he was ready for whatever came their way. They had planned for this scenario a very long time ago.

"Carl, do you want to take some time off?"

"You mean like a vacation?"

"Sure, if that's what you think you need."

"Maybe that would be a good idea for all of us."

"It's totally up to you, Carl. Whatever you want to do."

Carl said, "Maybe I'll go out on the boat for a while. Take the wife maybe and just head to the beach."

"Whatever you have to do, Carl, and whatever it is that has you frantic can be all figured out while you are away."

"It won't be that easy, Jeff. I'll be in touch."

Chapter 11

"Angie, a week has gone by and we haven't heard anything from Carl. Don't you think that's a little odd?"

"I do think it's a little odd, but maybe he just really needed some time away."

We were in Jeff's office when our office assistant came barreling through his door.

"Jeff and Angie, Carl's wife is on the phone, and she is asking to speak with him. I told her he wasn't here, and she demanded to speak with one of you."

I said, "Thank you. We will take care of it."

We put her on speaker so we could both hear what Anna had to say. She started ranting on about what sounded like nonsense.

I said, "Anna, we can't help you if we can't understand what you are saying. Can you calm down a little for us so we can help?"

She calmed down slightly but was still hysterical. It sounded like she had been crying, but she was out of breath, and we could barely understand what she was saying.

This was a very strong, well-educated, professional woman, and she was in hysterics. Whenever I had any contact with Anna, she was always put together. She could put any outfit together and make it look amazing. She was a fashion designer and was really great at her profession. Even if something was bothering her, you would never know. She was always very strong, almost emotionless at times. This was very unlike her.

She settled down enough to tell us that Carl was missing, and she hadn't spoken to him in a few days. She proceeded to tell us that she was traveling for business last week and last spoke to him on Friday. She mentioned that she was telling him her travel schedule to come home and he seemed very distant and very out of it.

Jeff said, "By 'out of it,' do you mean like he was on drugs?"

She gasped and said, "No, not Carl. He doesn't do drugs."

Jeff and I looked at each other, very puzzled but at the same time almost not surprised, given his actions last week when he was in the office.

"Anna," Jeff said, "Carl was in the office over a week ago, and that was the last time we saw or spoke to him." There was silence on the other end of the phone.

"What do you mean you haven't seen or spoken to him in over a week?"

We explained how frantic he was in the office and that Jeff had told him to take a vacation. There was silence again on the other end.

I said, "I don't want to be insensitive, Anna, but have you noticed anything off about him lately?"

She said, "He always seems to be off," trying to make light of the situation.

We all chuckled awkwardly but got right back on track.

"Anna, Jeff and I were trying to figure out what was going on with him, but he wasn't budging, so we don't know what was wrong with him the last day he was in the office. Has he ever been involved in drugs or anything related to crime?"

"Not since he came back after college, Jeff. I don't have any knowledge of that at least."

I went wide-eyed and looked at Jeff like my whole world just fell apart. About a million scenarios went through my head. I didn't understand what I was hearing. I could tell that Jeff was confused and even a little hurt. Did they know each other before? Before the business deal?

Jeff said, "Anna, what are you talking about?"

I couldn't understand why Anna was talking about Carl to Jeff as if they knew each other long ago.

"Carl came home right after college and—"

Jeff cut her off. "I don't want to hear any more. If we hear anything, we'll let you know, Anna. Call us if you hear anything."

"Jeff, what the hell is she talking about?"

Jeff answered, "I don't know, and I really don't care. I've had it with his nonsense. I don't know what she's talking about. I'll care when we have more info. He'll turn up one way or another—dead or alive."

I wasn't buying it. I knew he knew more, and I couldn't understand why he was trying to hide it, especially from me. I decided to give my husband the benefit of the doubt. He'd tell me when he was ready.

Chapter 12

At 3:00 a.m. the next morning, the phone rang, waking us up. I reached over to answer it, and before I could even say hello, I could hear Anna crying on the other end.

She said, "Hello, Angie, can I please speak with Jeff?"

Obviously something was seriously wrong, but again, I couldn't feel more left out of whatever was happening.

I handed the phone to Jeff and said, "It's Anna, and she wants to speak with you."

I made it very obvious that I wasn't happy. He got the message loud and clear.

Jeff didn't say much, but it sounded like Anna was talking a lot. I couldn't imagine what she was saying, but I knew it wasn't good.

Jeff said, "Anna, what do you want me to do?"

I rolled my eyes at his question.

He said, "Okay," a nauseating number of times and hung up.

"Well, what's going on?" I said.

Jeff said, "Carl is dead, Angie."

"What? When? Are you sure? What happened? Where is he?"

"They found his car in an abandoned parking lot mostly charred from a fire."

"That doesn't make any sense." I could tell that Jeff knew I was trying to put the pieces together right away, and he just let me talk.

"Anna said that his car was at home in the garage. How could they have found his car? If the car was charred, what did his body look like?" I started to feel panicked. *Who are these horrible people that we are now involved with? Who did this to Carl? We are directly linked to murderers.*

Jeff's face dropped a little, and he said, "They aren't sure the body is his yet."

"*What*? Then why does Anna think it's Carl, and what's the deal with the car?"

Jeff said, "The car was registered to him, but Anna knows nothing about another car. She didn't know he had it and obviously doesn't know where it was stored. She's now trying to get access to any finances, homes, apartments, vehicles, and anything else he might have been hiding."

"Jeff, do you know anything about all this that's happening?" I figured if he had anything to do with this or had any inkling of what might be going on, I would be able to tell in his face whether he admitted it or not.

He just looked at me and very innocently and honestly said, "No, it doesn't make any sense. Up until last week, there was nothing leading us to believe that he was involved in any foul play or leading any type of double life. Other than his frantic episode at the office, there would be no reason for us to believe he had any ties to people capable of doing something so awful."

I gasped overdramatically and said, "Jeff, you don't think he had another wife, girlfriend, or anything like that, do you?"

"Angie, there's no way of knowing that now, and sadly, I wouldn't rule it out as being a possibility. I would doubt it, but you never know, and at this point, anything seems possible."

I thought this was the perfect opportunity to ask Jeff if he knew Carl when they were younger. He and Anna shared some words yesterday, and they both seemed to hide what was behind it all. I couldn't bear the thought of Jeff not being the man I thought I knew and had loved for so long. He was my whole world, along with the kids, and I could not imagine what Anna was going through right then. I didn't even want to try to understand how she was feeling. Even though Anna and Carl didn't have the best marriage, they seemed to support each other in major decisions they made and always held it together as a couple. Anna was pretty upset for a woman in a struggling marriage.

Here it goes. "Jeff?"

"What's up, Angie?" he said in his deep, gravely voice. He looked at me with his big hazel eyes in wonder.

I lost my nerve. I suddenly became terrified of how he might answer. I didn't necessarily doubt that he was hiding something from me, but I thought he was trying to put the pieces together himself. He was clearly deep in thought. I wished I could read his mind. I could sense that he was recalling something in his memory, possibly from a long time ago, and I was almost certain that he knew Carl at some point in his past. I just needed to figure out when and to what extent. Were they childhood friends? High school friends? Were they friends at all? Did they have a falling out, or did they just drift apart?

"Nothing."

Chapter 13

Jeff walked around the office, asking everyone to make their way to the conference room.

"Good morning, everyone."

Some very somber good mornings grumbled around the room.

"I wanted all of us to come together this morning so I could tell you about Carl. For those of you who may not already know, Carl is missing."

A small ruckus broke out in the room, but no one actually said anything. They already knew something was wrong.

"We don't have many details, so we can't tell you much at the moment. I want to make it very clear that whatever you may hear on the news or read in the paper is most likely not true. We have been in close communication with the chief of police. He will provide us with any new details as they come about. We will communicate any new info to you as soon as it is received."

I added, "As Jeff said, we don't have much information ourselves. If you have any questions, please just ask. It will be business as usual here in the office until you hear otherwise."

We made it clear earlier in the announcement that we didn't have a whole lot of answers, but we would do our best to make this easier on everyone. There were a few questions here and there but mostly work related. Most of the questions made us realize that we didn't have as much of a handle on our business as we thought we did in regard to communicating properly with our employees. There were some really ludicrous questions, which again showed us the severity of ignorance throughout the companies. This was our fault. It came at a good time for us to address these issues.

We did ask all the employees if they had any information about Carl or anything they thought would help us or the police in getting to the bottom of this. We asked that they come to us in private so that we wouldn't cause chaos and start rumors. We suggested very sternly but respectfully that they not talk about the situation at all, as we did not want any rumors flying around to muddy the waters of this tragic time.

The meeting was over, and I went back to my office. I got settled back at my computer, and Derrick appeared in the doorway.

"Hi there."

"Hey," he said, walking into my office, and sat in his usual chair.

"What's up?"

"Nothing really. I just wanted to come in here and ask you how you're doing."

"I'm okay. This might sound heartless, but it could be worse. I don't want to worry too much until we have more information."

"What do you think is actually going on?"

"Knowing Carl, nothing."

"Really? You think he's just ducking life?"

I laughed. "I don't know, but that's always a possibility I suppose."

"Yeah, he's a strange bird as it is," he said with a smirk.

That smirk sent a rush of tingling through my body. *Just focus. Don't let him see it.* He just sat there looking at me for a few seconds and then stood up. He put his hands flat on my desk and leaned toward me, almost over my computer.

"If you think of anything I can do to help, just let me know."

"I will do that. Thank you."

He winked at me. I almost lost my composure.

"I'll see you later," he said and was gone.

I looked down and noticed that he had left handprints on the desk. My mind wandered to extremely inappropriate places.

Jeff walked into my office moments later.

"Hey, everyone seemed to comply for the time being, don't you think? I also think that went well, don't you?"

"Yes, definitely," I said very breathily.

"Are you okay?"

"I'm fine. Why?"

"Your cheeks are red, and you sound out of breath."

"Oh no, I'm fine."

"Okay. I can't help but think the hammer is going to drop and wonder how exactly it's going to happen. I have a feeling it's going to come in stages. That might be okay."

That afternoon, that was exactly what happened.

Chapter 14

The office phone rang off the hook that first afternoon, as we expected. Newspapers, magazines, the local news, existing clients, and so on—everyone you could possibly imagine was calling us, and I was hoping they were calling us and leaving Anna the hell alone. She didn't need this right then. With the whole thing really being up in the air and not having any answers at all, she didn't need people blowing up her phone or banging on her door for a story that wasn't there to tell.

Anna warned us that this might happen, but I guess Jeff and I didn't think it would be this soon. About 3:30 p.m., my assistant came into my office asking if I had time to speak with an Officer Fitzpatrick. She said, "He actually asked to speak to you and Jeff at the same time, but I know Jeff is in that meeting and he asked not to be disturbed."

I said, "Of course."

"Okay, he's on line 2 then for you."

"Hello, Officer Fitzpatrick. How are you today?"

"I'm fine, ma'am. Under the circumstances, how are you and Jeff?"

This was the first time I'd spoken to this man, and he acted like he'd known me my whole life, which, I guess, was exactly what he was trying to achieve. He didn't sound a day over twenty-five, and I thought that was a good thing—young blood on a case like this. It made me feel like he would work to the bone to get to the bottom of what was going on with Carl.

"I'm sorry, but there are some things that I'm not at liberty to share with you at the moment, but I will be able to share them very soon. After I speak with Anna. Would it be okay if I swung by the office tomorrow to meet with you and Jeff? I have some questions for you guys. I also have some questions for your employees. I know you feel the need to protect them, but if it's okay with you, I would like to speak with all of them?"

"Officer, are you saying that you think someone here is involved?"

"No, ma'am, I just want to try to get some details about Carl that we might be missing, something that can possibly give us another clue and give us better direction."

"Okay, Officer, that's fine with us. Do you know when you might want to come by the office?"

"I was hoping that I could come by tomorrow first thing in the morning."

"What is your first thing in the morning?"

He laughed and said, "How does nine work for you and Jeff?"

"That would be fine," I said.

I hung up the phone, and by then, Jeff was out of his meeting. I walked into his office and told him about my phone call with Officer Fitzpatrick. He wasn't very happy but didn't look at all like he was nervous about meeting with the officer.

"Jeff, do you think he thinks one of us had something to do with Carl's death?"

"Disappearance," Jeff said.

I cocked my head, and Jeff looked at me and said, "We don't know if he's dead yet, Angie."

"Oh yes, sorry about that. I'm just thinking the worst because I don't know what else to do."

"To answer your question, Angie, no, I don't think that they think anyone here had anything to do with it, but they need to exhaust all options, and the way it sounds, they don't have any leads at all right now."

"How credible can these guys be, Jeff?"

"What do you mean, Angie?"

"I mean, most of them have a history of drug abuse and a criminal record."

Jeff smirked a little bit and said, "That may be true, but that is all the more reason to ask if they noticed if Carl was involved in something he shouldn't have been."

I looked at Jeff, confused a little, which seemed to be the norm for me these days. I had to pull myself together. I was an educated, knowledgeable woman with a great deal of professional work experience who could handle a crazy situation with her eyes closed. Why was I not thinking straight in this instance? I seemed to be detached. I needed to focus on whatever I had control over. That way, I wouldn't look so stupid.

"I guess you're right," I said.

"Think about it," Jeff said. "Most of them are now buying houses, and they are getting custody of their kids and getting married. They have also been clean and sober for years at this point. They are perfect candidates to know if something isn't right. They are very observant, and they are thinking very clearly."

I could see exactly what Jeff what saying, and I thought the opposite. With all he said, I couldn't help but think they wouldn't want to get involved or be bothered—not necessarily that their opinion wasn't credible. They had enough going on in their own lives that they wouldn't want to put themselves or their families at risk. Carl didn't deal with the employees as much as we did, so if there was enough loyalty to us and the company, that might be the only way they would talk, if they had anything they wanted to share.

Chapter 15

I got to the office very early the next morning. I needed to get a number of things done before Officer Fitzpatrick graced us with his visit. My mom was truly my savior during this mess. She had the kids again. I was sitting at my desk, making some pretty good headway, and heard footsteps in the hallway. I looked at the clock, and it was 6:45 a.m. Most of the guys started showing up around that time. They started at 7:00 a.m., but most of them came in early to get some coffee and shoot the shit. With Officer Fitzpatrick coming in that day, that schedule was going to change.

I looked up from my computer, and Derrick was standing in the doorway. I loved my husband very much, but there was something about Derrick that just made my skin tingle. We always had great conversations in the office and strangely had quite a bit in common. I would always laugh because a number of his stories started with "When I was in prison." He once said, "I feel so stupid because most of my stories start with something that happened to me in prison."

I said, "You don't seem to be ashamed to talk about them, so don't worry about it."

He did often speak of his wife and kids, and I thought that was so cute. The connection that Derrick and I had was definitely on an intellectual level, so it was never weird or uncomfortable. Although he was very handsome and he definitely got to me when he looked at me, I always tried to keep it very professional.

He was lingering in the doorway but didn't say anything.

I said, "Hey!" with a bright smile. "What's up?"

He was looking sort of awkward, and I wasn't sure how to respond. I never saw him like this. He usually wore a uniform for work when he was going to see clients, but he hadn't put it on yet. He was wearing a tight white

T-shirt and fitted navy-blue pants with his work boots. I tried as hard as possible not to visibly look him up and down. I maintained eye contact. He kept flicking the lid of his lighter open and closed. Clink, clink, clink, clink. As I looked into his eyes, I felt like the clinking started to sink with my increased heart rate.

"You know you shouldn't smoke," I said.

With his devilish smile, he said, "Is it bad for my health?"

"Well, it's not good for you," I said with an odd motherly tone.

"I tend to gravitate toward things that aren't good for me."

Even the motherly tone didn't deter him from flirting with me.

He looked genuinely concerned about something, so I was trying my hardest not to have my mind wondering. I really couldn't help it; as soon as he spoke, all those naughty thoughts drifted away, and I was able to focus, thank God.

"Ang?" he called me Ang, as if *Angie* weren't short enough for *Angelina*.

"Yes, Derrick?" I said.

"I just wanted to say that if you need anything during this time, you know you can trust me, right?"

I said, "I assume you are referring to this mess with Carl?"

He said, "Yes, but even beyond this situation with Carl, I want you to know that you can trust me with anything no matter what happens." He wasn't scaring me at all, but it seemed as though he was trying to say something without actually saying it.

"Is there something else you want to say?"

"No, Ang, but I need you to understand that if you need anything, you can come to me, and I will do everything I can to help."

"Derrick, I really appreciate you saying all this to me. I know our conversations are usually fun and mostly revolve around our hobbies, but this is obviously way more serious than the norm."

"Yes, Angie, but I really value what you and Jeff do for us here in the company, and I enjoy working here, so I will do whatever I can to help."

"Thanks again, Derrick. It really means a lot to me and Jeff to hear you say that out loud."

"Ang, it's not just me that feels that way, so we'll all get through this as a family. You have done so much for all of us, and I can't speak for everyone else, but from what I have been hearing, everyone else feels the same way I do about the situation."

"It will make it much easier to know that we have everyone's support, so thank you again."

Derrick stood in the doorway for what felt like an eternity just looking at me. In reality, it was only a few seconds, but his piercing blue eyes looked like they were reading right through me in that moment. I was a little uncomfortable, but I didn't want him to look away. I felt so terribly like he wanted to say something else. He finally said, "I really enjoy talking to you. Great conversation as usual."

"I wish today's was under better circumstances."

He shot me that overwhelming little smirk and a quick wink and said, "There will be plenty of time for that."

After my heart stopped racing and my lower extremities weren't so weak, my mind took over and thought, *What was that supposed to mean?* It was almost like he knew something I didn't. Again, I felt like I did when Jeff and Anna were talking right in front of me—like I wasn't even there. What was Derrick talking about?

Derrick walked out of Angie's office and thought, *Wow, maybe Justin wasn't talking out of his ass this time for once.* Maybe he really knew what was happening, but how would he know? Did he have something to do with Carl? Was he connected to the situation some way? Just as he thought things were falling into place and starting to make sense, this popped up.

Chapter 16

Anna wasn't sure how this was all going to shake out, so she frantically made her way through the house looking for paperwork and old documents that could somehow incriminate Carl. The last thing she wanted was to have to explain his past—not that she would have any idea where to begin. She thought if she didn't have anything that the cops could find in the house, she would be one step closer to not having to explain it all to them. There was a very large portion of it that she didn't know herself, so she wouldn't be able to put the pieces together for the police. She believed that Carl set it up that way so if anything like this ever happened, she would be protected by her lack of knowledge alone.

The phone rang, and she nearly jumped through the roof.

"Hello?"

"Hey, it's me."

"Hi, what's the word?"

"We're not sure," the voice on the other end said hesitantly.

Anna said, "Do you know when you will know?"

"No, we are still looking into it all. We have about as much info as the police do, and you know where they are with the investigation. We do have a number of leads so at least we have somewhere to start."

"Okay, thank you. I appreciate that you are staying in touch."

"Of course, Anna. We know this is hard for you, and we'll try to let you know as soon as we come up with something. We're glad that you are cooperating, Anna, because we've had other situations like this where the wife is not so eager to help and it doesn't end well for her. This is by no means a threat; we just want you to understand that we are working for you and Carl, and we are truly trying to help."

"Thank you again," said Anna.

All she heard was a dial tone, and the man of mystery was gone.

This was not the first call from Anna's mystery caller. This was part of Carl's past. She was sure of it. She didn't know who they were or how to contact them. They contacted her and said they would keep her in the loop as they did with the wife. These were experienced people. *Experienced in what?* she wondered. It made her cringe. They were very nice and supportive and nonthreatening. She felt protected, but at the same time, she didn't know who these people were or if they were eventually going to turn on her even though they assured her that was not how they operated.

There was a knock at the front door, and she nearly had a heart attack. *What now?* Like the phone wasn't enough to scare her to death. It was Officer Fitzpatrick.

Anna said, "Hello, Officer. Please come in. Can I get you something?"

"No, thank you," the officer said.

Inside, Anna started to panic a little bit. She envisioned him saying, "We have a warrant to search the house," and a flood of cops and detectives barging through the house. What would she do? How could she possibly stall a shitshow like that?

"Officer, what can I do for you today?"

"I just wanted to drop by and let you know that I will be heading over to the business today to speak with Angie and Jeff."

"Okay, that's great."

"Is there anything that you want me to ask them? I will be meeting with some of the employees as well. Is there any one specific employee that I should focus on?"

"Officer, I don't mean to come off as being rude, but I recall telling you that I don't know anything about Carl's business so I wouldn't even know where to begin. Angie and Jeff have never been anything but nice to Carl and me the few times I've dealt with them. Carl spoke very highly of them both during the acquisition, so the chances of them being involved in any of this would be pretty slim. They are just as shocked and worried as I am. They would know more about which employees to focus your efforts on in the investigation."

Officer Fitzpatrick looked very skeptically at Anna and said, "Are you sure about that, Anna?"

Anna wasn't sure what to say. It was obvious that he knew something that she didn't or was trying to get in her head, and she wasn't sure how to react. She thought he was testing her, and she didn't like that one bit.

"Officer, is there something you want to tell me?"

He said, "I think I can ask you the same question, Anna."

She started to get very anxious. The last thing she needed was for the cops to think she was involved when she was in the dark just as much as they were. She kept her composure; no way was she going to show him that she was starting to get very nervous. She needed to talk to Jeff as soon as she could.

"Officer, I think it's time you leave. It sounds like you are accusing me of something, and I don't like it at all. This has been going on long enough, and you and the police department don't have any information regarding Carl, not even a single lead."

Fitzpatrick backed off and saw himself to the door with a ridiculous smirk on his face. The door closed, and she locked it as soon as he was gone. Anna raced to the phone to call Jeff.

Chapter 17

Jeff's cell phone rang and went to voice mail after the fourth ring. Anna hung up and dialed again. On the third ring, Jeff picked up.

"Hello?"

"Jeff, it's Anna."

"Anna, how are you? Are you holding up okay for now?"

"Jeff, Officer Fitzpatrick just left the house."

"Wow! He's an early riser. He's supposed to be here in about a half hour to talk to me and Angie."

"I know; he told me when he was here. Jeff, he asked me if there was anything I needed to tell him before he came to question you and Angie along with the staff. Why would he ask me that?"

"I'm not sure, Anna. Let's see what he has to say when he gets here, and we can compare notes. Do you want me to call you when he leaves and you can come down to the office?"

"Yes, I would really like to come down to the office."

"Absolutely, I'll call you when he leaves to let you know it's safe to come down."

"Jeff, he was acting really strange, and I wasn't comfortable at all. Don't let him talk to anyone without you being present in the room."

"Okay, Anna, thank you for the warning."

"Okay, see you later," Anna said and hung up.

Jeff thought to himself, *What the fuck is this kid doing? What's he trying to prove?* Jeff didn't need him in the way now.

—◦◦◦—

Jeff called me in my office and told me about the conversation he just had with Anna. I wasn't sure what to say. Yet again another opening for me to ask him if he was hiding something from me, but I pushed the urge way down deep inside. I said I would give him the benefit of the doubt, and if he had anything to tell me, he would tell me when the time was right. It was big of me to think this, but I knew in my gut he was hiding something.

I said, "Fitzpatrick should be here soon, right?"

"Yes, and Anna is going to come down here as soon as he leaves. I think we should compare notes. The last thing I want to happen is for us to get blindsided with some bogus accusation from Fitzpatrick after he leaves here and tells the chief something that isn't true."

Fitzpatrick showed up ten minutes later. He was very polite but sniffed around the office almost like he was looking for something but wasn't really. He was acting a little strange and very unprofessional. He was looking through a stack of mail that had been delivered earlier that morning. He even hovered over the customer service representative trying to hear the conversation. We were expecting him to come in and ask how we were doing and proceed to explain how he was going to conduct the day's questioning. All we knew was that we both thought Fitzpatrick was acting very odd. Maybe it was only because we had just spoken with Anna and we were expecting him to be odd. We weren't sure if he was actually going to ask us any questions or just look around. He was like a police dog looking for drugs, but he was looking for clues to find Carl. We didn't know what he thought he was going to find here among the office paperwork.

Finally, he said, "Where were you both on the night of Carl's disappearance?"

Jeff and I looked at each other and almost burst out laughing. It was like a bad cop show with a rookie questioning the first suspect. The question was ridiculous. We didn't know exactly what day he disappeared.

Fitzpatrick looked at us both and said, "Well?"

After an awkward pause, Jeff said, "Officer, that's a little hard to answer because we don't know what day he went missing. He took some time off from work, and the next thing we knew, Anna called us saying his car was found and he was missing. We had no idea what was going on or how long he was missing until we heard from Anna."

Fitzpatrick looked very angry, as if he thought we were mocking him. "Jeff, don't fuck with me here. We know you were in contact with him that week."

I looked at Jeff as if to say, "What the fuck? Are you kidding me?"

Jeff said, "Excuse me? I was most certainly not in contact with Carl the week he took off. The whole purpose for him taking vacation was to get away and work through some family issues."

Fitzpatrick had a smirk on his face, and Jeff looked ready to choke him. Jeff said, "In case you missed it, we are very upset about Carl's disappearance, as is Anna, and we don't appreciate you coming in here with your empty accusations. It sounds like you are really fishing for a lead, and in turn, you are just insulting all of us instead of finding Carl. We want you to leave."

Fitzpatrick was getting very angry now. He went from lunatic to pure psycho in the short period of time that Jeff was handing him his new asshole.

"I will do no such thing as leave this office until I finish my questioning."

Jeff said, "You haven't done anything but accuse us of who knows what, and it sounds like you are just making shit up now to create a worthless lead. You will not speak to my employees with this accusatory tone either."

Jeff continued, "You know as well as I do that you have nothing in this investigation. For you to come in here and start pointing a finger with no proof of anything is insulting to me and Angie, as well as all of our staff, not to mention Carl, wherever he is. Please leave now. If you want to talk to us again, please call, but you are not welcome in here any longer today. I know my rights, and in my place of business, I don't have to talk to you unless you have legitimate questions and I have a lawyer present. I will be talking to the chief about this, and if you fuck with us like this again, I will file a formal complaint with the department. Get the fuck out!"

Fitzpatrick left, but it was evident that he wasn't happy about what just went down. Jeff said, "Can you believe that asshole? What a jackass! The nerve of him coming in here and trying to accuse us of having something to do with Carl's disappearance."

"Jeff, do you think we need to call Demetri?"

Jeff said, "I'm calling the chief of police, and then I'm calling Demetri. I didn't think we would need him until now. Angie, can you call Anna and ask her to come to the office?"

"Of course, I'll call her right now."

"Thank you, honey."

Jeff gave me a quick kiss, and we headed for the phones.

Chapter 18

Anna raced down to the office after we spoke. When she got there, I explained what had happened with Fitzpatrick. Anna was appalled to hear what he had said to Jeff and me.

She said, "What is his problem? I thought he was trying to help us. I understand he's trying to find a missing person, but why is he attacking us? Maybe he's not at all trying to help. We are the ones trying to figure out which milk carton to put him on."

I chuckled, and Jeff and Anna followed. It was nice to have a laugh together during this absurd nightmare we seemed to be living. I think all of us thought that any day Carl would just show up like nothing had ever happened. That would be something Carl would do, especially because he and Anna didn't have the best of relationships and she was always on the road traveling for work.

"Jeff's going to call the chief of police to let him know what happened with Fitzpatrick, but we wanted to talk to you first. He wants you to tell him about the conversation he had with you and the fact that he just showed up on your doorstep at the ass crack of dawn."

Anna said, "He basically did the same thing to me. He kept asking me if there was anything I wanted to tell him. He was definitely trying to say that I was hiding something from him."

"Okay, I'm going to call the chief now," Jeff said. "Should I put him on speaker so we can all talk to him?"

Anna and I agreed that would be the best thing to do as long as the chief was okay with it.

The line was ringing, and the chief picked up.

"Chief DeNardo speaking, how can I help you today?"

"Hey, Chief, it's Jeff."

43

"Hey, buddy, what's up? How's everything over there under the circumstances?"

"As good as it can be, but we have a problem."

"Oh no, what's the matter?" asked the chief.

Jeff went on to tell him what happened with Fitzpatrick that morning. As soon as the name *Fitzpatrick* came out of Jeff's mouth, the chief said, "What? Shit! Jeff, I'm so sorry. I was going to call you this morning to tell you that we fired Fitzpatrick last night."

"Wait. What do you mean? He visited Anna at her house early this morning in full uniform and came to our office right after he left her house? What do you mean you fired him last night?"

Anna and I looked at each other, and I could see in Anna's eyes she was really creeped out. She said, "That man was in my home this morning. I was with him alone in the house. He could have killed me."

Chief said, "I'm coming right over to the office to get your statements about Fitzpatrick."

———❦———

He showed up in about four minutes. He must have turned his lights on and run every red light. He came through the front door, shook Jeff's hand, and then rushed over to Anna. "Are you okay?" he asked. "Did he lay a finger on you?"

Anna said, "I'm fine. He didn't touch me at all, but he kept saying that I wasn't telling him everything, almost as if he'd heard something about me or us or something that would explain Carl's disappearance. He even looked at me as if to say, 'I know you had something to do with all this.'"

Jeff said, "He did the same thing to us ... well, to *me*. He said, 'We all know you were in contact with Carl the week he was out of the office. I most certainly was not in contact with him the week he was out. Check the phone records, and they'll prove it. He asked where Angie and I were the day he went missing. We don't even know when he went missing, so how would we know what we were doing?"

The chief was very upset about this and didn't know what to say to make it better.

Jeff said, "We called our lawyer."

The chief was nervous. "Why did you call your lawyer?"

"We thought a cop was accusing us in Carl's disappearance, so we didn't know what else to do."

The chief was relieved. He had thought they were going to come after the police department. Jeff could sense all this going through the chief's head and said, "Don't worry, man; we're not coming after the police department."

The chief said, "How did you know I was thinking that?"

Jeff said, "We've been friends a long time, so I know when you are on edge. It's not your fault Fitzpatrick took it upon himself to continue the investigation after he got fired. This whole situation is getting weirder by the minute. You know, it doesn't seem like there is actually an investigation."

The chief said, "We don't have much to go on, so there's not a lot we can do. We already know the last time you saw Carl, and since Anna was traveling, we know the last time she heard from him via her cell."

"What do you think prompted Fitzpatrick to say, 'We know you talked to him while he was out of the office'?" Jeff asked.

The chief said, "I have no idea. We don't have any record of that at all. We haven't even looked at the phone records, so there would be no evidence that you spoke with him that week he didn't come to work. Sounds like he was just fishing. Why and for what, I'm not sure."

I was listening and just taking it all in, but I heard the chief say they had no evidence of Jeff speaking to Carl the week he was on vacation. Then he said they didn't even check the phone records yet. How could he know if they had or didn't have evidence of Jeff speaking with Carl when they hadn't even checked the phone records? Something wasn't right. Maybe the chief was just flustered with Fitzpatrick. Maybe because they hadn't checked the phone records, he was just saying they didn't have anything, but why would he say it like that?

"What are you going to do, Chief?"

"I'm not sure, Jeff. I'm not quite sure why he's trying to get information about the case. It's not like he's involved."

"Are you sure about that?" asked Anna.

The chief looked at her and said, "No, I guess I'm not sure, but now it's my priority to find out. I took your original statements, but Fitzpatrick followed up, so I'm going to have to review his original notes. If I have any questions, I'll let you know."

"Thanks, Chief."

"Sure thing. I'll be in touch."

Chapter 19

A few days had gone by since Anna had received word that the body in Carl's car, which she knew nothing about, was most likely not Carl's. Relief obviously swept over her, but in the end, he was still missing.

The police chief contacted all of us and asked if we could have a meeting at the office, as he had some information about Fitzpatrick that he wanted to share with all of us and he preferred to do it with all of us together. It was like we'd all been in a fog since he was there to see us. It was like time had stopped.

The chief showed up at the office, and he looked like he hadn't slept since we'd seen him last. I asked him if he wanted a cup of coffee, and he said, "Sure, that would be nice. Thank you."

"Okay, so I wanted to see all of you together again. I'm not sure how you will all react to what I have to say. It turns out Fitzpatrick has one fucked-up past, going all the way back to his childhood. His father left his mother before he was even born. His mother got remarried to a pretty decent man. They decided to expand their family. The mother got pregnant and developed an aneurism. Then she ended up miscarrying the baby, and due to all the stress, the aneurism burst and she died as a result. Fitzpatrick lived with the stepfather until he started drinking and eventually started beating on him for fun. He couldn't handle the mother's death, so when Fitzpatrick was only eight years old, the stepfather committed suicide.

This is what all the documents say, but something just doesn't seem right. I just don't buy any of it."

We all glanced around the room at each other, and the chief said, "There's more."

He continued, "It turns out there was a very long history of mental illness in the stepfather's family, so his relatives weren't surprised to find out he had taken his own life. This left Fitzpatrick to either go into foster care or live with his aunt on his mother's side. After a series of stays in juvenile hall, he ended up assaulting his aunt, and before the cops could catch him, he ran away at age fifteen.

"At this time, we are not sure if his records are accurate."

"What do you mean, Chief?" asked Anna.

"What I mean, Anna, is there is a possibility that he faked his records to get into the police academy. He definitely attended the police academy and actually finished at the top of his class, but we are looking into how he was accepted."

"So where does that leave us?"

"Well, Jeff, I haven't even touched on the worst part of Fitzpatrick's past. We have sources who have confirmed that he was, at one point, involved with the McNamaras."

Jeff and Anna shared a quick glance, and there was no way I was letting it slip this time. Before I could say anything, Jeff said to Anna, "Do you know anything about Carl being involved with them?"

Anna, of course, said no, but again, that was the best attempt to hide the glance they shared. It was a sly move. I was almost convinced. I was starting to second-guess myself and think I was just being paranoid.

The McNamaras were a hateful, ruthless crime family dating back at least three generations when they first came to the States. They'd only gotten worse as the years passed. How could the chief not know that Fitzpatrick was involved with them? Fitzpatrick must have done a pretty damn good job of flying under the radar. How could a cop be involved with them and no one know about it?

The room was silent for a few very long minutes. Anna was shifting in her seat, and it looked like she was going to say something. She opened her mouth a few times, and I was waiting for her to speak. Finally, she said, "Since all of us are here and we are the closest to the situation, I need to make a confession."

Jeff said, "Anna, don't say anything without a lawyer."

She laughed and said, "I don't think I need a lawyer for this one. Carl and I haven't had a good marriage for quite some time now. We coexist for the most part. We don't hate each other by any means, and we seem to have become really close friends as the years have gone by, but we are not in love with each other anymore. Now that I think back, it seems as though he never really romantically loved me from the beginning of our relationship. We got along really well, and we seemed to be a power couple, but I'm not sure he loved me romantically … ever. Even though he still calls me 'Anna Banana' like he used to when we first started dating, he just seems so distant all the time, completely preoccupied."

There it was again. She glanced at Jeff, and I couldn't contain myself any longer.

"What is going on here with the two of you? I have seen you glance at each other each time something mysterious or unexplained pops up about the case and Carl's past has been mentioned. I can't let it go any longer. If I'm involved in this case and I am doing everything I can to help and try to make things better, I need to know what's happening."

"Angie, honey, I'm so sorry. This whole situation has been so stressful, and since you've been in every conversation I've had regarding it, I never thought that you would feel left out or that we were hiding something. I'm so sorry. Angie, I knew Carl when we were kids. We were really close when we were little but drifted apart through high school. I went away to college, and I'm not sure what happened to Carl.

"I know he moved away at some point for a while, and that's when he met Anna. I wasn't really sure that he even came home until years later when he started his own company. I believe that failed, so he started working with his father. The only reason Anna and I shared a few glances here and there is because we both know there is some time missing in those years before he moved away and met Anna. When I say missing, I mean Anna and I don't know what he did, who he was involved with, or even what he did for work. The glances were more shared of concern and lack of knowledge than anything else."

I looked at Anna, thinking she might not corroborate his story, but she said, "God's honest truth," and gave me a strange version of a cross-my-heart, Scouts honor signal.

"Angie, Jeff and I really have no idea what Carl was up to in those 'missing years,' as I like to call them. It's not for us to figure out but maybe that might have something to do with what's going on now. We will have to start doing some serious research."

"Anna, I'm sorry for the outburst, but I was starting to get really paranoid, and this was the last straw for me. I'm sorry I was so insensitive. Good marriage or not, I can't imagine what you are going through."

"Don't sweat it, Angie. We are all under so much stress that everything seems like a clue or sign of foul play. None of us are living a normal life at this point, so I don't blame you for getting a little crazy."

"Okay. Again, I am so sorry."

I still couldn't help but feel like there was more to this story, and there was no way I was letting it go. No matter what I had to do, I was getting to the bottom of Jeff and Anna's glances and all the secrecy. If it was, in fact, the "missing years" that were the issue, then we needed to find those years and put my freaking mind at ease. Although maybe we didn't want to know what went on during that period of Carl's life, it could very well be the answer to what was going on. It might even help us find him.

The chief said, "We are going to continue to do everything we can, including wrap up whatever else there is to know about Fitzpatrick. Unfortunately, my guess is if he was wrapped up with the McNamaras, there is a really good chance that the records we do have of him are sending us on a wild goose chase."

"What do you mean, Chief?" I asked.

"What I mean is the records we have could very well be bogus, and if that's the case, we don't actually know anything at all about Fitzpatrick. What scares me most is that the time line just doesn't match up. It's like he's everywhere but nowhere at the same time."

The hairs on the back of my neck stood up, and all I thought was we could be dealing with a true psychopath.

"Chief, what are you saying?" asked Jeff.

"What I'm saying is that the time line of his age doesn't match up. I think he's older than we thought. I wasn't going to say anything, but we all need to have our guard up."

"Why would that make us put our guard up?"

"Not that. If it's not his age that's off, he might not be working alone. Something just isn't adding up."

Chapter 20

It was 7:30 a.m., and Jeff and I were already in the office. My mom took the kids to school. Jeff and I were having a meeting in his office, and his cell phone rang. He looked at the number, bobbed his chin at me, and said, "It's the chief."

I got up and closed his office door so no one in the office could overhear the conversation.

Jeff said, "I'm in here with Angie, so I'm going to put you on speaker."

"Don't bother. I'm on my way if it's okay with you?"

"Sure, we're here. I already called Anna, and she's on her way to the office as well."

"What's up, Chief? Do you have something for us about Carl?"

"Well, sort of, but it's probably not what you were expecting. I'll see you in a few."

The chief hung up, and Jeff and I just sat there, of course thinking the worst.

Jeff said, "This can't be good. The chief only comes to the office when there is big news to share."

"Do you think they found Carl?"

"I don't know, Angie. I guess we'll find out soon enough."

The chief came flying into the office, and Anna followed shortly behind him. She came rushing over to me, and we hugged each other very tightly, as if to say, "Let's brace ourselves for this one." The look in her eyes showed how badly this was wearing on her.

The chief spoke. "So the body in the car registered to Carl is definitely not Carl's."

The three of us sighed in relief and shared a quick smile, assuming the chief had more to say by his earlier comment.

"The body, however, was identified by dental records, and it's confirmed that the body belongs to a Daniel Fitzpatrick."

The eeriest feeling washed over the room, and no one said a word. Confusion, worry, and utter dismay were the tone of the next few comments. We just sat there, blinking at each other and not understanding at all what the chief had just said.

Finally, in an emotionless and flat voice, Jeff said, "What?"

Anna said, "I don't understand."

I said, "How is that possible?"

The chief said, "I'm not really sure what to say or what this means, but obviously this is not the Fitzpatrick we know. Same name and the body seems to be the same age as Fitzpatrick. I am demanding some answers, but it's a very slow process.

"What I have to say next is bizarre, and, Anna, please know that I am trying to get all the information as quickly as possible. There was a fire that sent a house up in flames in South Beach, Florida."

We all looked at each other very skeptically, wondering what this had to do with Carl.

"Okay?" said Anna, questioning.

"Well, the deed to this home was in Carl's name."

"*What*?"

Anna always had her shit together. During all of this, I'd seen her in hysterics only a couple of times, but I'd never seen her like this. This was pure anger coming out now.

"It doesn't stop there. There are four bodies in the house—all male, no women or children."

Jeff and I were totally stunned. We had no idea what to say. We figured we would leave it up to Anna to reply.

The chief continued, "There is a boat dock that belongs to the home with a forty-foot yacht anchored on it. The medical examiner will be looking into the identities of the bodies. On the bright side, if there is one, the way this is all playing out so far, I would be pretty confident that none of those bodies belong to Carl either."

Anna asked, "The boat is also Carl's?"

"Oh yeah, Anna, no doubt."

We all looked at Anna, wondering what she was thinking or if she was going to say anything. We did not expect to hear what came out of her mouth next.

"I'm at a loss at this point. I'm sorry if you all think differently of me in saying this, but do you think it would look awful if I went back to work?"

The chief said, "No, and I wouldn't judge you at all for it either."

"I haven't heard anything from him, and we can't make heads or tails of what is happening. I have a very important fashion show in Paris next week, and I would like to be there since I've been preparing for it for the last six months."

She looked at the chief as if wanting his blessing.

The chief said, "If I hear anything, I will let you all know ASAP."

"Given our current marital situation, while I care deeply for him, I can't put my life or career on hold for whatever tricks he could be playing. I am partially afraid for my own life and what might happen. I don't believe he's behind this, but I do think something from his past is following him and bringing this mess to us now. I don't want to be around when it comes knocking at my door."

The chief said, "I know it's a lot to take in all at one time, but I'm afraid to say that Anna may have the right idea here to just move on with your day to day, and we'll let you know once we know anything further. This mess with Carl doesn't seem to have anything to do with the company and hasn't seemed to have infiltrated anything in your personal life, so there is no threat there as of yet. I don't say that to scare you, but so far, there is no evidence that it will affect the company."

"Not to be an asshole here, Chief, and I am not trying to be disrespectful to the department, but we don't seem to have much evidence at all in the case, not to mention a good lead."

"I know, Jeff. Please just let me do my job and understand that we are now working with another police department. It's not like they are in our backyard. There won't be anything quick about this."

Anna headed out and told the chief she would be leaving the following day for her business trip. "Please call my cell if you need to get ahold of me. I will have it on me all the time. See you guys when I get back."

"Bye, Anna. Be safe."

Anna was out the door and gone in seconds.

"Oh, one more thing," the chief said. "I'm so sorry I keep forgetting to tell you this one last detail. I have been debating whether or not to tell you this because all of Fitzpatrick's notes are under investigation. When he had the follow-up conversation with your employees, after Carl disappeared, Fitzpatrick's notes say that Derrick mentioned something about Carl being a strange bird."

"That's nothing that we don't all already know."

We all laughed after Jeff's comment. It was inappropriate, but we needed a laugh.

"Funny, Jeff, but Derrick said he ran into him early one morning in the office before anyone punched in for the day." I looked at Jeff, because no one was supposed to be at the office any earlier than 6:30 a.m. This was a company policy for overtime purposes and safety reasons.

Jeff looked at me and said, "The Wilson job."

"Oh yes, I remember."

Derrick had to get to this job early because the Wilsons were leaving for vacation, and they wanted to pay him before they got on the road.

The chief said, "Derrick mentioned that Carl was completely nuts that morning. He was babbling on and on about some lady named Alisa. Derrick said Carl was barely making any sense at all, but he said to Derrick—and I quote—'Women will kill you or at least try.'"

The chief asked us, "Do you know an Alisa, or have you ever heard Carl mention anyone by that name?"

Jeff said, "We have no idea who Alisa is or how she would have anything to do with Carl. He never mentioned an Alisa. Obviously, we don't know much about Carl, his past, his friends … really anything, so how would we know anything about an Alisa?"

The chief asked, "Is it possible that Carl would be stealing money from the company?"

Jeff laughed. "No way. I track every penny that comes in and out of the business so the answer to that is not a chance. Since he is just an employee now and not an owner, he does not have access to the bank accounts."

Jeff and I believed his thought process was to hide an affair from Anna, but it didn't seem like he was onto anything with that idea so he certainly never mentioned anything of the sort.

"Chief, are you going to tell Anna or ask her about Alisa?"

He said, "I was going to keep that under wraps until I have a little more information."

Jeff and I agreed that was probably the best thing to do, especially while she was trying to figure out what was happening. Also, her business trip seemed pretty important for her career, so why muddy the waters with something there was really no evidence for?

"Okay, Chief, thanks, as usual. I think Angie and I might take a few days off but stay close to home, so if you need us, just call my cell."

"Will do, Jeff. Talk to you soon—I hope with good news."

The chief left the office.

My cell phone rang, and it was Elle. I had been keeping her in the loop of what was going on with Carl—not only because she's my best friend but because I wanted her to know the truth and not what she heard from the gossiping mommy-and-me groups, not to mention the newspapers. I ignored her call and figured I would call her back later. Since Jeff and I were going to take some time off and have a staycation, I would go and visit Elle in the next few days. She didn't leave a voice mail but called back right away.

I answered it and said, "What's up, Elle?"

"Angie, you'd better get over here as soon as you can, and you might want to bring Jeff this time."

"Are you okay, Elle?"

"Yes, I'm fine, but I found something that you need to see."

"Okay, Elle, we're wrapping up with the chief, and then we are headed home. We'll come right over when we get home."

"Okay, Angie, but try to hurry."

Chapter 21

The kids were staying with my parents that night. Jeff and I were going to order takeout and just go home. I felt like this vacation would be good for the whole family. The kids were starting to bug me about staying home more with them. They threw it in my face that I had quit my old job to spend more time with them, and they were spending more time with Grandma than me. They were right, and there was nothing I could say to make it better. This vacation, I was hoping, would show them how much I loved them and how I could put work aside to spend good quality time with them.

We stopped at Elle's, and she was acting very strangely, like she'd had twenty cups of coffee.

"Elle, what's so urgent?"

She pulled up her computer and typed "Facebook" into the search box.

"I know you hate Facebook, Angie, but you need to see this. I was searching for Justin's page so I could leave him a review. I know he's not your favorite person, but he did a good job. It seems like he's trying to get back on his feet. I felt like I should let people know I was happy with the work."

Jeff said, "This ought to be interesting. What could that loser possibly have to offer besides his shady business that he runs without proper insurances? Not to mention cash only?"

Elle looked at Jeff, a little pissed off, but what could she say when it was mostly true? I wanted her to land the plane. She knew I hated Facebook, and I was looking through a page of someone Jeff and I were not very fond of after everything that went down at the company.

There were a number of photos of Justin with his son and some random women, both of whom looked like a hot mess. I was so bitter about this kid.

Elle finally stopped and said, "There, there it is!"

"What are we looking at, Elle?"

"Don't you see him in the background with his arm around Justin?"

I grabbed Jeff's arm, and he said, "What the fuck?"

There they were, in full color right there on the computer screen. In the background of a photo of two stupid girls clanking their bottles together was Justin with his arm around Fitzpatrick.

I gasped like someone was chasing me with a knife. "OMG! What the fuck? Jeff, we need to call the chief right away."

"And tell him what, Angie? That some deadbeat drug addict who used to work for us is buddies with Fitzpatrick?"

"Don't you think it would be worth him looking into to see if there is any connection? I'm worried that he's going to retaliate against us for what happened."

"Angie, let's sit back and think about what happened. We didn't do anything wrong, and Justin never held us responsible for what happened. He never blamed us for what went down."

"How do you know that?"

"We've both spoken to him a number of times since then. I know it's been years now, but at the time, he always took full responsibility for his actions."

"I guess, Jeff, but aren't you worried?"

"Honestly, Angie, I'm not. I don't feel like there is anything to be worried about. I will call the chief and let him know just so they can keep an eye on Justin since he is already looking for Fitzpatrick. I'll see if he can find a connection. Will that make you feel better?"

"Yes, Jeff, it would definitely put my mind at ease."

"Just remember, Angie, that Fitzpatrick's records are a shitshow, so don't expect much out of the chief to find a connection."

"You're right, Jeff, but just let him know so if something does surface, he's not blindsided."

"Okay, I will."

Elle was just sitting there, listening to our conversation, and I could see that she had a million questions. I knew Jeff wouldn't want us to share the details for our safety as well as hers, so I didn't say anything. I couldn't get away that easily though.

"Guys, what happened?"

"Oh, Elle, it's not as simple as just explaining the situation. It's a mess, and we don't have enough time in the day to go through it all." I figured she wouldn't push, and she didn't, so I kept Jeff happy with putting her off for a while.

"I don't need to be worried, do I?" I looked over at Jeff, but he didn't falter. Jeff jumped at the chance to answer Elle.

"No, Elle. Like I said before, there is nothing to worry about, and I'll talk to the chief just to put our minds at ease."

We hugged and kissed Elle good night and went home.

"Jeff, were you just saying all that to keep Elle from getting scared?"

"No, Angie, I really believe that we have nothing to worry about with Justin. I can say this though. We know nothing about this Fitzpatrick asshole, so that makes me really uneasy. I'm not sure what his motive is and if it's against us or Anna. I'm going to ask the chief to look into the relationship between him and Justin. I also want to know what Justin has been up to these days, why you saw him at the house down the street, and just his everyday activities. If he's involved in some shit like the old days, then I'll want to know what Fitzpatrick has to do with him for sure. Not only that, but I want to find out how hard they are actually looking for him and who is looking?"

"Those are all great points, Jeff. I'm going to try not to worry unless the chief can really give us something."

"Angie, tell me again what he said to you at Elle's that day you were over there when he was cutting down the trees."

"I didn't actually see him. I hid in the bathroom so he wouldn't see me and I wouldn't have to talk to him."

"Oh yeah, but he told Elle to tell you something to make sure you knew he was there and he saw you, right?"

"Oh yeah. He said, 'Tell Angie that Toph said later.'"

"What does that mean?"

"What do you mean 'What does that mean'? Is this a trick question?"

Jeff laughed at me. Thank God because I was trying to stall something fierce. I didn't have an answer that he would want to hear. I felt guilty because I was hiding something from Jeff, and that was not what we did.

"Angie?"

"What?"

"What does that mean?"

"I'm not sure, Jeff. Maybe a term of endearment for his big sis? I think he was just saying goodbye."

"Who's Toph?"

"I don't know." I kept my face as straight as possible. I didn't give anything away.

"Okay but why would he think you would know that?"

"I'm not sure."

Very wearily, Jeff looked at me but with a smirk on his face as if he could tell I wasn't quite being honest. I felt awful about keeping it from him, but I didn't need to give Jeff a reason for him not to trust me. It was nothing like that, but it definitely looked that way.

He came over to hug me. He kissed me on the forehead and said, "Let's go to bed."

Chapter 22

Anna was sitting in her hotel room in Paris, just looking out the window. She had a wonderful view of the city. She never wished that Carl was there with her, but today was different. She wanted him there just to know he was okay. She couldn't help but think how far apart they had drifted over the last few years. She always felt like he was a little distant since the day they met but not like it had been the last few years. She always felt like he had a wall up that she just couldn't break through.

They actually talked often, but they only spoke about the day-to-day, asking the same old boring questions. How's work? What's for dinner? They didn't discuss the details. If Carl was involved in some crazy drug ring or had some weird mafia connection, Anna would never know. She didn't know the details. He seemed to be home all the time though. If he was involved in something off the wall, she thought he would have been out a lot more often.

She certainly was no saint. Her mind drifted to those long nights she had away from home, the nights she would have had to lie about if Carl had actually asked. He never asked though. It didn't make it right, but she never had to explain herself. He never cared enough to ask.

She'd had a long conversation about them drifting apart with the chief, and he mostly just listened. She felt so awful that she wasn't able to add some earth-shattering piece of information to help the investigation. She felt like if she had paid more attention to him, she would have noticed something going on but then obviously he'd been hiding money, cars, and now houses. Maybe she wouldn't have noticed anything. She didn't know which end was up.

Anna's phone rang, and by the number on the caller ID, she could tell it was from her mystery caller. The voice on the other end was very subdued and steady as usual. "Any info from the police chief?"

Anna reluctantly said, "No, nothing yet except the explosion in the Florida home."

"Excuse me, ma'am?"

"The house in Florida, there was an explosion, and I guess four bodies in the house."

The voice said, "We'll be in touch, ma'am," and all she heard was the dial tone.

Anna was always so bothered by these calls, but she felt a sense of calm and safety at the same time. She wasn't sure why she felt this way, but it was a relief to not be afraid of the people who seemed to be trying to help. This time, though, he seemed just as rattled and out of the loop as she was. This made her uneasy. She was concerned that he seemed to have no knowledge of this current incident.

From the moment she received the first call from her mystery caller, she had assumed Carl was involved in something much bigger than anyone thought. Who were these people, and what did they want from her? She thought it was very odd that they didn't know what happened in Florida. Whatever their connection was to Carl, how could they not know about the explosion? Maybe Carl wasn't involved.

Anna's mind started to race. Maybe they did know, but they were surprised that she knew already. Maybe they just wanted her to confirm what exactly the police knew up to that point? They probably assumed that the police would keep her updated with anything new they discovered.

Something else Anna couldn't understand was why he wasn't trying to disguise his voice. Maybe he was, but he just sounded like any other normal guy. He was definitely using a burner phone so there was no way to get in touch with him. She was always so unprepared when he called, so she never had any time to ask him any questions. He also never asked for any money or anything to that effect, so she was really at a loss as to what his purpose was for calling her at all.

One more thing she noticed was that he usually called her by her name, Anna, but that day, he kept calling her "ma'am." Why? Why was he doing that? Maybe this was someone else? He sounded just like the other man who usually called, but maybe they were both disguising their voices. So odd, she thought.

She sat down at the desk and began writing a list of questions she was hoping he would be willing to answer the next time he called. Whenever that would be, she was hoping someone didn't have to die for him to call. That seemed to be the trigger for a new phone call.

Chapter 23

Anna finished writing her list and was hoping it wasn't too late to get a nightcap at the hotel bar. She checked her face in the mirror and applied some quick dabs of lip gloss. She went to get her heels that she had kicked off by the door when she first got back to the room. She put them on, grabbed her evening bag, and headed out the door.

Most of the people from the show were staying in the same hotel so she was bound to run into someone, which was okay with her. The elevator stopped on almost every floor on the way down. She thought she would never get down to the lobby.

Anna just wanted a quick drink, and then she would head back to bed. She bellied up to the bar and ordered a gin and tonic. The bartender was professional and had a soothing smile. She felt at ease after the long day she'd had.

She had been there only a few minutes when a woman came and sat down a few bar stools over from her—a strikingly pretty woman, for that matter.

She didn't say anything at first, and Anna just assumed she wanted to be left alone very similarly to how Anna was feeling. She seemed to be acting a little odd, and she was wearing sunglasses—not panicked but just odd, like she wanted to go unnoticed. Anna left her alone. She was rifling through her purse, so Anna just thought she was trying to find something.

Once she settled down, Anna called over the bartender for her just in case she wanted a drink. The woman took the opportunity to order a gin and tonic, but Anna didn't say anything.

The woman looked over at Anna and said, "Oh my! You're Anna!"

As Anna was turning her head to look over at the woman, she said, "I might be," with a playful smirk. She went stone-faced when she actually saw the woman sitting next to her at the bar. Anna was dying inside. This was the longest trending fashion designer in the, well, in the *world*, and she knew Anna by name. Anna was reeling from this experience. She could not believe what was happening. *Keep it cool, Anna*, she thought. *Compliment the hell out of this woman in a very nonstalker tone.*

"Well, Anna, it's very nice to meet you. You are a very talented woman. I love your new line. It's very classic and caters to almost every age group. It's the best line I've seen in a long time."

"Thank you very much, Josephine, I mean, stranger having the same drink I'm having in the hotel bar." Anna was petrified that she would take offense to this, but she knew they both had had a long week and the critics could be pretty brutal so they deserved a good laugh. She held her breath until Josephine burst into laughter.

"You were afraid I wasn't going to laugh, weren't you?"

"I will admit I had my doubts."

They laughed together, and Josephine held up her glass for cheers with Anna. She gladly raised hers, and Josephine said, "To the best show I've seen in years and to hell with the critics, whatever they say!"

They clinked their glasses together and shared a smile.

"Anna, I don't know you very well, but you seem to be a little preoccupied. Maybe it's just gas?"

Anna laughed out loud and with such a catchy laugh it forced Josephine to do the same.

"I didn't know you had such a sense of humor."

"Well, maybe we should get to know each other a little better."

"I guess so."

"We could start tonight over our first drink together after a great show."

"I'm down with that, and how ironic that we have the same drink?"

"Very ironic, but then again, we are two of the best fashion designers in the world, so we have that in common too … So you did a pretty good job of avoiding my earlier question."

Anna looked at Josephine and was very wary about her inquiry. She had just met her, so she certainly wasn't willing to trust her, especially given the bizarre situation she was in with Carl.

"Oh, you know, just your normal run-of-the-mill domestic troubles. Nothing worth talking about really. My husband and I are going through a little bit of a rough patch. That's all."

Anna saw Josephine's face fall. She was afraid it was something that she had said.

"Oh, I'm sorry. Did I say something to upset you?"

"No."

"That doesn't sound convincing at all."

Josephine gave a little chuckle and smile with her perfectly applied lipstick-covered lips. "I was married once, a long time ago, and things don't ever turn out the way you planned or hoped."

"Did you ever have any children?"

Josephine's smile fell again, and before she had the opportunity to answer, the bartender came over to tell them that he was going to be closing up in a few minutes.

"Okay, Josephine, well, I guess it's time for bed."

"I guess so, Anna. It was really nice to finally meet you officially. I do truly love your work." Josephine pulled out a business card and wrote her personal cell number on the back. She told Anna that she should call her anytime. She would love to catch up and share secrets.

"Josephine, it was truly a pleasure meeting you, and I would love to keep in touch. Are you heading back to wherever you call home tomorrow?"

"Yes, I am."

"Me too. Safe travels and I will definitely reach out when I start working on my next line ... which will be on the plane ride home most likely."

They laughed, and Josephine said, "I think you are my kindred spirit."

Chapter 24

Even though we were supposed to be on vacation, Jeff and I went into the office just for the morning meeting. We also wanted to see what the morale was like. We didn't want to be absent too long, just in case the employees had questions or anyone thought of anything to share. It was Friday, so the kids were in school. They couldn't hate me too much if they weren't around.

The chief came to visit us at the office because he had some news about the Florida home explosion.

"We got all the identities of the four bodies that were found in the house, and so far, not one person has anything to do with Carl that they can find—no connections, business-wise or family related. The bodies belonged to a bunch of young guys who were all friends and had no history of criminal records or drug abuse. They were looking into the rental companies to see if the house was rented to tenants with a lease or if it was rented weekly as a beach house. That seemed to be a dead end as well, but they wanted to make sure they covered all the bases.

"The most bizarre thing was they couldn't find any family members for any of them. It's like they were all orphans at one point. One drawback is that I am working with a Florida police department, so the long distance kills us. We are not exactly a priority for them. It's their case, and we're just here when they feel like communicating."

He told us that he received a call from Anna. She was still in Paris, but she was not dealing with this as well as she thought she would. "The more time goes by, the more she is thinking about what could be happening to him."

He said he'd continue to keep us in the loop with additional details once he got them. We thanked him, and he went on his way.

Derrick was lurking that morning for some reason, and I couldn't help but notice he wanted to talk to me.

"Hey, what's up?"

"Angie, if there is anything I can do to help, please just ask. I can sniff around a little bit."

"Derrick, I really appreciate it, but where would you even begin?"

"Well, Carl struggled with the bottle for a while, and I just happen to know some of the same people he used to hang around."

"I would never ask you to do that, but if you wanted to do it on your own, have at it."

He shot me his adorable smirk, and I just smiled back.

"Jeff and I didn't know Carl had a drinking problem."

"Apparently, Angie, it was a long time ago, so he's been sober for many years now. I'd be surprised if Anna even knows. The people I was referring to are the ones who helped him get sober."

"Whatever you decide to do, please just be careful, Derrick."

"It always feels good to know that you are so caring."

"I try, but I truly do care about everyone who works for us, and I don't want anyone getting in trouble."

"Your boy Toph always thought that of you."

It was a good thing I was facing my computer so Derrick couldn't see all the blood drain out of my face. I managed a chuckle and waved him out of my office. I could see him smirk out of the corner of my eye and couldn't help but wonder why he would bring up Justin and now of all times.

What does he know? Better yet, how does he know about the Toph.

I was also crabby at Derrick. He had never mentioned anything to me about Carl's rant to him when they were in the office early that morning. Why would he not tell *me*? No sooner did this cross my mind than Derrick came back around the corner to my office door and said, "Do you have another minute? I want to tell you something."

"Yes, of course. What is it?"

"I told the police this piece of info. Well, I told Fitzpatrick. I thought you should hear it from me. If they already told you, I'm sorry I didn't tell you first. The day I came in early for the Wilson job, Carl was here, and he was acting crazy. He was ranting on about some woman named Alisa. He said, 'Women will kill you, son, or they'll at least try.'"

I felt really good about Derrick sharing this information, since I thought he wasn't going to at all.

"The reason I'm telling you this, aside from not wanting to keep it from you, is when I first told Fitzpatrick, his face turned bright red, and he said, '*What*?' I told him again, and he got right in my face and told me not to repeat this to anyone. This information was not to be shared. I didn't tell the chief when he circled back with me about the interview because Fitzpatrick told me not to say anything."

"Derrick, now that he's gone, you need to tell the chief. He will need to know how Fitz reacted. This could shed some light on the investigation and possibly give him another lead." I could tell he wasn't very thrilled about doing that, but he agreed.

"I'll have Jeff call him and get him back down here so he can take your additional statement."

"Okay, Angie, if you think that's the best thing to do, I'll do it but just for you ..." He paused and then said, "And Jeff of course." With his adorable smirk, he walked out of my office and moved on with his day.

I called Jeff into my office to tell him what Derrick had just shared with me, and he agreed to call the chief right away and get him in the office the following morning to speak to Derrick.

"Jeff, I'm learning to just let this thing ride itself out, but I have to admit that this piece of information almost confirms that Fitzpatrick is involved somehow, maybe not in Carl's disappearance, but something has him sniffing around this case for what sounds more and more like personal reasons."

"Angie, I'm trying to be strong and not worry you, and if you know I'm worried or concerned, it will worry you even more. I can't control how smart you are, so there is no way for me to hide my concern in this new development."

I smiled very lovingly at Jeff because that was a very nice compliment and again showed how much he cared.

"I know this sounds crazy, but it makes me feel a little better that you are so concerned because I know your radar is up and you pay attention to the strange and unusual that may occur around us. It also makes me feel better because I don't think I'm such a neurotic mess."

Jeff smiled and flat out laughed at me. Then we laughed together and said we'd get through this one way or another. The best part was we had each other.

I was recalling a conversation with Anna in my head from that morning.

"You know, Jeff, when Anna called us earlier?"

"What's eating you, Angie?"

"Well, I know Anna and I aren't very close, but I feel like Carl going missing has brought us closer each day. Since she is still away, I thought maybe she might be starting to cope a little better. We didn't speak every day, but today, I could feel her pain. She is really struggling with blaming herself for not being able to help. I keep trying to tell her it's not her fault. I told her that Carl was just as guilty for being distant and not sharing everything that was happening in his life. She also mentioned that she felt like such an ass that he kept all those things from her. It was obvious that he kept all this away from her on purpose. She thought maybe he was going to leave her. He didn't want her lawyer to know about the other possessions. She might either try to take them or make him sell them to give her half the money."

— m —

Jeff's head was spinning after Angie's babbling. He knew she was worried for Anna, but this was over the top.

"Angie, slow down. Better yet, why don't you try not to think about it?"

"Really? How can I try not to think about it?"

"You have work to do, don't you?"

"Yes."

"Try to get some of that done so we don't fall too far behind. I would like the company to be the least affected by Carl. We bought this business to get him out of it. Let's try to keep him out."

Jeff was so heartless sometimes. Being business minded was one thing, but this was another. I just walked away from him back to my office.

I went back to the conversation with Anna in my head.

I told her not to start jumping to conclusions. "We hardly have any information at this point, so don't worry until we have reason to," I advised. She told me that she kept trying to tell herself that, but something new always popped into her head or she got a dreaded call from the chief. She did say that maybe Carl just said, "Fuck it!" and disappeared on his own to get away from everything. She said she hated all the different scenarios always crossing her mind.

"It's easier said than done to just put it all aside until we know more, but, Anna, you just have to do that for now."

"I know, Angie. I'll try. Thanks."

That last sentence seemed so rehearsed, almost like she was faking her concern.

Chapter 25

Jeff and I still had a few more days off from work and made it a longer holiday weekend. We reminisced about the days when we used to just get in the car and drive to different places. We would research a place on the internet and just go. We used to do it all the time but stopped when life got in the way. One day, I brought it up, and he said, "Let's plan a day and do it." Since we were taking some time off, we decided to map it out and get in the car. We never took the kids with us before, and since they had off from school for the holiday, we asked if they wanted to go. They jumped at the chance. They enjoyed hearing the stories about all the places we had gone and all the good food we ate. They thought we were a little corny because we had somewhat of a ritual. We would pick a place that was featured on a TV food show. We would watch the episode before we went in to eat.

This was the closest to normal we had felt since before this mess with Carl started. I thought it was a little odd that we hadn't gotten any information from the chief about Carl or the Justin/Fitzpatrick connection. I guess it was better than getting more bad news. Plus, I was really enjoying spending this quiet time with my family.

Elle and her family came over the next day to swim and grill. Even though her little princess was so much younger than my kids, they still all played so nice together, and the adults talked up a storm. It had been weeks since we were able to catch up with them, so we had so much to talk about; it was mostly work, but because we were all business owners, talking shop was something we could do for hours. We shared some secrets and helped each other with new processes to implement.

Elle and I went inside to clean up and get the dessert. Jeff made espresso, and, of course, we couldn't forget the Sambuca. Elle asked if we had any updates on Carl and if we were even allowed to talk about it. Sadly there was nothing I could say. We had no updates, and even if there were any, I didn't think I would be able to share. I spoke too soon, because as soon as the word *no* came out of my mouth, Jeff was barreling through the patio door, calling my name.

"Angie, you'd better come in here. I have the chief on the phone."

Elle asked if they should leave, and I told her, "No, the chief sticks to the facts, so it won't be too long.

"Chief, what's the latest?"

"Hey, Jeff and Angie, I really wish we could talk under better circumstances, but this one is for the record books."

"What is it, Chief?"

"There has been a fire!"

"*What*?" Jeff and I yelled at the same time.

We were afraid to ask what or where. The chief very somberly said, "Carl and Anna's."

"Oh my God! Anna! Thank God she's not home yet."

The chief said, "She is home."

"Is she okay? Where is she?"

"She's here with me."

"Can we talk to her?"

The chief handed her the phone.

"Hey, guys."

"Anna, my God, are you all right? Are you hurt?"

"I'm okay. I'm not hurt."

"What happened?"

"They lit the fucking house on fire, and the chief and I don't know if they didn't know I was home, but I had plenty of time to get out before it went up in what looked like a mushroom cloud. I'm exaggerating, of course, but that's what it felt like. I even had time to grab my purse and call 911. I ran to the neighbors' through the very shallow tree line behind us to the development back there. I watched the whole thing but never saw anyone— no cars, no people, nothing."

"Anna, do you have somewhere to stay."

"Honestly, I haven't even thought about that yet."

Jeff and I looked at each other, assuming that we would both be more than happy with her staying at our house.

"It's eight thirty at night. Can you have the chief take you here? You can stay with us as long as you need."

The chief, of course, agreed to take her over to our house.

I said to Jeff, "I know you are going to be mortified when I say this, but don't you find her story to be a little odd?"

"Angie, how can you say that?"

"I don't know, but she had enough time to get her purse and call 911? Why was she so calm, and why was she so calm talking about it just now?"

"Angie, are you saying you think she's involved too?"

"I don't know, Jeff. I just think that all sounds a little far-fetched."

"Whatever you do, don't say any of that to her. Maybe she's just in a mild state of shock, or maybe she just doesn't know what else to say. Let's get everything ready. She'll be here soon."

—⟋⟋⟋—

In the car, Anna had closed her eyes for a little while on the drive over. She didn't fall asleep, even though she wanted so badly to get some rest. As the chief turned the corner into the development, she couldn't help but think there was something so familiar about the block and the architectural details of the houses. She kept looking around for something she recognized. She turned her head to look out the opposite car window and saw the yellow house. She drew in a short, sharp breath and couldn't believe her eyes. So many emotions washed over her, from sadness to fear and even happiness and safety. She wasn't sure what to do or say, so she just kept her mouth shut. She wasn't quite sure about the chief yet. Was he really on their side, or was he just going through the motions to be polite? She thought it was best to just stay calm and quiet.

—⟋⟋⟋—

In the front seat at the wheel, the chief very cautiously eyed Anna in the rearview mirror, watching her carefully so she wouldn't see him looking at her. He watched her eyes dart around after she saw the yellow house. He knew she recognized it, but he wasn't sure why she was so on edge about it. *She must know*, he thought. *She must recognize it. This means that she's aware of the past.* What form of the past, he wasn't sure. He knew there was something there though. He wasn't sure what to make of her reaction.

She arrived at our house around ten. We had the spare bedroom all set up for her, and thank God, she was right about my size, so she could wear all my clothes until she could buy new ones. Jeff and I still had another day off, so I could take her around to get some new clothes and speak to the insurance company about getting her life back together. She would also need a new car. Anna had a great job and was paid very well, so lucky for her, she would not be without these things for long—except her house … and of course her husband.

"Angie, it was bad enough that Carl is missing and I had no idea about all the other possessions he had but now the house? What in the hell is happening? I can't help but think he's still alive somewhere, and they are just torturing him with all this violence. It doesn't make sense to kill him and then take everything away from him. What would he care if he's already dead? If they are targeting me, why? You know, I cut my trip short also so I wasn't even supposed to be home for another two days."

Before I could console her, Anna's cell phone rang. Her face turned a ghostly shade of white. She showed me the caller ID, and it said, "Carl."

Chapter 26

Anna tapped the green accept call button on the phone and said, "Hello?" She teared up in pure hesitation, wondering if it would really be Carl or just an unfamiliar voice she didn't recognize. She also thought it might be her mystery caller, but why would he put her through this? She had the most awful pit in her stomach, and even though she was not a very religious woman, she briefly prayed that it would really be Carl.

I raced down the steps to get Jeff. Our company had left, and the kids were in bed. Jeff and I ran back up the steps just to hear a bunch of static on the other end of the line. It wasn't static like a bad connection but like there was a struggle or someone dropped the phone. There was more static and then a dial tone. Anna snapped at the phone, yelling, "No!"

We all sat there looking at each other dumbfounded, obviously not knowing what to say. I felt like I needed to do something, so I put my hand on Anna's but didn't say anything. Jeff had his arm around me, and we just sat in silence for a little while.

I could tell that Anna wanted to tell us something, but she was feverishly searching for the right words. There was a lot of hesitation in her demeanor, and she kept glancing at us wearily.

Just as her mouth opened to speak, the phone rang again, and it was from Carl's number again.

Anna said, "Hello?"

"Anna Banana?" said a soft voice on the other end.

We all looked at each other in shock, not only had Anna just told us that was Carl's pet name for her, but we all recognized his voice.

"Carl!" Anna managed to half cry out.

"Anna, dear, I'm okay, but I don't think I have long to talk. Things are not safe right now, and I don't want to worry you, but you must leave the house."

"Carl, someone set a fire in the house, and I am with Jeff and Angie."

"Hey, guys, I'm so sorry about all of this. I don't know how to say how sorry I am for you having to worry about me. Wait. What? What do you mean there was a fire in the house?"

"Well, both houses."

"What do you mean 'both houses'? Anna, what are you talking about? There was a fire in our home? What other home?"

"Carl, the police said they found a car, which was charred from a fire, containing a body just as charred as the car. Then they found a house in Florida with a huge yacht docked on the boat dock outside. This house was blown to bits too, and there were four men inside the house when it blew."

"I'm sorry, Anna, but I'm not following. What do those things have to do with us?"

Anna hesitated. She was so happy to be hearing from him but so angry that all these possessions that she was unaware existed had popped up.

She very wearily said, "The police chief said they are registered in your name."

"How can that be, Anna? We own all of our possessions together. I don't understand."

We could tell that Anna was at a loss for words. She had thought the same thing but spent the time since she received this information from the chief trying to figure out why Carl would hide these possessions.

"To be honest, Carl, when I first found out, I didn't know what to think. I thought you were hiding these things from me."

"Anna, listen. I know things haven't been great for a while with us, and honestly, it's been my fault. I've been distant and totally closed off from emotion. You have been enjoying your work, and I just thought we would eventually work it all out together."

"Oh, Carl, I don't even know what to say. I've felt the same way for years but never wanted to say anything. I have definitely been caught up in my work. You know I love it."

"It's okay, Banana. I called to tell you to go to the bank and get everything in the safe-deposit box. There are some things in there that you are not going to want to see, but you have to trust me that this will all be okay. It will also explain the missing part of my past that you love to tease me about."

"Where is the key?"

"Well, it was in my sock drawer. You'll have to go to the bank and explain what's happening, and you mentioned the chief a few times, so take him with you if he's willing to help. Try not to mention that you spoke with me though."

"Why, Carl?"

Jeff and I looked at each other very skeptically, and Jeff interjected, "Hey, buddy! Where are you, and what are you doing?"

"Hey, man! I don't know. I must have been drugged. I don't remember anything. I don't even remember where I was when I was drugged or taken or whatever happened. I woke up and still had my cell phone so I said, 'Fuck it!' and called Anna right away."

"Why don't you want us to tell the chief that we heard from you?"

All we heard was a major commotion. We heard people yelling, and Carl whispered, "I love you, Anna Banana," into the phone. Then, the line went dead.

Anna yelled *No!*

Chapter 27

Jeff's head was spinning. He thought, *Is this it? Is this really happening?* He needed to call Demetri, his longtime friend and lawyer.

"Jeff?"

"Yes, Angie?"

"Are you in there?"

"Ha, yes, I'm listening."

"What do you make of all that?"

Jeff wasn't about to repeat everything that had just taken place in his head, so he just said, "I think there is more to the story here so we need to put our heads together and see what's in that safe-deposit box."

Anna was silent. What could she really say? Her husband was missing, sort of, and she had no idea if she'd ever see or speak to him again. I knew when my husband was lying, and something definitely wasn't right about all of this and what he just said. The pieces didn't fit, and he sounded way too calm.

"Anna, you should have seen him that last day he was in the office. He was a frantic, disheveled mess. He didn't know which end was up or down, and he looked like he was searching for something. I know we said this before, but if I never thought he used drugs in the past, this would be the time. He was a total disaster. If that was staged, he should get his Academy thank-you speech ready."

I was relieved to hear Anna say that she thought Carl was lying and something wasn't right. I didn't want to have to tell her what I thought and have her angry at me for not believing him.

"Angie, you'll still drive me around tomorrow for clothes and apparently now to open this safe-deposit box?"

"Yes, of course."

"Jeff, do you think you should come with us? And what are your thoughts about how much we share with the police chief?"

"Honestly, Anna, I'm not going to let the two of you out of my sight for quite a while. You can work from our office for a while, right, Anna?"

"Yes, I was working mostly from home remotely anyway when I wasn't traveling, so as long as I have an internet connection, I can work anywhere."

"That's settled then. As far as what we should share with the police, I'm not sure about that part yet. I will discuss it with our attorney, if that's okay with you, and see what he says."

"That's okay with me. While we're talking about all this mess, I have something else to say."

"What is it, Anna?"

"So, right after Carl disappeared, I received a mysterious phone call from a man who I don't know. I don't recognize the voice."

"Are they trying to blackmail you or something?" Jeff asked.

Anna laughed because she had originally thought the same thing. "No, it doesn't seem that way. They have never asked for money. They don't really ask me any questions. They just talk about the latest disaster revolving around Carl. They tell me it will be okay and usually just hang up. The Florida house was different though. I told them about it, and they didn't seem to know anything about that house either or maybe didn't even know it existed. I thought maybe they were just trying to see how much the police knew about that investigation, but I didn't have much info, so he said everything is going to be fine, and as usual, he hung up."

"Anna, are you thinking that you don't want to tell the chief about him either?"

"I think that's exactly what I'm thinking. I'm not sure it's the right move, but I need more information before I go spilling the beans about them. If Carl hadn't said not to tell the chief when we heard from him, then I would definitely tell him, but as far as the chief goes, what would I tell him? There is a random, mysterious guy calling me and telling me not to worry about my husband being missing and my life falling apart? I don't think he'd care anyway."

I asked Jeff what he thought, and he agreed with Anna. "I think we need to get more information before we start blowing the whistle here. The safe-deposit box, from the sound of it, should help quite a bit, and I'll talk to Demetri and see what his thoughts are on telling the chief about Carl and the mystery caller. Let's all try to get some rest so we are ready to hit the ground running in the morning."

Chapter 28

Jeff woke up the next morning, knowing everything was about to change. He was sure Demetri had more details. With the ladies sleeping, he decided to phone Demetri but wasn't sure he would answer so early. Jeff was up half the night, of course, thinking about the best way to approach the conversation with Demetri. He was waiting for Jeff's call but wasn't quite sure when exactly it would be coming through. This has been planned for quite some time, but they all weren't sure how it would come about and which plan of action they would need to use. Jeff thought this was different, and he didn't like it.

The line was ringing, which meant his phone was on at least. Ring, ring, ring.

"Hello, my friend!"

Jeff couldn't help but smile at Demetri's greeting. "Hello, Demetri."

"How are you?"

"Just fine. How are you?"

"I'm well. Are you calling why I think you're calling? I've been reading the papers and the local news. I sat on the couch with a Scotch and the physical newspaper, something I haven't done in months, and I opened it right to the article about Carl. I nearly choked on my Macallan 18 and dropped the glass on the floor. To be honest, I never thought this day would actually come to fruition."

"Haha, I know, man. Who would have thought we would actually have to have this conversation?"

"Well, we all thought that bitch was crazy from the beginning."

"Yeah, all of us but Carl."

"I think he always knew but just thought he could change her ways. I think he thought she would change after they got married and had kids."

They were both silent for a moment, and they knew why.

"So which plan are we starting with? Knowing Carl, we are starting at Z and working our way back to A."

Jeff let out a big belly laugh because Demetri was so right. "You are full of them today, Demetri. Actually, we are headed to the safe-deposit box today, so I think we are starting with A."

"Who's we?"

"Me, Anna, and Angie."

"Seriously?"

"Oh yeah, that crazy bastard called Anna last night while she was at our house. She is staying with us because the house blew up."

"What the fuck? Are you kidding me?"

"Yeah, you didn't read that in the paper, did you?"

"Um, that's a no. What in the world is he doing?"

"I don't have a clue, but I don't think he's doing it. I think this is the real deal this time."

"You do? You think it's really her?"

"Oh yeah. He let her name slip to one of our employees. He sounded genuinely confused when Anna told him what had happened so far."

"What's happened?"

"You don't know the half of it, so I'd like to meet you later today if that's okay with you? I told the ladies that I wasn't letting them out of my sight for a while, so would you be able to stop by the house later this afternoon? They'll probably go visit Elle right across the street so we can talk in peace while they are over there."

"Sure. I have court in the morning, but then my afternoon is pretty free."

"Great. Text me on your way over."

"Sure thing, buddy. See you then."

Jeff hung up the phone and started planning for what was to come that day. He knew there were a few options, but once they got their hands on that box at the bank, he would have a much better idea of what they, well, *he* was in store for in the upcoming weeks … maybe months.

Chapter 29

Anna and I woke up around the same time, and I could see that Jeff was up already. It made me happy that he was watching over the house.

I headed downstairs to find him. He was sitting at the kitchen table, having a cup of coffee and reading the news on his tablet.

"Good morning, handsome."

"Good morning, wifie. How did you sleep, hottie?"

Oh my, my brain flashed to Derrick standing in the doorway of my office last week. *Focus, Angie! What's the matter with you?* "I slept pretty well, considering."

We both heard Anna coming down the steps.

"Hey there! Did you get some sleep?" I didn't want to tiptoe around her and make her feel like a child, but I didn't want to be insensitive either.

"I did actually. I slept quite well. Thank you so much for letting me stay here with you both. I feel so much safer not being alone. I know you are taking a risk letting me stay here, and I really appreciate all you've done for me."

"We feel like we are all in this together, and we definitely think you are safer here with us."

"Is anyone hungry? I thought I would make some breakfast if anyone is up for it, and then we can get showered and head out for the day."

Jeff and Anna both said they were famished, so I made some eggs, toast, bacon, and even some pancakes. I felt like we needed a lot of protein for our long day and some comfort food too. Since we had heard from Carl, we could rest a little bit easier.

I fed everyone, including the kids. All three of us would take the kids to school on our way out.

"Angie, I called Demetri this morning, and he's going to stop by later this afternoon, just to get some facts from us and see how he can help or at least be on standby."

"Oh great. Anna, if there is anything you would like to discuss with him, please, by all means, take this time to do so."

"Thanks, Angie."

"I thought we could go visit Elle later today too if you want to meet her."

"That would be nice. I'd like that. I'll let her know we'll be over later. I'm sure Jeff will want to have some private words with Demetri, and we'll get out of their hair after we speak with him ourselves."

———⟋⟍———

Jeff was nervous for a minute, thinking that Angie could read his mind, but then he realized how stupid that sounded when he played it back in his own head. He was going to need her to be a neurotic psycho in the next few weeks, depending on how this all shook out. He would need her to follow some clues and solve some of this shitshow on her own. He had total faith in her neuroses, so he was not worried, but it would be a test to see if she could get Anna to conform to the roller coaster of events that would take place. Angie worked best under pressure. She always had, and during this mess, he could see she hadn't lost her touch.

"Anna, Jeff and I will clean up the breakfast dishes. You go ahead upstairs and get showered, and we'll get ready when you're finished. I laid out some clothes for you, and I even had some brand-new undies that I never wore that you can have until we get you some things of your own today."

"Angie, that's amazing. I will buy you some new ones to replace them today."

"Anna, don't you worry about me. We are taking care of you today, and come hell or high water, we will get some answers if it's the last thing we do ... and some new undies."

Anna and Angie laughed together, certainly making light of the shitty situation.

"If you think this is a stress reliever, wait until you meet Elle later today."

Jeff was convinced by this comment that Angie was on her game and ready for whatever came her way. God, he hoped so because the shit would hit the fan once they got to the bank.

Chapter 30

We dropped the kids off at school and headed for the bank. Anna was a nervous wreck, and I was a wreck for her. Who knew what we were going to find in that box. I thought for a minute that Anna maybe was in on this whole thing with Carl. Maybe they were going to file bankruptcy, and this was a last resort to get some insurance money to get rid of some other debt. It really didn't seem like Anna had a clue what was going on, but then again, given the way Carl was acting on the phone, like he was just calling to say hi, made me question this whole thing. I needed to stop thinking so crazy and start preparing myself as best I could for whatever we were going to find in that box.

We pulled up to the bank and all got out of the car. Jeff looked at me and asked, "Are you ready for this?"

"As ready as I'm going to be, I guess. How do we know if we're ready when we don't even know what's in there?"

"Great question, babe. I've been trying to figure that out since we spoke to Carl and he told Anna to come here."

"Anna, are you okay?"

"No, I don't have any idea what we are going to find in there, and I'm not sure I even want to see it. What if I see something in there that reveals that the last fifteen years of my life have been a lie and Carl isn't really who he says he is? What if he's some crazy spy or works for the CIA?"

"Haha!" Jeff burst into laughter and then recoiled when he saw the hurt in Anna's eyes. "Anna, I'm sorry, but I just don't see that with Carl. He's been a mess for what seems like, well, all the time, and I just can't see him holding such an important position as those you just named. I don't at all mean to hurt your feelings, but I just can't see that being true. I know Carl said we were going to see things in there that we weren't going to like, but it will hopefully make the pieces fit better for us all. I've known Carl a long time, and even though I wasn't in his company for years in between childhood and these most recent years, he's just not the type to be involved in something that big."

"I guess you're right, Jeff, but I'm starting to get really scared."

"I know, but we have to stick together and make sense out of what we are about to find. Let's not get too panicked until we find out what's in there."

"Shall we go into the bank, or should we wait for the chief?"

"We should probably wait."

"Okay, I don't like this either. I don't like lying to the chief just to get into the box."

"What did you end up telling him anyway?" asked Jeff.

"I just told him that I had some cash in the box, and I wanted to get it out so I could do some shopping."

"And he bought it?" asked Jeff.

"Yeah, I couldn't come up with anything better. Leave it to Carl to tell me that I can't tell the chief that I spoke to him. Then he suggested that I take him to the bank with me just in case they give me any trouble getting into it without the key. What an ass."

Just as they stopped talking about it, the chief pulled up in his cruiser.

"Hey, everyone," said the chief. "I'm not going to ask how anyone is because I'm sure you are no better than the last time I spoke to all of you."

Jeff said, "Yeah, definitely the same."

—⁓—

They shook hands, and he put his large hand on Anna's shoulder as if to say it would all be okay. All she could think was *Why do people keep telling me it will be okay? How do they know that? Do they know something I don't, or are they just trying to be helpful and consoling?* Either way, she was starting to get sick of it. With everything that had been going on, she was beginning not to trust anyone but Angie and Jeff. It didn't seem like anything was going to be okay.

"Are you ready to get this over with, everyone?"

"Yes," Angie said. "Let's do this. It's now or never."

Chapter 31

They headed into the bank together, and Anna knew once they let her back in that room, she would be all alone. She was pretty sure she couldn't take anyone else back there with her and part of her felt completely alone. The other part felt a little relieved because whatever was in that box could be humiliating to her, and she didn't want anyone to see that.

So many scenarios continued to race through her head as she walked up to the teller. She knew they would have to get a manager to open the box with her, and she was going to have to explain why she didn't have her key.

"May I help you?" said the chipper voice coming from the girl, who didn't look a day over eighteen.

"Yes, I'm here to open a safe-deposit box I share with my husband. The only problem is that I had a house fire last night so I don't have my key."

The young woman went wide-eyed and was at a loss for what to say. She stuttered a little bit, fumbled with her pen, and nearly fell out of her chair. Finally, she managed to say, "Okay, ma'am, please wait here, and I will get my manager."

Anna didn't bother to say anything. She just stood there and waited. The manager came over to speak with Anna.

"Hello, ma'am. I'm sorry, but I cannot open the box without a key."

The chief stepped in and showed the manager his badge to make it very clear he was not going to stand for any bullshit and he was expecting Anna to be treated with the utmost respect. "She was afraid you might say that, so she brought me along to verify what happened. The house was in fact set on fire. I cannot discuss the details of the situation, but I can tell you this. There must be some sort of protocol for the predicament she is in right now."

"Okay, so the only other option we have is for us to drill through the box, and unfortunately, you will have to pay the cost of a new lock and a new set of keys."

"Okay, that's fine, if that's the only option."

"I'm afraid it is, so let me make a phone call and I'll be back to let you know what kind of timing we are looking at here."

Almost fifteen minutes went by, and she finally returned to the desk. "Okay," she said. "I was able to get ahold of the locksmith, and he is on his way."

"Will I be able to empty the contents of it and take it with me?" asked Anna.

"Yes, that is not a problem. Whatever is in that box is yours to do with whatever you like. Do you think you want to close it altogether?"

"No, I don't think I do, so in that case, you can go ahead and order a new key. Do you know how much it will cost?"

"I will get that total for you before you leave, ma'am, and we can just debit it out of the bank account if that works for you?"

"Yes, that's fine with me."

"Can you please verify your Social?"

Anna wasn't sure how she was going to get the chief out of the bank. She definitely didn't want him to see what was in the safe-deposit box. She was also afraid that one of them would slip and say something about Carl.

The chief looked at Anna and said, "Are you okay to take it from here? Since Jeff and Angie are here and you can get into the box, I don't think you need me any longer." She must have had an alarmed look on her face because he proceeded to say, "I would need a warrant to see what's in that box during the investigation, and if Carl is behind this, it will come out sooner or later."

"What's that supposed to mean, Chief?"

"Nothing. I'm just saying that if someone kidnapped him, they didn't leave evidence in your safe-deposit box."

"That's a good point, but you said Carl was involved."

"I said if Carl is involved, it will come out sooner or later. What I'm getting at is whatever is in that box will most likely not help the investigation."

"Oh, I see what you are saying."

"If you need me, Anna, just call. I know you'll be with them for a while, but if you need anything at all, just give me a shout." The chief put a reassuring hand on Anna's shoulder again, and in seconds, he was gone.

That conversation left Anna's head spinning. She wondered what he was talking about and why he seemed so nonchalant and matter of fact. It almost sounded like he knew something about the case and wasn't sharing, like he had a gut feeling or an assumption and already had his mind made up about how this was all going to shake out in the end. Why did it seem like he didn't care about the contents of the box? Better yet, was the chief involved? It couldn't be … could it?

Chapter 32

"Miss … excuse me, miss?" The bank manager was trying to get her attention to let her know it was time to head back and open the box. "The locksmith is here, so we can get into the box now."

"I'm sorry; I was just thinking."

"It's quite all right. Take your time."

All Anna could think of was making a mad dash toward the front door, getting in the car, and driving as far away as possible.

"No, it's fine. I'm ready."

The hallway felt a hundred miles long, and Anna's forehead was starting to sweat, more because she was a nervous wreck than because the ten-foot walk made her tired.

They finally reached the room, and the locksmith got out his tools.

Anna asked, "How long do you think it's going to take to get in there?"

"It shouldn't take long at all. Longer to get my tools out than to get in the box."

Anna was hoping his answer was going to be different. She was hoping it was going to take much longer.

"One more turn and *dink*," said the locksmith.

She could hear the lock come loose and fall to the table. The bank manager was talking to her, but it sounded like she was underwater. Anna could feel her heart start to race, and again, she just wanted to run out of there and get away.

"Ma'am, we are going to leave the room so you have some time to yourself. You can just push the button when you are ready for me to come back. Since you mentioned you are going to take everything with you, I will just come back and take care of the box."

"Okay, thank you," said Anna.

Anna stood there over the box, just staring at it, prolonging the viewing of the contents. She didn't want to open it, and she didn't. She just continued to stand there and stare at it, wishing this wasn't happening and she was just going on with her life. So many thoughts about Carl and Jeff were going around in her head. She kept trying to put some pieces together but knew she couldn't. There was no evidence. There were no clues. She had nothing—no pieces to solve a puzzle.

She was hoping against hope that she wouldn't open the box and find hundreds of thousands of bills in ten different currencies. Next to that, she pictured a nine-millimeter Glock firearm lying on top of ten different passports with Carl's photo but not his name on the ID portion.

After picturing that mess, she couldn't help but chuckle to herself, thinking, *No way would Carl have all that stuff. He wouldn't even know how to get those items. He would probably try to buy it all from an undercover cop.* That would be Carl's luck and lack of planning. *Oh, Carl*, she thought. Her heart started to break all over again when she thought of him.

Time to get it together, Anna. It's now or never, she thought.

She slowly opened the box, and her eyes flickered. She blinked a few times in total disbelief. Just when she thought this couldn't get any weirder or more frustrating, this was the moment when it did.

She wasn't exactly in the mood for a scavenger hunt, so she was thankful that there wasn't a map in the box. Sadly, this was just as ridiculous. The only solitary thing in the box was a key.

"You have to be shitting me," she said out loud. It was definitely a key to another safe-deposit box, but which one and where? Was it even in this bank, or was it in another one?

Her only option was to get the bank manager and ask her if it belonged to this bank.

She pushed the button to call the manager and just waited.

Chapter 33

After leaving the bank, the chief headed back to the station with all the scenarios playing in his head. The end result, of course, was the one that continued to replay. Anna was a very smart woman, so she might very well be an asset in this case, and she appeared to have all her marbles in the same bag. She wouldn't be faltering anytime soon. He knew this would be a huge help when moving the pieces of the plan around. There were still some pieces missing, and that was where he came in to put it all back together.

If the chief wasn't all too familiar with the McNamaras, he would be researching them a little more, but as much as he knew, something was really eating at him. He thought if he kept thinking about it, he would come up with some connection or some sort of lead at least.

He was so frustrated with this whole case. Whoever was behind this was pretty damn good. They had no solid leads, and it seemed that every avenue to research came to a dead end. He had never worked such a frustrating case as this one in his entire career. As long as he'd been on the force, he'd never been in so deep as he was with this one either. They had spent so much time preparing for this, but it didn't come to them the way he'd thought it would.

He replayed every gruesome case he worked involving the McNamaras. He saw some really horrible things in those cases. This case wasn't too far off from those—dead bodies charred from fire so badly the skin was melted into what was left of the furniture. Even though he was still waiting for the autopsy reports, he had a feeling those people were already dead before the fire started. He had zero evidence to base this on, but something told him there was so much more to those creepy scenes. Working by phone and email with another police station hundreds of miles away didn't make anything any easier. They shared what they had, but he hadn't seen the full police reports, so he didn't know the fine-pointed details.

Recalling the McNamaras again, he thought he would pull some old case files out and start combing through those. Even though he knew each page and sickening detail by heart, he thought maybe if he read them again, he could recall something he'd forgotten over the years. He didn't want his ego to get in the way. Maybe he had truly missed something, and he would be looking at it from a different perspective now. He knew in his gut who was behind this, but he needed proof. He needed to be sure.

Since Fitzpatrick was gone, they replaced him with a female rookie. She was already on the force, but she actually took Fitz's position. The chief thought it would be a good idea to test her out with this case. He figured this would either make or break her, and from what he'd seen so far in her over the last few months she'd been on the force, he was sure she would handle it just fine. She had a keen sense of foul play and paid more attention to the details, which he chalked up to her being a woman.

The chief stuck his head out of his office door and yelled, "Hey, Smith!"

"It's Smythe, Chief."

"Yeah, yeah, see that's why you're so good with the details."

She rolled her eyes at her coworkers, who just laughed and snickered at her in response to the chief's old-school tendencies.

Smythe entered the chief's office and said, "What's up?"

"I need you to look through these files with me. I'll give you a brief back story of the McNamaras so you know what to expect."

"Chief, that's great! I did my master's thesis on them. At the time, I obviously didn't have the info you have access to, so I only know what is public knowledge."

"Smythe, get yourself prepared, because you haven't seen anything yet. You might second-guess your police career when you see this shit."

He was looking forward to how fun this was going to be, watching her expressions and hearing what she had to say as she unfolded each piece of the puzzle in her mind. There was no puzzle for the chief because he loved it. She had no idea what was to come in these files. He knew she was prepared. Being a cop, you had to know you were going to come across some really awful people committing some really heinous crimes, the unthinkable kinds of crimes.

"Chief, why are we looking through these now anyway?"

"I think some if this old shit might have something to do with a current case."

"You mean our current case?"

"Yes, Smythe, and please don't repeat that piece of information."

"Chief, why would I do that, and who would I tell? Why would I jeopardize—"

"Don't say it, Smythe. You young kids seem to go off the deep end sometimes, and who's telling what you might say?"

"I'm looking to advance in the police force, not screw myself into a permanent desk job."

The chief loved the young blood. They were always so eager to advance, even though they didn't even have enough experience to hold his gun. He laughed to himself but was looking forward to her doing a lot of the rookie legwork so he wouldn't have to do it anymore. Plus, he was out of practice. She would be happy to do something that he would rather stick a fire poker in his eye than have to do.

"Okay then, are you ready to study this gruesome shitshow?"

"Can't wait!" Smythe said with a smile. "Let's do it."

Chapter 34

Carl hated doing this to Anna, but it was the only way to get this over with once and for all and keep her safe. There was no telling what would happen to her if he didn't take care of this madness after all these years. He hoped, at the same time, to keep Angie and Jeff safe with his plan as well. He was banking on them helping Anna so he knew they would always have information, but he wanted to keep them protected.

If he needed to move to plan B, Jeff knew when to step in, and he had probably already spoken to Demetri and most likely to the chief to get everything in place. He knew this day would come sooner or later but wasn't sure when or how soon. He was mostly a total fuckup in the rest of his life, so at least he was smart enough to plan for … Elizabeth. He was smart enough get others involved to ensure he didn't fuck it up himself.

He watched Elizabeth sitting patiently, drumming her newly manicured fingernails on the table. She waited for her phone to ring. It would be her brother-in-law calling to let her know that the situation was taken care of and there wouldn't be any reason to worry any longer.

Elizabeth still had a body that would stop traffic. She had a smile that would almost paralyze any grown man, and those eyes … those eyes of hers sealed any deal for what she wanted. She used this to her advantage all the time. She could chalk up most of her professional success to her physical attributes as well. She was a very smart woman but always used her looks to get her way instead of working for it. Carl could never understand why she would do that. He felt it was lazy and so dishonest, but then again, that was Elizabeth, always breaking the rules and never wanting to do anything by the book. It only brought him anger to know that she had completely deceived him from the beginning. He wasn't even sure why she bothered with him in the first place. She clearly never had a real use for him … ever.

She'd been living in Italy for quite some time, so it wasn't like she could just knock on his door to track him down. She still had a few connections, but none of them would be willing to do some babysitting thousands of miles and an ocean away.

She lived her life much differently now from how she did in the old days, and thank God for that, or she would most likely be dead for real. There was no way she would have survived that lifestyle. She had a great career and did very well for herself. She had more than she could have ever imagined. Rotten to the core was Elizabeth, and that was how she got so far in her industry. She faked her college diploma and all the other credentials she needed to get where she was.

Carl had someone tracking Elizabeth, watching her every move. He was not going to let her know he was on to her and her games. He was as careful as he could possibly be, especially because he was not actually there himself. She thought she was winning and didn't even know he was about to strike. He had to wait until the time was right.

—⁓—

Her phone rang. It was the call she'd been waiting for, and the voice on the other end said, "Your situation was taken care of this morning."

"Thank you, but I need proof."

"You'll have it later this evening."

"Thank you."

The line went dead, and she suddenly had a sickening pit in her stomach. She wasn't quite sure why, but she started thinking she had made a huge mistake. She thought this might start a war, but then again, who would care if Carl was gone? Not his wife. She seemed to have her shit completely together at her fashion show in Paris. She thought maybe she should have just taken out Anna too while she was there. She had had every opportunity to do so. There would be time for that in the future if she chose, but in the meantime she could just rest easy, knowing Carl was dead.

Chapter 35

Back at the bank, Anna was waiting for the manager to come back and talk to her about the key. She quickly thought maybe she should speak with Jeff before she consulted with the bank manager. She wasn't sure she wanted her to know what was in the box, and now that they'd had to break it open for her, she wasn't sure what to do.

The manager walked right around the corner to meet Anna just as she was going to head out of the room.

"Are you all finished?"

"Yes, I am. Thank you. We can close it up. What do we need to do with it now that it's in this condition?"

"We will just be getting rid of it since it's of no use to the bank."

"I took everything out of it for now, so when the new box arrives, just let me know, and I can come back and put some things back."

"Okay, I will do that. Is there anything else I can help you with today, ma'am?"

"No, this will be enough." Anna gave the manager a sideways smile, like "Thanks for nothing," but the woman had no idea what Anna was going through. She certainly saw the news and read the papers, so she knew that Anna's life was upside down, but she couldn't feel the way Anna was feeling.

Before Anna walked out, she said, "Thanks again for your help."

The manager smiled and said, "Anytime, I will do my best to help with whatever I can. I'll be in touch."

Anna headed for the front of the bank, where Jeff and Angie were waiting.

—m—

"There was another freaking key in the box."

"What?" I said.

"Another key," said Anna. "Nothing else in the box but this stupid key. It was completely empty except for the little key sitting there right in the middle of the box. I was going to ask the teller if she recognized the key and if it belonged to this bank. I decided not to do that because I didn't want her to know what was in the box. It's really none of her business."

"Anna, this key looks just like our safe-deposit box key. There must be a safe-deposit box at our bank that this key will open."

I said, "Yes, Jeff, you're right."

Anna said, "Isn't that convenient? What are the odds of that being the case? Maybe it's a break for once?"

"Let's go, ladies. Our bank isn't far from here. If we get a move on, we'll get there before the lunch crowd swarms in to do their banking."

Angie and Anna piled into the car with Jeff to head over to the bank.

—m—

Jeff and Angie's bank was on Sixth and Broad, right in the middle of town. Anna never wanted to live in a big city as much as she did that day. She was wishing that people didn't know her, and she could just get lost in a big crowd. *Not the case today*, she thought.

She headed over to one of the tellers and let her know she needed to get into her safe-deposit box. Good thing the number was on the key, or she would have had no idea which box she needed to get into.

The teller said, "No problem, Anna. I will get the manager for you so she can help."

Anna was taken completely off guard, but then she realized that this woman must have been reading, watching, or streaming the news. How else would she know Anna?

The bank manager came racing over to Anna. She didn't want to be overwhelming, so she just said, "Hello, Anna. I know you don't know me, but I've been waiting for you. I wasn't sure when you would be arriving, but I knew you would be coming in sooner or later."

"Excuse me?" Anna said questioningly.

"I'm sorry, Anna, and maybe I am way out of line here, but I've been watching the news, and when Carl went missing, I figured you would be coming to the bank. I've been here a really long time, and I've known Carl only from here at the bank, but something always seemed off about him.

Very nice man and always friendly when he came in here but definitely a strange bird."

Anna couldn't say much, and she certainly couldn't argue with the woman. What would be the use anyway? What she said about Carl was definitely true.

"Why were you waiting for me?" asked Anna.

"I figured you would be coming in to get the contents of the safe-deposit box. We have strict instructions from the paperwork that Carl filled out that you are the only person who is allowed to get into this box, with the key, of course."

"Is that really how all that works?"

"It can if you know the right people," the teller said with a devilish smirk. "You want to get in this thing already or what?"

Anna said, "Yes, please, I thought you would never ask."

"Anna, you know how this works?"

"Yes, I do."

"Okay, let's get this thing open then, shall we?"

The manager took the key from Anna and opened the box. She did not look inside, of course. "I will leave you to it then, and when you are finished, you can just hit this button on the wall over here, and I will come in and close up the box. You can sign out at that point, and then you can be on your way. You can do whatever you want with the contents, including take it all with you if you'd like. Take as much time as you need. There is no rush whatsoever."

"Okay, thank you again," said Anna.

The manager touched Anna's arm as if to say, "It will all be okay," but how would she know? Then she was on her way.

Anna just stood there again staring at the box. She didn't want to open this one either. This box was twice the size of the last one, and this time, she picked it up to see if it felt like there was something in it. It was definitely heavier than the last one, but she wondered if it was only because it was so much bigger.

"Let's go, Anna. Put your big girl pants on, and let's open the stupid thing," she said out loud. She started to crack the box open and felt some tears prick the corners of her eyes. She thought, *Not now. This is no time to get emotional over something you don't even know yet. Get your shit together, and open this thing already.*

Chapter 36

Fitzpatrick was pacing his living room floor for what felt like days. He hadn't slept. He hadn't showered or even changed his clothes. He was a compulsive stress eater, so he'd eaten enough for six people in these few days. There were take-out boxes and containers all over the house. It looked like a garbage dump.

He had enough money stashed away to last almost a lifetime from his days of playing a bad guy. He owned the house free and clear, so he didn't have to worry about a mortgage. The address of this house, of course, was not the same one the chief had, so he wouldn't be looking for him there. The house was not in his name either, so there would be no finding him by searching deeds in the name of Fitzpatrick.

He was very uneasy about the comment that Derrick had made to him when he was questioning the employees at Carl's office. This didn't sit well with him at all, especially because he'd made enough phone calls to his old buddies to try to figure out what Carl was talking about and why he mentioned Elizabeth.

He was now obsessed with finding her and figuring out what the fuck she had to do with Carl. Why did he feel this sudden urge to track her down and get some answers? He was getting way too close to all of this but figured it would all pay off in the end if he could be the first one to find Carl. If he could find him first, then he would get the answers he was looking for, but he needed to be as invisible as possible.

He was certain everyone was already trying to find out what the hell he had to do with the case, and he was sure that the chief was already all over his records. The chief was a very smart man and had been a cop almost longer than Fitz had been on this godforsaken earth. Fitz was sure that the chief was all over his records, or lack thereof, and he would figure out there were a number of years missing in his whereabouts.

He needed to think fast and come up with his next steps. So far, no one knew where he was or what he was doing. He tried to keep his number of friends to a minimum and had very little contact with his family. He knew of only one person who could or might even be willing to help him, so he picked up his phone to make a phone call. This was the only person he could trust.

He punched in the numbers, and it started to ring.

"Hello?"

"Justin, it's Fitz."

"Hey, man. 'Sup?"

"Listen, buddy, I need your help."

"It's not illegal, is it?"

"I'm not sure, but it might take that turn somewhere along the way."

"No, man, sorry, I'm out," said Justin.

"Are you fucking kidding me?"

"No, man, I'm not risking going back to prison. All that shit they put me through back then was seriously not worth all that happened while I was in there and not to find out everything else that happened while I was away was total bullshit. They kept everything from me, and all that I did for them was worth nothing in the end. I'm not going back to that life. It's not worth it for anyone."

"What are you talking about? What happened?"

"That's for another conversation, my friend."

"Well, how about we have that conversation now?"

"I'm not in the mood to talk about that shit now, so unless you need something else that's not illegal, I'm getting off the phone."

"I'll be honest. I'm pretty fucking pissed that you won't help me, but I respect you not wanting to go back to prison."

"Fitz, what the fuck are you doing? I thought we were both done with that life?"

"I got fired from the force for reasons that I would prefer not to discuss."

"What? What are you going to do for a job?"

"I don't know. I'll figure something out, but right now, I have enough cash from the bad guy days."

Justin laughed out loud because it sounded so ridiculous coming out of Fitz's mouth. "The bad guy days, dude? What are you ten years old, playing cops and robbers in the backyard of Aunt June's?"

"Fuck you, dude, you never know who might be listening."

He laughed out loud. "I guess. You're a mess, man. Whatever you are considering doing, maybe you should reconsider. No one and nothing is worth going to jail for, especially at your age."

"This is worth it to me. I can't really talk about it though, at least not until I have more evidence."

"All right, man, whatever you say. I'll help if it's not illegal, but otherwise, count me out. If you can come up with something you need without me going back to prison if we get caught, let me know. You know how to reach me. Maybe you need to take a different approach to all this?"

"What is that supposed to mean?"

"I mean, who would want to help you when you are so angry and so confrontational? Being a dick isn't going to make anyone want to help you. You can't do this alone, so stop trying. Don't work against them. Try to work with them."

This really made Fitz think. Maybe he should calm down and try not to be so angry.

"All right, cous'. Catch you later."

"Later, man."

Who exactly is Elizabeth? And what does she have to do with Carl? Why the hell is he missing? The last he heard, the chief wasn't trying to find Elizabeth either. Why the fuck not? The chief didn't seem to care about Elizabeth. This was going to piss a lot of people off, but Fitz was going to do everything he could to track down Elizabeth, even if it meant he would die trying. He didn't want to hurt anyone. He just wanted answers.

Chapter 37

Anna was hovering over this safe-deposit box like it was going to bite her if she tried to open it. She opened the squeaky lid, and what she saw caused anger to start to rise inside her so much so that she wanted to take the box and throw it across the room. She had about had it with Carl and all this shit.

In the box, she found a huge wad of cash, a set of car keys, and a large envelope. She also found another box that she would need a key and a lock combination to get into. There was no key inside to get into the smaller box. She had no idea how she would be getting into that one. She figured it would be a waiting game for that to show up somewhere. Maybe another house would have to blow up, or, hell, maybe the actual bank would blow for her to get that key.

She decided to put all the contents into the bag she had brought with her, call the bank manager, and get the hell out of there.

The bank manager came to close up the box, and Anna darted out of the room over to Jeff and Angie.

Jeff said, "Well? Was there something in this one?"

"Yes, but another box. This one you need a key and a lock combo to get into."

Jeff, of course, already knew that Demetri had all that but wasn't sure when he would be presenting it to Anna, and obviously, he couldn't tell her that piece of information.

Jeff said, "Let's get out of here and head back to our house. We can discuss everything there and see what our next step will be for you, Anna. You still need to go shopping, and we need to get you a set of wheels."

"Here's what's interesting about that. There was a set of car keys in the box, so we just need to find out what they belong to. I assume I won't have to buy anything."

"This whole situation is just fucked up," Angie said.

Jeff and Anna laughed at the same time. It was a little out of character for Angie to swear, but Jeff knew that she had a crazy side, which was pretty much hidden away when the kids came along.

"I hate to say this, but maybe Carl isn't as clueless as we think," Anna said. "Even though we are still in the dark for the most part, I feel like up until this point, a lot has been planned out, like he knew all this was going to happen. Nothing else explains all this preparation."

Jeff played his part like he was supposed to if Anna started talking like this.

"Anna, you are definitely on to something. We just need to figure out what and how Carl, of all people, is pulling this off."

This pleased Jeff, as he knew that Anna was on her game, as was Angie. He needed them both thinking on their toes and ready to take on the world. Again, depending on how all this played out, he would need both of them.

Chapter 38

They headed back to the house so she could dissect everything she'd pulled out of that box. She didn't open anything until they got back to the house.

"Anna, do you want some privacy?" Angie asked.

"Thank you, Angie, but since I feel like we are all trying to solve this mystery, I want you both to see what all is in here."

Anna pulled each piece of what she had out of the bag separately and laid it on the kitchen table. The wad of cash came first. There had to be at least $3,000 there. This was obviously for her to have a decent amount of spending money. She was going to use it to put her life back together. She had money though, and Carl knew that, so why exactly was she going to need all that cash?

Then she pulled out the box. She was baffled at how she was supposed to get into the damn thing.

She pulled out the set of car keys, which had a BMW symbol on the key fob. She really didn't know how Carl could afford such a nice car that was just hidden away somewhere. This was another vehicle that she didn't know about, which made her angry, but she needed to focus instead of being pissed off.

The last thing was a big, thick envelope, sealed and taped with duct and masking tape like it was supposed to deter someone from seeing the contents.

Angie got Anna a pair of scissors so she could cut her way through all the ridiculous tape. She started cutting and was as careful as could be so she didn't damage anything inside. She cut and cut and thought the tape would never end. Finally, she got the last piece of tape off and opened up the envelope. She just dumped the contents on the table. There was so much stuff in the envelope she didn't know where to start.

There were wedding photos of Anna and Carl. Photos she hadn't looked at in years and some she didn't even remember seeing. It had been so long that she was so out of touch with these photos. She sat there for a little while, really taking them all in and looking at each one as if it was going to tell her something. Nothing that she could see looked out of the ordinary to her, but she would definitely go back to them after looking through the rest of the overwhelming pile.

There were movie ticket stubs from special occasions, including their first date. There was a bubblegum wrapper that had a joke on it, but the punchline was wiped away. Carl and Anna just made up their own. Every once in a while, one of them would tell the joke with another made-up ending. It was always so stupid, but it was their thing.

There was a smaller envelope with "Anna" written on the front of it, and it looked like a letter. Anna opened the envelope. She recognized Carl's handwriting even from the other side of the folded paper. It read,

Dear Anna Banana,

If you are reading this, it means you are probably with Angie and Jeff. At least I hope you are. That means you're safe. There are a lot of things in that envelope, and I want to make sure you know how much I love you.

If you are reading this letter, it also means that we've already spoken and you know I'm still alive. You need to understand some things. I said that you were going to see some things in this envelope that you won't be very happy with, but you need to know the truth after all this time.

Anna put the letter down. She needed to take a deep breath. She wasn't sure what she was about to read, and she wanted to brace herself for what was written in the rest of that letter. She also knew without a shadow of a doubt that Carl was missing on purpose and technically not missing at all.

"Anna, are you okay?" Angie asked.

"Yes, I'm fine. I just need to take a break. It sounds like we are going to get some answers in the rest of this letter."

Before we met, I was involved in some really bad shit with some very bad people. I did some things I am not

proud of, nor am I willing to share them with you in this letter. I am writing this because some of these people I am talking about are helping me take care of some "business" I've needed to take care of for a long time. I should have taken care of it long ago, but I thought it would just go away as time passed. You know me, always putting off the inevitable like I can hide from it. I can hear you laughing, and you have such a beautiful laugh. I know you are laughing at me, and that's okay, Banana.

I know you've gotten a lot of information since my "disappearance" from the chief, the media, and other outlets. None of it seems to make a lot of sense, but the history of this mess started a very long time ago, before we met. I had a whole different life back then, and there are things that we never discussed. That was to protect you from my past. I always hoped it wouldn't come to this, but it's finally come back to haunt me ...

Anna kept on reading, and she wasn't really sure how to react or what to say. She didn't say anything. It was pretty evident without spelling it out that Jeff was privy to each piece of the puzzle and what was going to be happening next. She didn't want to say anything out loud. She was pretty sure that Angie had no idea what was happening or what was to come in the next few weeks or months. She didn't know exactly what would be happening either, but she knew it was going to be a rough road ahead.

All she could do was sit back and wait.

Chapter 39

Jeff eyed Anna cautiously because he was not sure what she might say. He was pretty sure Carl's letter explained what was happening without going into specific detail. It seemed like she knew not to say anything in front of Angie, but he would have to continue to watch her closely.

Jeff was not supposed to tell Angie, but he wanted to so badly, especially now that Anna knew. Demetri would be arriving soon, so they would discuss the rest of the plan once Angie and Anna went over to visit Elle. He needed to tell Angie something, so he thought about what he could say without saying too much.

They were expecting Demetri at any moment. The doorbell rang, and Angie went to the door.

"Angie, honey, how are you?"

Angie and Demetri hugged and kissed hello.

"People keep asking me that, and I don't really know what to say. Come in and meet Anna. She is in the kitchen with Jeff."

—◊◊◊—

As Demetri and I entered the kitchen, it seemed as though we had interrupted Anna and Jeff in a conversation. I'd almost gotten used to it, but this time, it was different. It looked like they were making a plan or discussing something far more important than the glances they shared before. I could tell even Demetri was a little uncomfortable, but he didn't say a word.

Jeff and Anna both came over to us immediately.

"Demetri," Jeff said. They shook hands and gave each other a sideways hug.

"Hello, Jeff."

"Demetri, this is Anna. Anna, this is Demetri."

They said hello and shook hands. Demetri proceeded to say, "If there is anything I can help you with, just let me know. Here is my card. You can call me anytime. I know there is uncertainty here. When things start to unfold and we get more information about Carl, if you decide to seek legal counsel, I can help you with whatever questions arise."

"You sound so positive, Demetri," said Anna.

"Well, I like to stay positive in all situations. We don't know how any of this is going to end, so we want to stay as positive as we can. That will help us get through whatever comes our way. Have you looked through the contents of the second box?"

Anna was caught a little off guard. She looked at Demetri very warily and said, "How do you know about the boxes?"

"Oh, I'm sorry to alarm you, but Jeff told me about everything. He wanted to keep me in the loop."

"On that note," I said, "Anna and I are going over to see Elle. Anna hasn't met her yet, and we might be able to relax a little bit and have some girl time."

I kissed Jeff goodbye.

"Thank you and nice meeting you," Anna said to Demetri.

—m—

Demetri said, "Carl called me yesterday as planned. He's where he's supposed to be for now, and the call was made to Elizabeth saying that the situation was taken care of so, of course, she asked for proof. He is working on staging that so there is no question that he's gone from her perspective."

"Great, so it sounds like things are moving along and we can almost start checking things off the list."

"Yeah, so far so good. Anna and Angie seem to be holding up pretty well under the circumstances. It also sounds like they are doing exactly what we thought they would, so that's a major sigh of relief."

"Yes, but I'm starting to feel guilty for not telling Angie what's happening. We share everything with each other, and now that she's been working with me in the business, we really share everything. It's just so awkward sometimes when I want to tell her something and I have to stop myself because she can't know."

"I know, man, but this will all be over before we know it, and we are in control of most of it, so there's not a whole lot to worry about."

"Yes, but those few aspects that we are not in control of leave me very uneasy. Don't they make you uneasy too?"

"They do, but the chief is all over it, and I'm confident in his knowledge and experience to figure out those missing pieces. Mainly, I'm concerned about Fitzpatrick. He seems to be off the reservation, and he's keeping everything very hidden. Not being able to figure out his past is what leaves me the most worried. What's his motivation in all this, and where the fuck is he? How did he just disappear like that? I'm starting to believe that he got himself fired on purpose."

"I know. I thought the same thing myself when the chief first informed us of firing him. He's such a little weasel. We need to find out what his connection is to Justin sooner rather than later. The next couple of weeks here are going to be a nightmare for me if we can't figure out that connection."

"Don't worry about that. You know all other parties can be trusted, and I will be here for whatever Angie needs." Demetri knew more about Fitz than he was supposed to, but he would tell Jeff when the time was right.

"I know, but you won't be here every minute, and that's where I'm worried."

"Carl wouldn't put anyone in danger during all this. He has spent the last, what, fifteen plus years plotting all this out? I know he's not the sharpest knife in the drawer, but he seems to have poured his heart and soul into the 'sting operation' and gotten all the right people involved."

Jeff and Demetri shared a good laugh when he said, "*Carl* and *sting operation* in the same sentence should be against the law."

"Let's get back to Angie," Jeff said. "I was thinking—"

"No way, buddy. Don't even think about it," said Demetri.

"I may as well tell you now then. I'm pretty sure this wasn't the plan, or maybe for Carl, it was all along, but he told Anna some things in the letter he left for her in the safe-deposit box."

"What?" yelled Demetri.

"Yes. I'm not sure exactly what he said, but I am pretty sure he mentioned Elizabeth, well, Alisa."

"What?"

"Like I said, I'm not sure what he said, but I know he mentioned her as part of his past because Anna asked me who Alisa is. She wanted reassurance that she was part of his past and not part of his present life. I reassured her that she is definitely a part of his past. That seemed to make her back off for now, but I wouldn't be surprised if she starts doing some snooping of her own."

"I am at a loss," said Demetri. "This was not part of the plan."

"I know, and that's why I want to tell Angie at least what might be happening in the next few days so she doesn't go completely crazy when the shit really starts to hit the fan."

"Listen, man, you do what you want, but I am advising strongly against it."

"Okay, definitely noted, and I will not say anything."

"Okay, good."

After the conversation that Anna and Jeff had while Angie was letting Demetri into the house, Jeff wouldn't have to tell Angie anything. Anna would do that all on her own.

Chapter 40

We were headed across the street, and I told Anna how she would just love Elle. She was a nice, normal woman who didn't get caught up in all the nonsense. She stayed home with her little girl and kept a nice home.

Anna laughed out loud at that one.

"What?" I asked Anna.

"Do you feel like even though we are working professionals, it's still like the fifties?"

I laughed and said, "You mean from the comment I just made about keeping a nice home?"

"Exactly. That was a little over the top."

"I guess you're right on that one. I feel that way now more than ever. I love Jeff, but I feel like he expects me to still do everything even though I work full-time. It's very tiresome, and I never feel like I have any alone time. Oh, Anna, I'm sorry."

"For what? Saying that you don't have any alone time, meanwhile my husband is missing or on a vacation … whatever he's doing? Don't worry about it. You know we lived such separate lives before all this mess, I was usually alone all the time anyway. I can't lie to you; I enjoyed being alone. When Carl comes back, I hope we spend a lot more time together, but I will still need my alone time."

I knocked on the one-hundred-foot-tall front door of Elle's very large house.

Elle came to the door seconds later. She opened it and said, "Come in! Come in!" She gave me a big hug and said, "I feel like it's been ages since I've seen you. You haven't changed a bit."

We all laughed.

"Elle, this is Anna. Anna, this is Elle."

They said hello to each other, and Anna held out her hand. Elle practically tackled her with a hug. Anna received it warmly, and I think it made her feel very good and at home.

"Come into the kitchen."

We walked into the kitchen, and there was a nice little spread of bite-sized hors d'oeuvres, small sandwiches, macaroons in every color you can imagine, and lemonade in mason jars with pretty cardboard straws.

"Jeez, Elle, you didn't have to go to all this trouble."

"It's nothing. How often do I get to entertain for you, and I thought maybe Anna could use a little time to sit back and take a deep breath. Plus, we have to eat, right? I just put the princess down for a nap so we have a few hours of peace and quiet."

Anna and I both thanked her, and we all dug right in.

I was looking out the sunroom windows in the back of Elle's house, and I said, "Hey, how about the tree line?"

"Haha, very funny, Angie."

I didn't want to leave Anna out of the conversation.

"I'm just teasing Elle about Justin, her convict tree trimmer that she hired on a whim because he was trimming the trees at the neighbor's house down the street."

—————

Anna thought this was too good to be true. She started putting some pieces together in her head. She couldn't believe this was happening. She'd been wanting to get Angie alone without Jeff to talk about some things she felt she should know. Even though she wasn't supposed to share with Angie, she knew they were going to be in this for the long haul, and what good was an ally if she was in the dark with no information?

"Anna, are you okay?" Angie asked.

"Yes, I'm fine. Can we speak freely here?"

"Of course. What is it?"

Anna said, "This Justin that you are talking about, does he have a funny last name that's hard to pronounce?"

Elle answered, "Yes, he does. Why?"

Anna replied, "He's my nephew. Well, Carl's really, well, sort of, but he's obviously mine by marriage."

Angie's mouth dropped so far open Anna thought it was going to smash into the island where they were eating. She looked like she felt like passing out.

Chapter 41

Elle looked at me with my face twisted in horror. I had no idea what to say.

I blurted out, "Are you kidding me?"

Anna said, "No, Angie, why? What's the matter? You look like you just ate a bug or something."

"Ate a bug? Really? Are you kidding?"

Anna said, "No, I thought we already covered this?"

"Justin is your nephew?" I asked Anna just to clarify.

Anna said, "Yes, Angie, I don't understand the big deal here. Do you know Justin, or do you just know him as the convict tree trimmer, as you referred to him earlier?"

I felt like a complete asshole. Not only was I mortified, but I seemed to have insulted Anna at the same time. She said it so nonchalantly ("Oh, he's my nephew"), like it was okay that he was her nephew. I thought maybe I was just being ridiculous. Jeff did say that I had nothing to worry about with Justin. Even so, I couldn't help but feel completely panicked. *Just calm down and get the scoop.*

"Anna, I can't help but feel like a total ass. I always feel like I'm apologizing for the stupid things I say."

Anna raised an eyebrow at me and said, "Well, then stop saying stupid things."

We all laughed, but I needed to get to the bottom of this Justin issue.

"So what's the story with Justin?"

"What do you mean?"

"Well, you said he's sort of your nephew. Did you mean because he's Carl's nephew or something else?"

"Why are you so enamored with Justin? I guess the better question is how do you even know such a—what did you call him—convict?"

———∽∽∽———

Elle choked on her drink. She found this to be a great question, since Angie acted like a teenage schoolgirl that day she and Justin were at the house. She hid in the bathroom like she had an acne-covered face that she didn't want him to see. On top of that, he made that silly comment that clearly sent Angie into some kind of frenzy.

"Okay, so Justin used to work for us at the company. We had some disciplinary issues with him. It seems like his personal life overlapped into the business. Without getting into the whole story, we ended up having to let him go because it just got to be too much, and we really didn't know what else to do to help him. I'm sure you know this, but he ended up going to jail not long after we let him go. Then there was that whole other situation that popped up, which I really don't understand."

"You mean the rape?" asked Anna.

Elle was dumbfounded and started to understand why Angie was so outraged when she found out Justin was trimming the trees at her home.

"Yes," Angie said.

"What do you think about it?" asked Anna.

"Honestly, I just don't see it. I don't understand it one bit. I'm not really familiar with rapists, but even if I were to hold on to a stereotype or even what statistics and research say, there is no pattern at all. I have been in his presence a number of times and have never once felt unsafe or creeped out, and to be totally honest with you, I almost felt protected and safe. I know how stupid that sounds, but I just felt like he was always watching, not in any creepy stalker way, but just, for lack of a better phrase, so that no one could fuck with me."

———∽∽∽———

They both laughed at me, and Anna said, "Bringing out the prison mouth because we are talking about a convict?"

I laughed and said, "No, really though. I always felt protected."

Anna acted like a light bulb went off above her head. I could see her eyes bouncing around as she was trying to figure something out, and finally, she said, "Wait a minute! You're Angie! Holy shit!"

Elle and I looked at each other, and Elle seemed to know exactly what she was referring to, but I was lost.

"Justin used to talk about you all the time. He said he always felt like you believed in him and that he could do anything he put his mind to. He said you and Jeff trusted him with things that needed to get done around the shop."

"Wow, I was unaware that I had such an impact on him."

"Really?" Elle said questioning. "I don't believe that for one second. You nearly freaked out that day he was here trimming the trees. That day you and Jeff were here when we were looking him up on Facebook, Jeff mentioned that he had some sort of weird brother/sister attachment to you. Wait a minute. Is he McHottie?"

Anna nearly choked on her macaroon. She had to drink some water just to stop coughing. "What? Who, Justin?" Anna asked. "McHottie? What? What are you talking about? Who are we talking about?"

"Yes," said Elle.

I interjected and of course said, "No. Justin is not McHottie. It's Derrick."

Anna said, "What in the world are you guys talking about or *who* for that matter?"

"Okay, okay, there is an employee that we have working for us who is very good-looking. He is very polite and respectful to me, and it seems as though we have a lot in common. He said something very nice and, keep in mind, respectful at a company Christmas party, and when I told Elle, she came up with this silly name."

"Do you need to talk about this Derrick?" asked Anna.

"I could talk about Derrick all day."

We giggled like schoolgirls.

"He is very handsome and very personable. He still needs to get some of his priorities straight, but he is doing pretty damn well for someone who went down a wrong path in life."

"Is he a convict too?"

"Still feeling like an ass, thanks," I said.

"Do you only hire people who were in prison?" asked Anna. "Carl must fit right in there with everyone."

"Carl was in prison?" I asked.

"No, but he probably will be after this shitshow is over."

We all laughed awkwardly because it was a big possibility. It was so inappropriate to laugh, but we all needed it, and again, no one knew how all this would shake out in the end.

Once we all calmed down, Anna asked, "Why were you Facebook stalking Justin?"

Shit! Why did she have to ask us that?

Chapter 42

I was totally speechless. I briefly forgot if the chief ever got the chance to talk to Anna about what we saw.

Elle could see that I was struggling to find the words, and it seemed as though she knew exactly what I was thinking. She jumped in and said, "Oh, I was trying to leave him a good review on his page for the tree service. I had a really good experience, and he asked if I would do a review."

"Oh," said Anna.

We dodged that bullet, but then again, maybe Anna knew what the connection was between Justin and Fitzpatrick. Maybe I should just come right out and ask her if she knew. Better yet, maybe I should ask her how exactly Justin was her nephew.

"How exactly is Justin your nephew?"

"Oh, that's a long story. Okay, try to stay with me here. Carl has a half brother, Ray. Ray is a very nice guy, but he doesn't exactly do nice things. Family means a lot to Carl and Ray, and since they only have each other left, they try to stay in touch and stick together when needed. Many years ago, Ray fell in love with a woman, Justin's mother. Justin was very little when they met. They ended up getting married, but Justin's mother was diagnosed with a rare blood disease only a few years after that, and not eight months later, she was gone. By the time she passed away, Justin was already calling Ray 'daddy,' and there was no way he was giving him up. He didn't want him to end up in foster care, and his mother's side of the family was a total disaster, so he decided to raise him himself. Ray was very much in love with Justin's mother. He thought Justin would always be a nice reminder.

"Unfortunately, due to the lifestyle that Ray led, even though he tried his hardest to keep Justin away from it all, Justin started acting out in his early teens. He missed his mother so much that he didn't know which end was up, and before Ray knew it, the boy was out of control. He ended up in juvenile hall for a few years in and out, and then finally, when he turned eighteen, he ended up in jail. He was there at least two or three times before he started working with you and Jeff.

"Ray never gave up on him even when he was in trouble. The family felt as though he would continue to enable him, but no one knows until they are a parent and in that situation what they would do with or for their child. The rest of the family tried to keep in touch with him over the years, but he distanced himself for a number a reasons—shame mostly—but he's coming around again and obviously trying to get himself back together."

"Wow," I said. "I didn't know all of that about him, never mind Carl. I guess you don't ask someone if they have siblings when you buy their company from them."

"So, Anna, I don't want to put you in an uncomfortable position, but what are your thoughts on his last conviction?"

"Oh, the rape?" Anna said. She said this so matter-of-factly, like oh that stupid thing.

"Yes, the rape." She turned it back on me for whatever reason. I didn't understand until I answered her.

"To be honest with you, I was disgusted with him and almost completely wrote him off, but then I had a conversation about it with Jeff. I realized then that I was more disgusted with the action itself. I took a step back and put it in perspective. Was that a crime that I even thought Justin was capable of committing?"

"Well?" Anna asked. "What did you come up with?"

"No, I don't at all think that is something that he would be capable of doing."

"You see, you answered your own question without me having to say a word. Not that it matters, but for the record, not a chance in hell do I think Justin raped that woman."

After a few minutes of silence, I said, "Maybe we can solve that crime too after we find Carl?

I smirked at Elle and Anna and they burst out laughing at me. I was so glad to have this girl time. I think Anna and I both needed it.

"Elle, we'll help you clean up, and then we'll head out. We still need to get to the mall to get Anna some new threads."

Chapter 43

Carl was feeling awful about this whole thing. He was at Ray's place, staging his gruesome murder to appease Elizabeth. They were catching up and reminiscing about the old days, the good times and the bad.

"Ray, your dad was such a flaming asshole. I don't know how you could stand him."

"He treated me a little better at least than he treated you, so he wasn't always awful. Maybe just because I belonged to him and you didn't. What a fucked-up family history we have. It's a miracle we turned out half decent."

"Bro, we are lying on my basement floor staging your murder to get that crazy bitch off our backs … How well did we turn out? I've been involved in organized crime as well as the largest drug ring on the East Coast for almost half my life."

"How about your dad, bro? He died and left you not one cent of that empire he built?"

"I can't really blame him for that. He knew I was a fuckup and anticipated my fucking up the business, and that's exactly what I did. He never had any faith in me. I'm convinced that's why he left our mother."

"She was screwing my dad because yours was such a bastard. That's why he left her."

"What a mess we are. Maybe when all this is over, we can just live normal lives. Whatever that means."

"I wouldn't count on it. Usually in instances like these, all sorts of shit comes out of the woodwork, and even though we have all this planned out, we need to plan for the worst possible thing we can come up with. As easy as we think it will be, our luck does not point in the direction of normalcy or well-thought-out plans."

"What is all that supposed to mean?"

"All I'm saying is that we need to be very aware all the time of what's happening and be ten steps ahead of this plan and everyone involved. The second someone fucks up or is even one second late on facilitating their portion of the plan, we need to start questioning."

"I don't want anyone pissed off at me thinking I don't trust them."

"That's your problem, Carl; you want to be friends with everyone, and that's simply not going to work for this type of plan. You'll know who your real friends are when this is all over."

"Ray, there is no money involved, so why would you think I'll lose friends?"

"Carl, if we need to move to plan F, you are talking about a whole different type of loyalty. I don't think you have enough evidence on anyone that will force them to get through that one with us."

"I understand what you're saying, Ray, but they all committed to this knowing that was a possibility—a last resort, but definitely a possibility."

"You're right, but all I'm saying is we need to watch our backs through the whole process."

"Okay, Ray, whatever you say, buddy. Now come here and make it look like you shot me through the forehead so that crazy bitch thinks I'm dead."

Chapter 44

Jeff and Demetri were just finishing up when Angie and Anna came back to the house. They were saying their goodbyes, and Demetri said, "I'll see you later in the week."

Demetri hugged Angie goodbye and shook Anna's hand. He said, "See you all soon," and out the door, he went.

"Jeff, why are you going to see him later this week?"

"I'm going to his office to sign some paperwork. Just some precautions for the business in case this thing takes another turn for the worse."

"Oh, okay. Are you ready to take us to the mall?"

Cough, cough. "I might be coming down with something," said Jeff.

Anna and I looked at each other and laughed.

"Very funny. I thought you weren't letting us out of your sight?"

"Oh yeah, I guess I did say that."

"The mall's not even open that much longer tonight, so we won't take too long."

Anna said, "I really don't want to sound like a stuck-up snobby bitch—"

"Too late!" I interrupted, and I crossed my eyes and smiled sideways at Anna.

"Seriously though, most of my clothes I designed, and I can't get anything like them here, so I'll just get some basics to get me through, and then I'll be out of there."

"Okay, ladies, time for a double date." Jeff laughed at himself, and we just rolled our eyes.

—∿—

The next morning, we all piled into the car—me, Jeff, Anna, and the kids. We took the kids to school and then headed to the office.

Anna just sort of hid away in my office. We had a small desk on wheels that we put in my office for the time being so she could work and not be bothered. I didn't want her to be distracted by the phones either. I had a quick meeting with the techs before they started their day. All was good in the office, and we didn't miss much while we were out for a few days.

The morning wasn't complete without Derrick popping his head in to say hello and check in on me.

"Hey, lady, how was your few days off?"

Without even looking at him, I felt my insides jump. I looked away from my computer to answer him, so I got the full effect. I could be so awful sometimes. I wasn't the only one though. I could see Anna look over at him out of the corner of my eye, and I also caught her doing a double take. I'm pretty sure she figured out it was McHottie at the door.

"Hey," I said back to Derrick as he was standing in my doorway with his hands reaching the top of the doorjamb. His sleeves fell to his shoulders, so his biceps were just sitting there naked.

"The few days off were pleasant. We had some running around to do with Anna to get some things figured out with Carl. Oh my God, I'm so rude! Anna, meet Mc—I mean Derrick. Oh my God."

Anna let out a tiny giggle, and Derrick just went along with the flow. I'm positive he knew we were eyeing him up like a side of beef.

"So I wanted to tell you something, but I can come back later if you're still here when I quit for the day?"

"It's up to you, but Anna will be here all day, so we can talk now if you want."

"Okay, I just wanted to say that I was so impressed when you told me that you play the piano that I felt like I needed to get off my ass and do something too, so I bought a used guitar and started teaching myself how to play."

"Oh, Derrick! That's wonderful news! I'm so proud of you! That's a big task to take on by yourself. Good for you. You will feel so good once you start playing songs that you really enjoy. You'll be like, 'Is that really me playing this song?'"

Derrick looked at Anna and said, "She's like a mother hen, always encouraging us to do more and be better. Thanks, Angie, I knew you would be excited."

"You know me, always aiming to please."

"I'm sure you are." He looked me up and down, cute smile on cue, and he was gone.

Both of us exhaled at the same time, and Anna said, "*Wowza*! Do you get to see him every day?"

"Usually only the days I'm in early when my mom takes the kids to school, so we lucked out today. He has a later appointment to start the day today."

"Jeez, I haven't seen someone that good-looking in a long time, and I'm in the fashion industry. Do you think he knows how good-looking he is?"

"I'm really not sure. He has such a great personality. He can talk about anything, so I'm not sure he does know. If he does, you would never know. He doesn't act stuck up one bit."

"Has he been to prison too?"

"Oh yeah."

"He probably even made that uniform look good."

We laughed hysterically like little schoolgirls, and then we were interrupted by the phone.

"I hope it's not the chief," I said with a frown.

"Me too," said Anna.

Chapter 45

Ray's guy, Danny, was watching while Elizabeth worked out in her own in-home gym. She still looked pretty damn good for her age, but as good as she looked on the outside, she was just as hateful and ugly on the inside. He was completely repulsed by her, knowing what she was capable of—this coming from a man who'd killed a few people himself in the past, the distant past, but the past nonetheless. He had left that kind of hatefulness in the past. His wife got really angry when he did something like that. He didn't like when she was angry.

If he had one good one left to do, he would take Elizabeth in a heartbeat, but her life was not his to take, another bummer, but as much as he would enjoy it, someone else would enjoy it more.

He was there to watch Elizabeth to make sure she bought the photo of "Dead Carl" when it came through to her burner phone. He would make sure she believed what she saw in the photo and didn't try anything stupid.

He sent a quick text to Ray to see when he would be sending the photo through. Ray replied, "Ten minutes max."

He sat tight and waited for the confirmation text that it was sent.

Meanwhile, Ray and Carl were getting him all set up, and Ray's phone rang.

"Really, Ray? Do you have to get that now?"

"It might be a client."

"Hello?"

"I know what you're doing, and you'll never get away with it." The voice on the other end of the phone was very familiar, but Ray just couldn't place it quite yet.

"Oh yeah, and who, may I ask, am I speaking with?"

"You know damn well who this is, and tell that piece of shit Carl that he'll never get away with it."

Ray was pissed, and whoever this stupid young punk was on the phone must know he was barking up the wrong old veteran tree. Ray didn't know who the fuck this kid thought he was, but Ray wouldn't deal with this rookie shit.

"Sorry, my hearing must be going bad. I'm getting older, you know? I've been in this business a long time, asshole, and since you sound barely old enough to have hair on your sack, you might want to consider who you are talking to. Do you understand what I am capable of doing? I'm not sure what you think it is myself or Carl are trying to get away with, but you'd better get your facts straight before you come at me like this again. Besides, jackass, don't you know that Carl is missing? Has been for weeks now. Why would you think he's with me or that I'm working with him?"

"If you don't know where Carl is, then maybe you can tell me who is this Elizabeth woman? Better yet, where is she?"

Ray had this nitwit on speakerphone, and he and Carl looked at each other with a little concern. Without skipping a beat, Ray said, "I don't know, man, but why are you asking me about her, and why are you so worried about her? Why do you think I know who she is?"

Ray needed to keep this young punk talking. He thought eventually he would recognize the voice, especially if it was someone who used to work for him in the business.

"It's none of your business."

"Then why the fuck are you bothering me?"

"I need to know where Carl is, or I'll find him myself."

"Wow, buddy, I'm shakin' in my boots. You have a pretty big set to threaten someone like me the way you are, and if the cops can't even find Carl, what makes you think you can?"

"I'm an ex-cop, and I have my resources."

"If that's the case, for the one-hundredth time, why the fuck are you bothering me?"

"Just so you know I'm looking."

"Sure thing, pal. You along with about fifty other people. Fuck off." With a tap on the screen to disconnect, Ray hung up on the young punk.

Carl said, "Do you know who that was? The voice sounded awfully familiar to me too."

Ray looked at Carl and said, "I'm not a hundred percent positive, but I think it was Fitzpatrick."

"I guess that's what you meant about being prepared for the unexpected."

"Exactly," said Ray. "I'm not worried about him, but you never know what people are capable of doing."

Chapter 46

I sat in the kitchen drinking my coffee while Anna was getting a shower. I was already showered and dressed. The kids were getting ready for school, and Jeff had a job site meeting that morning, and then he was off to sign paperwork with Demetri. This was the first time in a while that Jeff wouldn't be in the office all day.

It would be weird, but I had new interior projects I was working on for a couple who just bought a new house. We were gutting the whole house and finishing it, and then I was decorating all of it once the construction was complete.

The couple was going to visit their daughter in California for the weeks while most of the construction was taking place. They wouldn't actually be moving into the house until I'd completed the decorating.

Everyone came down the steps at the same time, and with the exception of Carl missing, life seemed to be moving along smoothly.

"Good morning, everyone! Did everyone sleep okay?"

Isabella, my daughter, said, "Why are you so chipper this morning, Mom?"

"Because it's a beautiful day, and I love my job!"

"I love my job too! Maybe not sharing an office with your chipper mom, but I'll take it, considering the rest of the mess in my life."

The kids looked at me like "Is it okay to laugh?" I nodded because Anna was laughing.

We all piled into the car and left the house. I dropped the kids off at school, and we stopped for some Starbucks on the way to the office. I wasn't exactly getting enough sleep these days, so there was no such thing as too much coffee.

We got to the office, and Anna sneaked through the back door and right into my office. She tried to avoid everyone as much as possible. They all meant well when asking how she was doing, but she could only hear so much of it before starting to get angry. I didn't blame her one bit. Some guys who didn't know what to say just stared at her as she walked by, and sometimes, she would prefer that to them talking to her. Even though the guys were already out on their jobs that day, she still came through the back door as a routine.

I was unprepared for my usual early morning visitor because we were later than usual. I was also unprepared to see him in the sales office, where we were all alone.

I was taking a quick inventory of supplies. My customer care representative usually did it, but she was on vacation that week, so I wanted to make sure we didn't run out of anything while she was gone. I told her I would take care of it so she didn't have to worry when she came back. She was my right hand there at the office, so the least I could do was keep up with the supplies while she was away.

My back was to the door, and I heard, "What a nice surprise."

I nearly died. He scared me half to death, but the two of us in that room together and Anna glued to her desk downstairs put such exhilarating thoughts in my head. *My God, Angie, calm down.* Why was I constantly telling myself to get my shit together when he was within five feet of me? *You love your husband and your family.* The little devil on my shoulder shouted, "A girl can dream, can't she?"

I always tried to play it as cool as humanly possible, even though I felt like I was burning up. Temperature aside, I kept my wits about me and said, "Good morning, blondie." *Good God, Angie, control yourself.*

He smiled his earth-shattering smile that left me hanging on every word that came out of his perfect mouth.

"How's it going today? What are you doing slummin' in the sales office?"

This set me up to make his temperature rise a little. I was wearing a black pencil skirt, a fitted white blouse, and of course my black patent sky-high Christian Louboutin pumps.

I bent over to pick up something from the bottom shelf and peeked out of the corner of my eye to see if he was watching me. He was. *Score!* One point for me.

I stood straight up and faced him head-on with a raised eyebrow and said, "Which question should I answer first?" I bit my lower lip just to see what reaction I would get.

He stayed completely cool. He exhaled and smirked slightly. He started walking toward me, and I thought, *Oh shit! What the hell did you do?*

He came within a foot of me and leaned against the eight-foot-high cabinet next to us. He crossed his arms and said, "Whichever one you want, just don't bend down again, or I'll have to move my crossed arms about a foot lower."

I'm pretty sure I flushed, but I kept it in complete control and said, "I'm better now than I was this morning, and I'm ordering supplies."

While I was bending down earlier and trying to provocatively entice one of my employees, a stray curl escaped the clip that was holding back my thick black hair.

Derrick moved six inches even closer than he was before. I think I actually started to sweat a little, and my breathing was completely hitched, or maybe I even stopped breathing. He looked down my body and right back up to my eyes, softly stuck his finger in the stray curl, and tucked it behind my ear. He licked his perfectly plump lips and said, "This is gonna be fun." He tapped his index finger on the tip of my nose. "Have a great day, Angie. See you ..." It sounded like he was going to say something else, but he just trailed off and walked down the steps.

I finished up my supply inventory and went back to my office.

"Angie, are you okay?"

"Yeah, why?"

"Your face is all red, and you look sweaty."

Pretty soon, Derrick walked by the office door saying, "Have a good day, ladies."

"You are the worst," said Anna in a sarcastic tone. "Well, your lipstick doesn't look smudged at all in case you were worried."

"Anna! I would never do that."

"Never say never, Angie. You don't know where life might take you."

I wondered what she meant by that. I drifted away in thought and certainly thoughts I should not be wrapped in ... ever.

Chapter 47

Ray and Carl were pretty much wrapping up and were ready to send the photo.

"Ray, how did you learn to do makeup so well?"

"I did theater makeup a very long time ago."

Carl laughed and said, "No, seriously?"

"Seriously, Carl, and if you tell anyone or ask me about it again, I'll …"

"You'll what? Put me in a headlock?"

Ray laughed hard at Carl. "You could always make me laugh even when times were really shitty. How did you let yourself get mixed up with this crazy bitch in the first place? I can understand dating her or maybe just having some fun but to marry her? How could you be so stupid? It's not like I didn't warn you back then either."

"I don't know," said Carl. "She was so hot back then, and she paid attention to me. I guess the thing that made the most sense was that we were both caught up in that terrible life. I figured it would be so easy because she understood it all. She wouldn't question where I was or what I was doing. It just made sense. I didn't know it was going to end so badly."

"I'm sure you never thought she was going to come back from the dead either?"

"Fuck off, Ray."

"Sorry, man."

"We had it all back then."

"Her father was the devil though, so you didn't really have it all. You couldn't even really think for yourself. Everything you did was either in fear of him or to please him, so it wasn't that great."

"I guess you're right, but you know me. For the most part, I need someone to think for me, or everything gets fucked up. He took care of me though."

"All true, so now it makes more sense to me why you would give yourself to that awful family. The McNamaras aren't what they used to be, especially since ..."

"Since what, Ray? Just say it," said Carl.

"Since the old man died."

"You don't still think she blames me for that, do you, Ray?"

"It's hard to say, Carl. If she does, why would she wait until now to get revenge? That doesn't make much sense."

"She had her chance many times, so for her to wait this long doesn't make any sense. Plus, it was her idea to disappear after that bloodbath involving her brother. There was nothing left for her here, and she wanted out of the life. Her mother was long gone from cancer, so there was nothing left for her here."

"We need to find out what the fuck her problem is now though. This makes no sense at all for her to come after you like this and to ask me to do it. I know she doesn't know that we have been close again for quite some time, but for her to think I would kill you is just crazy."

"I don't want to sound naïve—no comments, Ray—but maybe it's not her doing this. Maybe she's being blackmailed or something? Maybe it's someone else?"

"Why though, Carl? And who? Who would want to kill you? You were the most liked in the family, and you have led a mostly normal life since all that went down, especially after you met Anna. None of this makes any sense."

"Ray, what did she say when she first reached out to you?"

"The more I talked about it, she seemed delusional, like it was still the old days, like we were all still together and living that awful life. She just said, 'I need you to take care of him for me.' She asked if I would do that for her, and that was it. Of course I asked her why, but she just said, 'I just want it done. I can't live like this anymore.' Like I told you when I called you, as soon as I hung up the phone with her is when I called you to tell you what that conniving, evil bitch was up to."

"Since Danny is tracking her, maybe you can have him really look into her and what she's been doing."

"He has been, but he said her life is super boring. She goes to work and comes home. She travels sometimes, and he even follows her wherever she goes. Other than that, she doesn't do much. She's not married, and it doesn't appear as though she's seeing anyone. The only strange thing Danny noticed is that she has a woman who's always with her wherever she goes."

"Like a girlfriend?"

"Not romantically but like an assistant maybe. Danny thinks she's more than a friend because she's always carrying a briefcase or computer bag. He said it's bizarre."

Carl asked, "Does she go home at night?"

"No, but they definitely don't sleep in the same bedroom."

"Is it always the same woman?"

"Yes, it's always the same woman. Why do you ask that?"

"Remember when Mom was sick, and she had different caregivers?"

"Yeah, but Elizabeth doesn't seem to be down and out. She is living her life like normal, like nothing is wrong."

"Yeah, Ray, but she just reached out to you a few weeks ago so maybe she was just diagnosed and has a helper now? Maybe she only has a few months to live?"

"I think that's a little far-fetched, Carl, but I guess it's possible."

"Nothing else can explain what her problem is coming after me after all these years."

"I'll talk to Danny, Carl, and see what else he can dig up. I want him to keep his distance as much as possible, but I'll see what he can find out."

"Okay, now, let's send this ridiculous photo."

"Sent, and now I'm texting Danny to let him know it's sent. I want him to call me when he gets the chance. When he calls, we can explain to him what we think is going on and see what he can find out."

Chapter 48

I was getting ready to leave the office for the day. I texted Jeff to see when he would be home and if he wanted anything special for dinner.

Anna and I packed up our computer bags, got in the car, and headed home. I was so preoccupied with driving and maybe thinking about Derrick that I didn't notice that Jeff still hadn't texted by the time I got home.

When I got in the door and settled, I called his cell—no answer.

I didn't want to worry the kids, so I waited until they went upstairs to get changed to say something to Anna.

"Hey, Anna, I texted Jeff at least an hour ago, and he hasn't replied. I called his cell, and he didn't answer. He's only with Demetri, so there shouldn't be any reason why he doesn't answer."

"Why don't you just call Demetri?"

"I will do that."

I punched in the numbers, and on the fourth ring, the voice mail picked up. I left a message. "Demetri, it's Angie. I can't get ahold of Jeff, and I was wondering if he was still with you? Call me back as soon as you can please …Oh my God, Anna, what if he goes missing too?"

"Angie, let's calm down. We already think that Carl is missing but on purpose, so if something does happen where you can't get ahold of Jeff and he doesn't come home, we'll inform the chief and confirm with Demetri the last time he spoke with him. Maybe that's part of the plan?"

"Okay, I'll try not to get worked up until I speak with Demetri."

I made dinner, and after we ate, everyone helped me clean up. I got the kids to bed and came back downstairs to do a little work. Still nothing from Demetri or Jeff. Now I was really worried. It was not like Jeff at all not to call me. It was not like he was traveling or in meetings, and where the hell was Demetri? Why wasn't he calling me back either?

"I'm calling the chief. Do you think it's too soon?"

"It's probably too soon to file a missing person report, but you should at least let him know," Anna said. "Remember, we can't tell him that we heard from Carl either."

—⟋⟋⟍—

The chief continued to think about all of this, and his cell phone rang. He saw that it was Angie. He was expecting the call but not so early.

"Hello? … Angie, wait a minute. Slow down. I can barely hear you, and it sounds like you are crying. Please calm down so I can understand what you're saying."

"Chief, you need to get over here to the house right away. Jeff is missing!"

"I'll be right there. Is Anna with you?"

"Yes, she's right here."

"Okay, I'll be right over."

The chief packed up his computer and his paperwork. He was walking out of the office, and Smythe said, "Do you want me to tag along?"

"No, it's okay. When I know more, I'll get you involved."

"Okay, Chief, let me know."

He jumped in the police car and raced over to Jeff and Angie's. He wanted to at least make it look like he didn't know what was going on.

He pulled up to the house and ran to the front door. His large frame made him look like Big Bird running through the front lawn to the door. He knocked once he got up there, and Angie was waiting for him. She opened the door.

"Chief, thank God you're here. Jeff is missing."

"Angie, tell me what happened."

"Well, there's not a lot to tell. Jeff and I spoke briefly this morning. He was headed to a construction site meeting, and then he was meeting with Demetri. He said he wouldn't be at the office all day so I assumed he was going to have lunch with Demetri and then head to his office. Anna and I were packing up for the day to leave the office, and I texted him. He didn't reply so I called his cell phone. He didn't answer, so I left a message. By the time I got home, I still hadn't heard from him, and it's not like Jeff at all not to get back to me right away."

"Was he acting strange this morning at all?"

"What do you mean?"

Anna shook her head at my question.

"Did he do anything different than he normally does, or did he say anything out of the ordinary?"

"No, I don't think so. I would have to think about it. Oh, wait! Yes! He hugged me really tight and said he loved me but not like he usually does. He said it with a lot more heart and, well, feeling, I guess."

"Like he knew he might not be seeing you later today?"

"What? No! I don't know! I didn't really think of it that way."

I glanced at Anna because of what I was going to say next.

"We had just been talking about Anna and Carl, about what they must be going through, and he did all that immediately following that conversation so I just thought he was trying to comfort me and reassure me of our relationship. I didn't think he would go missing less than twelve hours later."

"Did you call Demetri?"

"Yes, and he's not returning my calls either."

The chief's heart picked up an extra beat or two because this wasn't the plan. This timing was way off, and where the hell was Demetri? Even he was starting to panic a little. Angie was now busying herself with something in the kitchen, and he couldn't see what it was, but he glanced at Anna because he knew she was already in the safe-deposit box. The first step revealed a small portion of the plan so he could see that she wasn't worried. She wasn't aware of the next steps. If she was, she would be a little more on edge.

"Angie, what are you doing?"

"Trying to dig out Demetri's home phone number. I called the office and his cell, but I don't have his home number in my cell for some reason."

"Don't call the house."

"Why not?" I asked.

"Because I don't want you to get his wife worried if there's no need for her to be."

"Good point."

"Why don't we just wait it out a little bit?"

"How can you say that when Carl is missing? I'm sorry, Anna."

"Stop saying you're sorry, Angie. The situation sucks, and it is what it is for now. I agree with you. Carl is missing, and now we can't seem to track down Jeff. I wouldn't want to sit tight either."

Anna of course was saying this because she didn't want to make it sound like she was not worried.

"Angie, I'll see if we can find Jeff's car in the area of Demetri's office, but other than that, there isn't much I can do until tomorrow or at least until we hear from Demetri."

"Do you want me to stay a while? I brought my computer and some work so I can keep myself occupied so I'm not in your hair."

"That would be great. You can set up at the kitchen table."

"Thanks, Angie, and let's try to stay calm."

Chapter 49

Danny replied to the text from Ray to let him know he'd gotten it. They also set up a time to talk about Ray's concerns. Danny committed to seeing this through to the end, so he knew it was going to be a long process. Danny was going to be getting a large sum of money for the work that he was there to do, so he was more than happy to put his time into the job. After all this time, they were finally going to get her once and for all. He was planning on retiring after this job. He and the wife would move away and just be normal people living their lives, finally, after all these years.

He was walking down a very empty street. With all he'd done and been through in his life, he was surprised how eerie it felt to be in a foreign country all by himself on an empty street. He kept looking over his shoulder, making sure he wasn't being followed. He wasn't sure it was really putting his mind at ease, but he would have to deal with it. Knowing Elizabeth as well as he had in the past, he was as careful as possible to make sure he wasn't made. He kept a substantial distance from her when he wasn't watching her every move. When he was watching her, he made himself as inconspicuous as possible.

When he got to the bottom of the hill, he met a far busier street, so he was more at ease. *I'm too old for this shit*, he thought.

He was heading back to his hotel to call Ray when he saw a woman out of the corner of his eye who looked just like Elizabeth. This woman was carrying on in the town square, making a huge scene, going on and on about someone stealing her purse. She was swearing and yelling, but most of it sounded like gibberish. The woman Danny had been seeing with Elizabeth was talking to a police officer nearby. He was starting to approach Elizabeth.

The policeman was talking to her like she was a small child. It looked like he was trying to calm her down, but he looked almost afraid of her himself. Danny watched all this from around the corner of a nearby building. Something was totally off about the whole situation. He tried to snap a few photos of the woman with her to send to Ray. He thought the photos might help Ray recognize her. He thought maybe she was from the old days. Even though he didn't recognize her, Danny thought maybe Ray might.

This whole scene doesn't make any sense. Why is she acting like that? Elizabeth is not one to ever call attention to herself. He knew it had been a long time since he'd spent any time with her, but he was pretty sure she hadn't changed that much after all those years.

She continued to carry on, and finally, it looked like the cop was trying to detain her, like he thought he was at risk of being hurt. Pretty soon, another cop showed up and headed over to the three of them.

Something definitely wasn't right with this situation. It looked like Elizabeth had calmed down. The cops were on each side now. Each man had an arm in his hand, trying to make sure she was stable? Or maybe that she couldn't get away from them?

The woman with her didn't falter one bit. She barely batted an eye at the situation. It was like she was used to it or expected it. Danny couldn't believe what he was seeing. They put Elizabeth in the back of the cop car and drove away. Danny got on the phone with Ray.

Chapter 50

Danny pulled out his phone to dial Ray and saw a message from his wife.

"Hi, honey, I know you're busy, but what do you think about living in the South of France?"

Danny replied, "Good God, Marie, can't it wait until I get home? I'm a little busy here."

She replied, "I know, but I'm just so excited to start the next chapter in our lives."

"I know, dear, me too, but let me focus on this last job, and then we can talk for the next thirty years."

"Okay, honey," Marie wrote. "I love you, and please be careful. Don't break a hip or anything. You're no spring chicken anymore, and you are a little old to still be doing that kind of work."

Danny replied, "I love you too, dear. I'll call you tomorrow."

Danny dialed Ray, and it barely rang before he picked it up.

"Hey, asshole. I'm here with Carl. You're on speaker."

Danny laughed out loud. He regrouped immediately at the thought of Elizabeth in the back of that cop car.

"Hey, guys. I've been thinking about this on my little trip here the last few weeks. Imagine what we could have done if we had all these gadgets back in the day when we were much younger? Could you imagine the damage we would have been capable of back then?"

"Yeah," Ray said. "But it would have been a lot easier to get caught then too."

"I guess you're right, and Carl really would have fucked everything up."

Ray and Danny laughed, and Carl said, "I can hear you."

Danny and Ray kept on laughing, and finally, Ray said, "Whatta you got, and what's up with those photos you sent?"

"You guys might think I'm totally off, but something isn't right about Elizabeth."

Ray and Carl glanced at each other. This was the whole reason for the call.

"How so?" asked Ray.

"Those photos I sent you were of Elizabeth and the woman that's always with her, but she was making a major scene in a high-traffic area today, calling so much attention to herself that people were stopping and staring at her. She was ranting and raving about her purse being stolen. The cops showed up and everything."

"What?" Carl and Ray both said at the same time.

"Yeah, and the weirdest part of the whole episode was that her purse was on her arm the whole time."

"What?" they said in unison again.

"Did you two swallow a fucking parakeet or something?"

Carl laughed stupidly, and Ray said, "No, sorry, but we're just trying to understand all of what you're saying and put some pieces together."

Carl asked, "Then what happened?"

"There was one cop at first, and then he must have called the second one for backup. Before I knew it, the second one showed up, and they were hauling her off in the cop car."

"Something definitely isn't right," said Ray. "Danny, I didn't say anything to you about this when I asked you to follow her, but Carl and I were talking about the initial discussion between myself and Elizabeth."

"Okay, what's up?" asked Danny.

"Well, she wasn't exactly acting weird; it's what she said that was weird. She was talking like it was way in the past, like she was still home and we were all working together in the 'Family Business' as she called it back then."

Carl said, "When I took some classes at the community college, I heard about that type of sickness. It's Alltimer's. Old people get it."

They could hear Danny breathing with his mouth open, probably in awe of how stupid Carl was.

Ray looked at Carl and said, "How did you get so stupid?"

"What?" Carl said.

Danny said, "It's Alzheimer's, and it depends on what your definition of old is. People have early-onset effects as early as age sixty and in some rare cases earlier than that. Carl, sometimes I wonder how you get through life most days."

"Fuck you, Danny."

"Sorry, man, but the things you come up with are over the top sometimes."

"Sorry to break up the fun here, guys, but what's our next step, Danny?"

"I'm going to have to keep digging and put a bigger push on following her. I know that's not exactly what we all want, Ray, but she's gotta go to a doctor or something if she's having those issues."

"What if she doesn't even know it yet?" asked Ray.

"Well, after she goes through questioning with the cops, there won't be any way to hide it if that's what she's trying to do," said Danny. "That would explain the lady that's with her all the time too. My wife's father had it, and it's truly a terrible disease."

"You ask me, couldn't have happened to a better person."

"I would agree with you, Carl, especially because she's *trying to kill you!*"

Chapter 51

The chief and Anna were working on their computers. I was trying to make myself busy and not focus on Jeff. There were so many emotions going through my head. I was nervous and worried, but then I shifted gears to anger. I was angry, because if Carl really wasn't missing, then neither was Jeff. Why didn't he tell me if he was going rogue? I realized maybe he couldn't, but he could at least throw something out there so I wasn't a nervous wreck.

My cell phone started ringing, and I nearly broke an ankle trying to get over to it on the kitchen island.

"It's Demetri!" I announced to the chief and Anna after I looked at the caller ID. "Hello?"

"Angie! What's going on?"

"I don't know, Demetri. You tell me."

"I don't know. Your voice mail said Jeff is missing. What do you mean he's missing? When did you speak to him last?"

I wanted to jump through the phone and strangle him.

"The last time I saw or spoke to him was when he left the house this morning. He had a meeting, and then he was going to see you at your office."

"He did come to see me at the office. We had lunch together and then went back to sign some paperwork."

"Okay, was he acting strange, or did he say he was going somewhere after that?"

"No, he didn't say anything odd that I can recall. We did go out for a quick drink before we parted ways. When we were finished, we shook hands. He said, 'Thank you for all your help with everything,' and then, 'I'll be in touch if we have any updates.' He didn't sound odd at all, and he certainly didn't say anything that led me to believe that he was planning on going anywhere else before he went home."

"What time did he leave the bar?"

"Maybe 3:30. I'm not 100 percent positive. It definitely wasn't any later than that because I got back to the office around 3:40, and the bar we went to was right around the corner from my office. Why?"

"Because I called him quite a while after that. What took you so long to get back to me?"

"I was in a meeting with a client who is going through a horribly nasty divorce. I literally just got out of it now. It feels like I never go home sometimes. Truthfully, sometimes I don't. Angie, please forgive me for talking about this now, but me and Jenna are separated. I just wanted you to know."

"What? Oh my God, why?"

"We can talk about it another time, but I wanted you to know before you heard it through the grapevine."

"Thanks for letting me know. If there is anything I can do, just ask."

"Thank you, but more important, back to you and Jeff. Did you call the chief?"

"Yeah, he's already here with me and Anna."

"What's his take on all this?"

"Well, the first issue is not enough time has gone by for him to really file a formal report, so we'll have to wait until tomorrow to do that, and Jeff is a grown man, so it's not like we are missing a child."

Demetri laughed, thinking back to when they were kids and Jeff was such a little wiseass, he was always making them laugh. He tried so hard to do something really stupid when one of their friends would take a drink of soda just so that it would come out his nose.

"Demetri, are you still there?"

"Yes, I'm sorry; I was just thinking back to when we were kids. Stress-free summer days of playing and acting stupid."

"Yeah, tell me about it," I said. "To be young and stupid again. Now we're just old and stupid, and what's the fun in that?"

Demetri laughed at me and said, "I'm sorry that I couldn't be more of a help. I assume if we don't hear from Jeff by tomorrow, the chief will be coming back in the morning?"

"I don't know; we didn't get that far yet."

"Okay, when you do, let me know what time he's coming back, and I'll come around the same time or right after he leaves. Make sure Anna is there too."

"Okay, Demetri, thanks."

"I didn't do anything, Angie."

"You finally called me back."

"Yeah, with no useful information whatsoever."

"At least I know you're there when I need you."

"Always have been. Why would I stop now?"

I said, "Thanks again. See you tomorrow," and hung up.

I thought back to college when I met Demetri for the first time. I actually went out on a date with him before I met Jeff. It was an epic fail. Demetri got so drunk he passed out before he could even take me home. He was the one who introduced me to Jeff. We had all been friends ever since college. Jeff and Demetri, however, were friends from childhood.

Anna and the chief were looking at me wide-eyed, like "Are you going to tell us what's happening?"

"Oh, sorry, I wish I had better news, but Demetri hasn't seen or spoken to Jeff since they had a drink together midafternoon. He said Jeff left him no later than three thirty this afternoon."

Anna said, "You called him quite a while after that, so he was already gone from Demetri when you reached out."

"That's exactly what I said."

The chief was scratching his head. "I know this doesn't sound like Jeff at all but maybe he went for another drink after he left Demetri and happened to run into an old friend, maybe just lost track of time."

"Maybe," I said, "but Jeff hardly ever drinks during the week, and if he does, he'll have a beer with dinner, and when I say a beer, I mean only one."

"Okay, we all have to remain calm and sit tight until he either shows up tonight or until the morning comes. I will come over in the morning around eleven to see if anything has transpired overnight, and then I'll take your formal statement. If he shows up or you hear from him, please call my cell. I don't care what time it is. Since I live alone, no one will care if the phone is ringing in the middle of the night."

"Okay, Chief, thank you," I said, and he left.

"Anna, I need to ask you something."

"Fire away, Angie."

"You might think I'm a total loon, and maybe you can't tell me if you know something, but this appears to be too well planned."

Anna could feel her insides jumping and was hoping that Angie couldn't see it on the outside. "How do you mean?"

"Well, the chief said he would be back tomorrow, and that's exactly what Demetri said."

"Demetri said he would be back in the morning, or he said the chief would be back in the morning?"

"Well, both, but he said, 'Let me know when the chief is coming back in the morning, and I'll come right around the same time.'"

"Angie, if it was planned, wouldn't Demetri already know when he was coming back?"

"That's a good point, I guess. It just seems like something is up, and I'm not sure why Demetri is coming in the morning. He did say to make sure you're here too."

"Why?"

"I don't know. I didn't ask. I just assumed because Carl is missing too that he wanted you here maybe to compare notes? I'm just assuming, but I have no idea. I didn't question him because he knows what he's doing."

Angie was looking at Anna so desperate to share information that she considered giving her a little insight into what she knew, which wasn't much, but she thought it wise not to just in case Angie went crazy. She had to know she could really trust her first.

"Anna, you look like you have something to say."

"Well, I guess all I can say is that we can probably assume Carl isn't really missing and something much bigger is going on here. We have the chief and Demetri, who are on us like flies on horse shit when we need something, so let's just relax and see what tomorrow brings. I've been looking at all this one day at a time."

"Do you think the chief is involved as well?"

"Oh God, I don't know. Do you?"

"I'm not sure. I'm going to get my pj's on, and then I'll come down and make us some tea."

"Oh, that would be great. Thank you."

Anna just looked out the window, wondering what was in store for them in the upcoming days, weeks, and months. She was hoping that Demetri was going to be bringing some sort of information with him. If this was going to drag on for a while, she didn't want to have to keep hiding everything from Angie.

Chapter 52

The sun had set hours earlier, and there was a new moon, so it was very dark outside—dark enough for Jeff to be moving around without anyone being able to make him out. He let himself in the back door of the house. He assumed everyone was in the basement, so he made his way through the very dimly lit kitchen and then through the living room. The house was large, so it took him a while to get through to the basement door.

———✐———

The guys heard footsteps up above on the first floor and assumed it was Jeff. The door flung open, and Jeff said, "Put your hands in the fucking air and don't move."

By the time Jeff got down the steps, Carl had almost peed himself and was standing with his face against the wall and his hands in the air.

Ray almost threw his back out laughing so hard at Carl because he was so stupid. He knew the footsteps were Jeff's. He was right on time.

Jeff nearly passed out from laughter when he saw Carl. "Man, you are something else. Sometimes I don't even know how we became friends."

Ray said, "He gets it from his father."

"You guys are so mean."

"Sorry, Carl," Jeff said, "but you're such a moron sometimes. I don't want to hurt your feelings, but you make it so easy sometimes."

"How's Angie?" Ray asked.

"I think she'll be okay once she sees Demetri tomorrow morning. I think she'll be more pissed at me than anything as long as he says what he's supposed to say."

"Do you want a beer, Jeff?"

"Uh, sure, I'll take a beer."

Carl got up to get him one.

"We have a situation," said Ray.

Carl blurted out, "Elizabeth has Alltimer's."

Jeff spit his beer clear across the basement floor.

"Oh shit, if only Demetri were here to see that. He used to hate when you waited for the perfect moment to do that to us."

Jeff said, "Carl, what are you talking about? I honestly don't know how you are not mentally handicapped."

Ray just shook his head with a facial expression that was beyond disgusted.

Ray said, "Jeff, Danny has been tailing Elizabeth as per the plan, and there was an episode earlier today that leads all of us to believe that she has early-onset Alzheimer's disease."

"You're serious, aren't you?"

"Like a heart attack," said Ray.

"This is serious."

"Ray, are you thinking that she doesn't really want to take out Carl?"

"I'm not sure now. I explained to Carl and Danny that she was talking all crazy on the phone when I spoke to her about Carl originally. She was talking like it was the old days, like we were still living in those times back then. I wasn't too worried about it until Danny sent me some photos. Told me about the scene she made out in public. Danny said it was so embarrassing. The cops put her in the back of the cop car and took her away. Danny said he almost felt sorry for her, and then he brought himself back to reality, reminding himself that it was Elizabeth. The sorrow subsided very quickly."

Jeff was completely floored by the situation and wasn't really sure what to make of it.

He asked, "Do we think she's faking? Do we assume that she knows we are following her and she is putting on this act so we lay off?"

"I don't know what to think," said Ray. "I was not expecting something like this at all. It threw me for a loop. Knowing Elizabeth, she is definitely faking, but what if she's not? What if we take her out because we only think she wants Carl dead? Meanwhile, she's looney tunes and doesn't even know what she's saying?"

"Does Danny have a plan?"

"So far, he believes that if she's really that sick, she will have to be treated by a doctor sooner or later. Also, he believes that if they are questioning her at the police station, they will figure it out right away. He's going to keep following her and see what he can unearth, but it's really just a waiting game for now."

"Shit, here I thought we were on track with the plan."

"This literally just happened minutes before you got here. We just got off the phone with Danny. Plus, we feel like we have bigger fish to fry. We think this Fitzpatrick punk is trying to sabotage this whole thing. We don't know why or what his fucking problem is, but he's gunning for something. Do you know anything about him?" asked Ray.

Jeff shot a quick glance at Carl, who was just listening and trying to absorb it all.

"The only thing I know about Fitzpatrick is that he's a little punk who got himself fired from the police station right before he questioned me, Angie, and Anna."

"Wait. He was on the police force?" asked Ray.

"Yes, but faked his records to get into the police academy. No one knows how he pulled that off. He graduated top of his class, but no one knows if he was even qualified to get into the academy in the first place."

Ray asked, "What is his problem?"

"No one knows what his deal is, and no one knows if he's somehow connected or even what he's trying to achieve. He just seems to be a total dickhead."

"I am pretty sure he was part of the crew when he was younger," said Ray.

"Maybe, but how old could he be? Even if that was the case, he probably wasn't even born yet when Elizabeth was around, so there's no way he could have known her, so why would he care? Plus, he just thinks Carl is missing so he wouldn't even know about Elizabeth being involved in all this shit."

As Jeff was talking about all this with Ray, he realized that Carl was pretty quiet, especially when they started talking about Fitzpatrick. Jeff wondered why and thought maybe Carl knew something. Then he thought Carl didn't seem to know anything. It was a wonder he even knew his name sometimes.

"Okay," said Jeff, "so now what? What do we do from here?"

"I thought maybe you could go to Italy and help Danny, or you could stay here and help us figure out what's happening with Fitz?" said Ray.

"Wow, I have options. Is this plan double D now?"

Ray laughed out loud because he knew Jeff was referring to Elizabeth's cup size. "Jesus, she could be really sick, and you are making references to her boobs."

"Yes, she may be ill, but she's still a vindictive, conniving, crazy bitch."

"Touché, Jeff. Touché."

"Are you staying here tonight?"

"I guess. I feel like I should go home, but I'll just end up disappearing tomorrow again anyway."

"Okay, take whatever bedroom you want, except the master of course. That's mine and Marie's."

"Oh jeez, how is Marie, and where is she tonight?"

"She and her mother went to visit Francesca in California for this week and next."

"Oh, that really worked out."

"Well, I told her bits of what was going on, so she wanted to get the hell out of here."

"Nice! Isn't it weird that you and Danny both married Maries?"

"Not really, 'cause they're cousins, both named after their grandmother."

"Crazy Italians."

"Yeah, but we love every bit of them and their insane families."

"That is so true." Jeff thought about Angie and how horrible he felt lying to her, but she would understand. She would have to. Their family depended on her forgiving him, and more important, he was banking on how she was going to play this whole thing out from her end. He needed her to be focused and on her game.

"Good night, Ray. See you in the morning."

"Yeah, man. Sleep well!"

Chapter 53

Anna and I got up and did our normal routine. The kids woke up and got ready for school, and I fed everyone. I felt like I was on autopilot with Jeff gone. I was as strong as I could be and certainly didn't need him to function with the day to day, but I just wanted him there with me.

I took the kids to school, and Anna came with me. We stopped for coffee on the way back home. I wanted to get showered and dressed before the chief came. I wanted to look like I had slept a little bit; I didn't want to look like a homeless person in my sweats.

I showered, got dressed, and put some makeup on, thinking it would help improve my current mental state. It helped quite a bit to have one small goal achieved today. Anna said it would be one day at a time now. My life had been completely altered in less than twenty-four hours, once again.

I headed down the steps to see what Anna was up to, and as soon as I entered the kitchen where her computer was set up, her cell phone started ringing. She looked at me unfazed and said, "It's my mystery caller."

Anna was expecting him now that Jeff was missing. Yet another unfortunate event in the midst of all this madness had occurred, so she knew she would be hearing from him sooner rather than later.

"Hello."

"Hello, Anna."

"Wow, no 'ma'am' today? I'm impressed."

"Sorry, ma'am."

"I prefer Anna."

"Anna it is then."

"What's the latest, my mystery caller?" Anna figured this guy sounded like he was on her side so it was time to lay back a bit with him and try not to keep it so formal. Plus, she wanted answers this time.

"So, Anna, what is it that you want to know?"

"How did you know I had questions?"

"I figured by now you would be frustrated with my calls, as the police have no more information than I do for you, and I also know you've been in the safe-deposit box."

"I have been. I also assume there is zero chance that you will tell me who you are?"

"You already know who I am, but it will be confirmed in time, less time than you think."

As creeped out as she was, there was a voice inside her head, yet again, telling her not to worry.

"I'm going to come right out and ask you since I've been in the box, what can you tell me? What are you allowed to tell me? What are you willing to tell me?"

"Well, I'm not allowed to say much, but I can tell you later today you will have more answers and you will be able to get them on your own. I'm not sure that you will be hearing from me anymore after this call, but I will be seeing you."

"Why do we have to meet? What are you going to do to me?"

"Oh, Anna, no! I will not be harming you. I am in this with Carl, and there is no reason for concern. I've been in contact simply to attempt to reassure you that things would be okay. I know my tone isn't the greatest and may not spark a great deal of confidence in the matter, but I am doing my best. Have I achieved some confidence in showing you that you are not alone in this and it will all be all right?"

"Yes, actually, you have. As bizarre as your phone calls have been, I always hung up with you having a good feeling of comfort in knowing that I wasn't alone. The fact that I couldn't contact you was very bothersome. I needed a little boost every once in a while, but then again, you usually seemed to call at the right times."

"Well, ma'am, I mean Anna."

Anna could hear the slightest bit of a smile in his tone.

"If you don't have any further questions for me, I will be going. The next time we speak, it will be in person. Things will not be back to normal at that time, but you will at that point have a direct dial to me and be able to reach me whenever you need me. I can say one more thing without being specific. I cannot give specifics yet because I myself am unaware of them, but I can say that things are going to get harder from here before it's all over. This is not to scare you by any means but to get you and Angie in the right mind frame. You are both strong, confident women, and you would not have been put in these positions if they didn't think you could handle it."

"Who's they?"

"You will soon find out."

"Okay, mystery caller. Till we meet then, I suppose."

"Yes, until we meet, and I am looking forward to it."

"Oddly enough, I am as well."

Anna heard the dial tone, and her mystery caller was gone.

Chapter 54

"Well, what did he say?" I asked.

Anna gave me the run down, and even I couldn't help but feel a little relief.

Then it hit me. "Anna, your mystery caller is now referring to my situation as well."

"Oh yeah, it's this whole mess that he's referring to, but it sounds like today we will have a lot more answers. One concern I have is that he said it's going to get much harder before it's all over, so I'm not sure what all that entails. It sounds like we are going to have to take some time off from work, and you might want to talk to your mom about the kids."

"Since school is ending in another few days, that shouldn't be a problem. Maybe she can even take them down to Florida for a few weeks when they go down for vacation. The chief will be here any minute, and then Demetri shouldn't be far behind."

No sooner did she say "Demetri" than the doorbell rang.

I went to the door, and there was the chief.

"Hello, Angie."

"Hey, Chief."

"Did you get some sleep?"

"No, you?"

"Not a chance. I just kept thinking my phone was going to ring. It would be you telling me Jeff stumbled in drunk at 3:00 a.m., and all was well."

"I wish that were the case, but as you can see, still no word."

"This might be a little out of line here, Angie, but you look pretty well for not getting any sleep."

"Ha! Thanks, Chief. Thank you for noticing, but I made an extra effort to clean up, knowing this was going to be a very long day ahead. We have Demetri coming very soon, and then we are still cleaning up some things from Carl. Even though Anna has her own vehicle now, we have still been doing things together. Signs seem to also be pointing in the direction of us getting more information today."

Anna looked at me as if to say, "Shut up! What are you saying?"

I mentioned this to see if I could get the chief to slip up. I was trying to figure out if he was involved or not.

The chief knew what I was doing. He was too smart to let anything slip.

"So I'm here to take your formal statement so I can get it submitted for us. I already wrote most of it up from what you told me yesterday, if you want to read through it to make sure everything is accurate. The only questions I have are were you at the office all day yesterday, did everyone work yesterday, and do you have the time records to show who was working and what their hours were for the day?"

"Yes, Anna and I were at the office all day yesterday, and I can pull up the time records and print them out for you right now."

"That would be great, and that's all I'll need. I do want you to read the whole report before I leave so I can make sure nothing is missing or incorrect."

"Chief, I trust you."

"It's not a matter of trust, Angie; it's a matter of me getting older and my memory not being as sharp as it used to be."

The chief looked at me with a sheepish smile, and I couldn't help but wonder why he never got married or found a love interest. I would have to ask Jeff—if I ever saw him again.

"Okay, Chief, let me print out these records for you, and then I'll read the report."

The report wasn't that big because there wasn't much to say. It took me no time to read through it all, and I made sure everything I knew or Demetri said was in there. I was sure the chief would be getting Demetri's statement as well.

"Demetri will be coming here shortly if you want to stay and speak with him."

"No, I think I will head out, as I spoke with him already this morning. I did tell him I would stay if I thought of anything else to ask him, but nothing comes to mind. I'll just call him if I need to ask him any further questions."

"Okay, Chief, the statement looks good. I don't see anything that needs to be updated or added. If I find anything around the house that looks odd or anything comes up, I'll let you know right away."

"All right, Angie, I'll be on my way then. I'll get this submitted and then get a start on looking for Jeff's car if it is somewhere to be found."

"Okay, Chief, thanks again. See you later."

With that last comment the chief made about Jeff's car, I looked at Anna and tried my best not to start crying.

All she said was, "Angie, they need us to be strong."

Chapter 55

"Anna, Demetri just sent me a text to let me know he's on his way. He said we have a lot to talk about. Looks like maybe we will be getting some info after all. I'm not sure what Demetri has to do with all this, but we'll see when he gets here."

Anna eyed Angie, wondering if she had the same information that she did.

———〰———

I could see Anna's inquisitive look. The comment about them needing us to be strong sparked a lot of questions for me. Why would Anna say that? What did she know that I didn't?

"Hopefully it's news we can use to get those idiots back."

I laughed at Anna's comment. She was feeling the same thing I was, although I was worried and was getting the feeling that this was a ridiculous master plan and those "idiots" she referred to were behind the whole thing.

The doorbell rang yet again, and of course it was Demetri.

"Hello. We have to stop meeting like this."

We laughed and hugged and kissed cheeks.

I brought him into the kitchen, where Anna was waiting for us.

"Hello, Anna." They normally shook hands, but this time, she went in for a hug, and he accepted it with open arms—literally. I couldn't help but notice she looked a little flushed afterward. He did as well, and he was gazing at her a little awkwardly. Well, it was awkward for me anyway. I eyed them cautiously until they remembered I was in the room.

My mind briefly slipped to Derrick and the moment we shared in the sales office yesterday morning. I could feel the instant sweat rising to the surface of the skin on the back of my neck. How could I be having these feelings when my husband was missing? What kind of person was I? Although Anna seemed to be having the same encounter with Demetri, she and Carl had a marriage that was just about in shambles when he went missing. Jeff and I had a great marriage. Why couldn't I shake this kid?

"Okay, ladies," said Demetri. "We have some things to discuss. I am warning you that some of the items we need to discuss you won't be crazy about and some will help you understand the chaos that's been happening around you since Carl went missing."

I looked over at Anna and said, "This ought to be good."

"Angie, you sound a little sarcastic."

"Honestly, Demetri, this whole thing is starting to become a joke."

"Aren't you worried that Jeff is missing?"

"Only as worried as you are and you don't seem that worried at all."

Demetri looked at me and said, "I'm a bad actor."

"On with it then," I said.

"I will start by saying that Carl and Jeff, among some other very old and dear friends of mine, are caught up in something from Carl's past. It's obviously a mess, a small one, but a mess no doubt."

"What kind of mess?" said Anna. "Like a real mess where the law is involved or a 'Carl' mess?"

Demetri laughed but kept on talking. "Well, right now, it's a Carl mess, but there is a chance that it will turn into a cops and robbers mess. We are going to try to avoid that as much as possible, and we are on the right track. Some of the horror involved in this mess, such as the situation in Florida and the car that was supposed to be Carl's was partially faked."

Anna asked, "How do you partially fake an explosion?"

"Well, the explosion was real, but the bodies were fake."

"*What*?" Anna and I both yelled at the same time.

Anna said, "The chief even came back saying that the bodies of the men in the Florida house were not connected to Carl."

"Yes, you're right because they weren't real people."

"Same thing with the body in Carl's car?"

"I don't have much information on that."

"What about my house for God's sake? Why set the fire?"

"So this is the part that you might not like very much. The car and the Florida house were part of the plan, but your house was not."

"Are you saying that someone else blew up my house?"

"For the most part, yeah. We don't know who or why. I know you don't want to hear this, but it actually works out in our favor."

"How is that even possible?" I asked.

"This is the part that I have been dreading telling you two."

Pretty soon, I heard someone coming through the front door. Around the corner came Justin. My heart nearly dropped to my stomach. Anna stood up and raced over to him.

"Hello, honey! How are you? Are you okay? Are you behaving these days?"

"Yes, Aunt Anna, I am. How are you?"

"I'm well, considering your stupid uncle is more stupid than ever."

Justin laughed and then looked at me and said, "Hey, Ang."

"Hey, Toph," I said and left it at that.

I looked at Demetri to find out what the punch line was for Justin being in my home when my husband was missing, and Derrick came around the corner into the kitchen. Instead of my heart being in my stomach, it was now trying to beat out of my chest. If Anna's eyes had gotten any bigger, they would have popped out of her head. The sweat from the back of my neck was creeping to the surface again. With every fiber of my being, I tried to stay as calm as possible and not say much of anything, but I didn't have to.

Derrick slowly walked over to me, and in this situation, his actions were very inappropriate, but his words totally trumped them. He put one hand on the small of my back and pulled me in close to him. He said, "Are you okay?"

"I'm okay, Derrick." He was so close to me I swore he could feel the sweat on me. As much as you would think I would be embarrassed with him, I was not.

Demetri, Anna, and Justin were chatting about what? I really didn't care at the moment. It gave me a chance to talk to Derrick while his arm was wrapped around me.

"What the hell is going on, Derrick?"

"I'm not really sure, Angie. I know, but I don't know the whole story. Something tells me we are about to find out from Demetri, but I wouldn't get your hopes up that we'll get any real answers."

"But why are you here?"

"I'm going to let Demetri tell you that."

Derrick had a very businesslike tone in his voice at the moment, but I could still see that hint of connection to me in his eyes. As I was thinking, thank God we're not alone, he said, "I think we'll have some alone time to talk later."

Oh shit, I thought. *What good could come of that? Is he reading my mind?*

I saw Demetri eye us very cautiously, but at this moment, I didn't care. He and Anna had practically undressed each other with their eyes earlier, and his wife was one of my closest friends. Some friend when I didn't even know they were separated.

If you asked me what I thought my life was going to look like now six months ago, I would have said not the total shitshow it was today. No one was dead yet—or at least I didn't think so—so that was a blessing.

Chapter 56

"Let's get on with this then, Demetri," I said. "Why are these two here?"

"Well, they are here to serve as your protectors."

"What?" I said blankly, not fully wanting to succumb to the idea of constant temptation. "I must be misunderstanding what is happening here."

"I told you there was a part of this that you weren't really going to be thrilled with. They are going to be watching over you both until all of this is straightened out."

"Watching over us how exactly?" I asked.

"Basically with you twenty-four hours a day, seven days a week."

"*What*? That's completely crazy! Do we have a say in the matter?"

"I'm sorry to say, no, not really."

"Derrick has a family. What is he supposed to do about them?"

"Derrick, I'll let you answer that for Angie."

"I volunteered for this. I am getting paid, and unfortunately, I am separated at the moment. The wife is staying in the house while I'm, well, going to stay here with you—and Anna and Justin of course."

Oh my God. This is not happening. There is no way I am going to sleep in my home with this man and Justin no less. Clearly any negative thoughts I had of Justin, prior to this, had now gone away or at least to the back burner. I didn't even know what to say. I turned to Anna.

"Anna, what do you think about all this?"

"Well, Justin here is my nephew, and I know pretty much all there is to know about him. Past and all, and you seem to be pretty chummy here with Derrick, so I don't know who else our loving husbands would have chosen to protect us. I'm comfortable with it … for now."

"I mean about them watching over us constantly? How do you feel about that?"

"Angie, in all reality here, it sounds like some shit is going to go down at any minute, so I personally would rather have people around us that we trust than be alone. I understand we can call Demetri and the chief at any time, and they will jump to our rescue, but Justin and Derrick will be right here with us. Listen, I know we are strong, intelligent, capable women, and it's not the ideal situation, but I will feel safer if they are here."

"I will be here as often as I can be as well," said Demetri as he glanced at Anna.

For about half a second, I didn't feel as bad for feeling the way I did about Derrick.

"So it's settled then," said Demetri.

"I guess so," I said, not happy about the situation at all. "Are we allowed to go to work?"

"You and Derrick can, but it's probably wise to not have Justin go into the office. Anna can actually go back to her office if she wants to, and she can take Justin with her because it's her company so she can have anyone in there that she wants. There is no past connection there with Justin like there is at your office."

So my thought went to Derrick and me spending every waking moment together.

"Derrick runs appointments during the day, so what are we supposed to do with him in the office all day?" I asked Demetri.

"Well, you could work from home and just keep him here with you while you work."

I flushed again, and there was that sweat creeping to the surface of my skin. *This cannot be happening.* I'm sure Derrick could sense my concern. I had to believe that he would be perfectly professional and not do anything unless I welcomed it, which meant I would have to initiate it, so the ball was in my court not to cheat on my husband with an employee. When I put it that way, I worried much less.

Derrick said, "Angie, at least we know this is only temporary. We'll get through it and adjust on the fly when needed. It will all be okay."

"Okay, Derrick, I feel much better when you put it that way, especially that it's okay for us to be together."

He raised a quick eyebrow at me without anyone seeing him, and I felt like my insides were on fire. How the hell was I going to get through this with the strength I needed to behave?

Demetri said, "I have one more thing for Anna. Anna, do you want to join me in the other room? I think Carl would like me to speak with you about this in private. After I leave, you may do whatever you would like with this info, including share it with Angie, but first I need to tell you alone."

"Sure thing, Demetri. I guess it's obvious that I share everything with Angie regarding this mess."

"Yes, that's why I said what I said."

"Okay, I'll join you in the other room."

"I'm going out for a smoke," said Justin.

This left me and Derrick all alone. The only difference from this time and the next, well who knew how long, was that everyone was still inside or outside. We were technically not alone.

Everyone was out of the room, and it was just me and Derrick. I didn't know why he did this, but he seemed to need to be physically close to me. I didn't think he did it on purpose, but it did cause me to wonder sometimes. I was pretty sure he knew how good-looking I thought he was. As I stood there, leaned up against the kitchen island, he walked over to me and stood shoulder to shoulder next to me.

"Hi," he said.

I didn't want to look at him, but I just couldn't help it.

"Hi," I said, looking to my right where he was standing. I always looked him right in the eyes. He always looked right back.

"I'm not really sure what to say to assure you that it will all be okay because I can't promise you that at this point. I can promise you that I will behave … as much as you want me to."

He smiled his usual subtle, trusting smile, which made me feel even better about the situation. It immediately occurred to me that he was saying he wouldn't lay a hand on me unless I wanted him to, which left it all up to me whether anything happened or not.

"I will say this, though, if I even think you're giving me a shade of green for a green light, I won't even question it. I'll do whatever feels right at the moment. Of course, it will only be between me and you, but then again, it seems like there will be a lot only between me and you in the near future."

I kissed him on the cheek and said, "There's a very pale shade of green while there are people in the house."

"This is going to be fun."

"Oh my God, you knew! You knew the other day when we were in the office that this was going to be happening, and you didn't say anything?"

"I signed a number of documents to swear not to say a word until you and Anna were made aware. There was no way I could have said anything. You're not really mad at me, are you?"

"Even if I was, I don't think it would be for very long."

"I'm not here to cause any trouble, and I never expected any of this to happen."

"I know."

When we were whispering, his lips were so close to mine that I could almost taste the cinnamon from the Big Red he was chewing. *How am I going to get through this and behave like a happily married woman? I think the answer is … I'm not.*

Chapter 57

Demetri and Anna were in the other room, away from Derrick and Angie. Anna was hoping to get to the bottom of Demetri's priceless information.

"Demetri, when is someone going to fill in all the holes for me?"

"What do you mean, Anna?"

"You know exactly what I mean. What is going on, and when is it going to be over?"

"Anna, I'm not sure. I don't have all the info myself, and this is all Carl's plan."

"You're joking, right? Who would ever follow a plan concocted by Carl? Are you all actually following along, and were you all drunk when you agreed?"

Demetri laughed at Anna's question and then smiled so she didn't take offense at his laughter. "Honestly, the plan seems to be well thought out, and he has enough people involved that we've got his back if he doesn't stick to the plan."

"How many people are involved?"

"A handful."

"How many is a handful?"

"I can't say right now."

"I assume you can't tell me what this is all about either."

"No, but you are closer than you think to some answers."

"What is that supposed to mean?"

"I wanted to pull you aside for this so if you want to share it with Angie I will leave that up to your discretion."

"Okay, what is it?"

Demetri put his hand in his pocket and pulled out a key. Anna was hoping she knew what it was going to open.

"Is that what I think it is?"

"Yes, and this will answer a lot of questions. If Carl hasn't already let some of the cat out of the bag from diverting from the plan, I would bet he is using this box as a tell-all to give you some missing pieces at least."

"I was hoping you were going to have that key with you today."

"It is so at least that mystery will be solved."

"When you said Carl diverged from the plan, what did you mean by that?"

"Jeff told me Carl called you while you were at Jeff and Angie's house."

"He did, but he didn't know I was there. The only reason I was there is because the house was torched. What scares me is that no one is talking about that. I know that was done on purpose, so who's behind that?"

"Anna, I don't know. I know that's the worst answer I can give you, but we are looking into that."

"I think it would be worse if you said Carl did that on purpose. I'd rather not know then for you to tell me that Carl had it done or better yet did it himself."

"Well, in that case, it's good news," Demetri said, laughing.

"I wouldn't say its good news, but it's better than the alternative."

"It's very interesting, Anna, that you are looking at all this the way you are."

"Like how? You mean open-minded?"

"Exactly, my wife would be a total mess in the sense that she would be so pissed at me. Maybe that's why we're separated."

"What?" said Anna. "You and your wife are separated?"

"Yes, I told Angie, and I thought she may have said something. I did ask her not to, so I guess she kept her word."

"Yes, she didn't say anything. If you asked her not to, why would you think she would breach your trust?"

"I'm not sure. You looked at me a little funny earlier, and I wasn't sure if that was why." Demetri was completely fishing, and Anna thought he was hitting on her.

"I gave you the same look you were giving me, which honestly felt like you were giving me a once-over."

Demetri laughed. He definitely was giving her a once-over. "I'm pretty sure that's exactly what I did, but I guess knowing Carl, I didn't expect you to look the way you do."

Anna flushed and didn't know what to say. "I didn't always look like this."

"Well, whatever you are doing, keep it up. I don't think I would be complimenting you if Carl was really missing."

"I would hope not. Talk about poor taste."

"Are you going to wait to open the box?"

"Yeah, and I'm not sure if I want to open it with Angie or not. I'm sure I will. I need to get myself psyched up to open the box. She and I can just disappear upstairs. How much do Derrick and Justin know about all this?"

"They don't know much at all actually, so if you don't want them to know anything, then don't tell them. We are not purposely keeping anything from them, and now that they will be here all the time, they will be witnessing quite a bit. It's up to you what you want to share with them."

There was a pause in the conversation, and Demetri looked over at Anna and raised an eyebrow. The corner of his mouth perked up.

Anna nodded. They shared a laugh.

"I think maybe we should talk after you open that box."

Chapter 58

Anna and Demetri walked into the room to meet Angie and Derrick. Anna couldn't help but notice they were a little closer than they should have been. They weren't touching, but if they had been an inch closer, they would have been. They didn't even seem to care that Demetri and Anna had entered the room. They didn't move.

"Hey, guys," I said.

Demetri said, "Okay, I'm going to head out. If you need anything, just let me know."

Justin came back into the house, and we all stood there looking at one another. It was such an awkward moment I tried to think of something to break the silence. I looked at my watch and thought it was too late to go into the office. I would never get anything done at this point in the day.

Derrick said, "Parcheesi, anyone?"

We laughed, and his comment certainly eased the stress of the silence.

Anna said, "I have some work to do, so I'm going into the study for a while. Angie, will you join me in a little while? I want to talk about some things."

"Yes, of course," I said.

Derrick said, "Yeah, I have some things I can do also, so if it's okay with everyone, I will go on the back patio and get on the computer."

I was curious as to what he had to do, but I didn't want to ask in front of everyone.

"Angie, do you think we could talk for a while? I would like to at least try to clear the air since we will be spending a lot of time together in the upcoming …" No one knew how long it was actually going to be until this was over.

"Sure, Justin, it's definitely a good idea."

We all sort of scattered into our own corners, and Justin and I stayed in the kitchen.

"Let me start by saying I understand that this is not the ideal situation, but Jeff trusted me enough to leave you in my and Derrick's hands during this fiasco."

My mind wandered to Derrick's hands being on me.

"This is something I take to heart because Jeff very well could have just written me off after everything that went down at the company. I want you to understand some things about that time in my life. Are you willing to listen and hear me out, Ang?"

"Yes, Justin, I will listen but on one condition. You need to tell me the truth. If I even for one second think you are lying, I will call bullshit on this whole conversation. You have given me reason to not trust you in the past, and especially now with everything happening, I don't feel like going down that road with you again."

"I understand, Ang, and I don't blame you for not trusting me after all that has happened."

"Okay, Justin. Jeff and I had a long conversation about you when I spotted you in the neighborhood."

"Wait. You saw me?"

"Yes, you didn't do a very good job of hiding yourself."

"Well, to be honest, I thought you were a workaholic, so I didn't think you would be home during the daytime, and I didn't know you quit your job to work with Jeff, so I thought I was in the clear."

"Well, you effed that up now, didn't you?"

"What did you and Jeff talk about?"

"I saw you twice and didn't mention anything to him until after Elle told me you were cutting down the trees. Jeff actually freaked out on me. I was over there at Elle's, and I guess he saw you walk out of the house. He didn't know I was hiding from you in the bathroom."

He laughed.

In retrospect, as I was talking it out, it really sounded ridiculous.

"I can't believe you were hiding from me. You know I would never hurt you. Don't you?"

I didn't answer right away because I wasn't really sure why I was hiding from him.

166

"No, I guess not. I think I was just hurt and angry that you acted the way you did at the company. I already knew what kind of things you were doing and people you were involved with, but I heard so much more after you were gone for good. I was infuriated when I heard about you getting arrested and the r …" I trailed off, barely finishing the word because I didn't want to make him angry or get myself angry just talking about it all.

"It's okay. We can talk about that too. That's one of the things that I want to cover while we are talking."

"When Jeff and I were discussing you being in the neighborhood, he was so pissed at first, but then he calmed down. He calmed me down too after a while."

"Wait … Jeff was pissed?" Since Jeff didn't get angry very often, Justin didn't understand why he was so mad.

I started with a laugh. "Yes, Jeff was pissed, but he sat me down to talk it through, and he simply said you have some issues and there was no reason for concern, that you wouldn't do anything to hurt us. I brought up some things we heard, and he said that we don't know if any of it was true and that we shouldn't dwell on the things that we can't prove. I, of course, brought up the arrest and the circumstances."

"Let me explain my side, and you can come to whatever conclusion you want. I have no reason to lie to you, especially because you are already disgusted with me and my actions."

"That's for sure," I said with a sympathetic smile, trying to show him I was going to give him the benefit of the doubt through the rest of this conversation.

Justin said, "Okay, here it goes."

Chapter 59

Back at the newfound bachelor pad, the sun was setting, and they knew in a few hours, they would be getting another visitor who was a part of this master plan. Jeff was tossing around in his head the scenario of Elizabeth possibly having Alzheimer's and said, "Man, where did the years go? Carl, it seems like just yesterday you were just dating that lunatic. Now we're old enough to have Alzheimer's, or at least someone from the old days has it? I need to do more with my life instead of working so much."

Ray said, "She is quite a bit older than us, don't forget. Once this is all over, we can relax once and for all and possibly reevaluate what we want to do when we grow up."

"Ha, that's a good one, Ray. Carl will never grow up, so maybe we should take a page from his book?"

The sun was now long gone from the sky, and Ray cooked a big spread of rigatoni Bolognese and garlic bread and made a huge garden salad.

"Angie makes a mean Bolognese, and that was pretty damn close to hers. Very good, Ray."

"Thanks, buddy. Justin's mother taught me how to cook. She could have been a chef she was so good. Talk about where did the time go? It seems like she was just taken from me yesterday. Do you guys feel much more emotionally as you get older?"

"Are you kidding?" Jeff said. "My daughter gets a base hit in a softball game, and I almost tear up. It's ridiculous."

"Get it together, you pansies!"

"Fuck off, Carl," said Ray. "You're such a putz. You have a great woman at home, and you don't even realize it. And you don't even have any kids."

Carl froze up a little and tried not to make it obvious. His thoughts were racing, so he got up and asked if anyone wanted a beer.

He needed to get out of there before he broke into a cold sweat. He bolted up the steps, and once he got to the top, he tried to get his composure back. He just wanted all this to be over, and he knew it was just beginning. So much uncertainty ahead.

Even though he had planned it all out, the new development of this Fitzpatrick douche and the Alzheimer's situation was getting to be too much for him to handle. He kept running some worst-case scenarios through his head. He could only focus on the worst possible things happening. He had good friends and family involved in all this, and he couldn't bear the thought of losing any of them. He was going to have to talk to Jeff or Ray about how he felt. Maybe they could calm him down.

He heard someone at the back door, and even though he knew they were expecting the last member of the group, he couldn't help but jump. He broke out into a cold sweat from fear, but then he saw the chief come through the door, and his mind was way more at ease.

"Hey, buddy. What's up?"

"You scared me half to death."

"You knew I was coming, and I'm right on time. Maybe you need to take a Xanax to calm you down. Or maybe just get some sleep."

"I guess. I'm glad to see you though, Chief."

"Me too. How's everyone holding up?"

"They are all good. It's like old times, so a lot of ball busting and, well, more ball busting."

The chief laughed a big belly laugh and asked where everyone was.

"They are all downstairs."

"Chief, can I ask you something before we head down there with everyone?"

"Of course, Carl. What's eatin' ya?"

"This Fitzpatrick asshole. What's the deal with him? Do you have any idea where he came from or how he's involved? It doesn't make any sense where he fits into the equation."

"I wish I had a better answer for you, Carl, but I have no idea. I've been racking my brain constantly and researching everything I can possibly think of regarding Fitzpatrick. I've been studying every file we have on him, and I've dug up some stuff on him, but I don't know what's real and what's fake. I've also been playing the conversation he had with Anna in your home over and over in my head. I'm trying to use that to come to some sort of conclusion." The chief eyed Carl very cautiously, hoping to appease him for the time being. The chief wasn't about to give Carl the truth.

"What conversation with Anna?"

"Oh boy. Let's go talk to Jeff. The morning after he got fired, he went to your house to talk to Anna, and then he went to the office to talk to Jeff and Angie. He questioned them something awful and then tried to accuse all of them of having more information than they were letting on. What concerns me is that Jeff did have more information. Did Fitz somehow know about the plan, or was he just trying to get one of them to slip up and lead him to believe most of this was all planned?" The chief knew this would throw Carl off.

Carl's head was spinning, and he didn't quite know what to say. He was also pissed that no one made him aware of this conversation.

"Why didn't anyone tell me about this?"

"We weren't sure that it was anything really to worry about. We're still not sure if there is anything to worry about. You do know he faked all his records to get into the police academy, right? Did Jeff tell you about that?"

"No, he didn't."

"Maybe he just thought it was insignificant."

"Maybe, but it doesn't seem like that anymore."

"No, but we haven't seen or heard anything from him since that day."

"That's not true because he called Ray yesterday."

"What did he say?"

"Just a bunch of shit that didn't make any sense. Sounded like he was looking for information about me and the fact that I'm missing. He was accusing Ray of knowing where I was and us staging the whole thing."

"That's basically what he accused Anna, Jeff, and Angie of doing."

"What is going on with the guy? Carl, do you know this guy?"

Carl felt the blood drain out of his face and could almost feel the sweat beading on his forehead. He tried to keep his cool.

"Hey, buddy, are you okay?"

"Yeah, I'm in way over my head here."

"Yes, you are, but you have all of us to protect you like always. I know we can't control everything that makes you nervous, but let's not get ahead of ourselves. I myself am looking in every direction I can think of to figure out who Fitz really is, and I also have my best officer helping me on the case. We will find something. Right now, I'm focusing on finding him."

"Okay, Chief. Also, I don't see how I could possibly know him. He's much younger than us, and it sounds like he's not really even from here, right?"

"Well, that's the odd part. He may have been born here, but he didn't grow up here. There's a lot involved in his story, but we are just trying to put the pieces together and figure out what's real and what's not real."

Carl's wheels were really turning now. He was more scared than ever, and he was hoping that after talking to the chief, he would feel more at ease. All the uncertainty was not making any of this easier.

"Let's go downstairs with the rest of the crew, and you can all brief me on how Danny is making out in Italy with the ice queen."

Carl was able to laugh, but he was still a mess. He was more of a mess than before. He was completely beating himself up because he was sure he had thought of everything, every possible scenario. Then again, he knew what a fuckup he'd been his whole life. Something was bound to go wrong, and now he felt like the whole plan was backfiring. He was even more puzzled as to why no one else was feeling the same way he was. No one else seemed the slightest bit worried, and usually everyone was when it came to him. He was starting to get paranoid. What did they know that he didn't, and were they all going to turn on him? He couldn't take it anymore.

Chapter 60

"Okay, you assholes. What are you hiding from me, and how fucked are we?" Carl yelled at everyone once he and the chief got into the basement.

"Carl, calm down. What's wrong?" asked Jeff.

"I feel like this is all falling apart around us."

Ray said, "What are you talking about? If Elizabeth has Alzheimer's, then we don't need to worry about any of this and we can just all go back to normal."

"How normal can it be? My house is a mess, and there is all that other shit that is supposedly in my name that I know nothing about. Not to mention this Fitzpatrick asshole that seems to be hovering over us like the grim reaper."

No one had anything to say. There wasn't anything they could say.

Finally, Jeff said, "Right now, we can only take one step at a time and stick to the plan as much as possible. We all have to agree to be totally honest with each other, and unless we are in a situation where we need to think fast, we have to consult with each other before we diverge from the plan. Whatever plan that might be at the time, we cannot change it in any way. This will only cause a shitty chain reaction."

The chief said, "Jeff is right, and there is no doubt that we are going to have to regroup, and it may be more often than we would like. I am looking into Fitzpatrick, but there is just too much that doesn't make any sense. The beginning of his existence is impossible to find, and from age eight to fifteen seems too crazy to be real. Then after that, we lose any and all info about where he was and what he was doing. Then he clearly faked his records to get into the police academy. Since the police academy, everything seems to check out, *but* we don't know where he is. His last known address does not actually exist. We do have reason to believe that he was part of the McNamara family business."

Everyone, of course, looked at Ray.

"Well, Ray?" asked Carl.

"Well, what? Are you asking me if I know him and have been keeping it from you all this time?"

"Yes, that's exactly what I'm saying."

"No, of course not. Chief, what time frame are we talking about?"

"Well, it's hard to say but maybe five to ten years ago."

"Oh, then no. I've been out too long to know any of the kids that started to come up through the business during that time."

Jeff said, "So we do have a slight problem, but I don't know what the connection is, so we have a small lead. Chief, maybe you can help us out with this one. Long story short, Angie's cousin had some tree work done at the house by Justin, and she hit up Facebook to give a positive review to Justin. She saw him and Fitz in a photo together."

The room erupted. The yelling and swearing was overwhelming. Finally, the chief was able to get some order over his friends.

Carl said, "Jeff, how do you not share this information with us? Now our wives are in the care of Justin, who may possibly be in on this with Fitz."

Ray was angry now. He said, "Carl, you are crazy to think that Justin has anything to do with whatever shit Fitz is trying to pull."

"How do you know that?"

"Justin has been doing everything possible to get his shit together and get back on his feet. I just don't see him being involved with anything so stupid."

The chief said, "I will continue to look into all connections to Fitz that I can find. I would really like to find out where he is actually living. Then I will work on how he even knows Justin. Wait … Ray, was Justin ever in juvie?"

"Yes, he was. Do you think there is some connection there?"

"Well, it's somewhere to start."

"I'll send him a message in the morning and just flat out ask him how they know each other. If something is going on, he'll tell me what he knows."

"Not if they are plotting to kill all of us," said Carl.

"You are so stupid. Listen, I understand that criminals can be capable of anything, but that's a long shot with Justin. He's a lover, not a fighter."

The chief needed to reign this in again. "Okay, guys, between whatever Ray can find out and Officer Smythe back at the station, maybe we can put some pieces together here."

Jeff said, "Maybe we can all get some rest and start fresh in the morning. Lots to do!"

Chapter 61

"Angie, I had a pretty great life thanks to Ray. I, however, let my emotions get the best of me instead of just being thankful to have Ray."

"Okay?"

"I lost my mom when I was little, and my dad was already gone before I was born. I guess Ray was attached to me when my mom died, so he decided to keep me. Ray was a great stepdad. Still is, but he was involved with not-so-great people. He always made sure I had more than I needed and mostly what I wanted. As I got older, I started obsessing about not having a mom—my mom, specifically. Again, Ray always made sure I was taken care of, but being that I was a boy, I think he gave me a little more freedom. It didn't exactly work out as well as he wanted. I don't think he wanted to suffocate me, which was good, but it backfired."

"You've always talked about your siblings, so were you lying about having a big family?"

"No, not at all. I do have siblings, but they belong to Ray's wife. She had children before they got married, so they are all stepsiblings."

"Oh, I see."

"So I got myself in trouble from a young age. It was easier to do bad than good. I was so bad by the time I was fifteen, I got caught stealing from the local supermarket, and because I had gotten in trouble too much, I ended up going to juvie."

"I'm surprised Ray didn't pull any strings to avoid that."

"There weren't any strings left to pull. He pulled his last one for the incident before that one, and there was nothing left to do to help me. Ray and I sat down to have a chat. I was so thickheaded and stubborn, I tried to be strong and refused to tell him I was hurting inside. Ray was at his wit's end because he was doing the best he knew how to take care of me.

Each time he did something nice, I would find a way to make it crappy. He suggested that I see a therapist. He even offered to go with me. I just couldn't see that he didn't need me to be strong. For some reason, I kept thinking I needed to be a man and not let my emotions show."

"Why do you think you were doing that?"

"I don't really know, but I think it's because my mom wasn't there to pick up the pieces, and I didn't think it was Ray's job to have to do that. I felt like a burden on him, even though he never ever gave me reason to think that way. He treated me like I was his own. I just had some serious issues."

"Wow, so you spent more time getting in trouble than just talking to Ray and telling him how you felt? Looking back on it, do you think he would have understood if you just would have talked to him?"

"Of course. I think he would have given me everything I needed emotionally if I just would have opened up to him. Looking back on all of it, I see what a great guy he really was and again still is and how much I really effed everything up. I pissed half my life away just because I couldn't open up to anyone. This may be a little bit inappropriate, but I always felt like I could talk to you. You were always very receptive to my nonsense. You always seemed to listen no matter what I had to say."

"Well, when you first started working for us, you seemed like such a lost soul. I felt like if I listened even just a little bit, you wouldn't feel like you were alone."

"I appreciate all the times you listened to me. I know you didn't have to, but you did, and that made me feel good."

"So this leads me and I think everyone to the question of Fitzpatrick. You don't have to tell me if you don't want to, but how do you know him?"

Justin laughed. He was a little uncomfortable. "I met him in juvie. That's how we know each other. We somewhat ran with the same type of bad kids, but we never really met before juvie. I'm sure you're thinking, *Well, that doesn't make any sense*, but it's true. We both knew of each other but never actually formally met before we got locked up. He got out before me and much earlier than his sentence. No one knows why, but he was there one day and gone the next."

"So then what happened? When did you meet up with him again?" I was keeping my fingers crossed that he didn't try to lie to me. After that photo of them together on Facebook, which Elle showed Jeff and me, we knew for sure they had met up again at some point. It was definitely a recent photo, so I knew the photo was taken in the last few months.

176

Justin began saying, "Not long ago actually. I don't know for sure but only a few months ago. He tracked me down via a cell phone call, and we haven't exactly rekindled an old friendship, but I saw him a few times since he reached out."

"Do you know what's happening with him?"

—m—

Justin tried his best not to let on that he had just heard from him a few days earlier and knew he was up to no good—never mind the shocking discovery in juvie. Justin and Fitz went down a road that they never thought they would explore, and the discovery was not what they were expecting. Justin still had his doubts, but Fitz was obsessed with finding out the truth. Justin believed that if he kept his distance, whatever Fitz found wouldn't come to get him too.

"What do you mean?" he asked, trying to stall a little but also making sure he could answer the question she was actually asking.

"Oh, I don't know, the fact that he was on the police force, got fired, and is now obsessed with Carl and this mess?"

"Oh, that," Justin said with a smirk. "Well, I'm not positive but even though he's acting like a jackass I'm not sure that his motivation is malicious."

"Justin, if you don't know why he's acting like this, then how could you know he's not up to no good?"

"I don't really, but from what I do know of him, it just doesn't make sense."

"Do you know of any way for us to find out what he's up to?"

"No, and I don't exactly know how to get ahold of him."

"I'm not accusing you of anything, but I feel as though you are hiding something from me."

"You're pretty good at reading me, Ang. I'm not hiding anything, but some things went down with Fitz and me in juvie, and it might have something to do with that. We swore we would never say anything about it, so until I'm sure of what he's doing, I don't want to start a shitstorm for no reason."

"Can you give me a hint?"

"No, because it doesn't make any sense right now."

"Okay, I'll trust your decision, and I can't fault you for giving your word to someone. You don't think he's dangerous, do you?"

Justin laughed harder than I had ever heard him laugh in the time I knew him.

"He's as dangerous as Carl is smart."

"Oh, Justin, you're awful, but that was really funny!"

We shared another laugh, and he said, "I want to come clean a little more about what happened when I left the company."

"Okay, like now or another time?"

"Now, if that's okay with you?"

"Sure, let's hear it."

Chapter 62

"Before you say anything else, Justin, I have some questions for you if you're willing to hear them?"

"Of course. What's up?"

"What is really going on here, and do Anna and I need to be worried?"

He looked at me sympathetically. He knew I was ripped up about not being in control.

"All I can say is that I can't say anything."

I smacked him on the shoulder, and he laughed at me. "You have to be able to tell me something?"

"I can tell you that you don't need to be worried, and if all goes well, this will be over in a week or so."

"Really?"

"Yes, really. Demetri will keep us informed if anything changes, but so far so good and everything is on track."

"What's on track?"

"Not so fast there, Ang. You can't trick me."

"Okay, okay, I'll lay off for a while. Let's get into the rest of your story."

Justin was not happy with the story comment, and he made it very clear. "It's not a story, Ang. This is what really happened."

"Yes, I'm sorry. I didn't mean story like it wasn't the truth. I just meant whatever it is you wanted to tell me, we can talk about now if you're ready."

"Oh, okay, well, here it goes. You are wondering about the whole rape plea, right?"

I went a little stiff because he said it so nonchalantly, like it wasn't a big deal and I should be completely comfortable with him in my home, knowing he was convicted of rape.

179

"Ang, I know you don't know me that well, but we have had enough conversations for you to form your own opinion if you think I'm capable of raping someone or not, right?"

"Yes, I suppose."

"You suppose? Really?"

"Justin, you have to understand that the construction industry is not something I was very familiar with before I started getting involved with Jeff and the company. It's a very interesting industry, to say the least. You must also understand that I am completely unfamiliar with addiction. In the short time I have been involved in the company, I have witnessed some things and some people that are disgusting, unbelievable, and downright repulsive—nothing short of acting like wild animals. So for me, and it's sad to say, but I don't believe much of anything, and I certainly don't get close to anyone. When they are here today and gone tomorrow, what's the point. I've also realized not to believe anyone. This makes it much easier to weed out the bad and focus on hiring better people."

"Ouch, that hurts."

"Sorry, dude, but it's the truth. This isn't something that you don't already know."

"It's sad to say, but it's true. So does this mean you are going to believe what I say or not a chance?"

"I will give you the benefit of the doubt and listen to everything you have to say."

"Well, it's not a long or involved story, but I will tell you what happened. Since you have most likely already drawn your own conclusion, I'm going to tell you each piece of the puzzle so you understand."

"Okay, I'm all ears."

"I know you're tired of hearing that we can't tell you all the details, and I'm afraid I have to stick to the mantra but—"

"Stop there," I interrupted him. "How do you expect me to believe anything else you say if you can't tell me everything?"

"I know it sounds a little ridiculous, but the only details I will leave out have to do with Jeff and Carl, which you will find out soon enough."

"What does your prison time and the rape have to do with Jeff and Carl?"

Justin could see the fear and partial disgust in my eyes. He knew he better think fast before he lost my focus and open-minded attitude.

"No, no, *they* don't have anything to do with me going to prison, but they may know some people from my past."

Relief washed over me, and I was thankful for his reassurance. I was still trying to keep an open mind with having a convicted rapist watching over me and my new friend while our husbands were playing cops and robbers ... or whatever they were doing.

"So let's get down to it and stop the suspense."

"So I started using drugs again and got this brilliant idea to start robbing houses. I really don't know what I was thinking."

"You clearly weren't."

Justin looked at me, a little surprised.

"You know, you are awfully brave talking to someone like that who just got out of prison a few months ago."

"Are you serious? To me, you are just that quirky guy who used to work for my company, a guy who has a lot of potential to do great things but is too stupid to realize it."

Justin was smiling his shy smile and said, "You always believed in me and didn't even know me. Why?"

"Mostly because almost from the day you started working with us, Jeff trusted you and everything he asked you to do, you got it done and he never had to worry about it, of course, until you ..." He knew what I meant. I didn't have to throw salt in the wound.

"Anyway," Justin continued, "Fitz was not really involved at all but somehow got dragged into the investigation. There was proof that he was with me that day, but no one could prove that he was with me at the actual house. The cops kept him as a person of interest mostly because of his prior record too."

"Has he ever committed a serious crime as an adult?"

"No, God no. He's a lot like me. Overall good guy who tries to do the right thing but gets caught up in the nonsense. Being that I was such a fuckup, it all happened so fast, and I wasn't ready to straighten myself out. Fitz was just accepted to the police academy, and I wanted to get the cops off his back."

"This makes no sense. So you pled guilty to rape because he was going to the police academy? How close are the two of you?"

"We were really close back in juvie, but as the years went by and he grew up but I didn't, we drifted apart. Just a few months ago, he reached out, and we saw each other a few times, but now he's involved in something that's not exactly my deal."

"Let me guess: you can't tell me all of it?"

"Now you're catching on," Justin said with a smile.

"Can you tell me anything?"

"Honestly, the only thing I really know is that he is searching for his biological family."

"I thought his family was all gone? What else is he doing?"

"I don't really know of anything else."

"Justin, did Carl or Demetri or Ray or anyone involved tell you what happened with Fitz and Anna? And then his visit to the office?"

"No. Why? What happened?"

"Oh boy, let's talk to Anna so you can hear her side of what happened."

"Okay, but, Ang, I need to know that you believe that I didn't rape that woman. Do you?"

"Justin, I don't think I really ever believed it, and Jeff doesn't believe it for one minute. Now that I know how much of a mess you were and that you took the blame for Fitz, it still doesn't make sense, but that's more believable than you actually doing it yourself."

"There is more to the story, and maybe we can talk about it soon."

"Okay, but did Fitz actually rape that woman?"

"No, Angie, he didn't."

Chapter 63

Justin and I walked into the kitchen. Derrick was still out back working on the computer, and Anna was walking out of the home office. She seemed to be happier than she had been before and possibly at ease. I wasn't quite sure, but she looked like she had game face.

"Hey, guys."

"Hey, Anna."

"Angie, can you come into the office with me? I think it's time to open this box."

"Anna, I thought you would have opened it by now."

"No, I wanted to wait for you. I'm not sure what I'm going to see in there, and no one told me you couldn't be with me."

"Okay, let's go. Justin, are you good?"

"Yes, Ang, but I want to continue our conversation before the end of the night."

"Okay, Justin, we can do that. I don't think I'm going anywhere," I said with a crooked smile and a shrug of the shoulders.

Anna said, "Let's go, Angie."

Anna and I walked into the home office, where her paperwork was laid out all over the floor. She was using her iPad as a second monitor with her laptop. I was glad she'd gotten herself settled in and hoped she could immerse herself in her work and get her mind somewhat off this nonsense.

"Angie, I am not going to harp on this, but since we have been pretty honest with each other, I have to ask. What's up with you and Derrick?"

"What do you mean?"

Anna looked at me, disgusted. I wasn't quite sure what else to say.

"Are you kidding me? After all this, you are going to play dumb with me?"

"Look who's talking? You practically mauled Demetri earlier this morning when he was here, and you just met each other."

"Really, I thought Derrick was going to plant one on you right in front of all of us."

"Okay, okay, let's not fight. I know we are both under a lot of stress and pressure here, but we need to stick together. The last thing we need is to be at odds with each other. To be honest, you are the only one I really trust. I trust Demetri, but he's withholding info from us, so I don't have a high level of trust like usual with him."

"You're right."

"Then you first."

I thought she would just let it go with Derrick, but she persisted.

"I know how it looks, but there is nothing happening with us. It's no secret that he's ridiculously good-looking, and I am very attracted to him, but it's more than that."

"*What*? Are you serious?"

"Not like I have feelings for him, but he's very easy to talk to, and we seem to have so many things in common."

"Oh my God, I can't believe you are saying all this. I thought you and Jeff were like the perfect couple?"

"No couple is perfect. I have some issues with our marriage. Jeff doesn't open up a lot. He doesn't express his feelings very often. I struggle with that. Just general conversation is a struggle sometimes. I'm happy. I never question our marriage, but there is just something about Derrick that has opened up a whole new outlook for me."

"Outlook? Like you're going to cheat on Jeff?"

"*No!* I don't think so. I mean, I don't plan on it. Oh God, listen to me. I'm sure I don't sound very convincing."

"Um no, no, you don't at all. I don't even know what to say to you right now."

"Well, start with Demetri and the moment the two of you shared this morning. That was just as intense as me and Derrick, and you barely know Demetri. What is that all about?"

"I really don't know. He is very captivating. For some reason, he came at me like I was the only person in the room. I don't really know what happened or why he was acting the way he was. We spoke a few times since you first introduced me to him about some legal questions that I had, and he was happy to answer them for me. He never said anything that led me to think that he was hitting on me. He never said anything complimentary of me, so I don't know where all that came from."

"I believe you, but that's not the way it looked from outside of your encounter."

"I was caught up in it, and it was very strange to me, although I did happily receive it."

"That's an understatement."

"Well, you know that things haven't been great with me and Carl, so the attention was exhilarating. Also, a few times when we spoke, it was so relaxing to speak with an intelligent man. It was effortless to talk to him. Carl can be so stupid."

"I'm sure, and you could see it all over your face."

"Well, let's stay on track here and be each other's support. At least I won't be with Demetri all day every day. Derrick will be here all the time."

"Yes, but so will you and Justin, so it's not like we will really ever be here alone."

"That's true, and that may just help you resist the hotness."

Anna looked at me wide-eyed all of a sudden, and she said, "Oh no! He's *McHottie*?"

"Oh yeah" was all I could say.

"Oh, Angie. Okay, let's get in this box and get our minds off this temptation that our husbands faced us with."

"Okay, where's the box?"

"Over here behind the computer." Anna walked over to the desk and grabbed the box.

"Are you sure you're ready for this?"

"Well, I don't really have a choice, right?"

"No, you don't."

Chapter 64

Fitz sat in his living room, knowing no one was going to find him out there since he didn't use this address on his application for the police force. He was still trying to put all the pieces of everything together, and he was at a standstill. He was hoping that Justin was going to help him, but he wouldn't. He understood that he didn't want to get involved just in case something went horribly wrong, and with Fitz's luck, that was exactly what would happen.

He got up and moved over to the dining room table, where he had everything laid out—no guns or ammunition, no drugs or anything illegal at all.

All he had on the table were notes and letters. He had a box full of old photos from his younger days.

He had a large packing box full of shit from his aunt's house. When she passed away, he went and got it all cleaned out. She didn't have any children of her own, and she left everything to him. She didn't have a lot of money, so most of what she had was of no value. He took what he thought might be worth something and got rid of the rest.

Sitting next to the box of his aunt's things was a smaller box. He flipped off the lid, and the photo on top instantly took him back to his early teenage years when he met Justin, when they went away.

They needed some serious discipline. They were both a mess and getting in way too much trouble. At the time, they both had the option of attending a new type of disciplinary facility. The instructors focused more on the good than the bad, and they had more opportunity to interact with the other students, learning about one another and taking actual classes so they would be able to go back to school when they were released. It was an interesting idea on how to make them better. It worked for Fitz but not so much for Justin.

Fitz leafed through the photos until he came across that shocking photo that first linked him and Justin together. Justin recognized someone in the background of a photo that Fitz had, but he wasn't sure how. It only took him a few days to recall that the woman in the photo that Fitz said was a relative Justin had seen in family photos of his own. He had never actually met her because she never came around to family functions.

The box of stuff from Fitz's aunt's house revealed much more about that photo—things that he'd always wanted to know and in his heart almost always knew. Still, there were missing pieces.

Chapter 65

Anna sat there in front of the box. She wondered how she was going to react to the contents and if it was going to change what she thought to be true of her life with Carl. She wanted to think the worst. She thought it would help to make whatever was in there better than the worst thing possible.

"Anna, maybe you should just open it. Like ripping off a Band-Aid."

"Easy for you to say."

"I know, but I was just trying to lighten the mood a little."

"Thanks." Anna smiled. She knew that I would be by her side every step of the way, no matter what was in that stupid box.

"Here it goes."

Anna put the very small key in the lock and turned it. She felt the lid come loose and spring up just high enough to see the bottom of some papers. She lifted the lid all the way, and on top lay a letter in an envelope. The outside of the envelope read "Anna," followed by a small sticker of a banana. Anna shook her head and in seconds felt love, which quickly switched to anger.

She opened the letter and started reading it out loud.

Dear Anna,

Now that you are reading this, Jeff is already "missing." He is safe here with me. I know you don't know where here is, but we are not terribly far from you. Jeff and I will be seeing you and Angie soon. That I can promise you. You are already with Justin and Derrick, so I know you are safe. The contents of this box are going to shed some light on this mess, and it will tell you some things that I never told you. I am sorry for that, but I'm glad it's all coming out now. I don't want to say everything will be back to normal soon, but I want it to be better than normal. I hope once this is all over, you will want the same thing.

I love·you, and I will see you soon.
Carl

"I was hoping for more in that letter."

"What were you hoping for?"

"I'm not sure. Something more about this annoying mess."

"Let's keep looking through this stuff. Maybe you'll get more out of that."

Anna was looking through documents that didn't make any sense. She couldn't understand why there was a random birth certificate of someone she didn't know. There was also an old passport, a charm bracelet, and some photos. Anna started looking through the old photos. Some of the photos were of people she didn't know, and some were of Carl, Jeff, Demetri, Ray, and another tall, lanky kid she didn't recognize.

"Look at this photo!"

"So they were all friends since childhood?"

"Yeah, obviously."

"Who's the chubby kid on the right?"

"Oh, that's Ray."

"Justin's stepdad?"

"Yep!"

"Demetri was even captivating as a young kid." Anna raised an eyebrow at me, almost making fun of herself.

"Anna, who's the tall, lanky kid in the middle?"

"I'm not sure, Angie." Anna pulled the photo closer to her face, and I was right behind her.

We both blurted out, *"Oh my God!"*

"Anna, is that the damn chief?" I asked.

"Angie, I think it is."

"He's in on this shit too?"

"Maybe not, but since he's in this photo, I would guess he is."

"What the hell? This thing keeps growing legs with each piece we uncover."

"No shit, right?"

Anna kept looking through the photos, and she came upon four photos of Carl and a woman.

"Who the hell is that now, Anna?"

"I'm not sure. I think this is the part where I'm supposed to be pissed at Carl."

"I'm sure it's obvious to you too, but she's beautiful."

"She is, Angie, and I hate to say it, but she looks really familiar to me. I just can't place her."

Pretty soon, Anna gasped deeply, throwing her hand to her mouth and dropping the photos in sheer horror.

"Oh my God, Angie! What the fuck!"

"What's the matter, Anna?"

"Maybe it's the situation that's making me so suspicious, but that's Josephine Romano."

"The Queen of Fashion?"

"Yes."

Very awkwardly and surprised, I said, "With Carl?"

Anna looked at me as if to say, "Seriously … now you are going to pull some sarcasm?"

I said, "Sorry. Are you sure?"

"I'm positive, but, Angie, you don't understand."

Anna was starting to worry me a little from the look on her face and tears starting to well up in her eyes.

"What is it, Anna? What's the matter?"

"When I was just in Paris, she sat down at the bar with me to have a drink."

"Whoa! What? Are you sure?"

"Yes, Angie, I'm positive. She knew who I was, and she was complimentary of the line I created and displayed in the show."

"Is that all she said?"

"We talked for a while but mostly just pleasantries and about how mean the critics can be."

"Do you think she knows who you are outside of the fashion world?"

"Now I'm thinking, she must. Maybe I should be happy that she didn't try to kill me over there."

I didn't know what to say to Anna. We needed to focus on this box.

"What else is in that box?"

"There are a bunch of newspaper articles. They look like the originals. They're not copies."

"What are they about?"

"I'm not sure. I need to read them. Something about the McNamaras. Sounds like they were some sort of crime family."

"Wow, look at this one."

The headline read, "Another McNamara Gone—Dead or Only Missing?"

> Only two months after Dermot McNamara, head of the McNamara crime family, was slain, his daughter Elizabeth McNamara goes missing. Looks like the family is slowly crumbling. The investigation is ongoing and there are still no leads. This could very well put an end to the crime family or at least keep them quiet for a while. It is said that Elizabeth was going to take over for her father and run the "family business." Other reports say that her husband, Carl, was slotted to take over if anything happened to Elizabeth.

Anna was baffled. She couldn't believe what she was reading. I was hovering over her shoulder. "Angie, are you reading this?"

"Yes, and I don't know what to say."

"This article can't possibly be about *my* Carl? Can it?"

"Well, Anna, I don't think it's a matter of opinion. I think this is hard evidence."

"Husband? I don't get it. Carl never said anything about being married before."

"It looks like he's telling you now. What else is in the box?"

"More articles." Anna was leafing through the rest of the papers, and she came across an obituary for this Dermot McNamara, who was mentioned in the first article.

Dermot McNamara—Obituary

1912–1972

Dermot McNamara, 60, passed away in County Hospital Monday night. Born September 4, 1922, to Daniel and Alisa (Fitzpatrick) McNamara …

"Holy shit!"

"What is it, Anna?"

"Read this, Angie."

I nearly choked on my gum as I read the obit. The hair on the back of my neck stood up, and at that moment, I realized this was way bigger than we and whatever little game we thought Carl and Jeff were playing were.

"Do you think we should call the chief? What are your thoughts on all this?"

"Well, obviously, Fitzpatrick has something to do with this family, but what? More important, we need to figure out what the hell Josephine Romano has to do with Carl."

"Angie, I think maybe we need to do some research of our own. This all had to be public record, right?"

"Oh boy, what are you suggesting, Anna?"

"Think this through with me. We need to find out what Fitz is up to and how he fits into this picture. Maybe we can get Justin and Derrick to help us?"

"Are you crazy?" I yelled.

"Shh, keep it down!" Anna scolded me.

"Sorry, but do you think for one minute we are going to go snooping around an old crime family just to find out what Carl and Jeff are up to?" Then it hit me. Derrick said he would be willing to help in any way he could.

"What is it, Angie? I see your wheels turning."

"How did you know?"

"You get a wrinkle in your forehead when you are thinking about something important."

"Jeez, I hate that I am so obvious."

"I don't think it's that; I just think we've been spending too much time together."

I smiled at Anna because I knew she was joking with the little smirk on her face.

"Derrick mentioned something to me when Carl first went missing. He said he would be willing to help in any way he could. I didn't want him to get in any trouble, and he said there was a group of people he knew who also knew Carl, and he would ask around if they could tell him anything. I think that he would be willing to help."

"That's great, Angie. What do you think about Justin?"

"I'm not sure about Justin. I think he would be willing to help you. Do you see how he looks at you when you talk to him so motherly? My only concern is that he might not want to get himself into any trouble. I wouldn't want that to happen either. I know he's trying to get himself straightened out. I would hate for him to get into trouble trying to help us. That's why I think it would be a good idea to get the chief involved."

"I don't know, Angie. Maybe not right away. You know what Carl said about telling him even about the lockbox."

"True, Anna. Well, let's hold off until we really need him."

"Okay, that's sounds good."

"Let's talk to Justin and Derrick and see what they think. They might even know where we should start."

Chapter 66

Carl, as usual, was starting to panic. He hid it well, but inside, he was a wreck. He was terrified of how this was all going to unfold and wondered if his friends would all be safe. Now he had reason to think that Anna wouldn't be safe and he had put her in danger.

Ray's phone rang, and Carl jumped.

Ray answered the phone. "Talk."

"So shit just keeps getting weirder and weirder over here. I am getting more reason to believe that Elizabeth is just flat-out fucking crazy."

Jeff said, "So Ray sent you all the way over there to find out something we already know?"

The whole room laughed, but Danny had more to say.

"I still can't get any evidence on the Alzheimer's situation, and I'm starting to get the feeling that I'm being followed. I don't know for sure, but I can't shake the creepy feeling I get whenever I leave the hotel room."

"Maybe you're just getting paranoid in your old age," said Jeff.

Danny laughed and said, "I wish that were the case, but I'm pretty sure someone is watching me."

Ray said, "Do you want me to send someone to meet up with you?"

"Ray, that's not the plan, so I don't think that's a good idea."

"Danny, I know it's not the plan, but it looks like there is going to be a lot of improvising in this plan. We didn't know Elizabeth was going to stump us all with her current state, and now this Fitzpatrick asshole seems to be stirring up some kind of shitshow to be determined."

"Ray, it's up to you. It couldn't hurt to have someone else here to look over my shoulder with me, especially if something does go wrong."

Ray put Danny on speaker so he could hear the conversation. Who would volunteer, if anyone, and what was the new plan going to be?

"Okay, moving on to plan 67 or triple Z or whatever the fuck we're at by now—who's going out there to meet up with Danny?"

The room was dead silent, and they all looked around at each other. It didn't make sense for anyone but Jeff to go out there. He knew her the least out of all of them, and it had been more years than he could count since he'd seen Elizabeth. He felt like Angie was in good hands with Derrick and Justin, and the kids were going to be heading to Florida for most of the summer with his in-laws.

"I'll go," said Jeff.

"No," said Carl. "No, you are not going to another country, leaving your wife here with maybe someone we can't trust and putting yourself in danger with that nut job. I won't let you do that."

The room erupted.

"Whoa, whoa!" said Ray. "Carl, what's the problem? We are all in this together. Are you having second thoughts about all this?"

"I don't know, but I'm starting to freak out. I don't know why I decided to do this in the first place. It was so stupid of me to get all of you involved, and now I'm a mess. We don't know what that woman is capable of. She could kill us all."

Ray walked across the room and sat next to Carl on the couch.

"Listen, buddy, it's all okay. We will all be fine. We've been planning this for a while now, and I don't see how anything can go wrong."

"How can you say that, Ray? That woman is crazy, and now we don't know what's going on. Danny is one of the best in his field, and even he can't figure out what she's up to. He's been doing this most of his adult life and now to make things worse, he thinks he's being followed. Maybe we should just get him home and call this whole thing off?"

"Carl, calm down. We didn't force Danny to go there; this is something that he wanted to do for you. This will be his last job, and he figured he would go out with a bang. No pun intended." Ray shot a quick smirk across the room.

Ray said to Jeff, "Is this something you would really be willing to do?"

"Yes, of course. I wouldn't have offered if I wasn't committed to actually doing it. I don't quite have the experience that Danny has, but if I go instead of one of you, it will be way less conspicuous. I think there will be way less concern on her end if she sees me. There will be no reason at all for me to be there, so maybe that will throw her even more—that is, if she sees me."

Danny chimed in, "That's not a bad idea. I can tell you exactly what to do, and it would mostly be just to show her that I'm not alone and you could watch my back."

"This is an awful idea. I can't let this happen. Jeff has no experience in this, like he just said, and I would never forgive myself if something happened to him."

Danny said, "You don't have anything to worry about. We are not threatening her or screwing with her in any way. There is no reason for her to go after Jeff especially. I think sending Jeff out here is our best bet. We will keep you updated every day and let you know what we find."

"I'll book a flight for tomorrow night, and I can be there in less than twenty-four hours."

"Looks like it's a done deal then," said Ray.

"Carl, everything will be fine, and if it's not, we'll just have to manage," said Danny.

Carl was worried. He was afraid of how much Jeff was actually going to find out over there.

Chapter 67

Anna and I walked into the living room, and Derrick jumped up off the couch and said, "Angie, can I talk to you alone for a minute?"

"Sure, Derrick, but, Anna, I want to talk to you and Justin first before we do anything else."

Anna found something so familiar about Derrick's voice. She had been in his presence often lately, but she just couldn't put her finger on it.

"Okay, what's up?" asked Justin.

Anna started talking first. "We need to know a few things from the two of you, and we will not take 'I don't know' for an answer. You must know something, or else you wouldn't be here 'protecting' us."

I was so impressed with Anna and how she was carrying herself. She had more confidence at that moment than I'd ever seen in her, and that was saying a lot. She was a pretty tough cookie—on the outside at least.

Justin and Derrick looked at each other, and Justin said, "I know more than Derrick because I'm closer to the situation. Only because I'm family. What is it that you want to know?"

"So many things, from who is Elizabeth, who killed her dad, and what the fuck does Carl have to do with any of them? And this Fitzpatrick asshole? What's his deal, and when is someone going to find out what he's looking for or trying to accomplish?"

Derrick and I stood there with our mouths practically gaping open.

Justin was very calm and collected as usual.

"Anna, how do you know all these things? Why are you asking all of this?"

She took the handful of things that we found in the box and laid them out on the kitchen island. Derrick walked over to where she had laid everything out and leafed through the pieces like he was looking at some vintage baseball cards signed by the greats.

"Anna, I wouldn't even know where to begin with all this. The old newspaper articles are way before my time, so I don't really know what they mean, but obviously, they are not good scenarios. People seem to be dead or missing. As for Fitzpatrick, I know he's up to something. I don't know if it's no good or what, but he asked me to get involved and I said not a chance. I already knew I was going to be watching over the both of you when he asked so I was already committed to this."

"Let's go back to the dead or missing. There is nothing in here that says anyone is missing. What gives you that idea?"

"I don't know; I just remember hearing stories about people saying that someone was dead even though they weren't."

"You mean like they faked someone's death?" I said.

"Exactly," said Justin.

"What does this have to do with Carl?"

For the first time, I could see Justin looking a little uncomfortable, more uncomfortable than I was comfortable with him being. As stupid as that sounds, I thought if he was nervous, we should all be nervous. Derrick didn't seem to care much about anything. He was there to do a job, and he was focused on that job.

"My next question is can you find out what Fitz is up to? We need to know how he is involved and how we can make sure we don't get caught up in whatever it is he's doing."

"I can certainly try to find out, but I'm not so sure he'll tell me if I'm not willing to help."

"Fair enough, but I at least need your word that you will try."

"I will try. I can call him first thing tomorrow morning."

"I need to look through all these papers and actually read them. That might spark my memory a little on the people involved and what they have to do with Carl or any of this."

"Okay," said Anna, "I'm going to go to bed. I'll see you all in the morning, and maybe we can come up with some sort of plan on how we are all going to coexist."

"Angie, is it all right if I just crash in the rec room?"

"Yes, of course. I wasn't sure what the sleeping arrangements would be going forward. I haven't given it much thought throughout the day. That's fine with me. There is a pull-out in there, and there are blankets and pillows in the bench seat under the window."

"Thanks. I'll take this stuff back there with me and get to it then."

Derrick and I said good night at the same time, and Derrick looked over at me with the devil in his eyes.

Chapter 68

Jeff arrived safely in Italy, and Danny met him at the airport. He was exhausted. He just wanted to sleep, but he knew that was not an option.

Danny and Jeff shook hands. They knew there was no time to bullshit.

"Danny, what's the plan?"

"Well, now that you're here, it frees me up to get some things done. I need to hear her conversations, and since I've been alone, I haven't been able to do much without having a lookout. The last thing I need is to get caught."

"Danny, do you think she knows you're here?"

"She's not stupid, but I've been as careful as possible. The only way she could know I'm here is if she just assumes that Ray sent someone to watch her. Okay, she has someone watching me."

"What are the chances?"

"Knowing Elizabeth, pretty good, but if she's truly sick, she most likely wouldn't even think to do that."

"Carl is a mess, and I'm getting the feeling that he's not telling us everything?"

"After I heard that Elizabeth called Carl's brother to kill him, I think anything is possible."

Jeff smirked at Danny with a very half-hearted chuckle.

"So what are we actually going to do today?"

"I wanted you to fly in today because she seems to be out all day on Tuesdays, so I thought today would be a great day to get in there and get the house wired. This should give us a much clearer picture of what's actually happening with her. Let's head right over there. We'll stay far enough away so we can see her but she can't see us. Once she leaves, I'll head inside, and you be my lookout."

Jeff and Danny watched as Elizabeth pulled out of the driveway and headed down the street.

Jeff could see that something was eating at Danny.

"Danny, what's up?"

"Elizabeth always has her sidekick with her, and she's nowhere to be found today. She wasn't in the car with her, and her car isn't here either. Her car is always here because she doesn't leave her side."

"So what do you want to do, Danny?"

"I'm not really sure. Let's just wait a little while. Maybe we'll see some activity, and if not, I'm going in."

As the time passed, Jeff started to get a little uneasy about the whole thing. Danny looked uneasy too, and that made Jeff even more unsure of all this. He needed to play the part anyway.

"Okay, Jeff, I'm going in."

"Okay, I'll be here. Make sure your phone is on and not on silent. Are you sure this is the best way to do this?"

"Unless you come up with a better way."

"Sorry, I should just keep my mouth shut. You're the one who's been here for what seems like ages tracking this woman."

"This is true. Okay, I'm going in."

"Okay, I guess I'll stay here."

Danny walked down the road to the house. He took a good look around to make sure no one was there. Jeff stayed in the car. His phone buzzed on the passenger seat next to him. He picked it up and saw the message. He smirked and put the phone down. He looked in the rearview mirror, and a small twinge of excitement caught him below his belt.

"Hello, handsome."

"Hey, baby. Miss me?"

"Of course I did."

—m—

Elizabeth's bizarre sidekick threw her arms around Jeff after he got out of the car to greet her. She slipped her hand under his sweater and pulled him in close. He lowered his head so he could go in for a kiss. She backed away a little but then gave in to his tight grip on her. She had missed him too much to turn him away.

"Wow! It's been too long."

"It's only been a few months, but it feels like a lifetime."

"Tell me about it."

"So tell me, Jeff, where do we stand with everything?"

"Everything is on track so far. I wouldn't keep your hopes up that everything will work out according to the plan."

"Why? Why do you say that?" She was getting nervous. She was doing everything she was supposed to do, so what could go wrong?

"Well, we think Carl is going off track. We also didn't anticipate Elizabeth having Alzheimer's."

Her face fell like she was hiding something—or it was all getting out of hand and she knew it.

"Jeff, I don't really know what to say about that."

"What does that mean?"

"I mean I don't think she's really sick."

"You don't know? You're joking right?"

"No, I wish I was, but I'm not really sure what's going on. I don't think she's really sick. I'm 99.9 percent positive, but I have a small bit of doubt. You know Elizabeth. She should have been an actress."

"So they are both out of control, and we're basically all just watching?"

"More like babysitting, it seems."

"So what now?"

Jeff's phone buzzed again, and it was Danny.

"He's on his way back. You should go."

"Will I see you again before you go back …?" Her voice trailed off because she didn't want to think about another few months without seeing Jeff.

"I'm not even sure when I'm going back, so I'm sure I will see you. I'll be in touch."

"Okay." She kissed him slowly and softly, trying to savor the moment. She backed away from him and ran off to her car to be out of sight by the time Danny got back.

Jeff got back in the car and sat back, wondering how he could have let all of this get so out of control. And Angie, how could he do this to her and for so long?

Chapter 69

Fitz wasn't sure what his next move should be or what he was even going to do next. He knew it was time to get this all out in the open. He kept contemplating how and struggled with whether he really gave a shit that people might get hurt. He hadn't planned to intentionally hurt anyone physically or emotionally, but he knew that was going to happen no matter what—unless he kept his mouth shut, of course. He didn't end up so bad for what he went through in his childhood. Why should he pull any punches with all this information that he had? It was time to get it all out in the open. He was still missing one piece of information, but he really didn't seem to think that was very important. He was sure that what he didn't know wasn't significant in all this.

When he followed Anna to Paris, he was shocked to see her talking to Elizabeth. He thought he was utterly crazy to think that Elizabeth and Anna were hanging out at a hotel bar. At first, he was totally caught off guard, but then he realized that Elizabeth and Anna didn't actually know each other.

There was a knock at his door. *Who could that possibly be?* He peeked out the curtain in the living room and was completely astonished to see Carl right there on the doorstep. He'd been trying to find this asshole from the beginning, and there he was, knocking on his door. Why was he there, and what could he possibly want?

He could open the door, sucker punch him, and drag him into the house. Maybe it was a trap. There was no way he could open the door. But how could he not? He'd been trying to find him since he went missing, and he was standing outside his door. He wasn't prepared for this. He wasn't ready.

"I know you are in there, you little punk. Open up."

Fitz just stood there, trying to be silent and hoping Carl would just go away.

"Like I said, I know you are in there, and if you don't answer the door, I am going to kick it in. This is not a game, and my patience has worn very thin with you during the last few months."

At this point, Fitz knew he didn't have any choice but to answer the door and talk to Carl. He wasn't sure what he would say or what the hell Carl could possibly want from him. More important, how did this absentminded fool find him? He was sure Justin was the only one who had some idea of where he was hiding. He was kicking himself for not being ready for this.

Fitz walked to the door and opened it. His jaw gaping open, he saw Carl standing on the doorstep with the chief. He did not see him a minute ago when he looked out the curtain. Where the fuck did he come from?

"Fitz," said Carl.

"Carl," said Fitz. "What do you want?"

"No, no, you don't get to ask that question. I should be the one asking you that. What are you trying to pull? You are a major pain in everyone's ass, and you haven't even told anyone what it is you want. You are just making a fool out of yourself."

"If I was making a fool out of myself, you wouldn't be worried about me, and you sure as hell wouldn't be on my doorstep. What do you want?"

"Again, you little asshole, what are you trying to pull? We are about sick and tired of trying to find you and figure out what the fuck your problem is, and why do I have to keep repeating myself?"

"I have every right to do whatever I want to do, and it doesn't seem like anyone can stop me."

"That's why I'm here," said the chief. "I'm hauling your ass to the police station."

"On what grounds?"

"Lying on your résumé, making up a fake name, and forging legal documents. Should I keep going?"

Fitz, shocked, said, "I can't believe you actually figured all that out."

"Listen here, dumbass, Smythe helped me with some last-minute details, but I was the one that researched your past."

"I don't even know all about my past, so how could you?"

"I know enough to arrest you, and anything you did before you broke the law to come and work with me, I don't give a shit about."

"Oh, I thought we might be able to put an end to all of this," said Fitz.

"What are you talking about?" asked Carl.

Broken down and clearly defeated, Fitz said, "That's why I've been such a dick. That's why I've been trying to get all the details about whatever Carl here is trying to pull."

"What the hell are you talking about, Fitz?" Carl was getting angry, and the chief was starting to think that Fitz was mentally unstable.

"Somehow your group of fucked-up yuppie friends is connected to my childhood."

Carl took a step back, and the chief thought he was going to punch Fitz square in the jaw until he realized that Carl was caught way off guard. It looked like maybe shock even, almost like he knew what Fitz was talking about.

"You're fucking crazy, kid. Now you are just talking gibberish. What would we possibly have to do with your childhood? I know you are connected to Justin from your juvie days, but what does that have to do with us?"

The chief was convinced that Fitz didn't even know what he was talking about. He thought Fitz was still trying to figure everything out himself. Wouldn't this be the first time that Fitz and Carl met face to face? The chief was looking at them like they'd known each other forever.

Fitz just stared at Carl while Carl stared right back at Fitz.

The chief looked from Carl to Fitz and back to Carl. While he was watching all this, he couldn't help but feel his skin start to crawl. He couldn't explain it, but he was pretty sure at that moment he knew exactly what Fitz was talking about. He was pretty sure Carl, as usual, was clueless.

Chapter 70

I stood there looking at Derrick. I could feel my cheeks getting red and that recent damp feeling of sweat that was starting to rise to the top of my skin. I felt like a teenager, and it was really starting to eat at me. *Please say something so I don't have to.*

Derrick crept closer and closer when he should have stopped. He was in my personal space, and he just kept coming. No way was I going to stop him. I hadn't up until then, so why would I this time?

"I swear that curl falls in front of your face just so I can move it."

As I smiled at him and giggled, it gave me a second or two to think of the right thing to say. Luckily, I didn't have to say anything because he started talking again.

"I want to tell you something, but I want you to swear that you won't laugh."

Already laughing, I asked, "How can I swear to such a thing?"

"You have to swear, or I won't tell you," he said with a pleadingly desperate smile.

He was obviously very serious, and I assumed he wanted to talk about whatever he had disappeared outside to do earlier. I was hoping anyway. I didn't want to have to ask him, and it really was none of my business, so I didn't want to be nosy.

"Okay, I swear I won't laugh. You know I'm one of your biggest fans and supporters so I won't laugh. What is it?"

"I have been working remotely with a guy I know from my younger days, and we have been life coaching."

I stared at him blankly because I thought it was wonderful on one hand, but on the other hand, his life was kind of a mess.

"Derrick, that's great! How did you get involved in that and why?"

"You sound only half excited for me."

"No, not at all. I think it's great."

"Yeah, me too. I know I'm not living the best life I can at the moment, but you know what they say. The plumber is usually the one with the broken toilet."

"Ha, when you look at it that way, I guess you're right."

"Yeah," he said with a laugh. "There are some really great people that I met when I was younger who got into lots of trouble, and I'm trying to get them back on track. These are good people, and they deserve a second chance."

"I think that's wonderful. Are you still learning the process, or are you actually coaching already?"

"I am actually coaching already, and I have three clients. Things are working out very well so far, and they are making a good amount of progress."

"That's really great. Why haven't you told me this before?"

"Well, like I said earlier, I didn't want you to laugh, and I wasn't sure what you were going to say about it. I didn't want you to think that I didn't want to work for you anymore either."

"Well, you know I love having you in the company, but I see bigger things for you in the future."

"Really? Like you see me moving on?"

"I do. I don't see you doing this work forever."

"Well, the work I am currently caught up in is one of the best jobs I've had. It's so good it doesn't even feel like work."

I wasn't sure how he could get any closer to me, but somehow he found a way. He was behaving since we discussed the ball being in my court if I wanted more than just conversation. I was hoping he would break that rule so I wouldn't be the one to initiate. Why did I make a rule that I didn't even want? Stupid, stupid, stupid.

I raised my eyebrow at him and smiled, hoping this would be enough to give the green light.

"Yeah?" he said, like a teenager trying to contain himself.

"Yeah," I said.

He put one hand on the counter and wrapped the other arm around me, putting his hand on the small of my back. "Come here," he said.

I leaned into him, putting one hand on his rib cage. I tilted my head up to meet his, and he kissed me.

He pulled away after the sweetest kiss I'd had in a long time. He just put his forehead on mine and said, "I know this isn't right, but I just feel so good when I'm with you. Up until now, just talking to you put me in a good place. Now this ... I don't even know what to say. I've wanted to do this for so long."

"Wow, you at a loss for words? Is that possible?"

We laughed, and he pulled me in tight. This time, he kissed me on the forehead and then made his way down to my lips and kissed me again.

Looking down at me, he said, "What do you think about spending a day together?"

"Like just me and you?"

"Yeah, just me and you."

"I would like that. I would like that a lot."

"How about tomorrow?"

"I need to go into the office for a little while, but then I'm all yours."

"You're mine all day then."

I looked at him, questioning.

"You can't really go anywhere without me, remember?"

"Oh yeah. How could I forget?"

Smiling at me adorably, he moved the curl out of my face and said, "Let's go to bed so tomorrow will get here faster."

I couldn't help but smile, and the butterflies started jumping.

Chapter 71

Danny turned the corner and stopped dead in his tracks. He could not believe what he was seeing. He thought it was a joke. He thought maybe Jeff was caught and decided to play dumb, to turn on some charm to get the attention off himself or maybe even Danny. Maybe Jeff thought Danny was caught, and he would try anything possible to make it look like it was not what it seemed.

Danny didn't know if he should run or find out what was happening. He just couldn't figure out why the hell he would be kissing Elizabeth's partner, caregiver, or whatever she was. What the hell was happening? He was disgusted with the thought that Jeff was in on Elizabeth's sick game. He thought he was not safe. Worry washed over him, and he didn't know what to do next. As close as he was with Jeff, he would now have to watch his back and figure out what the hell was going on. He waited for her to leave Jeff.

Danny walked around the side of the car on the passenger side and got into the car.

"What's up? What did you see?" Jeff was totally calm and seemed like he genuinely didn't know what Danny had seen at the house. Danny didn't know what to make of it, so he went along with it. He hesitated to tell Jeff anything, given the possibility that he was a traitor.

Danny eyed Jeff very warily and finally said, "I saw a number of pill bottles on the counter in the kitchen. Other than that, I didn't really see anything. The house looked immaculate. It didn't look like there was anything out of place. Everything was nice and tidy—clean carpets and not a dirty dish in the sink. Either she's really clean, or she's not really living here."

"Are you surprised?"

"Not really, but you would think there would at least be a pile of bills or magazines or something laying around."

"Maybe, but we're talking about Elizabeth. She was always a neat freak."

"I guess so. I did get some photos of the med bottles. I am sending them to Ray now to see if he can find out what they are, and maybe we can confirm if she's really sick."

"Did you do what you needed to do?"

"Yep, it's done."

—m—

Danny sent the photos and texted Ray to call as soon as he got them.

The phone lit up within seconds, and Danny picked it up but got out of the car just to pace and hopefully talk to Ray without Jeff hearing him.

"Ray."

"Danny, what's wrong, buddy? You sound rattled."

"I am a little. Did you get my photos?"

"Yes, I will get on this right away to see what they are and all the reasons to take them. I will talk to the doc to see what he says just to confirm. What's wrong?"

Danny fumbled over his words and could barely form a sentence. He kept looking back at the car to make sure that Jeff wasn't listening or watching through the rearview.

"Danny, I can't help if you can't talk to me. What are you trying to say?"

"So I didn't really have a lot of time to process what I saw. I was looking around Elizabeth's, and Jeff was in the car waiting for me. I walked out of the house. I came around the corner to get back to Jeff, and there was a woman in the car with Jeff. I stepped back so he wouldn't see me but just far enough out of sight that I could still see them in the car. I wasn't sure if we were made or what. I kept watching, and in a split second, she leaned in and started kissing him."

Ray must have been drinking something because Danny heard him spit something out and from the sound of it all over the phone. He started coughing.

Finally, he choked out, "Are you serious?"

"Ray, why would I waste your time joking about something like this?"

"Well, who was she?"

Danny paused and said, "The woman who has been attached to Elizabeth's hip."

The complete silence on the other end wasn't very comforting.

"Ray, are you quiet because you already know what's going on, or are you afraid Jeff is going to kill me?"

"Danny, I'm sorry, but I don't really know what to say. I have no idea what he's doing. It's becoming clear that there are more layers of this mess than we thought."

"What does that mean?"

"I don't know this to be true, but I think Carl is hiding something from us."

"Like what?"

"I'm not sure yet, but there is something not quite right, something that doesn't add up."

"Well, what am I supposed to do about Jeff?"

"You have separate rooms, right?"

"Yes."

"I would go to your room, lock yourself in there, and don't be alone with him."

"How am I going to do that? We've been together since he got here. We'll probably get some dinner and then head to bed."

"Well, whatever you feel comfortable with, but I would try to avoid him at all costs. Better yet, why don't you just come home?"

"How can I do that? What am I going to tell Jeff? That's definitely not the plan, so what do I say, 'Sorry, Charlie, you're on your own'?"

"No, I guess not. Give me some time to think about it. I'll get back to you."

"Okay, well, try to hurry up. I told you after this job, I am retiring. I'm not going to die on my last job."

"Okay, man. As much as I would like to say don't worry about it, you know I would be lying."

"Thanks, jackass. Call me as soon as you figure out what to do. I'll just use my experience to keep me safe for now."

"Okay, good luck, and I'll be in touch ASAP."

Chapter 72

Danny got back into the car with Jeff. It was not what he wanted to do, but he would just have to keep his guard up like the old days. He never would have thought he would have to watch his back with one of his oldest friends, especially Jeff. Jeff was not a man who went around killing people—that Danny knew of anyway. It was crazy to even think this. Jeff was a businessman, not a hit man. He needed to have faith in his friend and not think the worst but keep his guard up at the same time. How was he possibly going to do this and talk to Jeff like nothing was wrong?

"Danny, you're awfully quiet. Everything okay? Is Ray researching the uses for the medication you found?"

"Yeah, yeah. He said he's going to get on it right away."

"Oh, great. That will get us one step closer and hopefully get us the hell out of here sooner rather than later."

Danny couldn't help but eye Jeff very cautiously. *Is this for real? Is he for real? How can he be acting like this when he's hooking up with Elizabeth's ... whatever she is?*

"Let's get something to eat, Danny. I'm starving. Since you've been here for a while, what's good to eat? I'm sure you are going to say everything, but you pick where to go for dinner."

"Um, I'm not really hungry. I thought maybe we would just go back to the hotel and just get room service."

"Really? Are you okay? Don't be flaking out on me now. We have a lot more work to do. Come on; let's just go get a drink and some good food. Then we can call it a night."

Danny felt the panic rising, and he tried to keep as cool as possible. He did not want Jeff to know that he knew about the connection between him and the lady they were stalking.

Danny gave in to dinner. "Okay, there is a place right across from the hotel. Best seafood I've had so far during my stay here. Maybe the best ever. Let's go there."

"Now you're talking. So we're heading home soon, right?" asked Jeff.

"I guess. I'm not really sure that there is anything else for us to do here. I don't feel like we are getting anywhere with Elizabeth. She's crazy, which we already knew, and that woman that's with her is obviously useless." Danny threw that comment out there to see if Jeff would say anything or even flinch at the put-down. Danny watched him very carefully to see a change in expression or anything. Maybe even a comment ... but nothing.

"So we're really just waiting on Ray with his update from the doctor." As if on cue, Danny's phone rang.

"Hello. Listen," said Ray. "The doc said one bottle is for anxiety, one of them is for high blood pressure, and the third one is to minimize a flare-up of gout. Not one of them is for Alzheimer's. If you ask me, it's all an act."

Danny said, "Well, if that's the case, then she must know we're here. If she doesn't, why is she putting on the show? Now what?"

"I'm leaving it up to you guys. I know the plan was to 'take care of her,' but again, it's up to you."

"Guys," Jeff said, "I have to come clean on something."

Thank God, thought Danny.

Ray was thinking the same thing. They both let Jeff talk.

"So I think we are all in the same boat in taking some sort of extra step or precaution with all this. Knowing that Carl plotted out most of this plan, I know we all have our doubts. I wasn't sure what exactly I was going to do or how I would do something to contribute to helping us all, and then one day, I didn't have to think about it anymore."

"What do you mean?" Danny and Ray asked in sync.

"Well, you both know I've been traveling a decent amount in the last few years. I was on a trip roughly two years ago, and I bumped into an old acquaintance from college and ..." Jeff trailed off a little.

"And what?" asked Ray. "What are you saying, and what does this have to do with Carl and that crazy bitch?"

"Well, I got a little carried away with this old friend. I've seen her a number of times and, well ... we've been having an affair."

"Are you fucking kidding?" said Danny.

Danny and Ray knew exactly whom he was talking about, but why was this woman attached to Elizabeth's hip?

"Listen, I'm not proud of this, but the reason I am telling you is she is the woman we've been seeing with Elizabeth."

"What are we missing here, Jeff?" asked Ray. "And are you that unhappy with Angie?"

"No, not at all. I love Angie with everything I have, but I got involved with Franny, and I just can't stop. I don't see her but only twice, maybe three times, a year. I'm not saying that makes it better or even okay. I'm just saying that it's not a constant occurrence."

"Okay, so talk us through this. You knew this woman a long time ago. You ran into her on a business trip and started having an affair with her? At what point does Franny come in contact with Elizabeth, and why?"

"That's where it gets a little odd."

"It's not already odd," Ray sarcastically added.

"Well, after the second time I saw her, which would have been a year and a half ago, she told me she met someone that knows me. I was interested at first, and once she told me who she was, I was totally caught off guard and confused. *Franny is a special agent.* She's been following Elizabeth for years, trying to get close. She finally got close and—"

Ray cut Jeff off. "How the hell do you know Franny is telling the truth?"

"She doesn't have any reason to lie to me, I saw her badge, and I know she went into the field after college. Look, I'm not saying this isn't a total shitshow of a situation, and I can't exactly say she's on our side, but I do trust her."

"I don't even know what to say or what the eff is happening right now. How does Franny know that Elizabeth knows you? How does that come up in conversation?" said Ray.

"Like I said, she just brought it up. They didn't actually talk about it, and Elizabeth doesn't seem to know that Franny knows me or knows that Franny and I are even in contact."

Ray was now very angry and didn't know what else to say. He was beyond disgusted with the soap opera that this had become, and he just wanted it to be over.

Ray said, "Danny, what is your plan from here?"

"Ray, I wasn't really sure what to do with all this info, so we called you. I propose we come home and figure out what we're going to do from here."

"Good idea," said Ray. "Jeff, will you be coming home with Danny, or will you be rendezvousing with your new girlfriend?"

Ray knew by the silence on the other end of the phone that Jeff would not be getting on a plane with Danny.

"See you when I see you then. There is nothing I can do to protect you once Danny leaves, Jeff."

"I know, Ray. I put myself into the rest of this mess, so I know my risks."

"Ray, I'll see you tomorrow then," said Danny.

"Okay, see you tomorrow. Be safe."

Danny looked at Jeff. "I thought you were going to kill me."

"*What*? Danny, why would you ever think that? I would never do that to you. You are one of my oldest friends."

"I saw you kissing the woman we now know as Franny on my way back to the car, and I thought you were in on this with her and Elizabeth."

"Oh, I'm sorry. I guess when you put it like that, I could see how you would think that. But again, I would never do that to you. Why didn't you say something when you saw us?"

"There was nothing to say."

Chapter 73

I could barely sleep. My mind was racing from the evening. I couldn't help but be a nervous wreck with anticipation of tomorrow. We had no plan, and I didn't have any idea where the day would take us. What was I going to wear? What should I be prepared for? Why was I doing this? What was I thinking? Every question possible raced through my mind. I needed to get some sleep. I just kept thinking about Derrick being in the house. I was finally able to relax enough to fall asleep at a decent time. I faded off into a deep sleep.

My alarm buzzed on the nightstand, but I was already awake. The sun wasn't even up yet, but it was time to get into the shower and get ready for the day. I knew I shouldn't have waited until this morning to figure out what I was going to wear. Now I was stressing about something I shouldn't be. I'd dress for work and then maybe just bring a change of clothes, or maybe we'd come back here after the office and change for the day. Maybe he had a plan? I hoped he had a nice outfit to wear. He didn't seem the type to have nice clothes. Wow, if I didn't calm down, I was going to have a heart attack.

I got out of the shower and was glad to see the mirror fogged up. I didn't think I could face myself with all the dirty thoughts racing through my head.

I got dressed and spent time on my hair like I was going to the prom. My makeup was perfect, and not a hair was out of place.

I walked out of my bedroom and heard laughing and talking coming from downstairs. *Sounds like the house is up and alive.* This put a little more pep in my step, and now my nerves had turned into excitement. I needed to stay calm and on my game.

I walked into the kitchen to find Justin, Anna, Derrick, and Demetri eating from a wonderful spread on the island that Demetri no doubt brought for breakfast. I wasn't expecting him, and my thoughts somehow took me away from really seeing Derrick that morning.

I almost stopped dead in my tracks. Derrick was dressed in slim-fitted khaki pants, a pale-blue dress shirt, and something that looked like a mix between a jacket and a sport coat. He looked amazing. I was used to seeing him in his work clothes, so this was a welcome surprise. His tight white T-shirt and ripped jeans floated through my head. Wow.

He caught my eye, and he looked so happy to see me. I could tell that he was trying to hide it from everyone in the room but not from me.

"Good morning, everyone."

Everyone said, "Good morning," all at the same time.

"Demetri, how are you this morning? To what do we owe the pleasure of this early morning visit?"

He laughed and said, "I don't know really. I just thought I would check in with everyone and bring some breakfast."

"Well, that was nice of you."

"Yeah, I thought so."

We all laughed.

Demetri said, "So what is everyone doing today? All sticking to the plan?"

I said, "Yep." I left it at that. I wasn't going to get into it with Demetri. I was surprised he wasn't going to try to take Anna away from Justin for the day, but then again, it was not really his job—that I knew of anyway. Who knew what was going on or who was supposed to do what in this alternate universe we were living in these days.

Justin was going to take Anna to work today, and for Derrick and me, it would be, well … the best day ever.

The unexpected breakfast party started to break up, and Demetri said, "Anna, would you like me to take you around today instead of Justin?"

We all looked at each other, as Demetri and Anna were already lost in the idea. Derrick looked at me as if to say, "Maybe they have the same idea as us." I certainly didn't want Demetri taking her under his wing today. I didn't want him lurking around if Derrick and I were going to be together all day. But then again, if they were up to no good, they would want to be on their own. I would try to hide Derrick and me from them as much as I could. Derrick looked at me like "Stop overthinking all of this."

I snapped out of my neurotic trance to hear Anna say, "That would be great. Justin, do you mind?"

"No, of course not. I don't mind at all, and in reality, Demetri is the one calling the shots on this job."

Derrick frowned at me and shook his head like "This is not a job."

What are we doing? What is happening, and when is all this going to end? I slipped right back into my trance. I was starting to get angry with Jeff for putting me in this position. I was not blaming him for my actions, but I thought our marriage was more than this. I thought he was committed to taking care of us and working on our business. He was acting like a stupid college kid who was more committed to his fraternity brothers than his family. It was ridiculous. What made me even angrier was that he didn't even call me. There was no way he couldn't pick up the phone and call me at least to say hello.

Anna and Demetri left, and I didn't even realize it. With the most adorable smile, Derrick said, "Hey, are you ready?"

Derrick's deep, soft voice snapped me out of my trance for good, and I said, "Of course."

Justin walked into the kitchen and said, "Guys, I'm going to head out for a while. Derrick, you think that's okay?"

"I don't see why not. Demetri took Anna, so I don't know what you would need to do here today. We might all meet up later for dinner, so we'll let you know where we are."

"Sounds great. Later."

With his back to us and a wave, he was gone. The door closed, and we heard him pull out of the driveway.

My stomach was in a knot, a good knot but a nervous one. The look on Derrick's face said that I needed to commit to this, meaning if I was going to throw myself at him, I better know exactly what I was willing to get myself into. I didn't see us leaving the house just yet.

Chapter 74

After Fitz and Carl eyed each other up like two lions fighting over a female, Fitz broke the silence by saying, "You are not taking me to the station."

"Yes, I am, and there is nothing you can do about it. I am arresting you."

"I don't think so, old man. You didn't read me my rights, and how much proof do you actually have that I—"

Carl cut him off by saying, "Listen, we need to get this settled. I don't think you are going to kill me or my ... What did you call them? My yuppie friends?"

"Kill you? Why would I want to kill you?"

"I don't know," said Carl. "I'm not sure what your problem is, but I do know you are a serious pain in the ass. You have been acting like a complete asshole, and each and every one of us is trying to understand why you are involved. And my wife. Who the fuck are you to talk to her the way you did? And, more importantly, why did you light my house on fire?"

"Wow, Carl! What are you talking about? What fire?"

"You lit my house on fire."

The chief hoped Carl didn't pursue the fire situation.

"I did not light the house on fire. I will admit that I spoke to Anna a little out of line, but I was trying to figure out where you were and what ridiculous 'master plan' you came up with but more importantly why? What are you hiding from, and why? Is someone after you? Are you running from or toward someone?"

"Not your business, of course, and who's to say I'm up to something?"

Fitz looked at the chief like "Is this guy really this stupid?"

The chief tried not to let even a hair twitch on his face. He didn't want Fitz to think that he doubted Carl at all. Even though he totally doubted him, he wasn't going to show Fitz. The chief needed to keep still through all this.

"Carl, you do remember that I was working on your missing person case? I guess I found you." Fitz chuckled and looked at the chief.

The chief was again trying not to make any facial expression that would play into Fitz's joke.

Carl seemed to be taken off guard, but he rolled with it just so he wouldn't look so stupid.

"Yeah, so what happened that you went rogue? What is it that you want from us?"

"I just want to talk to you. I don't want to hurt anyone. I just want to talk."

"About what? What could you possibly need from me? Whatever it is, why should I give it to you after the way you've been acting? You are acting like a child. You would have learned more if you didn't get yourself fired."

The chief didn't move.

"As you already know, there are some serious gaps in my childhood. There is just too much that doesn't make sense. Too much that doesn't add up."

"What does that have to do with me? Why would I know anything about that?"

"I'm going to say this in front of the chief because I'm sure he already knows. If not, I'm really sorry. Truly I am."

"Quit babbling, and get it out already."

"I know you used to run with the McNamaras a long time ago—"

Carl cut him off. "Listen, kid, I'm about a hair's width away ..."

The chief thought, *What the fuck does that mean, Carl? How did you get so stupid?*

"A hair's width away from wringing your neck. I want to kill you right now. I just want you to leave us the fuck alone. Get your shit together, and leave us the fuck out of it."

"No, no, you can't just brush me off like that."

"Watch me. Let's go, Chief. Either bring him to the station, or let's get out of here."

"No!" said Fitz. "I know your nephew Justin."

This stopped Carl dead in his tracks as he was starting to walk off the porch. He wasn't sure how to react, so he just paused for a minute, and when he turned back around, Fitz's face was pleading for him to just stay and listen. The chief's face was full of sheer intrigue. The chief was questioning how Fitz was going to spin this to keep Carl from asking too many questions.

"Okay, kid, I'm listening." Carl's emotions were all over the place. He went from wanting to knock this kid's teeth down his throat to something similar but with less hate.

"I met Justin when I was younger, when we were away together."

Carl knew what he meant by "away." He was intrigued just like the chief. He almost felt bad for Fitz.

"Okay, kid. I'll hear you out, but if you don't cut to the chase, me and the chief are out of here, and you are hauled away in the back of the police car."

"I don't want to hurt anyone. I just want to know what you know about my childhood."

"Okay, okay. I have to be honest with you and say that I don't know anything about your childhood."

"Are you serious?"

"Yes, I didn't know you as a child, so how would I know anything about you as a child? All I know is what the chief has shared with me from his research. Of course I'm curious about Justin. He's my nephew, but just because you met him doesn't mean I know anything about your past."

"Yes, of course. I understand that, but Justin said he recognized a woman in one of my photos that I was allowed to keep with me. I had it posted on the bulletin board. He said he never met her in person, but he saw her in some photos of his dad's ... well, Ray's."

At this point, Carl was starting to sweat and wasn't sure where this was going, and he sure as hell didn't know how he would explain it to the chief.

"Okay, so what does this have to do with me? Or my yuppie friends?"

Fitz thought Carl was trying to make light of the situation, but he wasn't sure. He laughed just to ease his stress. Carl wasn't responding to the laugh.

"Well, I don't know. That's what I'm trying to figure out. Would you look at the photo and tell me if you recognize the woman?"

Carl was starting to sympathize with the kid.

"Sure, I'll take a look at the photo."

Fitz turned to walk inside, and the chief stiffened and said, "Sorry, kid, but I'm going to have to come inside with you."

"It's okay, Chief. At this point, I don't have anything to hide. Why don't you both come inside, and I'll dig out my photos."

Carl and the chief eyed each other to make sure they were both on board with this. The chief showed his gun to Carl. Carl was assured they would be okay.

They all walked into the house together.

The chief was starting to sweat. He needed to play the part, for everyone's sake. He already knew who was in that photo.

Chapter 75

Jeff sat in his hotel room, more relaxed than he thought Ray and Danny would think he would be, even though now they knew he was not usually alone on his business trips, which were few and far between these days. He still didn't worry.

The knock at the door gave him the thrill that he first felt two years earlier when he had reconnected with Franny. He opened the door, and there she was in a winter-white pantsuit with her long black locks flowing over her bright coat. There was just something about her that made his knees buckle. He felt so comfortable with her, and she was just so laid back—no games and no nonsense.

"Hi," she said with a leap into his arms.

"Hey, baby."

"I'm so glad you stayed a little longer, even if we only have the afternoon. We can have a bite to eat, and you can be on your way."

As much as Jeff wanted to throw her on the bed and peel off her clothes, she was just as happy with a bite to eat and spending quality time together. God only knew why, but that was just fine with him.

"I did arrange to spend the night ..."

Franny was elated but didn't want to look too excited.

"That's wonderful news. Then we can do both," Franny said, wide-eyed.

Jeff said, "Both?"

"Oh, I'm sorry. I thought you were thinking about throwing me on the bed and then taking me out to dinner?"

Shocked by how they were always on the same page for hardly ever seeing each other, he smiled at Franny and said, "How is it that you always know what I'm thinking?"

"Well, I am a trained professional." Jeff's face fell slightly, but Franny saved it by saying, "If I didn't care about you so much, I wouldn't know or care what you were thinking."

"Is that right?" asked Jeff.

"Oh yeah," said Franny.

Since it was lunchtime, Jeff said, "Lunch first and then …" Jeff raised an eyebrow and bobbed his head toward the bed.

Franny laughed and said, "Yes, I'm famished. I was hoping you would say that. I need to work later this afternoon, but it's nothing that you can't hear, so I don't need to leave you for a second."

"Thank goodness," said Jeff. "I wasn't wanting to spend a second without you today."

Smiling from ear to ear, Franny said, "What time is your flight tomorrow?"

"I am taking the red-eye."

Franny was suddenly so sad, and Jeff knew she thought he meant tonight so he quickly said, "But not until tomorrow night. I have a manufacturer to see tomorrow, so I will travel over to him for a late-afternoon meeting and then head over to the airport after dinner."

She practically leaped toward him and tackled him onto the bed. They stayed standing because Franny was just too small to knock him over.

"Where should we go for lunch?"

Jeff said, "Let's just go to La Cucina on the corner."

"Okay, good. Closer to the room," she said, while the side of her mouth perked up.

They walked out of the room hand in hand, and Franny looked at Jeff and said, "I'm really sorry about this."

Before Jeff knew what she was talking about, he felt something hard and heavy smack against the back of his skull, and it was lights out.

Franny and her partner, Joey, pulled Jeff back into the hotel room and hoisted him back onto the bed. She knew his crew wasn't going to go away without a fight, and that was what she wanted, but she didn't want him getting hurt once this all made its way back to the States. She figured if he was delayed getting home, the worst of it would be over and they probably didn't need him anyway. Also, she didn't want him getting arrested for no reason. This was so much bigger than Jeff, Carl, and their washed-up crime family friends. She wanted to be the one to take Elizabeth down for good, and their little game was going to lead her team right to her. If she had paid enough attention in the last two years of getting to know Elizabeth, she knew that by the next morning, Elizabeth would be in the United States if she was not already there.

Joey said, "It's confirmed that Elizabeth is back in the United States. She touched down there early this morning."

"Oh good. Glad we're on schedule."

"Yes, almost ahead of schedule, ma'am."

"Ma'am? Really, Joey? I'm not that much older than you."

"Yes, but I report to you, so you are ma'am to me."

"How about we stick to detective? Then I don't have to feel like a grandma."

"Okay, Detective. If that's what you prefer."

"I do."

"Okay, ma—I mean, *Detective*." Joey smirked, and all Franny could think was *This kid is going to break some hearts if he hasn't already.* She was glad to have such a focused partner.

"Detective, why are you looking at me like my mother on graduation day?"

She laughed out loud. He had quite the sense of humor too.

"Because you're a good kid, and I'm glad to have you as a partner."

"Aww, shucks! Thanks."

She laughed again and said, "Come on. We have a lot of work to do and a very long flight."

Franny felt awful, but they left Jeff to his nap and headed back to the office to get their things and catch their flight.

Chapter 76

"I need to get my computer bag and some paperwork from the office before we leave," I said to Derrick.

He didn't say much. The way he looked at me sent a shiver right through me. I didn't want to show that he'd gotten to me. He'd gotten me so good I could barely function. I started walking toward the home office to get my things, and he followed me. I looked back at him, and he very confidently said, "What? I'm supposed to protect you ..." I knew he was going to follow me all the way into the office.

We walked into the office seconds later.

I turned to face him, and he was so close my skin was tingling. I wasn't sure what he was going to do next, but either way, he wasn't taking no for an answer.

"So, we're all alone," he said while slowly running his index finger from my collarbone to the top button of my blouse. He cleared off the desk in one fell swoop, picked me up by the waist, and sat me down roughly on the desk. He grabbed the back of my neck and pulled me in to kiss him.

"I can't wait any longer," he said. "I need to be with you."

He leaned in, kissed me on my cheek, and gave me a quiet raspberry. I giggled. It was so cute. I really liked being with him, but I wasn't going to tell him that.

Derrick said, "I really enjoy being with you."

OMG! Did he just read my mind? What do I say? I was just thinking the same thing!

"Were you just thinking the same thing when I said it?"

I laughed and said, "How did you know?"

"I just felt it, so I said it. You seem so at ease with me, so I can tell that you enjoy being with me. I didn't know you were thinking it at that moment, but I figured as much at some point."

I grabbed his hips and pulled him in close to me. Wearing a skirt was a good idea.

"Are you sure you are ready for this?" he asked.

I was sure but didn't want to sound too desperate.

"Never more sure than right now."

Derrick smiled very widely, showing his happiness. Sometimes I thought he must be broken inside from all he'd been through.

He kissed me again, and I grabbed for his zipper. To my surprise, it was already down. His shirt was covering it, so I didn't know. With a breathy kiss, he muttered, "One step ahead of you."

I inched my body as close as I possibly could to his without falling off the desk. I wrapped my legs around his waist. His hand slid under my skirt. He was so soft and gentle. I was surprised. I knew he didn't want to be. My excitement picked up a little to show him it was okay to loosen up. He caught on pretty quickly.

Reaching for my undies to take them off, he realized I wasn't wearing any. The shock on his face was so thrilling to see.

"You knew we were going to do this?" he said.

I raised an eyebrow, and he smirked. His blue eyes sparkled with something I couldn't quite place.

I couldn't bear waiting another minute. I reached for that already opened zipper. Saying he was ready to go would be an understatement. He was bigger than I thought he would be. Nice surprise.

"What? You underestimated my manhood?" Derrick said in a mockingly manly voice. He put his hands on his hips like a superhero.

I laughed like a schoolgirl.

"Don't laugh just yet."

He slipped his hands under my butt to tilt it upward. He shifted his hips so we were perfectly aligned. I gasped in pure pleasure. I felt all of him. I let out a managed moan. He seemed pleased with himself as he leaned in closer to kiss me.

"You good?" he whispered.

"Oh yeah," I said, almost breathless.

With all the buildup, it didn't take either one of us very long.

We fell completely into each other, breathing very heavily.

"Why did we wait so long to do this?" he asked.

"Good question, but I think the reasons are obvious."

"Oh yeah, boss lady," he mocked. "Let's get ourselves together and get on with this *best day ever*." He smirked as adorably as always.

"Sounds good. You'll have to move so we can get out of the room at least."

"Oh yeah, I guess so. I don't want to let go just yet."

My insides were leaping with his adorable comment. I squeezed him in a hug and kissed him on the cheek. He kissed me back, and we pried ourselves off each other.

He put his hand out to help me off the desk.

"Let's get out of here."

Chapter 77

Demetri and Anna were headed out of town for the day. She always felt so safe and more than content with Demetri. She enjoyed sitting in the fine leather seat of his very high-end sports car. The tinted windows kept them out of sight from the general public, and she didn't worry as much when people couldn't see them. That day was different. It was publically acceptable for them to be together. There was no one on earth who would have a problem, and she was going to flaunt every minute of it. Demetri was so handsome, and Anna did a great job of keeping not only her spirit young but, most importantly, her body.

Demetri put his hand on Anna's as they drove to their destination. She looked over at him lovingly. He never felt so loved or more wanted than when he was with Anna. Now that he and his wife were separated with no chance of getting back together, this was the first time he felt this happy with Anna.

At the exact same time, they sighed and said, "This is wonderful."

They looked at each other and laughed. "Jinx! You owe me a beer," they said together. They brought out the hiding child or maybe teenager in each other. They felt so free and young again.

"So how do you foresee all this going down?"

"Well, it's not going to be pretty, but it needs to be done. It will only get ugly if she puts up a fight. Once the chief gets her to the station, we'll have a better idea of how's she's going to react and if she has someone working with her or not. We don't have any idea if someone will be waiting for her here or if she's working with someone here in the States."

"Do you assume she is?"

"It's hard to tell. I would think so. I can't see her coming home after all this time and not having someone to stay with or help her or at least someone her cold heart can abuse while she's home."

"Wow, you really have it in for her, don't you?"

"I don't necessarily have it in for her, I just don't like the woman. She was a coldhearted, crazy bitch back in the day. Obviously, with her upbringing, I don't think she would have turned out any other way. I don't think anyone can grow up in that family and not be coldhearted."

"You don't think she was that far involved, do you?"

"Anna, she was definitely that far involved."

"Do you think she actually killed people?"

"I am 100 percent sure she did. I'm not proud of some of the things that I did in my early adulthood."

Anna looked at Demetri, wondering whether she should be scared of what he was going to say. She was starting to become skeptical of how much she actually knew about him. He could see it in her eyes and shyly laughed.

"No, no, I never killed anyone, but I was in the general vicinity of situations involving Alisa."

"Alisa?" Anna said with a question.

"Oh yeah, I mean Elizabeth. I'm sorry, but Carl used to call her Alisa. She was named after a crazy old aunt she had. She would get mad when he called her that, but it was more of a playful mad. This aunt was the old man's sister. She got married young to some commercial developer, and he had a heart attack. She never remarried. She figured she never had to because he left her more money than either of us could imagine. She never worked, but she did a lot of charity work with the homeless and foster children. She never spent money like she had it, but that gave her the ability to volunteer and give her time to all those kids in need."

"Wow, she sounds like a great lady. I'm surprised—never mind, scratch that."

"What?"

"I was going to say I can't believe that Carl never told me about her, but then again, I didn't even know that Carl was married to Elizabeth, so why would he tell me that she had some crazy old rich aunt?"

"Let's try not to talk about him, especially because I'm falling in love with his beautiful wife. Well, I've been in love with her for some time now."

Anna got wide-eyed and smiled at Demetri with such awe and contentment.

"What do you think will happen to Carl by the time all this is over?"

"Honestly, with any luck, Fitz or Elizabeth will kill that jackass."

Anna was so shocked that he actually said it. She knew Demetri had always disliked Carl, but with some respect to him for being Anna's husband, he tried not to bash him all the time.

"I will be happy when all of this is over, Demetri."

"Me too, Anna. After all this time hiding each other, we can finally be together once and for all."

Chapter 78

As the landing gear touched down on US soil, Elizabeth thought this would normally spark a panic attack, but she was never more confident in what she was doing than right then. She knew Jeff was still in Italy and that damn special agent who tried to pass herself off as her confidante would be following her to the States. Jeff would soon follow. She was going to have to do her best to hide out and leave no trace of her even being in the United States. If anyone could go into hiding, it was Elizabeth.

She knew she couldn't stay with family so she decided just to get a hotel room. She had plenty of alternate IDs, and she certainly had enough US currency. She kept a boatload of it from when she was there so many years before. She had traded some of it out when the new crazy-looking bills started to be printed. She knew the old bills would spark some suspicion if she ever came back.

She needed to make sure the coast was clear before she headed over to the old homestead. It had been so long since she'd been there, but she would need some things before she set out on her mission. She would definitely need a gun, but more important, she would need some common clothing. That was all at the house. She paid a cleaning service to keep the house in order since she couldn't be there, and she had family members living there off and on over the years just so it wouldn't look like a scene from a bad horror film if she ever came back to stay there. She had made sure the house was well kept.

When she got off the plane at the airport, she was dumbfounded to see that the airport hadn't changed a bit since she had left all those years ago. As she made her way to the baggage claim, she noticed some updates and some decent upgrades.

She wasn't sure if she would ever come home again. In the back of her mind, she always thought she might have to, but she wasn't sure in her heart that she could bring herself to actually go back home. She wasn't sure this was something she would actually go forward with, but after all these years, she knew she had to get it done. This thing she was about to do, it wasn't like the old days when something like this would be a big deal. Now she figured no one would care. It was time to meet this thing with Carl head-on. She knew he would be ready for her, but she was going to do everything possible to catch him off guard. She was more worried about Jeff, Demetri, and that chief. As stupid as he looked, he was much smarter.

She felt her phone buzz in her pocket. She dug it out. It was the call she was waiting for and right on time.

Chapter 79

Carl walked into the house and shivered, not because of the cold but with a feeling that he'd been there before. The house looked like it hadn't been touched in thirty years. It was clean and well-kept but so old.

Fitz started, "I understand how all this looks, and believe me, my past doesn't help matters. I know you won't believe anything I say, but please at least hear me out."

Carl said, "We came inside with you, didn't we? If we weren't willing to listen, we wouldn't be here."

"Fair enough," said Fitz. He brought out a huge box of photos. It hit Carl again. He knew this box, but why? Or how? The chief picked up on Carl's reaction. It was slight, but he saw it. The chief was trained for this, so he was pretty sure Fitz had picked up on it as well.

Fitz opened the lovely flowery box of photos. This box was so old, it looked like it was going to fall apart right there in Fitz's hands. It was much older than the house. The box was the length of a Monopoly board game box but three times as high. It was huge and filled to the top with photos and some other paperwork.

"There's a lot here, and I'm not going to go through all of it with you, but there're a few things that I want to show you."

He dug out a handful of photos. Underneath those were a few newspaper clippings. Carl felt the blood slowly drain out of his face. He put his hand over his mouth to try to hide his reaction from Fitz. The chief didn't say anything, but he already knew what was happening.

"I know it sounds like I keep trying to explain myself, but I guess that's what I'm doing. I'm not trying to hurt anyone, and I feel like I'm losing control. I knew something was up with you, Carl, and I thought it might be related to what I'm trying to figure out. Again, possibly far-fetched, but I needed to give it a shot."

Carl said, "Why should we believe you?"

"You have to. I haven't done anything wrong. I haven't hurt anyone or committed any crime."

"Well, you falsified your records," said the chief.

"Yes, that's true. I'm not trying to hurt anyone, and I did all that so I could try to get closer to finding out about my past. There is so much missing, and the information that I do have doesn't make any sense."

Carl looked at the chief.

"Listen, Fitz," said the chief. "I've been saying that since I started looking through the records I found. There is a lot missing, but I just assumed that you could fill all the missing holes."

"You would think that I would be able to fill in all the holes because I actually lived it. I'm sure I can fill in some holes for you, but the people in my life don't make sense. You can ask me anything you want about my past, and I'll tell you whatever you want to know. The problem is that it doesn't make any sense."

"What exactly do you mean by that?"

"Like I said before, the people in my life don't make any sense. Some random stepdad that killed himself? My mother, that's a whole other story. Again, it doesn't make sense. That's why I want to show you these photos."

Carl was getting nervous. He didn't know what he was going to see in the photos and better yet what it had to do with him. He was pretty stupid sometimes, but he was starting to put some of the pieces together.

Fitz put them on the table in a pile and then showed them one at a time.

Fitz said, "The first photo is of some older people. I don't have any idea who they are."

Carl didn't say a word, but he was sure he had seen them before and possibly even met them.

"The second photo here is of a baby sitting on the floor playing. I'm not positive, but I'm pretty sure that's me."

"How do you know that?"

Fitz pulled out some old ratty photos from his pocket and said, "Well, this photo here was given to me by my aunt when I moved in with her after ... you know, and who knows if that's even true?"

Fitz was referring to his stepfather's suicide. He showed Carl and the chief the photos side by side, and the babies were identical.

The chief and Carl recoiled.

"So either it's the same baby and it's me, or neither one of them is me. Either way, they are definitely the same baby, but I don't know if it's actually me or not. The kicker here is the third photo."

He picked up the third photo and put it on the table.

"So now you can see my utter confusion and why there are so many questions. I don't even know what to say about this. The last photo might blow your head off if this one didn't already."

"Holy shit!" exclaimed Carl. "Are those triplets?"

"It certainly looks like it. They all look exactly alike, and they all look like me or like the kid in the photo that's supposed to be me. Even if this photo I have isn't me, how did my 'aunt' get this photo? What connection do I have to these kids?"

The chief looked at Fitz and said, "I don't know, kid, and sadly, this doesn't fill in any holes at all. If anything, it muddies the waters even more."

"Yeah, that's what I thought too."

Carl said, "I'm still not understanding what this has to do with me."

"Well, that's what the fourth photo should tell us."

Fitz put the last photo on the table and didn't have to say a word. Carl nearly passed out. All the memories flooded his head. They came back to him like a kick to the face. He looked at the chief and back to Fitz.

Fitz said, "Carl, since you are in this photo, maybe you can explain."

The photo was of Carl and Elizabeth—*together* and in this very house that he and the chief were standing in with Fitz. The chief eyed Carl very warily. He didn't want him to say anything in front of Fitz that could give him any more information than they all wanted him to have. They still weren't sure if they could trust him or not.

Carl raked his fingers through his hair and opened his mouth to speak.

The chief was ready for damage control.

Carl closed his mouth and didn't say anything. So many memories came flooding back to him about Elizabeth and their life together back then.

"I remember this day. We were here for a birthday party. Elizabeth had such a big family and so many nieces, nephews, and cousins I couldn't keep track of them all."

"So you know who these babies are?" Fitz looked at Carl with pleading eyes, hoping against hope that Carl could put all the pieces together.

"I'm sorry, but I don't know who they are. They weren't taken the same day. I've never seen these babies and certainly never met them. Listen, I know you're trying to figure out your past, but I don't think I can help you. I will certainly try, but these photos aren't helping me put the pieces together. I have to ask you this. How did you come to live in this house?"

Fitz looked at Carl and thought, *Oh shit.*

Keeping his gesture from Carl, the chief nodded at Fitz.

Chapter 80

Derrick and I got to the office so I could get caught up on some things. Since he usually worked in the field, I wasn't sure what he was going to do while I was at my desk working on the computer.

"Derrick, what are you going to do while I work?"

"Don't worry; I have enough to do." He winked at me, and my insides started jumping.

"We'll have to behave at the office, you know."

"Are you sure about that?" He gave me a playful, sad face.

I just shook my head and giggled.

I sat down at the computer, and he sat on the other side of my desk and set up his computer as well. I didn't know that was what he was thinking, but I was more than okay with it. I didn't know how much work I would actually get done but just being there was probably good enough for the time being.

I asked Derrick, "What do you want to do today?"

"I have some ideas," he said with a very intense look in his eyes.

I dared not giggle at this comment. I took him very seriously and said, "I have a few more things to do, and then we can get out of here."

"I was hoping you would say that."

My cell phone rang, and it appeared to be Jeff. It had been too long that he didn't bother to call, and I was angry. I let it go to voice mail. I felt a small pang of guilt in my heart, but as I looked across my desk at Derrick, the guilt quickly faded away.

I couldn't help but recognize that this was so effortless with Derrick. There were no awkward moments, no awkward silences. It was just easy. It was so nice. I knew this fantasy land wouldn't last forever, but I was going to ride it out as long as I could. My husband was missing but not really, and my children were thousands of miles away vacationing with my parents. I was here doing something I shouldn't be doing, but I didn't care. It felt so good to be free and alive again.

I wrapped up everything that needed to get done for the week, and I was ready to head out.

"Are you ready?" I asked.

Derrick said, "Ready to spend the day with you?"

I believe I blushed a bit.

"Hell yeah, I'm ready to spend the day with you," he said.

We were in the office alone. I walked around my desk toward Derrick. He grabbed my hips and pushed me toward the wall. He kissed me. He pulled away and grabbed my hips again. He moved in and kissed me again.

"I don't want to stop kissing you."

"I don't want you to, but we should probably go before someone catches us."

"Okay, if you say so," he said with his head hanging low.

He closed his computer and threw it in his bag, and we walked out together.

Chapter 81

Jeff rolled over with a splitting headache. It took him only a few minutes to remember where he was. He reached out to the nightstand to find his phone. He needed to know what time it was and if he had missed his flight. His phone was not on the nightstand, and he wasn't sure why he thought it would be.

Still trying to figure out exactly what happened, he knew it wasn't Franny who had hit him. Did she set him up? Did she have this planned all along?

This whole plan was unraveling right in front of them, and there was nothing they could do about it.

He sat up, got out of bed, and looked for his phone. He found it lying on the floor by the hotel room door. It was upside down, and he feared that the screen was shattered. He picked it up and turned it over to find the screen all in one piece. He was so grateful for that—one less thing that he needed to worry about.

He had a voice mail from Franny. He pushed the voice mail button, and Franny started talking in his ear.

"Hi, Jeff, if you are listening to this, you are obviously awake. I'm so sorry about what happened. I know you are wondering if I had planned to knock you out and leave you in the room by yourself, and again, I'm sorry, but, yes, that was the plan. It was a last-minute decision. Something has transpired, and I needed to get out of town—back to the United States to be specific. You might be wondering why I didn't just tell you. I know you would have argued with me, and I couldn't afford for that to happen. If all went as planned, I am already on a plane. If you don't completely hate me, call me when you get back to the States. I will see you there. Miss you, and please don't be mad."

Jeff was pretty pissed, but he wasn't as mad as he thought he would be. How could he be that mad at Franny? Every minute she was involved in his life, he felt more alive and reckless, but he didn't care.

He thought about home and wondered why he was being so stupid. He loved Angie, but he couldn't help but feel like he needed to do this. He picked up his phone to call Angie just to make sure she was okay. He just wanted to hear her voice. He'd know just by her voice how she was doing.

The phone started to ring, and after the fourth ring, it went to voice mail. He debated whether he wanted to leave a message. What would he say? What could he say? Nothing he said would make it better. He knew that now.

The beep sounded for him to leave a message.

"Hey, Angie. It's me. I just wanted to tell you I love you and it won't be long until we can see each other again. I'll call you again as soon as I have the chance."

He knew the voice mail wasn't enough, but she couldn't say he didn't call.

He gathered all of his things and headed to the airport.

Chapter 82

After Joey and Franny landed back in the United States, Joey broke away from her for a few minutes. He had planned this very methodically. He spent so much time on how he was going to execute the call and how he was going to keep it from Franny. Franny was a great lady, but business was business and family was family. He could barely stand the amount of time, just the few seconds it was taking for her to pick up.

"Hello?" said Elizabeth.

"Hello!" Joey said very enthusiastically.

"Hello, darling," said Elizabeth. "How was your flight?"

"Very nice. I upgraded us to first class. I couldn't bear to fly coach internationally."

"That a boy!"

"How was yours?"

"Very nice. I haven't slept like that in a long time. How's my best friend, Franny? Still clueless that I'm on to her and her real profession? The fact that I know she's a special agent and acting like she's my friend? She's ridiculous."

Joey laughed. "Well, at least you have me. You have me to report what her next move is so you can stay a few steps ahead of her."

"Yes, thank goodness for you, dear."

"Are you still on schedule?"

"Yep, still on schedule. You know where to find me."

"Okay, I'll see you later tonight."

"Sounds good."

Joey hung up with Elizabeth. He had waited so long for this day. Elizabeth told him it would come. He knew she didn't really believe it, but they talked about it a lot, so much that there was no way it couldn't happen.

He pushed and pushed hard. He pushed hard and planned most of this out himself. He knew she needed help to actually get it done.

Little did Joey know, Elizabeth had her own agenda. She planned on giving Joey what he wanted, but there was so much more involved, so much more that he didn't know. She knew he might be heartbroken in the end, but that was the chance she had to take. He would understand. If he didn't, she was willing to lose him to follow through with what she needed to do.

Elizabeth got her luggage and headed to the parking lot. She got the feeling that someone was watching her. She was usually dead on when she got this feeling, but she couldn't imagine who it would be. She didn't tell anyone she was even coming except for Joey. Of course, she already knew that Franny knew she was there, but Joey had her under control. The thought briefly crossed her mind that Joey might be double-crossing her. She couldn't rule it out as a possibility, but she had to follow through with the plan. She was a little out of practice with this life, but she always believed she was meant to do it, that it was in her blood. She was going to get this done once and for all and never look back. She said she would never look back again, but here she was back home.

She got in the fire-red sports car that Joey left for her in the parking lot. She was glad to not be doing this on her own. She just had to have faith in Joey. She would be really pissed if she found out he was working against her.

Her thoughts drifted to what she'd lost. She still couldn't bear the thought of what happened. She had tried to do the right thing and did her best to salvage what she chose to give up so long ago. The recent loss was so much to even take sometimes. Some people had so much courage. They were so much stronger than she was, stronger than she was even back in the day when she was really a badass. She was really good at putting up a tough front, but she was just a crying little kid inside. She was sure this last incident was going to put her right over the edge. Surprisingly, it didn't, and she was at peace with what had happened.

She was headed to her aunt's house. She wished her aunt was still living. They'd had such wonderful times when she was little and she would visit her. She was the cool aunt who never bothered to discipline the kids. She was so much fun that the kids all behaved for her. Even as most of the nieces and nephews grew older, they stayed close with her. They began confiding in her with things that they couldn't talk to their parents about. It'd been so long since Elizabeth had been back to the house. She was looking forward to a little peace and quiet before all hell broke loose. She planned on relaxing and finding some comfort in the good memories of the old days.

Chapter 83

Derrick and I decided to take a drive out to the lake for the afternoon. We wanted to be alone, and it was a beautiful day. The weather was nice and warm, and the sun was shining bright in the sky.

We pulled into the lot and threw a blanket on the grass. We plopped down like two teenagers ready to get into some mischief, even though we were adults just trying to get away from reality.

"Derrick?"

"Yes, Angie?"

"What do you think will happen by the end of all this?"

"Oh, Angie, I don't know. I'm not privy to anything that's really going on. All I need to do is make sure you're safe."

"Oh, is that what you're doing?"

I must have had a frown on my face without knowing it because Derrick quickly said, "Oh no, Angie, that's not what I meant."

"What?" I said.

"Oh, sorry. I thought that it sounded like I was only here to protect you, and that's it. When it's over, it's over."

My eyes got wide because the one thing I'd been avoiding talking about just came up without me even realizing. I didn't want to have that discussion with Derrick. I didn't want to even think about what was to come when this was all over. As fun as it was running around with one of the hottest guys I'd ever personally known, reality was going to set back in eventually—the new reality of my husband coming home, my husband whom I thought I knew but now knew that I didn't know at all. Then, of course, there were my children. Reality would be a rude, rude awakening. Maybe I could just put it off, the longer, the better. How would I ever trust my husband again? What would I do with Derrick? This situation, as effed as it was, was one of the best things that had ever happened. Even though I loved my family, this escape was like being young again, with not a care in the world, and being so much wiser made it all that more fun. When I was forced to join reality again, there would be a lot of change in my life.

"Hello … Angie? Are you in there?"

I had drifted off thinking about everything, and I was completely ignoring Derrick. It was like he wasn't even there.

"Hi, yes, sorry about that. I was thinking."

"About what?"

"Mostly about what you said. I was thinking about us, but I was really just wondering if you knew anything about this shitshow that is my life these days."

Derrick laughed and said, "You are so adorable."

I could feel the red start to creep up in my face. I knew I was going to blush, but I didn't care anymore. I was pretty much past the embarrassment stage with Derrick.

"You're pretty cute yourself."

He blushed, and he was even cuter than usual. I didn't know that was possible.

"Can I kiss you right now?"

I wanted to leap at him and say, "Yes! You can kiss me for the rest of your life!" I didn't.

"You don't have to ask," I said with a raised eyebrow.

"I was hoping you would say that."

He leaned in to kiss me and very comically pushed me backward. He was lying next to me, perched on his elbow with his arm around me.

"How great would it be if we could stop time for a while?" he said.

"I am all for that."

We kissed for a while like teenagers. It was a little much, but I didn't care. We finally peeled ourselves off each other, and he said, "Do you want to text Anna and see if she and Demetri want to meet us out for dinner? Or at least some drinks?" he asked.

"Yes, I will do that right now."

I grabbed my phone out of my purse and saw there was a message from Jeff. I didn't listen to it. I still didn't care what he had to say.

"I don't have service, so maybe we should start to head back?"

"Oh, already?" he said in a whiny but adorable voice. "How about one more kiss? Or ten or twenty or—"

I kissed him very sweetly and couldn't help but wonder what everyday life would be like with him. I quickly put that out of my head until he said, "The thought of not being able to kiss you anymore makes me sad."

"Uh-oh." Was Derrick falling for me? Falling for me like I was falling for him? What on earth were we doing? And why did either of us think this was a good idea?

He stood up saluting me, if you know what I mean. He looked down and then at me, and we both laughed hysterically. He put his hand out to lift me up off the blanket. I got up, and he threw his arms around me from behind. He hugged me, kissed me on the cheek, and said, "Let's go."

We got into the car and started to head back. Not five minutes later, I got service back, and my phone was ringing through the car. It was Anna.

"Hey!"

"Hi, Angie. How are you guys making out today?"

I couldn't help but chuckle at the unintentional innuendo. I glanced at Derrick, and he snorted out a laugh.

"We're good. How about you guys?"

"We're good. We just wanted to know if you guys wanted to meet up in a couple of hours for dinner?"

"That's so funny because we were wondering the same thing."

"Okay, great. Shall we meet at the house?"

"Yep, we are on our way there now."

"See you soon." Anna hung up.

Derrick said, "Does this mean I have to keep my hands off you for the rest of the night?"

"God, I hope not, but it's a possibility."

"Well, if that's the case, I better get my fill now." He sweetly put his hand on my mid-thigh and just left it there."

I thought, *Angie, you'd better get your head on straight because when reality hits, you are in for that rude awakening you keep trying to ignore.*

Chapter 84

The chief just sat back and kept his mouth shut. He wasn't going to get involved unless Carl needed him, and Carl was doing just fine on his own, surprisingly.

"Fitz, are you going to answer me?"

"Well, I don't really know how to answer that question."

"How hard is it to answer how you got this house?"

"I received a letter one day from an attorney saying that my old aunt died and the house was left to me."

"What?"

"Yeah, it was the strangest thing. There was always some confusion about my aunt. I don't think she was really my aunt, but supposedly, she was my mom's sister. Even that doesn't make sense because any aunt who owned this old place would have been old enough to be my mom's aunt. Something was never right about my whole family dynamic. It never made sense to me."

"Listen, kid," said the chief. "So are you saying that you don't know who you really are or where you came from?"

"Yes, that's exactly what I'm saying. The life I remember is not the life in these photos. Like I said, I don't know these people. My aunt seems to know them well, so how could I not know them?"

The chief felt bad for the kid. Even though he was a huge pain in the ass, he really felt like he was a lost soul.

"I don't know, man, but I wish I could help you."

"Does any of this look familiar at all?"

Carl tried to hide his concern about the familiarity he couldn't shake. He could feel that he knew these people, and he definitely knew the house, but the people in the photos weren't all family.

Fitz said, "I can see it on your face that you know something about these people."

"I can't quite figure it out myself, but I'll let you know if something comes to mind. How can we get ahold of you?"

Fitz gave Carl his cell and said, "Call me anytime. Chief, I want you to know that the records I gave you about by past are all I have. I don't have anything else that says otherwise about my life. I know it looks like I faked some things, but just because it doesn't make sense doesn't mean I lied about it."

"Listen, son, I can't say I believe or don't believe you, but I'll keep digging myself. If I come up with something that makes sense, I'll take it into consideration."

"Into consideration for what?"

"Whether I am going to charge you or not."

Fitz just dropped his head and said, "Oh, Chief."

Carl said, "We're out of here. We'll be in touch."

The car pulled away. When Carl and the chief were a few blocks away, Joey walked down the steps. "God, I thought they were never going to leave."

"I know, right?" said Fitz.

"That was a pretty good story you just fed them. They didn't show it, but I think you finally have them on your side. They may not believe all of your story, but they sure seemed sympathetic to what you were saying."

"Yeah, I think I put on a pretty good show for them. I played the asshole for these few weeks. Now I'm playing the victim."

"Well, it suits you," Joey said with a smile.

They looked at each other, still with amazement.

Fitz said, "I still can't believe you found me. I'm so thankful. It sure is crazy, this whole thing."

"I can't believe I actually found you, and who would have thought it would have been like this and in this town. With all my connections, it didn't take very long. I had some help, but it was like you were waiting for me."

"What do you mean, Joey?"

"I mean all the events in your life led you back here. You didn't know it, but every decision you made, good or bad, illegal or by the book ..." They both laughed. "... led you back here and put you in a situation where it was easy for me to find you."

"Oh, I see what you're saying. Like it was meant to be?"

248

"Yes, exactly. I think no matter what happened, our paths would have crossed."

"Yeah, I guess it was inevitable."

"Elizabeth will be here very soon, so let's get this place cleaned up so she doesn't freak."

"You don't think she's going to freak anyway?"

They laughed. They both knew she was going to more than freak once she saw them together.

Chapter 85

Elizabeth waited for the chief and Carl to pull away. She waited long enough to make sure they were completely gone to get out of the car. She got back in the car and decided to call Joey.

Joey answered the phone saying, "What's the matter?" Elizabeth was not supposed to be calling him.

"Why did I just see the chief and Carl walking out of the house and driving away? What were they doing in the house alone?"

If they thought she was coming, why wouldn't they wait until she got there? Knowing the chief, he saw her in the car. When Carl's radar was up, he could be pretty good at this life. There was a good chance he saw her in the car too. She knew there would be someone coming to scope out the place. They would want to know her every move. She would have to be as careful as possible.

"I'm already here."

"So you spoke to them?"

"Not exactly. Just come in." Joey hung up and waited for Elizabeth to come into the house.

Fitz was a nervous wreck. Joey kept telling him to relax, but he just couldn't. The plan was for him to be standing in the doorway to greet her. He had so many emotions running through him. He was so afraid of how she was going to react.

"Here she comes," said Fitz to Joey.

"Just calm down. It will all be fine once she understands what's actually happening and who you really are."

Elizabeth walked through the front door, and Fitz greeted her as planned. She walked up to him with her luggage and said, "Hello, darling.

How are you? It looks like your trip has agreed with you. You are awfully dressed down, aren't you?"

Fitz said, "Hi, Mom," and threw his arms around her. He tried his hardest not to cry.

"Honey, you are acting like you've never seen me before."

Joey came out of the kitchen to show his face. He wanted Fitz to have the initial moment all to himself.

Joey said, "Hi, Mom. Surprise!"

—⁂—

Elizabeth thought she was dreaming. She didn't know what was happening. She felt like she was having an out-of-body experience. She was confused but only for a moment until she realized what was actually happening.

"Oh my God!" Elizabeth screeched. She looked back and forth between Joey and Fitz. They looked so much alike that she didn't even know it wasn't Joey who hugged her. Of course they did. They were twins after all. She never thought she would have them in the same room together. She never thought she would see Fitz again. She was lucky enough to find Joey. Tears welled in her eyes, but she stayed in control of the situation.

"Come here, Joey. Come and let me hug you both at the same time." She wrapped her arms around the both of them. She didn't want the moment to end. Joey was relieved. Even though he told Fitz not to worry, deep down, he was afraid Elizabeth would freak out.

"We need to celebrate. I would love to go out, but we know that's not an option."

"Already ahead of you, Mom. We stocked the fridge. We can make a nice big meal and have some good wine. We need to all catch up after all."

The boys disappeared into the kitchen to get started.

Elizabeth was wary of this. This was when she would have to explain to Fitz why she gave them up so long ago, why she did it and what she'd been doing since then. She thought she would have to explain why she only wanted to find Joey and not him. She faded briefly, thinking of everything that Fitz didn't know, what she and Joey had orchestrated, the fourth and fifth pieces of their family. How would Fitz react to what they'd done? Would he do anything about it? Would he fight them on what was to come? Even though he was her son, she didn't know him at all. Was blood going to be enough to keep him on their side? She was very happy to see him but so skeptical of why Joey had brought him into this. She wasn't sure it was the right decision. As usual, she began to feel betrayed.

She needed to get Joey alone to have a word with him about what part Fitz was going to play in all of this. How was she going to get Fitz out of there so she could talk to Joey alone?

Fitz resurfaced and said, "I'm going to run out quick to pick up dessert. I ordered something that I think you'll like, so I'm just going to run over to the bakery."

That was much easier than she had thought.

Fitz appeared to be happy. He hugged Elizabeth and skipped out the back door to the car. He had been overjoyed when Joey found him, but he wasn't sure if Elizabeth was going to accept him. Now that he knew she did, he figured everything would be much easier from there on out.

Joey, however, knew otherwise.

Chapter 86

Jeff got settled at the airport and got something to eat. His flight wasn't for another two hours. Even though this wasn't close to being over, he was really happy to be going home.

He dug his phone out of his pocket to see if Angie had called. Maybe the phone was on silent and he missed her call. There was no message. There was no missed call and not even a text. Now he was worried. He was quickly reminded that if something was wrong, Demetri would let him know, and he hadn't heard from him either.

Now that he thought about it, why didn't Angie answer the phone? Why hadn't she tried to reach out to him yet?

Was it too late? Was she already pushed to the point where she didn't care what happened? Had he tarnished their marriage to the point it would be unsalvageable? He had to get home to her. He picked up the phone to call Ray. He needed to know what was next for this shitshow and let him know he was on his way home.

The phone was ringing, and finally Ray answered, "Jeff! You okay? Where are you?"

"I'm at the airport."

"What on earth is going on over there?"

"I'm a complete idiot. I got caught up in all of it and took a crap on my life."

"Yeah, that's what Danny seems to think too."

"I figured he already told you what was happening."

"Only what he knew so far. There is obviously something missing. The part where you didn't come back home with him because of some woman? What the hell are you thinking? Are you in this or not, and are you in love with this woman?"

"Calm down. It's not as bad as it sounds."

"Not as bad as it sounds? I think it's actually worse than it sounds. Tell me everything and don't leave a single damn thing out."

"There's a woman. I don't know what else to say."

"That's it? A woman, goddamn it! How can you be so stupid?" Ray's voice thundered through the phone.

"Yes, a woman. I met her about two years ago on a business trip. I did some stupid things, and I haven't been able to shake her since."

"I already know all this. You already told me yesterday! Okay, we've all been there, but what does she have to do with this?"

"Well, I was with her in the hotel room and her partner knocked me out. When I came to she was long gone. I had a voicemail from her saying she was already back in the States and would see me when I got back. We need to figure out where she fits into all this."

Ray's anger was now very evident. "Are you kidding me?"

"I wish I was. I didn't know until I saw her. Then obviously I realized it was her. It gets worse. She is in some sort of high level of law enforcement and is obviously following Elizabeth for other reasons than ours."

Jeff heard Ray throw something across the room. He was pretty sure it was the phone. Jeff just waited for him to come back on the line.

"How could you be so careless?"

"Listen, asshole, I met her before any of this came about. How was I supposed to know we would actually be caught up in this shit? More importantly, how was I supposed to know she would have anything to do with this?"

"I've seen the photos of her, so I get that you weren't thinking with the head above your shoulders. Have you given it the slightest thought that she was playing you from the beginning?"

The silence on the phone told Ray that Jeff was very naïve to the fact that he didn't meet Franny by accident.

"Jeff, are you really that clueless here?"

"Yeah, I guess I am. I never really thought about it. How would Franny even know all this was going to go down when we didn't even know?"

"If she's been spending all this time with Elizabeth to get close to her, she knew that she was going to pull this shit. She obviously knew we were going to retaliate."

"How, Ray? How would she have known anything about what we would do if this ever came about? There is no possible way she would have known that. Even if Elizabeth told her all about us, she wouldn't have known about the plan."

Ray wanted to scream, "What plan?" This was so out of control that they needed to reconvene and fix this shit. "Jeff, this is a mess now, and I'm not sure we are going to be able to get out of it. At this point, I think we should just cut Carl loose and let him deal with it."

"I would say the same thing. I'm exhausted, played, and I'm pretty sure Angie isn't even talking to me. I think she's gone from worried to not giving a shit at all in less than a few weeks."

Ray had been talking to Demetri, so he knew Jeff wasn't so far off in thinking this.

"Are you still there, Ray?"

"I'm here. Listen, don't worry about Angie until you get home and she gives you something to worry about."

"Okay, about that, I'm not sure what I'm going to do when I get back."

"What does that mean?"

"I'll call you when I get back, and you can tell me what's going on."

"Just come back to my house, and we'll talk it out."

"Where's Carl now?"

"He's with the chief. They are on their way back here. They were just with Fitz."

"Wait! What? Why?"

"They decided to scare him a little. Shake him up to find out what his problem is."

"What did they come up with?"

"They said he crumbled but gave them some sob story about his childhood and not knowing who he is and where he came from."

"So they didn't get anything?"

"No, they still have no idea what his motive is in all this. Elizabeth is home, but I'm sure you already know that. Do we need to worry about Franny?"

"What is that supposed to mean?"

"What I mean is did you tell her anything about all of this?"

"No, I didn't say a word."

"Okay, I'll see you when you get back. Come right here when you get back, and I'll make sure everyone is here so we can get our next plan together."

Jeff didn't want any part of it, but he said okay just to get Ray off the phone. Jeff could only do one thing when he got home.

Chapter 87

Elizabeth and Joey had some time to talk, not much but enough to regroup before Fitz came back.

"I'm sorry, Mom. Are you mad?"

"No, I'm not mad. Taken by surprise but not mad. I'm so grateful to have you both under the same roof. It's too bad ..."

"No, Mom, don't blame yourself for—"

Elizabeth whispered, "No, don't say his name."

"Mom, he was sick. I know it's hard to hear but he didn't have much time left. He volunteered to burn up in that car."

"What kind of mother am I to ask my son to die in a fire? Just to get revenge on his ..." She didn't want to deal with this right then. She knew she was getting soft, but this was too much. The older she got, the worse it got.

"Mom, please don't beat yourself up over this. We all agreed this is what needed to be done. He didn't know that Carl is our father."

Elizabeth turned her head from Joey. She was hiding something.

"Don't you feel like we betrayed him?"

"No, Mom, I don't. It's better that he didn't know."

"Why, because you don't think he would have done it if he knew?"

Guiltily, with a sheepish look on his face, Joey said, "Probably not. There is no way to know if he would have or not if he knew. I can say this though. He barely knew you, and he was so sick. I think he would have done anything at that time. He was going to die in only a few weeks, and he wanted to go out with a bang."

"Joey!"

"What, Mom? I know it's insensitive, but it's true. You know he wanted to be part of something bigger, and he never would have had that chance if we didn't approach him with the car fire."

"I guess so. What about … Fitz, is that what you call him?"

Joey laughed. "Yes, that's what I call him. What about him?"

"What have you told him? Does he know everything?"

"Yes, he knows pretty much everything. He doesn't know about Carl being our dad. The thing is, Mom …"

"What is it, Joey?"

"Well, I didn't want to read too much into it, but he already knew about you it seemed like."

Elizabeth looked at Joey very skeptically, shocked at what she thought he was saying. "What do you mean? How could he know anything?"

"It seems like he's been trying to figure out who he really is and who his real parents might be. He was sniffing around the investigation of Carl and that mess he created. I don't think Fitz is as stupid as he's making himself out to be to everyone involved."

Elizabeth looked at her son, so thankful that she was able to find him—even more thankful that he was willing to be part of this chaos. She was a little disappointed in Fitz that he even gave an inkling to Joey that she had already been in contact with him well before that day. She had to make sure all her i's were dotted and her t's were crossed. She couldn't afford to have all of this fall apart when she was so close.

"Did he actually say anything to you about the situation?"

"Not exactly, but he found some photos in a box that he thinks are him. He thinks he is part of the family that used to live here."

"Well, he is, and I don't think it's a big deal for him to know that."

"Mom, there are photos of you and Carl in that box."

"What? No, there can't be. There shouldn't be any photos of me and Carl anywhere."

"Here, see for yourself." Joey handed a pile of photos to Elizabeth.

She looked through the photos one by one. There were people in those photos she hadn't seen or even thought of in so many years—well, at least until she got the bright idea to come back home. She looked over at Joey, and for the first time, she truly wondered what the hell she was doing. Why was she doing this? Why was she lying to Joey? Why did she hate Carl so much?

He killed her father.

Chapter 88

Derrick and I walked into the house after a wonderful afternoon. Again, I was living in a dream world. Who knew how long it would last? I was going to absorb every minute of it.

"Angie," Derrick said with his very gravely voice. It sent a thrill right through me.

I turned around to see Derrick standing there, pulling his shirt off. "I'm going to get in the shower, okay?"

I quickly had to gather myself and push back the overwhelming desire to tackle him right there in the living room. I slowly smiled at him and said, "Are you asking my permission?"

"Ha ha!" He quietly laughed. "That wasn't my intention, but I can if you want me to."

"No," I said with a smirk. "I don't want you to. It sounded like you were asking."

"Oh, I'm sorry. I was just letting you know. Just in case." He slowly started walking toward me.

"In case what?" I could feel the heat rising in my face. It was like a shock of electricity was flowing through my body.

"In case you wanted to join me." As he spoke, he bashfully looked me in the eyes. One arm wrapped around my waist while his opposite hand cupped my butt cheek.

Oh my God. I inhaled a sharp breath.

"Are you okay?"

"Uh, yeah. I'm fine."

He kissed my neck once, and with that voice, he said, "You don't sound okay." He kissed me again on the neck, working his way up to my face.

"Oh yeah, I'm fine," I managed to choke out.

"Does this mean you do or you don't want to join me?"

I moved my head to face him, and he said, "Check yes or no." He proceeded to laugh.

I was so falling for this guy, and in the current position that I was in, it was completely ridiculous for me to have these feelings. I needed to snap out of it. I had some things to take care of before we figured out the rest of the night.

"You are so adorable I can't stand it sometimes."

"Is that bad?"

"Oh no! Sorry, I was just being dramatic, I guess."

"Oh, okay. I was worried for a minute."

"You were?"

"Yeah, not in like an I'm-falling-for-you kind of way, more of like, uh ... well, sadly, I guess that's exactly what I meant." He frowned.

What the ... What do I say to that? How can I even reply without spilling it all out there myself? Just keep calm.

"Well, that's a relief. I thought it was just me that felt that way."

Derrick beamed. His face lit up like a Christmas tree.

My cell started jumping on the island, and the amazing cute smile on his face slowly faded as I slithered out of his grip to see who was interrupting my dream land.

"It's my mom. I'm sure the kids want to talk."

"Okay, I'll be in the shower. Be back in a flash." He made a hysterical superhero gesture, and I was cracking up.

"Hi, Mom." I tried to have some happiness in my voice but also show concern.

"Hi, honey. How are you?"

"I'm okay. As good as I can be, given the situation."

"Yeah, I understand. At least you know he's okay for the time being."

"Mom?"

"What's the matter, dear?"

"I've gone through so many emotions during this mess and very quickly for that matter. I'm to the point now where I really don't care."

"What does that mean, honey?"

"What I mean is I'm not sure what's going to happen when Jeff comes home."

"Are you saying what I think you're saying?"

"Well, I don't know how I can trust him anymore. He's not exactly the person I thought he was, and I just have a feeling there is more to this than they are saying."

"Well, honey, I won't tell you what to do, but you should wait until he gets home to make any rash decisions. I know you are angry and sad and who knows what else, but know you are not alone. Your father and I support you in whatever happens, but just think about the kids and all you've shared with Jeff over the years."

"Yeah, I know, Mom. I've just felt so …"

"What, Angie?"

"Free."

By the silence on the other end of the phone, I knew my mom disapproved of my comment, but at least I got it out there. It felt so good just to say it out loud to someone who got me. She might disapprove, but I thought she expected it from me.

"I thought you might say that, and it's okay. We feel how we feel sometimes, and there is nothing wrong with that. There have been times where I could see that you felt like a caged animal, just looking to get out and be free. I know that's how you feel now. I can see it when I look at you. It's been long before this mess though. I don't think this has anything to do with it. Take a look at what you really want or need in life, and see how everything can fall into place."

"Thanks, Mom. I knew you would understand."

"I do, honey. What are you doing tonight?"

"Not sure yet. I think we are all going to go out for a bite to eat and then maybe something fun. What, I don't know, but something to clear our heads."

"Okay, honey, text me later. You know I'll be up all hours."

"Okay, Mom, I will. Can I talk to the kids, or are they in the pool?"

"Wow, you do know your kids pretty well. They are in the pool."

"Tell them I love them please, and I can't wait to see them."

"Okay, honey. Bye bye."

"Bye." I hung up the phone. I felt so much better just to get all that off my chest.

I got off the phone just in time to see Derrick coming down the steps. In just his towel.

Chapter 89

Jeff went to the bathroom. Then he headed for the newsstand to get some snacks and maybe a book for the plane ride back to the States. He was debating whether to get a healthy snack or just chips and candy. He couldn't help but catch his ridiculous question. His life was falling apart, and he was worried about his snack choice in the airport.

His pocket was buzzing from an incoming call. He dug his phone out of his pocket and just caught it on the fourth ring.

"Hello."

"Hi."

"Hi."

"Before you say a word, I'm sorry," said Franny.

"I know, but did you have to let him hit me that hard?"

"I never thought he would hit you that hard, but he needed to make sure he knocked you out."

"I get it but jeez."

"I know. I'm sorry. He is a trained professional, so I wasn't worried that he would hurt you too badly."

"Professional what, boxer?"

Franny laughed. She had an excruciatingly great laugh, which was filled with what Jeff thought was love.

"Okay, Franny, so where do we stand with everything?"

"So Joey is with Elizabeth. As far as I know, he has no idea that we are on to him. I spoke to the chief. He called me right after he and Carl left Fitz's place. Smythe is on her way over there now to watch the place. I know it's her job, but I'm sure she's wondering how she got caught up in this mess. Rumor has it that she's obsessed with the history of the McNamaras. That's

261

a good thing for us because she should understand a little bit about how Elizabeth might function from here on out."

"I lost you at Elizabeth."

Franny laughed again at Jeff. "Oh, stop. You'd better be paying attention to me. We are in this together, you know."

Jeff was now walking through the airport and happened to walk past some reflective glass. He caught his reflection for a few seconds and didn't like what he saw. He was so angry at himself for falling for this woman the way he had and letting it linger for so long. He never intended for this to happen. He just felt so alive with Franny.

"Jeff, are you still there?"

"*Yes*! Sorry about that. I'm here."

"Your flight is still on time, right?"

"Yep, so far."

"I miss you, Jeff."

Jeff stiffened. He missed her too, but he needed to slowly bring this thing to a close. He could not keep this going. It would be very difficult, but he was going to try.

"It's only been a few hours," he said it with the least amount of emotion he could muster.

"Oh, okay. Everything all right?"

"Yeah, sure."

—◁◁◁—

Franny knew something was wrong. Jeff was never that short with her. She figured he'd been through enough lately, and she didn't want to push it. She also knew he was married. They never talked about it, but she knew. It was her job to know these things. As confident as she was in her performance, he always wore his wedding ring. He never hid that he was married. They'd never been in the States together so she wasn't sure how that was going to work out.

"Okay, so I'll see you when you get here."

"Yeah, I'll see you, Fran."

She wasn't positive, but that sounded like a goodbye to her. She knew Jeff needed her until this thing with Elizabeth was over, but what was going to happen after that? She didn't want to think about it now. ·

Chapter 90

Demetri and Anna were in the café at the little table tucked into the corner. This was the only place they were able to meet in public, although that day was different. It was acceptable for them to be together. They had met there before. All the other times, they just needed to see each other.

Anna said to Demetri, "Do you feel even just a little bad lying to Angie and Jeff like we have been?"

"You know, I really don't, mostly because I know the truth will be coming out soon enough and all we can ask for is them to forgive us. I think, well, I hope, that they will understand once it's all over. If we weren't truly in love with each other, it wouldn't matter at all, but given the situation, I think they will understand."

"Yeah, I hope you're right, Demetri, especially because I put on such a show about Carl. It was painful, but I needed to make it look like I cared."

Demetri laughed at Anna's dramatic eye roll.

"What? Why are you laughing?" Anna asked with a smirk.

"You are just so darn cute!"

They were sitting next to each other, so it was easy for Demetri to kiss her.

"Okay, we better stop. Our visitor will be joining us soon."

"Okay, okay." Demetri put his hands up like he was surrendering.

"After this is all over, the four of us can spend more time together."

Demetri just looked at Anna emotionlessly. He was hoping she wouldn't bring it up. He still hadn't decided if he wanted to tell her or not. He wasn't sure what would happen, and he didn't want to put her in a bad spot. But he did love this woman, so he felt that telling her the truth was the best thing to do, especially because of all the uncertainty surrounding them all.

"Anna, there is something I need to tell you about Jeff."

"Oh boy, you sound pretty serious. I guess I should brace myself."

Demetri smiled at Anna and started with, "Well, I'm not sure what you are going to think, and you might not care at all, but—"

She interrupted him in midsentence. "Out with it already!"

"Okay, okay. So Jeff and Angie might have some issues when he gets back."

———ɯ———

Anna's eyebrows rose, and the corner of her mouth curled up with some worry. She was very careful not to say anything. She had a pretty good idea that something was going on with Angie and Derrick. She didn't want to let on to Demetri that she suspected. She wanted him to say it himself. He was Jeff's friend, and Anna was becoming very close to Angie. She didn't want to throw her under the bus.

Anna said, "What do you mean?"

"Well, it appears that Jeff has been having an affair."

"Wait … What? *Jeff* has been?"

"You say that like you're surprised that I said Jeff is having an affair."

"Well, uh, I'm not quite sure I understand." Anna was trying to keep her cool and understand what Demetri was talking about. She was sure he was talking about Angie and Derrick, but she was wrong.

"Jeff shared with me that he was traveling for work about two years ago and met a woman. This woman apparently lit his world on fire. He said she made him feel young again." Demetri was mostly telling the truth. Jeff actually told Ray who then told Demetri, but he didn't want to bring up Ray to Anna.

"Oh, so does Angie know now about the affair?"

"No, but Jeff is going to tell her when he returns."

"Which is when?"

"I don't know. Should be very soon, but I don't know exactly."

Anna just shook her head and shrugged her shoulders as if to say, "Yikes! We'll see what happens." She looked at her watch and started getting a little nervous.

Demetri said, "You seem nervous."

"I am a little. I don't know why. I've been looking forward to this day. I'm mostly looking forward to some closure and putting this behind us."

"I like that you said 'us.'"

Anna smiled and continued, "In just a few moments, we're going to get some answers, and as thrilling as it is, it's also very nerve-racking."

"You're right about that. We should get on separate sides of the table," said Demetri with a very adorable smile.

Minutes later, Anna and Demetri heard the bell on the café door ding. Their heads both snapped in the direction of the door. Their visitor had arrived.

Demetri stood up to shake Fitz's hand.

Chapter 91

I just stood there staring at Derrick, not with my mouth gaping open like I was wanting to do but just looking at him.

He said, "I forgot that all my clothes are down here."

"Oh, and here I thought you were trying to make me spontaneously combust."

Derrick laughed. "You never fail to amaze me, Angie. No one makes me laugh like you do."

We stood in what for most people would have been awkward silence but not for me and Derrick. We seemed to be able to just look at each other without talking at all.

He walked toward me, and that familiar heat started rising inside me. God, he just did something to me. He put his index finger under my chin and pushed up to tilt my head up toward his. We were looking into each other's eyes. He kissed me long and soft. I didn't want this to end.

Derrick's phone beeped with a text message. "It's Justin. He's coming over."

"Do you know why?"

"No, he just said he was heading over now."

"Okay." I looked down. "You'd better get dressed and cover that up," I said with a smile.

He kissed me again and disappeared to get dressed.

Minutes later, Justin was at the door.

"Hey, Justin."

"Hey, Angie."

"I was hoping we could finish our conversation?"

"Sure, Derrick is getting changed, but I'm sure you don't mind talking about it in front of him."

"Well, I'd prefer not to, but if I have to, I will."

"Okay, well, then let's hear it."

"Is everything okay, Angie? You seem to be on edge."

"Yes, sorry. I'm fine. I'm just trying to clear my head, just trying to put all of this out of it and try to enjoy the rest of the day and evening."

"Oh, okay."

"Hey, buddy, What's up?" said Derrick as he came out of the other room.

"Hey, Derrick."

"You guys look a little intense here. Should I leave you be?"

I said, "It doesn't matter. Justin and I are trying to finish a conversation from the other day."

"Okay, I'll leave you guys to it," said Derrick.

I panicked for a minute that he was going to leave, and then I remembered that he couldn't.

I looked at Justin, and he was fidgeting. I didn't blame him. I knew it was important to him for me to believe what he was about to say.

"So, Angie, again, there are things I can't tell you, but I will tell you as much as I can."

"Okay, I'm all ears."

"Getting mixed up with the family is the worst thing I could have done. Ray didn't want that for me, but it came so naturally, I think he was almost proud—not proud of me getting caught because I was reckless. In that business, you didn't get caught. You should lay low and act like you don't exist. I did not follow the rules. Fast-forwarding to where we left off with Fitz. He's a really great guy. You just need to get past the conspiracy theorist in him."

I laughed. It was funny. I didn't know that about Fitz. I just thought he was an asshole.

"What we believe is that the woman in the house was never actually raped. It doesn't make any sense because there was never anyone home when everything went down. She claimed that she was there, and she caught us stealing from her. It was a load of crap. We still to this day don't know why she made all that up. I admit that I was a total mess, but I am *not* a rapist."

"Justin, Jeff said the same thing. He said he never believed that for a second."

"The kicker, Angie, is that the woman never went to the hospital. She never had a rape kit done. She never had evidence at all that she was raped.

I had been in so much trouble by then, I didn't stand a chance against her in court. My lawyer was really good, but I think Ray convinced him to lose so I would go away. I think Ray thought that's what I needed to get my head out of my ass."

"Are you serious? I don't think that was the best way to handle things."

"I didn't either at the time, but looking back, it was the best thing to have happened to me. I can tell you I don't ever want to go back to prison. Ever!"

"Well, I'm glad it worked for you. I have to be honest in saying that I braced myself for the rest of this conversation, and it was almost a letdown."

"Angie! Are you serious right now?" Justin said, laughing at me.

Laughing myself, I said, "Yeah, sorry, but I was thinking you were going to bring much more than that."

"Well, sorry to disappoint."

"No problem."

We laughed together.

"Justin, I'm really glad that you are getting yourself together and trying to set things right."

"I have a long way to go, but so far so good. I'm trying to stay out of all of this as much as possible."

"Yeah, I thought you were supposed to be watching over us?"

"Yeah, I was, but Demetri swooped in and sort of cut me loose."

Derrick came walking into the room at just the right time. Justin and I were winding down with our conversation. I wasn't sure that he was really telling me everything there was to tell, but I thought the truth would come out eventually if there was more to tell.

"Okay, guys, I'm out of here. Later." And he was gone.

Chapter 92

Demetri shook Fitz's hand and asked him to join them at the table. Fitz sat down and looked at Anna. He took her hand in his and said, "I'm so sorry I treated you the way I did in your home."

They all had a good laugh. It all made a lot more sense. It didn't actually happen.

Anna said, "One thing I didn't like about all that was lying to Jeff—well, really, I didn't like lying to Angie. Wait until later tonight when we tell her what's really going on."

"Yeah," said Fitz. "She's a ball of fire that one, so who knows how she's going to react?"

"Well, I think she's past the state of shock. So I don't really know that you will get that big of a reaction out of her."

"I hope not. Maybe I won't even have to tell her."

"What's happening on your end?" asked Demetri.

"Well, she's at the house with Joey. Joey and Elizabeth are at the old house, and so far, she thinks that Joey is on her 'team.'" Fitz held up his fingers with quotes.

"Okay, so she has no idea that Joey is a cop working with his partner to arrest her?"

"No, she has no idea."

"Are you sure they are not playing you?"

"No. One thing this mess has taught me is you can't trust anyone and almost nothing is what it seems. I don't know of any reason why Joey would lie, and I don't think there is anything I can bring to the table for him."

"So the only reason he's after her is because she's planning on killing Carl, and she confided in Franny about it?"

"That's what I gather from Joey. The only reason he got me involved is to try to make her think we are one big happy family. We've been in touch for years now since he found me, so I don't think our relationship will change. At least I hope it doesn't. I like being in contact with him."

"Fitz, are you excited about going back to the police force?" asked Demetri.

"I am very much so. I don't like acting like I'm on the run. It's ridiculous, and I'm so bored."

"Yeah, the chief misses you too. He's got that Smythe, who's doing a great job, but I think he misses your antics."

"Oh, I'm sure he does. I'm going to ask Smythe to marry me once this shitshow is over."

"Oh my God, Fitz! That is wonderful!" said Anna.

"Yeah, it's time. She knows all about my past, and she doesn't judge me for it at all. She knows I'm a good man and that I will do anything to stay on the straight and narrow."

They took the rest of the time discussing what the next step of the plan was going to be for Fitz. He was going to continue meddling in Carl's day to day so they could all keep him off track. They didn't want him falling into a trap with Elizabeth.

It was also time for Demetri and Anna to let everyone in on the plan. They would explain it all later when they met up with everyone.

"Okay, guys. I'll keep you posted on anything new that transpires on the home front. I don't anticipate there being any issues, but then again, you never know," said Fitz with a sideways smile.

"Okay, buddy, sounds good, and maybe get a hobby to pass the time. It should all be over very soon," Demetri joked.

"Yeah, that's funny. Thanks for getting me involved in this and not leaving me out in the dark. I'll talk to Angie when I see her later on and apologize for my behavior at the office and with the employees. Once she understands what's happening, I'm sure she'll forgive me."

Anna chimed in, "She definitely will. She's at a point where nothing is going to surprise her, so no worries."

Fitz looked relieved and at ease that Anna was good with everything happening. It really couldn't have worked out any better. She had clearly moved on from Carl, and it was good for her. She was way too good for him from the beginning—at least he thought so anyway.

"I'll see you guys later at the house. You'll let Angie know I'm coming before I show up and she shoots me?" Fitz was dead serious. "She's a tough cookie, and I would prefer her to know I'm not crazy before I get there."

With a big belly laugh, Demetri said, "Yes, we'll give her a heads-up so she doesn't strangle you before you even get through the front door."

"Okay, good." Fitz stood up, and Demetri started to get up as well to shake Fitz's hand. Fitz said, "No, no, don't get up." He patted Demetri on the shoulder and touched Anna's hand. "See you guys later." Out the door, he went.

"He's such a good kid. It's a good thing he turned out so well. It's obviously better that he was raised by those crazy people instead of criminals," said Anna.

"That's definitely a positive way to look at his situation," said Demetri and laughed.

Anna said, "Are you ready to head over to Angie's?"

"I am but not without a quick kiss." Demetri leaned over to Anna and kissed her.

Chapter 93

"Derrick, what should we do tonight?"

"It doesn't matter to me. We can go out or stay in. Whatever you want to do. I'm flexible."

"Maybe we'll go out to eat and then just come back here?"

"That's good. Let's see what they want to do, and if that's good with them, then that's what we'll do. They'll be here in about an hour, right?"

"Yes, I should get in the shower."

Derrick flushed, and my insides started to jump. He grabbed for my hand and pulled me in close. He examined my face, which he hadn't done before. He usually just leaned in and kissed me, but this time was different. There was a lot of emotion in his eyes. I knew better than to ask. If he wanted to share, I wasn't going to force it. He kissed me slowly and softly. He put his forehead against mine and didn't say anything.

I waited a few minutes to savor the moment. I backed away far enough to speak without barking in his face.

I whispered, "I'm going to get in the shower." I wanted him to join me, but I didn't think we were quite there yet.

"Okay, I'll be right down here waiting for you."

He opened his mouth to say something and then closed it.

"Whatever you have to say, you can tell me."

Derrick asked, "How did you know I was going to say something?"

"Well, you opened your mouth slightly and drew in a short breath. I've seen that before. When you're ready, you'll tell me."

"You get me. I love that."

I smiled at Derrick. "I'll be upstairs."

I went upstairs and showered pretty quickly. I wasn't sure what we were going to do, so I did my hair and makeup just in case we decided to go out.

I dressed fairly casually for now, knee-length summer skirt and a little T-shirt. I could always change later if I needed to. I headed downstairs and heard Derrick talking. Demetri and Anna must have already arrived.

I got downstairs, and Derrick looked at me like he'd never seen me before. I made a silly face at him, and he laughed. Quickly, his laughter turned to a look of defeat. I was concerned. What could be wrong? Demetri and Anna were there so I couldn't ask him.

"Hi, guys! How are you? Did you have a nice day today?"

Anna jumped to reply. "Yes, we did. We didn't do anything special," she lied, "but it was nice."

"Good, I'm glad."

Demetri began, "Angie, I want to talk to you about some things. It's nothing to be alarmed about, and I want you to know that Derrick has nothing to do with this. He can certainly be involved, but he does not know what I'm about to say."

Derrick slowly slid next to me in what seemed to be a very supportive gesture. I felt protected. I felt like anything that happened, he would be there to help me through it.

Demetri continued, "So I want to discuss Fitz."

"Oh God, why? Did you find him?"

"Well, that's the thing. He was never really lost."

I stood there in much less shock than Demetri thought I would be in at this statement. Nothing could surprise me at this point, and I was about done with the whole thing. I was hoping I could just move on soon. Although what was about to come out of Demetri's mouth intrigued me.

"Okay, so what's happening?"

"Fitz was not fired from the police force. He did not set fire to Anna's house, and he is just in hiding. He's in hiding helping us figure out what is really going on with Elizabeth."

"What?"

Anna spoke up. She really didn't want Angie to be mad at her. "I'm coming clean also. There was never a fire at all at my house. It was all staged to make it look like someone, Fitz, was going crazy and he had something to do with what was happening."

"Anna, how could you lie to me like that?"

"Angie, I am so sorry. We started getting close before that, but then once I started staying here with you, we became much closer. I didn't know that was going to happen, and I felt awful about lying to you. That's why we're telling you now. We weren't supposed to say anything at all, but I

273

needed to come clean with you. I couldn't bear the thought of you being angry with me and losing our friendship."

"So when you say 'we,' you mean you and Demetri have been part of this since the beginning?"

"No," Anna said. "I was not involved until that day the chief came knocking on my door. He informed me of Fitz and that the fire was going to be faked. He wasn't sure I would agree to it all. I was already at the point of saying eff it, so I just said whatever."

"Oh, well, that makes me feel a little better."

"Fitz would like to come over and apologize if you are okay with that?"

"No, it doesn't matter. I don't need an apology from him. As long as he is working for us and not against us, that's all I care about. Have we decided if we are going out or staying in tonight?"

Demetri, Anna, and Derrick all looked at each other in awe at the fact that I could truly have cared less about what was happening with Fitz. I was totally checked out.

Demetri said, "Let's go out. I made a reservation just in case."

Okays all around and Anna and I disappeared to get changed.

Chapter 94

Fitz was now back at the house after his visit with Anna and Demetri.

Joey was pleased to see him back home.

"So how are Demetri and Anna?"

"They're good."

"How is Anna with everything?"

"She's okay. She seems to be good with everything that's going down. She's way more at ease now that she knows I'm not a lunatic trying to kill her."

Joey laughed and shook his head. "Who says you're not a lunatic?"

Laughing, Fitz said, "It's a stretch, but I like to think I'm pretty sane after everything we've been through."

"We both turned out pretty well considering."

"We sure did. Where's mother of the year?"

"She didn't say. All she mentioned is that she was going to visit an old friend."

"Oh God, I'm not sure anything good can come of that."

Joey laughed again and said, "Yeah, I agree, but Franny is following her, so we'll know exactly what she's doing. Knowing Mom, she'll try to lose her. The only thing we have to worry about is if she's out of practice or not. If she's as good as she used to be, then we should worry."

Now Fitz was laughing. "Yeah, well, let's just have faith in Franny. She is the best at what she does."

"That she is, my little brother."

"Little brother? By what, like eight minutes?"

"Haha, it's still funny."

"It's definitely funny."

Joey's phone was ringing, and it should be Franny. He looked at the caller ID and said to Fitz, "It's the chief."

"I wonder what he wants."

Joey answered the call. "Hey, Chief. What's up?"

"Hey, buddy. How's things there?"

"It's all good here."

"I know you are already aware that Jeff is on his way back, but I just wanted to let you know that's the story on my end as well. I could see this going south pretty quickly with just one person not following the plan. This has been quite the ride for me. It's been a lot of fun, but in the end, that crazy woman, no offense, could really screw us if we don't keep a close watch on her."

Joey said, "Yeah, Chief, I know. This has been one wild ride with everyone. I want to thank you so much for everything you've done for us."

"Hey, no problem. You are such good kids, and you all deserve what's coming. Fitz and Smythe is just wonderful. I wish them the best of luck. You and well …"

Joey knew what he was referring to.

He said, "Hey, man, I will be in touch once this is all over, but as planned, please let us know if something goes off the tracks on your end."

"Definitely, kids. You will be the first to know."

Joey always felt good when the chief called him "kid." He felt protected. Even though he didn't need to be protected, he felt like the chief cared about him more like a dad than a colleague. It was a good feeling. Now Joey understood why Fitz stayed on the local police force instead of moving on to bigger and better things. With his talent, he could have had his pick of any city. The chief was like a father to him.

As Joey was hanging up with the chief, Franny was calling on the other line. He finished up with the chief and answered.

"Hi. How's it going?"

"Let me tell you something. Your mother is quite the woman. She just walked in the coffee shop that Fitz was just in talking to Demetri and Anna. Listen, Joey, I can't help but feel like she's laughing at us. I think she's one step ahead of us."

"Are you serious?"

"Yes, I am. I can't see how it's a coincidence that she's in the same exact shop less than an hour after he was there with them."

"Well, what's she doing?"

"She's drinking coffee and reading a fashion magazine."

"Really?"

"Yes, really."

"She said she was visiting a friend, so she already lied."

"Well, she might be waiting for someone. I'll stay here and see what she's up to."

"Okay. We would all be lying if we said we trusted her."

Elizabeth sat in the coffee shop, reading her magazine. She knew Franny was outside watching her, and she didn't expect anything less. She needed to be careful. She had to plan out her next move. She needed to lose her but long before Franny realized she was gone. She didn't even want to cut it close. Her next visit could not be witnessed by anyone, especially Franny.

There was a back exit, but she thought for sure Franny would have that covered, so she needed to be slick in how she was going to get out. There was a back door for employees only. This was her only way out. She sent a quick text to make sure her ride was on the way.

She walked up to the cashier and said, "Hi."

She sensed that the young woman behind the counter was very self-conscious. She was quickly looking for a way to use this to her advantage.

The cashier said, "Hi. Do you need something else, ma'am?" with a pretty but shy smile.

Elizabeth had a plan, but she didn't need one after the few words that came tumbling out of her mouth.

"Oh my God! Are you Josephine, the world-famous fashion designer?"

Elizabeth felt her face flush unexpectedly. She was usually calm, cool, and collected. She was very taken by this young lady. Seconds earlier, she had been trying to figure out how to manipulate her, and now she was so pleased this fragile woman recognized her. But just as quickly as she was flattered, she was mortified. This wasn't supposed to happen like this. She was supposed to be incognito. She needed to calm down and think fast.

"Oh my, you know your fashion, young lady. Yes, that's me."

"Wow," said the cashier. "I am such a huge fan. You are just amazing. Decade after decade, you just get better. I didn't want to say anything before. I didn't think it could possibly be you."

Elizabeth felt flattered but old all from the same comment. This set off her ruthless side, and she thought, *Game on, kid.*

"I am dying to have a few puffs of a cigarette. I know the shopping center doesn't allow smoking on the grounds."

The cashier interrupted with a short laugh. "The employees go out back all the time. It's just me and one other employee working today. I'm sure she'll be fine if I let you go out there for a few drags. There is a customer exit. You will have to use the employee exit though."

This was perfect.

"That would be great. Let me grab my stuff real quick."

She grabbed her purse and jacket and headed toward the back of the shop. She thanked the barista and gave her some words of encouragement. She tapped her lightly on the nose with her finger and slipped through the door.

Her ride was waiting for her right there at the back door—out of sight from the back exit, where Franny had someone watching.

She opened the car door and climbed in.

Chapter 95

Anna and I were upstirs getting ready. I could tell that she wanted to talk to me. I wasn't mad at her. I was more pissed at Jeff for putting me and everyone in this situation. This was ultimately Carl's stupid plan, but Jeff was just as much to blame for this stupidity.

"Anna, I'm not mad at you. I promise."

"Oh, Angie, thank God. I was so worried that you were going to be angry with me."

"No, don't worry about it. We're fine. Once this is all over, we'll still be fine. I want to stay close. I know you didn't have anything to do with this from the look on your face when you opened that deposit box. Anything that has come about since then is out of your control."

"I'm so happy to hear you say that. This is one twisted mess we're in."

"It sure is. Let's go out tonight and have some fun."

"I'm all for that."

Anna and I came down the steps while Derrick and Demetri were talking. They both stopped talking as soon as we came into their sight. They were stunned. I whispered to Anna, "Looks like we still got it."

She giggled at me, knowing exactly what I meant. Even though Derrick had looked at me in the same way just a few hours earlier, this time, it was way more intense.

Derrick walked over to me and Demetri to Anna. Derrick behaved in front of Demetri. He didn't want to make this any more obvious than it needed to be. Demetri, in contrast, didn't care what was made obvious in front of Derrick and me. He kissed Anna right on the mouth, not in a creepy, get-your-own-room kind of way but in a very loving way. Derrick and I looked at each other, envious of their lack of caring who noticed.

We got to the restaurant and sat at the bar for a drink. I'm pretty sure Derrick didn't even notice the women. Every woman we walked by was staring at him like she'd never seen a good-looking man before. Even if he did notice, he never took his eyes off me. If they only knew this stupid mess I was in. Just the time I got to spend with him was worth it.

"You look beautiful tonight," Derrick said.

"Just tonight?" I teased with a raised eyebrow.

He laughed and said, "You are always beautiful, but tonight you are exceptional."

My stomach flipped in the way it did when he shot me his million-dollar smile. He was so freaking cute, and I was not sure he even knew.

"You look pretty amazing in that suit."

"Gee, thanks," he said in a goofy voice. He put his hands on his hips and turned his head to the side like a superhero. We burst out laughing.

Demetri and Anna were in their own world, which worked out for us. It gave us time to chat without worrying what we were saying.

A few drinks and dinner later, it was time to go home. We had a great night, but it wasn't over. We pulled into the driveway, piled out of the car, and walked into the house. Derrick looked at me with that familiar devil in his eyes. I'd seen this look before, and it lit my insides on fire. I needed to figure out a way to be alone with him.

Demetri and Anna disappeared together. Could it really be this easy? Derrick looked at me wide-eyed, thinking exactly what I was thinking. He walked over to me slowly. My insides were jumping.

Derrick wrapped a hand around my waist. The other was grabbing the back of my neck. He could be so intense at times. He looked me right in the eyes and then kissed me. This time was different. This time, he held on like he never wanted to let go. He was holding me like we'd been doing this forever but with all the excitement of a new relationship.

He pulled away a little and softly put his forehead on mine. He took my hand and led me up the steps.

"Angie?"

We heard Anna calling my name.

I fell into Derrick with my head on his chest. He hugged me.

"I guess we shouldn't have thought it would be so easy."

"No, I guess not," I said.

We walked downstairs together, and Demetri and Anna were waiting for us.

"Demetri, are those what I think they are?" I asked.

"Yes, they are. Is everyone in?"

I laughed out loud. "I haven't smoked pot since college."

Derrick's head snapped in my direction. "You've smoked pot? I don't believe it."

Demetri added, "She certainly smoked her fair share."

"I never would have thought that about you."

"Now you make it sound like I'm some sort of derelict."

"No, no, I'm just surprised. That's all."

Demetri again asked, "Who's in?"

"Light 'em up," I said.

Derrick leaned over and whispered in my ear, "I think I'm falling in love with you."

I nearly passed out. What a random, unromantic time for him to say that—thrilling but unromantic. There was nothing romantic about this disaster.

We smoked until it was all gone. We had so much fun just laughing and acting stupid. We watched an old movie about a bunch of high school kids who constantly got high. It was full of a bunch of no-name actors who ended up making it pretty big. The night was the most fun I'd had in a long time.

Chapter 96

Jeff landed pretty early in the morning. He had a decent drive back to Ray's house. He called Ray to let him know he had landed.

The phone rang, but there was no answer. Jeff left a voice mail.

"Hey, I just landed. I'm going to get my bags. I'll probably stop to get something to eat on the way back. I'll see you around noon. Call me if you need to tell me anything."

Jeff was exhausted. He'd slept a little on the plane, but the situation with Franny had started to hit him hard. He was going to have to tell her that he couldn't see her anymore. He was sure she would react calmly, and she definitely wasn't going to fight for him. He was pretty sure even if she wanted to fight for him, she wouldn't dare let him know she was heartbroken. He wasn't sure how all of this got so out of hand.

He kept thinking about Angie and how much he had hurt her. He'd hurt her so badly, and she didn't even know it yet. How was he going to tell her? Was he going to tell her at all? He didn't want it to happen like this, although if it hadn't, it might never have ended. Did it actually end? How was he going to tell Franny that he didn't want to see her anymore?

His head was spinning. He needed this to be over. His cell phone rang, and it was Ray.

"Hey, buddy, what's up?"

"So Carl is off the grid."

There was silence from Jeff's end. He was so done with this asshole and this ridiculous situation.

"Jeff, you still there?"

"Yeah, I'm here. For all I care right now, he could have killed himself."

"Jesus, Jeff, what's your problem?"

"Really, Ray? What's my problem? This is a total shitshow. Carl is a jackass. He got us all involved in this stupid game for what? So all of our lives could be thrown upside down? Now he disappears, and we're supposed to give a shit? Well, I can say that I no longer give a shit."

"Jeff, you agreed to be in this until the end. Why are you being such a dick?"

"Really, Ray? Why am I being such a dick? Carl is off the grid, you said. Was that part of his genius plan? Was that part of Demetri's backup plan in case Carl was too stupid to follow through on his plan? Was that part of the other ten backup plans in case Carl continued to fuck up?"

There was silence from Ray. He didn't know what to say. Obviously, Jeff was pissed, and he knew why.

"Is this about Franny?"

"Sure, it has something to do with it, but that's my problem. I made that bed, so I am going to have to lay in it, but Carl? That's not my problem. I am sick of this mess, and no one even knows what the endgame is. Where is this going, and what's the next move?"

"Jeff, you know the answer to that."

"Yes, plan ZZ, right? Who even knows what that is? Carl's missing, and we know that he wasn't kidnapped, right? Are you pretty sure he just went off the grid on his own?"

"Yeah, I'm pretty sure he just decided to do his own thing."

"So now we just sit and wait, right?"

"Yeah, I know it sucks, but we just have to wait for this to all shake out on its own."

"Are Danny and Justin there?"

"Justin's here because he lives here, but Danny went home to his wife. He'll be here shortly."

"Are you serious?"

"Yes. Why?"

"Nothing. Never mind. Where's the chief? Wasn't he just with Carl yesterday?"

"Yeah. He's at the station. He's the only one that is supposed to be living his normal life, remember?"

"Oh, I remember all right. Where's Demetri? And why the fuck is Justin there and not at my house watching over my wife? Wasn't that the plan?"

"Well, that's something we are going to have to discuss when you get here."

"Fuck it, whatever. I'll see you in a few hours." Jeff hung up on Ray. He knew it wasn't his fault, and he knew that Ray would understand his asshole tendencies on the call.

Chapter 97

I just ran through the house like a madwoman, trying to figure out how I got into my borderline sexy pajamas. What happened last night? Where was everyone?

I got back to the top of the steps, and Derrick was standing in the doorway of the spare bedroom. My heart skipped a beat. He was wearing cotton pants with a drawstring, which were sitting low on his hips, and no shirt. His crystal-blue eyes were sleepy, but they had managed to take all of me in.

He nodded quickly to the side, summoning me to join him in the bedroom. I quickly obliged.

"Good morning, beautiful."

Good thing I was lying down again, because my body went limp.

"Hi," I said softly but with confidence. He knew he got to me, but I didn't need to be so obvious about it. "What happened last night?"

"What do you mean?"

"I mean, I don't remember much about last night."

Derrick's face fell. "You don't remember anything from last night?"

"No, no, I remember all of it except how I got to bed."

"Oh, okay, well, that I can help you with. I put you to bed. I just carried you upstairs. You woke up. You went to the bathroom and got dressed. You came out of the bathroom and fell into me, and I put you in bed."

A wave of relief came over me.

"You look relieved. What did you think happened?"

"I wasn't sure."

"Did you think I—"

"Oh no! God no! I just—"

"You did think … Why would you think I would do that to you? Come over here."

I rolled into Derrick's open arms. He hugged me tight and kissed me on the forehead. I felt so safe. I felt like no matter what was going on in the real world, I just wanted to stay there forever.

He put his hand on my hip. He took his finger, dragging it over my skin, outlining my body. Just a simple touch from him sent fire right through me. He rolled onto his back, and without even thinking, I rolled on top of him. He grabbed the back of my neck and pulled me down to kiss him.

He rolled me over onto my back and inched my PJ bottoms down far enough to slip inside me. I let out a quiet moan. He was holding me tight. He pulled away enough to look at me. He made a funny face, and we laughed. I thought I heard the front door shut, but I tried to ignore it.

"Angie!" a voice thundered through the house, and I realized it was Jeff.

Chapter 98

"Holy shit," Derrick whispered.

"Oh my God! Why is he here?"

"Well, he does live here."

I playfully swatted at Derrick. "I'm going into my bedroom. Stay here and lock the door."

We peeled our bodies off each other. I grabbed my pants and slipped out the door. I tiptoed into my bedroom and ran into the bathroom. Jeff was walking through the house, so it gave me some time to get myself together. I put on some sweats.

I walked downstairs. When this first started, I envisioned our "reunion" with me jumping into Jeff's arms, kissing him all over, so happy to see him.

That was not the reality of what was going to happen. I wanted to crawl back into that bed upstairs and finish what I had started this morning.

I got to the bottom of the steps, and Jeff came barreling through the living room. He stopped dead in his tracks. It must have been the look on my face that stopped him.

He managed to choke out, "Angie."

"Hello, Jeff," I said, very monotone.

He just stood there staring at me. I knew he wouldn't have much to say. He could only say, "I'm sorry," and his usual lack of emotion would lead me to think he was lying. I was prepared for the emotionless words that were about to come out of his mouth.

I figured the less I expected, the less disappointed I'd be when I didn't get what I wanted, when he didn't actually try to make things better.

I couldn't believe what I was seeing. Jeff stood there with tears in his eyes, his mouth beginning to twist from holding in the sobs. He took a deep breath, clearly to gain some composure.

"Angie, I'm not sure there is anything I can say to make this okay, anything that will make it better. There is so much to say, and I don't even know where to begin."

"Well, start from the beginning." This was all I could say without losing it. Usually, my version of losing it would be screaming and yelling at him. I'd always been the more emotional one in this relationship. Now it was his turn. I didn't even know if he knew everything that was actually going on. I knew I didn't.

"Where are Justin and Derrick?"

"That's your biggest concern? Do you have any idea what's going on?"

"Just what Demetri and Ray have been telling me."

"What do you mean what they've been telling you? Haven't you been with them?"

Jeff looked away from me. I was starting to think there was a lot more to this than I had thought—maybe not more to Carl's story but more to my husband's. After what I had heard about Fitz, I knew there was definitely more about Carl's mess than Jeff even knew.

"Did you know, Jeff, that Fitz is working with the chief? He's not actually working against us?"

He just looked at me with a blank face. He was hiding so much. I could see it on his face. I didn't know what he was hiding. I'd never seen him like this, so I knew it must be pretty awful.

"Angie, it's all gotten pretty out of control. It's a mess, and no one really knows where Carl has gone."

I laughed. "Let me guess? He's missing," I hissed. I laughed again with a cocky eye roll.

Jeff looked even more defeated than when he got here. I didn't feel the slightest bit of sympathy. As the house usually made noise when it settled, I glanced at the steps, thinking of Derrick upstairs. My mind drifted briefly to him and what we were doing before my husband came barreling back into our home. The thought of Derrick even in this moment sent a shock of electricity through me.

"Angie, I'm going to go. I'll be back later tonight. We can talk it all out then. Is that okay?"

If Derrick weren't upstairs, I might have asked him to stay, but I wasn't ready to hear what he had to say. I also wasn't ready for him to be back full-time. This new freedom that I had was amazing. I wanted it to last as long as possible.

"Okay. Where are you going? Where have you been staying?"

"You won't even believe me if I tell you."

"Well, whenever you come back, maybe you can tell me everything."

"I would like that. I just have a few things to take care of, and then I'll be back."

"Don't rush back home." It was so coldhearted, but I didn't care.

I took a few seconds to push the anger aside, and I raced up the steps to Derrick. I peeked my head in the door of the bedroom. My legs were like Jell-O just at the sight of him. He was completely naked with just the bedsheet covering his lower body. He had a very approving smile as I walked over to him on the bed.

"How did that go?"

"It was interesting. This whole thing is a joke. I'm over it. I know reality will be setting in very soon."

"So about that … reality thing …"

I put my finger to Derrick's lips. I didn't want to talk about that either.

I crawled over closer to him and resumed the position I was in before the temporary interruption.

Chapter 99

Franny called Joey to let him know his mother had slipped out the back door of the coffee shop she was "hiding" in at the moment. She didn't know where Elizabeth was going. She was pretty sure whom she was with though, and that was the end of the line for Franny. She didn't know how this was going to play out. Her backup out back of the coffee shop ran the plate of the car she got into. It was 100 percent the answer that she needed to call it quits.

There was nothing Franny or anyone else could do now that Elizabeth had reconnected with her partner. This wasn't the way Franny thought it would go, but she had known it was a possibility.

"Joey."

"Yeah, what's up? What's happening?"

"She slipped out the back, and we ran the plate. She's definitely with—"

Joey interrupted, "Don't say it, Franny."

"Okay, Joey, I'm sorry. Is there anything else you need from me?"

"No, I don't see what else there is left to do."

"I'm really sorry, Joey."

"Don't be. There is nothing you can do about it. At this point, we are past the need for the law. I guess it's all true after all."

"Joey, at least you know the truth now. It should almost be a blessing in disguise." Franny wasn't quite sure what to say to Joey. This should give him some closure, but she knew it was a hard pill to swallow.

"Thank you for all your help thus far, Franny. You are a great friend and partner."

"Anything for you, Joey. If you need anything else, just say the word, and please just let it go from here. I know it's hard, but there is nothing else we can do."

"Yeah, as much as I want to seek her out, I know this is the end of the road—that is, if I want to stay on the straight and narrow. It's tempting to pursue it, but if what we think is happening is, there is nothing I can do about it."

"It's true, and there is no sense in fighting it. I get that you might need to talk to her, but wait until she reaches out to you. Be prepared that she might not but also be prepared if she does."

"Okay, Franny. Thank you again for everything. I'll see you back at the office on Monday."

"Sounds good, Joey. Tell Fitz I said hello, and I'm so proud of the both of you for who you've become."

"Okay, I'll see you."

"Hey, I'll stay close just in case."

"Thanks, Franny."

Franny hung up, but she wasn't convinced that Joey was going to leave it alone. She hoped he would, but she wasn't sure that was going to happen.

As Elizabeth opened the car door, her stomach was upside down. She was perfectly fine up until this point and almost lost it.

"Hello, Alisa. How I've missed you, you crazy bitch."

"Hello, you stupid asshole. I don't think I've missed you at all."

"Right back at it we are after all this time," said Carl to his estranged wife.

"Just drive. Let's go talk to our children. What's left of them."

"Yes, dear."

Carl and Elizabeth pulled up in front of the house where they had spent some time so many years ago. He wasn't sure how all this was going to go down, but it was time to get it all out in the open.

They walked in the back door, and Joey and Fitz both greeted them with guns drawn. Carl looked at Elizabeth like "What the hell. What are you trying to pull?"

She looked at Carl and said, "Calm down. This isn't my doing. I will explain."

Fitz and Joey both looked at Elizabeth and in sync said, "Mom?"

"Put the guns down, boys. It's just us."

"Us?" said Fitz. "Are you for real?"

"Let's put the guns down so we can all talk."

"Us? We?" Joey said. "What are you talking about? Did you play us?"

"I wouldn't say that we played you. We just wanted to protect you."

"From who? This crazy bastard was supposed to be the enemy."

"Yeah, about that. This crazy bastard is your father."

Joey and Fitz just stood there with their mouths gaping open, guns still drawn, and now they were eyeing Carl like he was a lion just let out of its cage. Even though Carl looked scared shitless, the boys were trained professionals. It was going to take them a few seconds to adjust to the situation.

Fitz finally muttered, "Father? Sorry, but how is that possible?"

"So Carl and I were married a long time ago. I left on some very bad terms, and he never even knew I was pregnant with the three of you."

Joey and Fitz eyed Carl when Elizabeth mentioned the *three* of them. Elizabeth picked up on the concern.

"Carl knows about your brother. It was Carl's suggestion that he sacrifice his life for us."

"What kind of person are you? Who wants their own child dead just to advance themselves?"

"We all know he was sick, and he had been going on about how he didn't want to suffer any longer. That awful disease he had decreased his quality of life horribly. You were both okay with it, and now because you know I was involved, all of a sudden, it's not okay? That's a little hypocritical, don't you think?"

Fitz blurted out, "You are a walking hypocrite 'Dad.'"

"That's enough, everyone." Elizabeth stepped in before they all killed each other. "I know this is a terribly awkward situation for all of us. Carl and I are obviously to blame for all of this and everything you boys have been through."

Carl eyed Elizabeth in defense.

"Just to clear the air here. This is actually your fault. I never even knew you were pregnant. You didn't even give me a chance to know my boys. Then you shipped them off like they were unwanted dogs. You didn't keep any of them."

Joey interjected. "Wait! You didn't even know we existed?"

"No, Joey, mother of the year left without a word, and I never knew she was pregnant. Never mind with three of you. And all boys, no less."

"That's not fair, Carl."

"How can you say that? It wasn't fair to me, especially after everything else that happened."

"Don't even bring it up. You're lucky you yourself are still alive after what you did."

Carl pulled a letter out of his pocket. It was weathered and clearly very old, certainly older than the boys.

"You need to read this. You refused to listen to me. You refused to hear the truth about what actually happened, Elizabeth!"

Carl handed the letter to Elizabeth. She unfolded this very old piece of paper. Tears filled her eyes at the sight of her father's handwriting.

Chapter 100

My phone was ringing, and I didn't want to answer it. I didn't care to know who it was because I didn't want to be bothered. I picked it up off the nightstand.

With a finger swipe, there was my mom on the other end. "Hello."

"Hi, honey. I thought I would have heard from you earlier today."

Just those simple words sent so much guilt through me. She had my children, and I was recklessly living life like they didn't exist.

"Hi, Mom! How is everyone?"

"We're all good. We are coming home tomorrow. What's happening there? Shall I bring the kids home to you when we get back?"

I was typically a very practical woman who did the right thing. There was no reason for the kids not to come home. No one was in danger, and everything was out in the open now. I looked over at Derrick, and my heart sank. I knew this was stupid, but I was falling recklessly head over heels for this guy.

"Angie, are you there?"

My mom's voice brought me back to reality.

"Yes, Mom, I'm here."

"Angie, you sound preoccupied. I'll leave you be once you let me know what to do with your children." My mom had a very stern tone now. She was a very intelligent woman. She could see right through the silence on my end of the phone.

"I'm sorry, Mom. Yes, please bring them here when you get back." I was watching Derrick the whole time I was on the phone. This comment forced his smile to race off his face.

"Okay, honey. We'll see you tomorrow. I'll text you where we are and what's happening throughout the day."

Good thing the conversation with my mom was coming to an end. Anna was calling, and I didn't want to miss her. I did, however, want to go to Derrick before he got up, got dressed, and ran out of there like his ass was on fire.

"Okay, Mom. Thank you, and I'll see you tomorrow."

She was gone, and I answered Anna.

"Hey, lady! What's up?"

"Demetri and I are coming over."

"I guess I didn't even realize you left." I laughed. "When are you coming over?"

"We'll be there in about an hour. We figured you would need some time to get ready. I'm sure Derrick could use a shower too," she whispered.

I'm sure I blushed. Derrick saw it all over my face.

"Uh yeah, okay, sounds good."

"He's right there in front of you, isn't he? Now you're trying to hide your flushed face from him." Anna was laughing.

"See you soon. Goodbyyye." I needed to get her off the phone.

"Was that Anna?"

"Yes. They are on their way over here. She said they'll be here in about an hour."

"What else did she say?"

"Why?"

"Your facial expression gave it away."

We sat in silence for a little while until he said, "So the kids are coming back tomorrow?"

I wanted to ignore the question, but I knew I couldn't. "Yes, they are." I bobbed my head, and the side of my mouth curled. I quickly changed the subject. "I'm going to jump in the shower quickly so I'll be ready when Demetri and Anna get here."

"Okay, you know we are going to have to talk at some point." I was hoping to avoid that comment by changing the subject, but it didn't work.

"I know." My face hardened, and I was shocked at the overwhelming urge to fall into his arms and cry. "We still have tonight."

"We do. We should make the best of it."

—❦—

I got out of the shower and got ready. Derrick was ready before me, of course, because he was a guy and they were ready in fifteen minutes.

I was ready just in time for Demetri and Anna to walk through the front door. Hugs and kisses all around, and Derrick and Demetri shook hands.

"So what's going on? You guys have an update for us?"

Demetri said, "We do," as Anna walked past me and into my home office.

Anna walked back into the kitchen, where we were all standing. She held the safe-deposit box.

"Oh boy." This was going to be interesting.

"There is a lot of paperwork in this box, some I've already seen before I got into the box and some I've never seen before. I'm sharing these with you all so that you can understand exactly what's happening here."

We all rifled through the newspaper articles, the letter that Carl had written to Anna, and the letter that Elizabeth had written to Carl. I was mostly taken by the gun hiding under all the papers.

I questioned, "What's the gun about?"

"That's where it gets a little confusing. Well, it's not confusing at all, but I could see how it could get confusing."

"Do I need to sit down for this? Derrick, do you know what Anna is about to say?"

"No, Angie, I don't know what's happening. In fact, Demetri, do you want me to step out for this?"

"No, Derrick. You can hear all of this."

Anna continued, "Carl killed Elizabeth's father. Elizabeth vowed to make Carl pay for killing him. The question is why did Carl kill the old man? In this pile of shit, there is a letter from the old man to Carl asking him to kill him. He had stage-four lung cancer, and he didn't want to suffer through a treatment that would end up killing him anyway."

"Jesus," muttered Derrick.

"So if Elizabeth knows this, why is she still trying to kill Carl?" I asked.

"Well, that's the kicker. Fitz, as I told you, is on the up-and-up and not crazy like we thought he was. Elizabeth was pregnant when she 'died.'"

"What do you mean she died? What does Fitz have to do with Elizabeth?" asked Derrick.

Anna laughed because it was all so ridiculous. She continued, "They faked her death so she could start a new life. She was pregnant when she left, and Carl never knew. She had triplets. She gave all of them up for adoption. She was young and didn't want any part of being a single mom. Fitz is one of the triplets."

There was silence around the room.

"What? This just keeps getting better," I muttered.

Demetri spoke up. "So the latest is that Carl is now gone."

"What do you mean gone?" asked Derrick.

"He hasn't been in contact with anyone in the last twenty-four hours. He's supposed to be checking in, but we haven't heard from him."

"No shit," said Derrick. "So he's actually missing this time?"

I laughed. "Oh, the irony. So we are pretty much free of this nonsense?"

"For the most part," said Demetri. "We aren't looking for him. He's off the grid on purpose."

"Anna, are you okay?"

She looked at Demetri, and he put his arm around her. "Never been better."

I looked over at Derrick, and while I saw on his face that he was happy for them, his eyes showed sadness for our future.

Chapter 101

Carl was clearly pissed at Elizabeth, which was nothing new, but now the boys were getting angry.

Elizabeth was reading the letter, and the sobbing was getting worse. She was clearly very upset. Then Fitz wanted to comfort her, but with the new knowledge he had about her leaving them, he trusted her even less than he did before. They were never really on her side, but it felt good to have a real parent in their lives.

"I don't understand."

"What don't you understand, Elizabeth? It's all there in black and white, right from your father."

She just collapsed on the kitchen chair.

"You never wanted to hear the real story. You shut me out after everything happened and left. I didn't know where you were or what happened to you. You could have actually been dead for all I knew."

"Yeah, that whole faking your death thing was a little much, don't you think?" asked Fitz.

"It was all so overwhelming, and I didn't know what to do."

"You should have just talked to me about it all. We could have done it together, but instead, you left me here with your crazy family, not to mention the house. We had that big, beautiful new house, and you left me in it all alone."

"Carl, I loved that house. It was such a pretty shade of yellow."

"I know; we picked it together. It wasn't my favorite, but you loved it, and I didn't want to say no."

Carl and Elizabeth were looking at each other like long-lost lovers. Fitz and Joey looked at each other like "Now what?" They were there because they thought these two were going to try to kill each other. Now it looked like they needed to get a room.

"I hate to break up this wonderful family reunion, but I think it's time I head out," said Fitz very sarcastically.

Joey didn't argue. He just said, "Yeah, me too."

—— *m* ——

Fitz was very pleased to be mostly freed of this ridiculous spectacle of crime. He couldn't wait to get home to Smythe and return to the police station. This feeling of unease was getting to him. Even though he knew it was all going to work out in the end, there was always that small piece of doubt in the back of his mind, making him believe that this was going to end very badly.

Fitz called Joey.

"Hey, I'm so glad to be out of there."

"Yeah, man, me too. It really is a wonder how we turned out the way we did."

"I know. They are a mess."

"Isn't that the truth?"

"Joey, do you think this is all going to work out the way it's supposed to?" Fitz asked very skeptically.

"Fitz, at this point, I think it has to. We need to just do our best and stay on top of everyone. It should be easier now for you since you'll be back at work. You can watch everything from out in the open now instead of like a fugitive."

"Ha! Yeah, I guess that's true."

"We need to make sure that Anna does her part, and Demetri is on top of her. He says she's still on pace to do what we need her to do."

"Okay, that's good to hear for now. Do you know when she's going to do that?"

"Supposedly tomorrow."

"Oh."

Joey could hear Fitz frown on the other end.

"I was hoping to sleep in."

"Haha, that's funny."

Fitz laughed. "Okay, buddy, I'll see you soon."

Chapter 102

We all stood there sort of staring at one another, wondering what was next. A very big part of me didn't want any of this to end, but I knew by the next day, when the kids came home, I would have to deal with all of this once and for all. I didn't know where Jeff went after he left this morning, and I hadn't even tried to call him. I did have that night with Derrick, and that made me happy, certainly much happier than I should have been at this point in my life.

"There are a few things that I need to take care of tomorrow," said Anna. "I will be in touch with you, Angie. I'll let you know what's happening with me."

"Please do. I want to make a habit of spending time together."

"I will. I've packed up all my things so we will be heading out now. We will be staying at Demetri's. Even though my house didn't actually go up in flames, I don't want to go back there ever again. I know I have to, but I don't have to go today or tomorrow. I'll go when I'm ready to clean it all out and sell it."

Demetri and Anna left. Derrick and I were together for the night. My heart leaped, and my stomach flipped. I was like a schoolgirl once again.

The door closed behind Anna and Demetri. Derrick was already in my personal space. The ease of being able to let go and not having to hide was exhilarating. I could enjoy every bit of him without my head getting in the way.

He kissed me softly and pawed at me like a cat. It was adorable.

He pulled away and looked at me with a concerned brow. "What do you think Anna is going to do tomorrow?"

"I don't know."

"Do you think she's going to file for divorce?"

"Can you divorce someone that's missing?"

"Ha! Angie, you're funny."

Derrick slid his fingers through my hair and pulled me in to kiss me. "What are you doing for the next few hours?"

I raised a playful eyebrow and smiled at him. I had an odd ticklish spot that he seemed to have found in the last week. His hand crept slowly over to that spot, and I giggled. He swept me off my feet and carried me up the steps to his temporary bedroom.

Chapter 103

Franny was in her apartment, wondering how this whole thing was going to end. She had a bad feeling. It didn't seem possible that it could end any other way than badly. Her doorbell rang, and she jumped to get it.

"Hi," she said as she opened the door to let Jeff inside.

"Hey, beautiful."

"I couldn't wait to see you. I'm happy this mess is coming to an end."

Jeff did not seem happy to see Franny, so she knew what was coming next. She braced herself for what he was about to say.

"Franny, we need to talk."

"I know, Jeff," she snapped.

Jeff looked at her sadly, knowing that she was upset.

"I'm sorry. I've just been dreading this conversation."

"I know, babe. It's not easy, and the whole thing sucks. I got myself into this, and we need to talk it out together."

Franny was surprised. If he was going to break it off, what was there for them to discuss together. She got her hopes up. She cared for Jeff so much. She knew it was wrong, but she didn't care.

"I've been thinking about all of this, and the right thing to do is sit here and tell you I can't see you anymore. We both know it's the right thing to do, and yet I can't seem to actually say the words."

"Well, you sort of already did," said Franny with a comforting smile.

"Leave it to you to make me feel better about being an asshole."

She smiled at him and put her hand on his face. Tears pricked the sides of her eyes. "I don't want to let go of you. It just hurts."

"I know it does, and I'm sorry I even put you in this position."

"Don't blame yourself, Jeff. The way we met was so crazy. What were the odds of us meeting the way we did or at all for that matter?"

"I often think that it was somehow planned for us to meet the way we did. We met in a foreign country while you were infiltrating Elizabeth's life. Meanwhile, I'm directly connected to Carl and ended up right in the middle of this mess with Carl and Elizabeth. It's crazy, but it crossed my mind a few times that you set it all up to meet me like that. That was the only way I could accept that such a beautiful, loving, caring woman would be put in my life. I didn't want to believe it was a coincidence. Why would I be put in such a position to have to deny you and test my marriage?"

Tears were now rolling down Franny's face.

"You're even beautiful when you cry," said Jeff.

He continued, "I would be a coward to say that I know Angie is more than pissed at me, and I'm pretty sure she's checked out of our marriage. I would love to sit here and say, 'Hey, let me see if my wife still wants me, and if not, I'll come back to you.'" Jeff was hopeful that Franny would think that was a good idea, but he knew he could never do that to her.

Franny laughed. "Yeah, I still have some self-respect."

They sat together and talked for a while about everything. They reminisced about all the things they had done in the two short years they had been seeing each other—the sights they had seen and all the things they had done that they shouldn't have.

"Franny, I should probably go."

"Where are you going to go?" As the question slid off her tongue, she realized that she didn't want to hear the answer, but it was too late. She had said it, and he was already answering even though she knew the answer.

"I'll just go back to Ray's for tonight and then deal with everything else at home in the morning."

This was not the answer she expected, but it left the door open for her to ask, "Why don't you stay here for a little while?"

Jeff looked at Franny, and that was all he wanted to do. He didn't want to be anywhere else but there with her at that moment. He would even take it as far as staying with her for the night. It was a terrible idea, but he would definitely give in if she wanted him to stay.

"Just stay here with me."

"Well, you don't have to ask again."

Jeff stayed against his better judgment. He would deal with his mess of a life tomorrow, but for right then, he just wanted to be with Franny.

Joey nodded off on the couch. He woke up and realized he'd been asleep for two hours. He had left Franny a message earlier. He was pretty sure they were going to have to deal with Elizabeth sooner than next week. He grabbed his phone, thinking that maybe he had missed Franny's call while he was asleep. There were no missed calls, texts, or messages. He found her name and dialed.

"Hello," said Franny in a whisper.

"Hey, are you okay?"

"Yeah, Joey, I'm fine."

"That doesn't sound too convincing."

Franny huffed a quick laugh.

"Yeah, I'm okay."

"Is Jeff there?"

"What would make you ..." She wasn't even going to try to lie to Joey. "Yes, he's here."

"Okay, I know you are a big girl, but if you need anything, please don't hesitate to call."

Joey knew she needed her space when it came to Jeff. She was already involved with him when she and Joey became partners. It wasn't the ideal situation for Joey, but he had his own demons and past that Franny understood. Joey couldn't help but think differently this time about the situation. He wasn't quite sure why he felt this way.

"Okay, thank you. Joey, did you want something?"

"Oh, yeah, I think we are going to have to deal with Elizabeth sooner than we thought."

"Why?"

"I just have a bad feeling. I can't explain it, mostly because they are together and she hid it from us, but it's even more than that."

"Okay, Joey, I'll call you in the morning, and we can get a game plan together."

"Okay, Franny. Thank you."

She said goodbye to Joey, and Jeff rolled over. "Everything okay?"

"Yeah, everything is fine." It was the second time in two minutes that Franny had lied, telling a man in her life that everything was fine. Nothing was fine, and she felt like her life was crashing down.

"I'm going to head out."

"It sucks, but it's probably the best thing for both of us." Franny was holding back the tears now. She needed to be strong, or she would never get through this moment without going all *Fatal Attraction* on him. "You have my number if you ever want to talk or just say hello."

Jeff was a strong man, and since he was not very emotional, this didn't visibly seem to be hurting him as much as it hurt Franny. She knew deep down that it was bothering him just by what he had said earlier.

Jeff kissed her goodbye, and a single tear rolled down his face. He walked out the door, and her heart broke at the wrenching thought of never seeing him again.

Chapter 104

Jeff walked through Ray's back door. Ray was sitting in the living room with Danny. Jeff looked defeated and miserable.

"Hey, Jeff, you look like shit. Where you been?"

"Doing something very stupid."

"You were with Franny?"

Jeff looked at Ray and bobbed his head.

"What's happening with that?"

Jeff didn't want to talk about it, but he knew Ray would keep questioning him.

"Nothing anymore. I said my goodbyes and came here."

"Wow, well, at least you got your head out of your ass and realized that you have a family and you're not eighteen anymore."

"Fuck off, Ray. You're not perfect, you know."

"No, Jeff, I'm not, but I've led a life full of crime. I never claimed to be a saint. You have this perfect life full of love and happiness. You run a successful business. Your company actually cares about their employees. You seem to have your shit together."

"Well, I guess I don't."

"Are we done with this shit now? Can I finally go home?"

"Are you planning on going home now?"

"No, I'll wait until the morning. I don't want to stumble into my house in the middle of the night."

"You mean you don't want to go home without taking a shower."

Jeff just looked at Ray as if to say, "Not now. I'm not in the mood for your shit."

"To answer your question, Jeff, yes, you can go home. It's over. Well, it's over for us. We are loose from the clutches of that jackass."

"Thank God. Where is he? Why isn't he here?"

Ray and Danny looked at each other.

Ray said, "Did you speak to Demetri lately?"

"No. Why?"

"We don't know where he is. He's just gone."

"Are you serious?"

"Yep, he's just gone. Does anyone care?"

"Does it look like we give a shit?"

"I'm guessing no?"

"You got it. I don't give a shit if that lunatic finally got him once and for all. We were all in this because we were good friends. All we did was back a friend and uphold a stupid bargain we made when we were practically kids. It's over. I don't know what's going to happen from here, and I guess I don't care."

"I'm going to bed."

"Yeah, get some good rest. When we all wake up tomorrow morning, life will never be the same. For any of us."

Chapter 105

With my head lying on the pillow, I looked across the bed at Derrick. He was staring right back at me. How could I possibly stop seeing him? The thought crept from my head and slowly made its way down to my heart.

"Hey, why so sad?"

I just frowned at Derrick. I didn't want to talk about it. I didn't want to face the fact that reality was going to set in tomorrow. I knew my life was going to be completely changed but in what capacity? Was he still going to be a part of it, or would this all really be over?

"I don't want to talk about it."

"You know we have to."

"I know."

"I'm going to just throw this out there. It might help our conversation. Are you still in love with Jeff?"

I didn't want to answer that. I also knew I couldn't avoid the question. I admired Derrick for being so blunt.

"We've been together a long time, and the kids …"

"That didn't really answer my question."

"I know. I've been struggling to figure out if I'm just really angry and it will go away or if I've fallen out of love with him."

"Okay, so what do you think you're feeling?"

"I really enjoy talking to you. Our conversations are great. We laugh; we get to know each other. It's just great. I could just talk to you for days. The rest of it is all a bonus. It's wonderful, but it's actually spending time with you that I enjoy the most."

"Yeah, I agree."

"What about your situation? What does the future hold for you two?"

"Well, it's pretty much over for us. There's just too much that was said, and she's seeing someone else now. He can give her things I could never give her."

"We pay you well enough that you should be able to get her anything."

Derrick laughed. "That's not what I meant. It's not material things that she wants from me."

I looked at him, very puzzled. "I don't understand."

"I'm not emotionally in tune with her needs. She needs more, and she doesn't think I'm capable of giving that to her."

Again, very puzzled, I asked, "How can that be? I feel like you give me everything you have. I feel your emotions just when you look at me."

Derrick's head was down, and he grabbed my hand. "I don't think I have ever cared about anyone the way I care about you. I feel like a different person when I'm with you. I feel like I can be myself and I don't have to put on a show. I feel like you like me for me and not what I look like. We've been friends a long time, and we've gotten to know each other so well recently that I want to see where this goes."

Wow. What do I say to that? What could I possibly say to him after all that he just said?

"Are you saying that you care about me more than your wife?"

"Angie, that's exactly what I'm saying. We got married really young and have drifted apart over the last few years. There is nothing there anymore for us, and we're both okay with it. It's better to end things now while we can still be friends and not hate one another, especially for the kids."

I didn't want to refer to Derrick and me as an "us" or a "we," but I couldn't help it.

"What are we going to do?"

"Angie, it's really up to you now. I'm pretty much free to do whatever I want. Now it's a matter of what do you want?"

This was an awful situation, and I couldn't stand to think about what else Jeff was hiding from me. I knew if there was more, I wouldn't be able to trust him ever again. What kind of life would that be?

"Derrick, I will just have to sort all of this out when he gets back. I will say this: I am not willing to give you up … give this up. In the beginning, I thought this was just for fun, and somehow, it turned into so much more than that."

"Angie, it's been a long time that this has been more than just fun. Long before this charade with Jeff and Carl, I cared about you more than as just a friend. If my situation were different at home, I don't think I would have gotten emotionally attached. I can say that I wouldn't, but I don't know exactly how it would have worked out. If I did care about you, I don't know that I would have told you."

"What are you saying?"

"I'm just saying, as much as it sucks, I understand your situation. I won't try to force you to feel a certain way or tell you what to do. I know no one can force you to do anything." He smirked.

He knows I don't take direction very well, and I sure as heck will break the rules if they suck.

"Thank you," I said. "This is going to be awful tomorrow. Let's just make the best of tonight and take one day at a time."

Derrick was not okay with this, but there was nothing else he could do. He had to believe what we shared was real and hope that would be enough to get us through this.

"I just want you to know that I wouldn't trade this time with you no matter what happens."

"Derrick, don't say that like this is over."

"I would be naïve to think that it's not over."

"No! It's not over. I won't let it be over. I'm not willing to lose you."

"So you're saying that we have a chance."

"Yes, I am saying we have a chance."

"Well, that's enough to keep me happy … for now." He smiled.

Derrick was so good-looking, sometimes I couldn't even look at him. I looked away to keep my composure. One thing I had learned in the last few weeks was that he was just a normal guy who had flaws. I'd always known he was a goofball, but this experience with him had shown me that he would let his guard down and let me in to know the real him.

A small ping of panic caught my heart. What if he was not what he seemed, just like everything and everyone else in this mess?

Chapter 106

The next morning, Demetri and Anna woke up together. It was a wonderful feeling for both of them. The road ahead would be a little rough, but they were ready for the challenge. They would control whatever they could and deal with whatever came along together.

"Are you ready for this?"

"As ready as I'm going to be."

"Are you positive you want to go through with it?"

"Yes, I decided this as soon as I got the contents in that stupid box. This is the only way for him to learn his lesson. He needs to pay for what he did and getting everyone involved in this mess."

"Okey-dokey. This puts me in a bad spot with everyone, but I'm not worried."

"I hope not, because you know this is something that I need to do. Everyone else is off the hook, and since I'm his wife, I call the shots. You may have all had your plan about how this was going to end, but it's my decision."

"I love a woman who knows what she wants and isn't afraid to take the bull by the horns."

Anna laughed. "I have been so independent for a very long time. I'm not letting someone stand in the way of my happiness and what's best for me."

Demetri kissed Anna on the forehead and pulled her in close for a hug. "Are you ready to head to the police station?"

"Yep, let me grab all my things."

Demetri and Anna walked into the police station and asked for the chief. He came right out to greet them. The chief wrapped Anna in a big bear hug.

311

"Hey, lady, how are you?"

Anna nodded and said, "I'm better than ever. So glad this is over and I don't have to worry about it anymore."

Demetri added, "You know there will be a trial, and you'll most likely have to testify."

"Yes, of course, and I have no problem with that. What's most important is that I can move on with my life and not have him lurking in the background not contributing to the house or the marriage."

Anna handed over the gun and the letter to the chief, the letter admitting that this was the gun that killed Elizabeth's father and Carl was the one who pulled the trigger.

"Thank you, Anna. I know this is hard for you, but it sounds like you are looking to the future."

"I am. It's a whole new world for me, and I can't wait."

Fitz came out of the back office. "Hello, Anna. How are you?"

"Hey, Fitz. Thank you for all your help in all this. I can't imagine how hard this must all be for you and Joey."

"You know, Anna, I said to Joey that we didn't know Carl. Yes, he is our father, but he didn't raise us, and he certainly didn't have anything to do with us joining law enforcement. The irony, right?"

Anna mustered a respectful laugh, along with a smile. "I'm also sorry for your loss. I know it couldn't have been easy to lose your brother in the car setup."

"Again, Anna, I didn't know him either. He was so sick with cancer when we finally tracked him down that he was happy to do it. It was actually his idea to do it, but we let Carl believe it was his direction that led him to sacrifice what was left of his very sickly life. He was so sick and wanted one last hurrah. He got it."

"So where do you think he is?"

"Since you are his wife, you will find out soon enough."

"I just can't get over the fact that he planned this whole mess just to throw everyone off and make himself look like the victim. What an ass."

"That he is. I can't even say thank God I take after my mother. Which is the lesser of two evils?"

Anna patted Fitz on the shoulder. "You should be proud of what you have done with your life, considering where you came from—or who—for that matter."

"Thank you, Anna, and again, I'm sorry for everything you've been through the last few weeks. I'm heading out, so I'll see you guys."

Demetri and Anna just smiled as he walked out the door.

"Anna," said the chief, "did you hear anything from the insurance company about the home and the boat in Florida?"

"I did actually, and they are sending me a check for all the damages. It will, of course, have Carl's name on it too. I know a good lawyer to get that taken care of for me." Anna winked at Demetri, and he reciprocated with a boyish grin.

Chapter 107

Carl and Elizabeth sat in the house planning their next step. Carl was not prepared for this.

"Carl, how are we going to get the money?"

"We aren't getting any money, Elizabeth."

"What are you talking about? What do you mean we aren't getting any money?"

"Why don't you tell me what's going on?"

Elizabeth's eyes welled up with tears. She refused to look at Carl. She didn't want him to see her so weak. He killed her father, so she didn't know what he was capable of doing.

"Please, Elizabeth. It's been a long time, and now that the truth about your father is out, just talk to me. I don't expect that you will fall into my arms and we will live happily ever after, but you have to talk to me."

She finally turned around to look at Carl. He could see the tears in her eyes. His face softened even more than his voice.

"What is it, Alisa?" he just blurted out the nickname.

"I know Danny was following me."

Carl stiffened, not enough for her to notice though.

She went on, "I was acting erratic. I was acting like I was crazy. The crazy was just an act to throw Danny off, to make him think I was off my rocker."

At this point, Carl was hanging on her every word. He was looking at Elizabeth and thinking she was still so beautiful. He was so angry at her for leaving him all those years ago.

"Why are you looking at me like that, Carl?"

"Like what?"

She smiled and said, "You know exactly how you're looking at me. It may have been a long time since we've been together, but I never forgot that face."

Carl, very shyly and with a serious lack of confidence, shrugged his shoulders. With a crooked smile, he said, "As angry as I am at you, you are still so beautiful." He was getting a little choked up.

"Please don't do this, Carl. I don't think I can handle it right now."

"What? Elizabeth McNamara not be able to handle emotion? I don't think that's possible."

She laughed. "Carl, even after all this time, you are still the only one that can make me laugh."

Very proud of himself, he puffed out his chest. "I aim to please, my Alisa."

Her eyes filled with tears, and she was filled with sadness. "I love when you call me that. I always loved that you had a nickname for me."

Carl thought of Anna and how he seemed to have a nickname for all the ladies in his life.

"Carl, I need to talk to you about something." Her eyes were still full of tears.

"What is it? What's the matter?" Carl was never really good at this kind of thing. Being supportive wasn't his strong suit. He had a heart the size of an elephant, but it was like he never grew up.

She was trying to get herself together. It wasn't happening as quickly as she would have liked.

"There is a trust in the amount of eight million that my father made before he died."

"*What*?" Carl exclaimed, mouth gaping open.

"The catch is that we have to be together to call it ours."

"What do you mean together? Like husband and wife, or just in the same room together?"

She just shook her head and smiled at him. "No, we don't have to be married; we just need to sign all the paperwork together with proper photo ID and some other information."

"Oh, okay. So why are you so upset?"

"I do have early-onset dementia."

Carl just stood there, staring at Elizabeth. He didn't know what to say. As much as he thought he hated her, he thought about the last twenty-something years that he had spent without her—all that time wasted because she didn't know the truth about the past.

"What? That can't be. You're too young."

"We're not young anymore, Carl."

"You're still young to me," Carl said with a smile.

"Oh, Carl, I've done some really stupid things in my life, but leaving you so long ago may have been the dumbest thing I've done."

"Okay, so maybe you really are sick," Carl said with a sheepish laugh.

"Oh, Carl, you really do still make me laugh."

"So, Elizabeth?"

"Call me Alisa please, Carl."

Carl looked down, trying to hide his grief, his sadness, his anger. "Okay, Alisa. What do you want me to do? Do you need me to come back with you? Do you want me to take care of you?"

"Oh, Carl, are you offering to do that for me?"

"Yes, of course." The words just slipped out of his mouth. How was he going to do that? How was he going to tell Anna that he was going to move across the ocean to take care of his dead ex-wife? What the hell was he saying?

"You are sweet, but I don't want that."

"Then what do you want? What can I do?"

"I want you to kill me, Carl."

Chapter 108

Joey picked up his phone and answered, "Franny! Thanks for getting back to me so quickly. What are you doing?"

"I just got dressed. It was getting harder to ignore the calls coming in every second." She could hear him laugh on the other end of the line. "What's up?"

"So like I said last night, something isn't right with my mother and Carl."

"Um, is that something new?"

Joey was just breathing on the other end now, no more laughter. "That's not what I mean."

"Well, what are you thinking?"

"We need to go to the house."

Franny never felt threatened by Joey. She thought he was a dedicated agent and never worried about his loyalty to her or the force. This was different. Elizabeth was a shifty character, and Joey might be blinded by the fact that she was his mother. She didn't want to get too paranoid, but she needed to stay focused.

"How do you know they are at the house?"

"Where else would they be? I don't know for sure, but I just have a hunch, I guess."

"So what are you saying? You want to go over there? What are you going to say? Surprise. Don't kill each other?"

"Maybe they already did."

"Joey, why do you want to get involved?"

"Well, I don't trust either one of them."

"I wouldn't either, but you have to figure out what your motivation is to go over there to that house. If you just want to see what they are up to, then you don't need me. If you want to arrest them, then you need to get me involved."

"I get what you're saying, Franny, but what if I just need a friend?"

"I'm there for you 100 percent, but if that was the case, why wouldn't you just take Fitz?"

"What if I find one of them not okay?"

"Well then, you would need me, but you don't know that will be the case."

"I don't know what I would do. I guess maybe it would depend on which one it was that was not okay."

"Really, Joey?"

"Yeah, well, maybe not, I don't know. I don't really have a relationship with either one of them, so I don't really know what I would do."

"Well, maybe you need to figure that out before we just go barging in on them."

"Yeah, I guess you're right, Franny. I can't help but feel like we need to go over there together."

Franny was very wary of the situation. She wasn't sure what to make of Joey's gut feeling. She was always taught to go with her gut, but this was different.

"Fitz is calling me on the other line. Can you hang on, or do you want me to call you back?"

"I can hold. What else do I have to do?"

"Don't think you are off the hook about Jeff."

Franny's heart skipped a beat. It was already aching because she had to deal with the fact that she would never be with Jeff again.

"I don't know what you're talking about," Franny said dryly.

"Okay, I'll be right back."

"Hey, what's up, brother?"

"I have a bad feeling about our wonderful, loving parents," Fitz said very sarcastically.

"Wow this must be the day of sarcasm."

"Why?"

"Because I have Franny on hold. She was slightly sarcastic with me right before I put her on hold."

"Ha! She's a good woman. I like her style."

"Yeah, me too." Joey briefly faded off into his own world.

"So I was thinking ... I don't have a good feeling about all this. I know that's obvious, but something just isn't right. I think it is way beyond what we thought wasn't happening."

"That's exactly what I was just talking about with Franny."

"Shocking that we are on the same page."

Joey was smiling. Even though they didn't grow up together, they were still on the same page. He decided it must be a twin thing.

"What do you think we should do?"

"I think we need to go over there."

"That's what I just said to Franny."

"What if they kill each other?"

"Ha! That's what I said, but I don't think that's the case."

"I don't either, but something is just off."

"Yeah, I think they are at the house."

"There's no doubt that they are at the house. Where else would they be?"

"Do you want to head over there?"

"Yeah, I think we should."

"Do you mind if I bring Franny?"

"No, I don't mind at all. That will give me some piece of mind. Even though we should deal with this on our own, who knows what we will find. For once, we won't have to figure out how to hide it. It's all out there in the open now."

"I agree. Okay, I'll let you know when we are on our way over."

"Okay."

Fitz hung up, and Joey went back to Franny.

"You still there?"

"Yep, still here."

"Thank you for waiting. He agreed that we should go over there."

"Okay, so when are you thinking you want to ambush your parents with a special agent in tow?"

"Are you making fun?"

"I'm not. I just think this whole thing is getting a little out of hand, especially because there is nothing I can really do about them now."

Joey took a few seconds to take in what Franny was saying, but he wasn't sure that was exactly accurate.

"Let's just go over there to make sure they aren't planning to blow up the earth."

Franny knew he was being sarcastic, but she agreed it was worth the trip.

"I'll be ready when you get here."

"Thank you. See you soon."

Chapter 109

"*What*? Are you crazy? Sorry! No, of course you're not. Forget I said that."

Elizabeth laughed at Carl's stupidity. He had no idea what this disease was about.

"Listen to me, Carl. You did this for my dad, and now I want you to do it for me."

"Ummm, I'm retired."

"Ha! Still making me laugh, dumbass. I know this makes you uncomfortable, but this is something I really want you to do."

"How do you propose I pull this off? Your dad was a whole different story. He had connections. Hell, he was the connected." Carl was pacing and running his hand through his hair.

Elizabeth shook her head and laughed at him. "Some things never change."

"What do you mean?"

"You look exactly like you used to when my brother told you that there was another job for you."

"It all scared the shit out of me back then. It still does. I was not cut out for that business. So back to you. How do you propose we do that, and what about all that money?"

She pulled out a small pouch from her purse. She opened it, and there was a syringe and a small vial of liquid. Carl's eyes went wide. "Where did you get that?"

"Does it really matter? Do you really think I can't still get anything I want?"

"Yeah, okay, I got it. What do you want me to do with that?"

"I want you to kill me with it."

"Are you insane? Aside from your sickness, you have seriously lost it! Was this your plan this whole time?"

"What does that matter?"

"It matters. It matters because this whole thing looks like you set me up."

"I did set you up."

"So you knew that I killed your dad at his request, not because I wanted him dead?"

"I was pretty sure that's what happened, but you confirmed it."

"You are something else, you know that?"

"I know. Listen, this is what I want to do. I want to get the money, and then we can take care of me."

"You say that like you're a business transaction."

"Well, my future is awfully dark, so at this point, I just want it to be over. I've come to terms with it, and I'm good. I want you to split my half with the boys. However you have to get it to them, I don't care. You'll figure it out. I'm sure Demetri will help you."

"Oh God. That smug bastard hates me."

"I'm sure he does, but you know he will help."

There was a knock at the door.

"Are you expecting someone?" Elizabeth asked, eyeing Carl.

"Are you serious? No, I'm not expecting anyone."

Carl walked toward the door.

"Maybe we shouldn't get the door," said Elizabeth.

"Why not? Maybe it's the kids."

"You say that like they are coming home for Sunday dinner. Maybe it is them, but what if it's not?"

Carl put his hand on the doorknob and turned it. The door opened. Carl was sorry.

Chapter 110

It all happened so fast. There was a woman standing at the door whom Carl had never seen before. He didn't recognize her one bit. He did recognize Joey, his son. Carl's heart rate quickened.

"Hey, Dad," Joey said sarcastically. "Can we come in?"

Carl panicked. He looked at Elizabeth for consent or maybe confirmation he could say no. Before Elizabeth could answer, Franny pulled her badge. Her badge was far beyond the local police force badge that Carl had seen from the chief on numerous occasions.

"Carl, this badge says that I can come in. I'm not going to touch the place. We just want to come in and chat for a little while."

By the lack of surprise on Elizabeth's face, Franny knew she already knew who she was.

"Elizabeth."

"Franny."

Carl said, "You two know each other?"

"You could say that," said Elizabeth.

"Why are the two of you here?" Carl asked Franny and Joey.

"We figured you were here ... together. Franny followed Mom to the coffee shop, and when she disappeared, we both assumed it was you who picked her up out back."

"You both think you're so smart, don't you?"

Franny stepped in and said, "We are trained professionals, so it wasn't very hard to figure it out."

Elizabeth reached into her purse, and Franny put her hand under her jacket. She put her thumb on the safety of her Glock. She wasn't sure what Elizabeth was up to.

She pulled out a tube of lip balm. Franny left her hand on her gun. She wasn't taking any chances.

"So why the antics? Did you think we wouldn't catch on to the two of you working together?"

Carl looked at Elizabeth. She was usually the one who spoke for them when they were up to no good. Carl saw it in her eyes that she wasn't in any shape to respond.

"I was just trying to get a grip on the situation. It got way out of control. I figured if I spoke to her myself, she would be willing to find some common ground. As you know, we have some history together." Carl tried to be coy, but Franny and Joey weren't amused.

Elizabeth was busying herself with something in the kitchen cabinet. Franny was eyeing her very cautiously. She had a bad feeling about all of this—worse than usual.

Joey and Carl were chatting. Joey was attempting to get to the bottom of why they were in the house, how Elizabeth knew that Franny was following her, and why Carl came to get Elizabeth away from Franny in the coffee shop. He wasn't getting very far.

Franny saw a brief flicker out of the corner of her eye, and she watched as Elizabeth spun around with a gun in her hand.

Just as Franny saw the gun, Fitz came barreling through the back door right into the kitchen. Joey heard the click, and his gun was out. It was aimed right back at Elizabeth. She fired at Fitz as he walked through the door. She missed. Joey fired at her and hit her right where he aimed.

Elizabeth stumbled backward into the counter. She coughed. Her eyes were glazed over, but not because she was dying. Her mental state was detached from her surroundings.

Joey aimed for her shoulder. He needed to think fast. He didn't want anyone to die, especially his mother—even if she was a threat to mankind.

Elizabeth wasn't going down that easily. She needed to end this once and for all. She fired her gun again, this time aimed at Franny. Joey was all over it and shot at Elizabeth again. This time, he shot to get her down. She went down, and Joey kicked the gun out of her hand. He wanted to be sure she wasn't going to shoot again. From his accuracy, Elizabeth wouldn't be doing anything again.

Relief swept across Carl. Maybe he wouldn't have to do the unthinkable after all. Then it set in what had actually happened. His first thought was he wasn't going to get to say goodbye. His second thought was *What about all that money? Where would it go? Who would get it?*

Franny ran to Joey. She held him. He was much more under control than she imagined he'd be during something like this.

Fitz dialed the chief. The chief was waiting by the phone. He was on his way and called the ambulance to meet them there.

Chapter 111

Jeff got up, said goodbye to the guys, and headed home. He wasn't ready for this. He knew Angie was pissed. He knew she was already pissed, and she didn't even know the half of it.

He pulled up to the house. He shut the car off and took a deep breath. He needed to tell her exactly how he felt, and he needed to tell her about Franny. As much as he knew the possibility of losing her was very high, he needed to tell her. They could hopefully move on with their lives. No more secrets.

He walked into the house and found Angie at the piano. She was playing the many songs she knew by heart. He just leaned up against the doorway and listened. He was so sad. He knew once she looked at him, she might let her guard down, but he didn't want to play that card. He gathered himself.

"Hi," said Jeff when there was a lull in the beautiful music.

She sat still and stayed facing the piano. She played something else. Tears were now rolling down Jeff's face. He recognized it right away. Hope filled his heart with the sound of their wedding song.

I only played the first few bars and stopped. I turned around to look at Jeff.

"Hi," Jeff said.

I gave him a sideways smile. He was fully aware that I wasn't going to talk. I didn't have anything to say. I could do a lot of yelling and screaming, but I was past that point. I didn't care enough to yell. I could see on his face that there was so much more to tell me than just Carl's poor excuse for existence.

"Angie, I won't pretend to know what you're going through or even what you're thinking. You obviously don't have anything to say, or you would have said it by now. All these years of marriage, I still know you pretty well."

"Yep, I guess you do."

"I have something to tell you. Here goes nothing," Jeff said. It was now or never.

"You know I have been on a number of business trips in the last two years."

I just stood there and stared at him blankly. I wasn't about to show any emotion. "Yes" was all I wanted to say.

"I met a woman while I was traveling." Jeff opened his mouth to keep talking, and I stopped him.

"I don't want to hear anymore."

With my words, the front door clicked shut, and Derrick came whistling through the house. He saw Jeff and slowed his pace.

I was standing between them, Derrick on my right and Jeff on my left.

"Hey, Derrick," said Jeff. "Thank you for all you've done and taking care of my ... taking care of Angie. I really appreciate your time. Did you speak with Demetri?"

I looked at Derrick. This was already awkward for me, but it was going to get a lot more awkward very shortly.

"Yesterday, but I haven't spoken to him today yet. Why?"

Jeff was confused. "Why are you still here?"

I looked at Derrick with confidence. I looked at Jeff. I said, "Oh, sorry, sir, has he been relieved of his duties?"

Jeff didn't pick up on my facial expression toward Derrick.

"Wow, you must really be pissed at me. Angie, before you say anything, Derrick should leave. I don't want to air out our dirty laundry in front of him."

"Jeff, Derrick has been living through our dirty laundry while you've been God knows where. Now I know where, screwing some stranger." Derrick looked at me. His face twisted with an "Are you serious?" questioning expression.

"Jeff, all those years we talked about the yellow house down the street, and you knew the whole time this Ray person was living there. Now you're telling me about an affair with a random woman. I don't even know what to say."

"I know you're mad. I understand that you are upset with me."

"Upset? Are you serious? Upset doesn't even scratch the surface of how I'm feeling." I knew he wasn't going to beg or plead with me. I knew he wasn't even going to take responsibility for any of it.

"What do you want me to say?"

"How is it possible that you don't already know what to say?"

He didn't say anything.

"I think you should leave, Jeff."

"I live here. Where am I going to go?"

"You haven't been here in weeks, so don't pull the I-live-here card with me."

I was fighting back some tears. I didn't know what the future held for my family or me and Derrick. One thing I knew was that I didn't even want to look at Jeff right then.

"You need to leave."

Epilogue

One Year Later

Demetri sat at the café table for four, waiting for his guests—his first round of guests anyway. He was prepared as usual, dressed a little more casually than he would have been for a business meeting. After his business meeting, which he hoped was brief, he was meeting with friends.

He heard the door open, and the first to arrive was Fitz. Demetri stood to greet him.

"Hey, Fitz. How are you? Getting ready for the wedding?"

"I'm good. Yes, getting ready for the wedding. Smythe is super excited. I thought she would be driving me crazy at this point, but she's pretty mellow about it all. Nothing has gone wrong yet, so not sure how she'll react if that happens."

The men laughed. Just as they sat down, the door opened, and the next man arrived. It was Joey. Demetri and Fitz stood up to greet him.

"Hey, bro," said Fitz.

"Hey! Smythe driving you crazy yet?"

Fitz and Demetri looked at each other and laughed.

"Demetri and I were just talking about that. She's been awesome so far."

Joey said, "Glad to hear that. Now let's get this show on the road."

Demetri said, "Let's just wait a few minutes."

"Demetri, why are we waiting? What's going on?"

"Yeah, what's going on?" asked Fitz.

The door opened for the third time, and in walked Carl.

Fitz looked at Joey, and they rolled their eyes.

"Daddy dearest," said Fitz.

"Play nice, boys," muttered Demetri.

Demetri had the whole meeting planned. He wanted to keep everyone on track. He wasn't in the business of trying to herd cats, which was how this could go if he didn't dominate the meeting.

"Okay, gentlemen," Demetri started. "I want to stay on track and keep this brief. I will answer any questions you have, but I don't want to get off topic. Are we all in agreement?"

They all nodded.

"I need a verbal yes from each one of you."

They mostly just grunted, but it was good enough for Demetri.

"Your mother ..." Demetri looked from Fitz to Joey, addressing them separately from Carl. "She was sick when Joey ..."

"It's okay; you can say it," said Joey.

Demetri continued, "When Joey shot her, she was sick."

"What do you mean sick?" asked Fitz.

Carl jumped in. "She had very early-onset Alzheimer's."

Demetri was impressed that Carl had finally learned how to pronounce the illness.

"What?" Joey and Fitz said in unison.

"Why didn't we know about this sooner?" asked Joey.

Carl began, but Demetri mildly cut him off. "Lots of legal issues and red tape. We're telling you now."

"Okay, so go on then," said Joey.

Demetri took a pile of papers and envelopes out of his briefcase.

"What is all that mess?" asked Fitz.

Demetri said, "Your mother had quite the estate. I do pretty well, and she had more money than I would even know what to do with."

"From what?" huffed Fitz.

"Mostly from her success in the fashion industry. Carl and I also believe that her father took care of her when she 'died.'" Demetri held up his fingers in quotes.

Joey and Fitz were disgusted because of the ridiculous statement.

Carl clarified, "The first time. I know it sounds so stupid. When she was pregnant and left."

Demetri continued, "So she had old money, new money, just flat out a lot of money. She wanted to split it evenly between the three of you. I received a phone call after her death from a man who was taking care of her finances over the years. She told him that I would be able to get in touch with all of you. She put my name on everything, giving me the ability to give you what she left to each of you."

Demetri handed out the envelopes to each one of the men at the table. Carl's was empty, but he and Demetri knew why. The boys didn't need to know.

Joey and Fitz opened their envelopes to find a few very large checks and each a deed to two different properties.

"You weren't kidding when you said she had more money than you knew what to do with. Smythe won't have to worry about anything now."

They all had a laugh.

Joey and Fitz stood at the same time. They thanked Demetri, and all shook hands. They looked at Carl, and they both went in to hug him— awkwardly, but it was still a hug.

"Carl, if you want to come to the wedding, I don't think Smythe would have an issue."

Carl was dumbfounded. As usual, he didn't know what to say. Demetri was stunned. Joey didn't seem to be fazed by the comment, as he already knew Fitz was going to ask Carl.

"I would like that very much and so—"

Demetri held his breath.

Carl continued, "I would really like that."

Joey eyed him cautiously.

Then Fitz and Joey left. Carl and Demetri stayed to chat.

"You are so stupid sometimes."

"At least I know I'm an idiot. I caught myself."

"Yeah, and you almost gave me a heart attack."

"Sorry. I'm going to get out of here."

"What time is your flight?"

"In a few hours."

The two men shook hands.

Demetri said, "Tell Elizabeth I said hello when you get there."

Carl just nodded at Demetri and disappeared out the front door.

Fifteen minutes later, Anna walked through the door to join Demetri for lunch.

"Hello, handsome."

"Hello, beautiful."

They kissed, and Demetri threw his arms around Anna.

"How did your meeting go?"

"Much better than I thought it would."

"Great! I'm happy. Did you order us some drinks?"

"No, I wasn't sure what you would want, so I waited."

"Okay, just as well. They'll be here any minute."

The door opened, and Demetri and Anna stood up to greet me and another familiar face.